MW01644643

Other Books by Phillip J. Adamczyk:

The Chronicles of Terra: Seeds of Chaos (Book Two of *The Chronicles of Terra* series)

Coming Soon:

The Chronicles of Terra: Traces of Darkness (Book Three of *The Chronicles of Terra* series)

THE CHRONICLES OF TERRA: THE ADVERSARIES

(Second Edition)

By Phillip J. Adamczyk
Cover Design and Illustrations by JoMarie Bentzler

This book is a work of fiction. People, places, events, and situations are the product of the author's imagination. Any resemblance to actual persons, living or dead, or historical events, is purely coincidental.

First edition published 07/2005
Second edition published 04/2018

ISBN-10: 1492730602
ISBN-13: 978-1492730606

Printed in the United States of America

To the folks who encouraged me to continue writing, and to my family and my friends – you know who you are. To Jo, my wonderful illustrator and dear friend, whose work has helped further my vision of the worlds created within these pages.

And in loving memory of and dedication to Michelle Sperberg, who reminded me that no dream is ever impossible.

-Phillip J. Adamczyk

Dedicated to my two amazing daughters, Alaina and Alexis – the two halves of my whole world.

-JoMarie Bentzler

Temple of The High Council
Mountains of Hope
Bright River
Serene Lake
Sapphire Falls
Ocean of Peace
Ruins of the Pure Ones
Aurora Lake
River of Happiness
Topaz Falls
Mystic Gardens
River of Light
Torchlit Vista
Ivory Pass
Raindrop Lake
Palace of Apollo
Ruby Falls
Marsh of Wisdom
Sunset Village
Forest of the Mystics
Tower of Apollo
Ruins of the Wise Ones
N
W
E
S
50Miles

Ocean of Antiquity
Ruins of the Ancient Ones
Forest of Light
Pristine Vista
Hills of Thunder
Moonside River
Twilight Vista
Moonlight Marsh
Tasha Magnolia's House
Morning Star Vista
Mountains of Forgetfulness
Starlight River
Desert of Tears
Hills of the Saviors
Palace of Torrent
Emerald Falls
Diamond Falls
Forest of Visions
Tower of Heaven
Village of Prophecies
Tower of Torrent
Sunrise Village
Topaz Lake
Serenity Hall's House
Twilight Pass
Onyx Castle
Forest of Antiquity
Gospel Marshes
Village of Memory
Scarlet Desert
Ocean of Discovery
Waterfalls
Lakes
Plains
Forests
Marshes
Deserts
Hills
Mountains

Waterfalls
Lakes
Plains
Forests
Marshes
Deserts
Hills
Mountains
Ocean of Sadness
Unholy Forest
Temple of the Infernal Council
Gates of Sorrow
River of Flames
Chapel of Shadows
Lake of the Damned
Castle
Fearsome Keep
Lost Isle
Forest of Deception
Hills of the Bluebells
Ocean of Darkness
Windfall Marsh
Nightmare Keep
N
W
E
S
50Miles

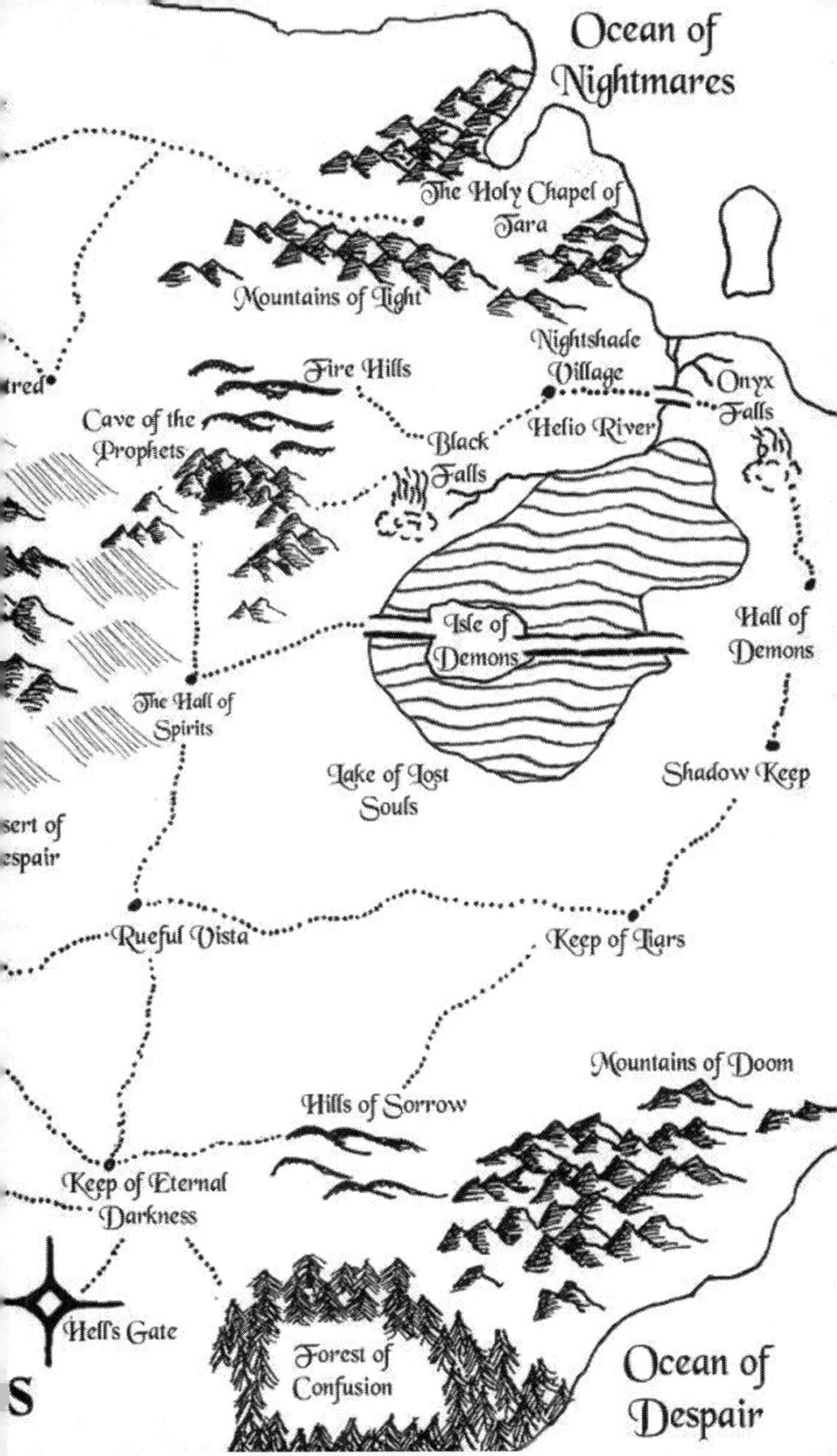
Ocean of Nightmares
The Holy Chapel of Tara
Mountains of Light
Nightshade Village
Fire Hills
tred
Onyx Falls
Cave of the Prophets
Black Falls
Helio River
Isle of Demons
Hall of Demons
The Hall of Spirits
Lake of Lost Souls
Shadow Keep
sert of
espair
Rueful Vista
Keep of Liars
Mountains of Doom
Hills of Sorrow
Keep of Eternal Darkness
Hell's Gate
Forest of Confusion
Ocean of Despair
S

The Chronicles of Terra
Volume One: The Adversaries

Prologue........1
Chapter I: The Beginning........2
Chapter II: Keepers and Keybearers........9
Chapter III: Ginger Molloy, Keeper of Love and Beauty........14
Chapter IV: Cody Bell, Keeper of Music and Dreams........21
Chapter V: MJ Holmes, Keeper of Strength and Wisdom........34
Chapter VI: The Invasion Begins........55
Chapter VII: Serenity Hall, Keeper of Peace and Prosperity........64
Chapter VIII: Tasha Magnolia, Keeper of Life and Youthfulness........73
Chapter IX: Daniella Borealis, Keeper of Truth and Honesty........91
Chapter X: The Cry of Terra........112
Chapter XI: The Visions Begin........128
Chapter XII: Tinuviel Seren, Keeper of Sanity and Hope........136
Chapter XIII: Adam Zirconia, Keeper of Justice and Reason........146
Chapter XIV: Autumn Firestorm, Keeper of the Elements and the Seasons........160
Chapter XV: The High Council........168
Chapter XVI: The Pure Ones, the Wise Ones, and the Ancient Ones........187
Chapter XVII: Michelle Harmonium, Keeper of Unity and Faith........202
Chapter XVIII: Tier Sundrop, Keeper of Light and Happiness........212
Chapter XIX: Aurora Lightly, the Emperor's Counsel........219
Chapter XX: The Prophecy........226
Chapter XXI: Into the Darkness........231
Chapter XXII: The Emperor's Tears........235
Chapter XXIII: The Hall of Demons........240
Chapter XXIV: The Cave of the Prophets........251
Chapter XXV: The Holy Chapel of Tara........270
Chapter XXVI: The Hall of Records........287
Chapter XXVII: The Temple of the Infernal Council........299
Chapter XXVIII: The Chapel of Shadows........307
Chapter XXIX: The Hall of Spirits........327
Chapter XXX: Hell's Gate........338
Chapter XXXI: Final Bastion........351
Chapter XXXII: The Castle of Souls........355
Chapter XXXIII: The Throne Room Awaits........362
Chapter XXIV: War of the Emperors........366
Chapter XXV: Oblivion........374
Epilogue:........380

PROLOGUE

Through the mists of time and space,
Exists in mem'ry a magical place.
Lit by starlight, suns, and moons,
Which reflect off its blue lagoons.
Enchanting to you, does all this seem?
Well, perhaps you've seen this world in a dream.
For humans, yes, a dream it is only,
So we shine down our rainbows to the saddened and lonely.
The time has come to all unite,
And embrace the universe with pureness and light.

-Emperor Gavin Moonstone

CHAPTER I: THE BEGINNING

PAST THE MYSTIC GARDENS, OVER THE HILLS OF Undar, and high on a plateau above the spans of the planet called Terra-Quenlist sits the Crystal Palace, home of the wise and powerful ruler, Gavin Moonstone. Created from a powerful surge of memories and magic one thousand years earlier, Terra-Quenlist continued to grow and had already spanned, in proportion, to one-fourth the size of Earth—and was growing larger and more beautiful every day.

You may have guessed already that Terra is different from Earth. It is called "The Realm of Light," as only good and peace reign there. This is a planet where dreams come true. A planet where magic is everywhere, visible to everyone. It lies past the rainbows, through time and space, and beyond a portal of mist, in a universe far from any known civilization. To all other planets, Terra is hidden, cloaked by a powerful magic spell to protect it from invaders. All planets, that is, save for one. This planet, however, will be later explained. Now, back to Terra and its inhabitants.

The wise ruler, Gavin Moonstone, was on the eve of his one thousandth birthday and still resembled a young man. He maintained a stature of average height, white-blonde hair, and shocking green eyes that changed color with his moods. With a mild temperament and fair rulings, he and his kingdom were loved by everyone.

Gavin, in cognitive respects, had the wisdom equal to one thousand geniuses on Earth. In physical respects, he was about average. For what Gavin lacked in the physical, though, he made up for with his immense psychic abilities. Physical strength was not really the key on Terra-Quenlist; it was the magic that counted.

One must keep in mind that the laws of time and space are different on Terra than on Earth. Time remains the same, but space, in essence, does not. On Earth, a person's lifespan usually lasts about seventy-five to eighty years. On Terra, however, a lifespan can last anywhere from two hundred to three hundred standard years.

Perhaps you've heard the phrase "knowledge is power." This statement is very true. The height of power lies in the amount of knowledge acquired. Knowing this important fact, Gavin constructed great academies as soon as Terra sprang into existence.

The academies were equivalent to schools and colleges on Earth. However, these great academies were much more enjoyable and took about ten years less to complete (the people of Terra have a much bigger and more efficient learning capacity).

There was a problem, however. Even though the academies were functioning extremely well, none of them taught the magical arts needed to control abilities and powers. This posed a big problem indeed, since Terra could not exist without magic. Also, with uncontrolled abilities, people could be dangerous to themselves and others.

Fearing for the stability of Terra and its people, Gavin constructed five great palaces, each honoring one of the five magical and sacred elements: Earth, Air, Fire, Water, and Spirit. At each of these palaces, magical beings would be trained according to the elemental sign they were born under. Each of the palaces honored specific associations.

The Palace of Apollo was associated with the element of Fire. Students born with fire as their strong element stayed there to master all magics associated with Fire. Their strongest weapon was the wand or staff.

The Palace of Torrent was associated with the element of Water. These students learned powerful magic, such as creating rain or moving oceans. Although wands and staffs were powerful weapons of magic, students of the water element used chalices or cauldrons as their weapons.

The Palace of Zephyr was associated with Air. Here, students could practice magic such as circulating air currents or gathering air into a concentrated space. Preferring physical weapons such as swords and shields, mastery of physical fighting was taught as well.

The fourth palace, the Palace of Gaia, played quite an important role in the growth of the planet. Associated with the element of Earth, these students possessed a great gift—the ability of life. From the earth, they could bring things into existence, such as trees, flowers, grass, plants, and animals. They could also move foundations and manipulate almost any planet-bound organism. They normally used only one weapon to help them direct their magical energies—the pentacle, a symbol both sacred and powerful. Evil was repelled by its purity.

The fifth and final palace was built when war began among the other four elemental palaces. Though each was positioned at a certain location of Terra, all were in conflict with one another. The four existing elements believed that each was acting toward war against the other, so they, in turn, caused internal battles to erupt.

The final element was added to provide balance among the warring elements. The Palace of Powers was built in the direct center of the others. Honoring the element of Spirit, these students were trained in astral abilities. The most powerful abilities were possessed by the rare Spirit-born students. They were trained in the high arts of magic, being able to move things with their mind, levitate, and alter time. These were just a few of the many abilities that they possessed.

With the final palace in place, peace finally reigned over all elements. Several years later, representatives from all five elements combined to construct a great palace atop a giant plateau overlooking all of Terra. They called it the Crystal Palace and appointed the creator of their world, Gavin Moonstone, Emperor of Terra-Quenlist. The palace would be home to the royal family and had been stationed on the Plateau of Kindness so the emperor could look out upon all.

Now, there was one planet that the people of Terra dreaded. It appeared out of nowhere one day and terrified all. It was named Chaos, the Realm of Darkness. As a total eclipse appeared one unfortunate day, the light of Terra faded. When the light returned, a terrible planet had appeared out of thin air. The magical cloak protecting Terra-Quenlist could not hide the good planet from the evil eyes which looked out from this new and horrifying dark planet.

This planet did not always exist. Like Terra, it was created, but by a very evil man who also seemingly appeared out of nowhere. His name was Helius Rue. He had crowned himself emperor of the dark world. If ever there was a man with a heart of complete darkness, it was he.

Helius was a very tall man, with short, dark hair and a small goatee. His composure was a shade of deathly pale and his eyes were like black holes, destroying happiness and feeling whenever they were gazed into. Resembling a skeleton, his tall and extremely thin figure was feared by even his minions. He wore only black, except for a long crimson robe worn to suit his evil rule. On his head sat a crown of obsidian, and attached to a black belt rested a wand made from Belladonna. The wand was Helius's most prized possession, as it carried a great deal of his power. This is what he used to help create his nightmare; Chaos was the result of his nightmare brought to life.

Filled with hatred, greed, and ruefulness—as his name suggests—Helius used his dark magic to combine all his evil and cruel thoughts into Chaos. With this planet, Helius also created a powerful empire. Little or nothing grew on most of Chaos, and the world was filled with terrible monstrosities that, to the people of Terra, had only existed in their darkest nightmares. Despite his success at the creation of his world, Helius was not satisfied. It was then that he created twelve skilled magical beings, christened keepers, to help him govern, each with a different power. These powers included: insanity, dishonesty, confusion, hatred, war, shadows, nightmares, deception, injustice, death, despair, and darkness. These twelve proved assets to Emperor Rue, who immediately set to looking for other worlds to control in his insatiable quest for power and domination.

Because he had used so much of his dark magic to create his world, Helius's power was not yet strong enough to reach out to any other planets or galaxies, except one—Terra-Quenlist. Using most of his remaining magic, Helius created a portal that linked Chaos to Terra and stepped through, ending up inside of a dark castle. Upon opening the doors and stepping out into the sunshine, Helius was almost destroyed by the overwhelming happiness and light that surrounded him. Far in the distance, he saw a large outline of a plateau, glorious and welcoming. On top of the plateau sat a shimmering castle, brighter than any of the other things on this new world. Wondering how powerful Terra's ruler was and how long it might take to conquer this world, Helius began his journey toward the Plateau of Kindness and the Crystal Palace with a fiery and dark determination, closing the portal to Chaos behind him, which lay inside of the Onyx Castle.

Let us pause just a minute so all can understand the significance of the Onyx Castle. Before Helius appeared, Terra was filled with only happiness and pure light. This happiness was distorted when he opened a portal to Terra with his dark magic. The result of a dark power surge on a source of good magic warped the space and resulted in the creation of the Onyx Castle.

The castle was made of pure black onyx, as its name suggested. It towered higher than all other structures, except for the Plateau of Kindness. This was the one place that evil was protected from the pure; the castle was a sanctuary for any form of evil.

It took Helius much less time than a human to reach the Crystal Palace. In about three hours, Helius had reached the palace walls. Guards admitted him warily, stepping aside, but leaving their weapons at the ready as he entered the great hall, walking into the throne room. Gavin Moonstone sat on a throne of crystal, not clear like the palace, but instead shining all colors of the rainbow.

As Helius approached, the members of Emperor Moonstone's cabinet shrank back, sensing a terrible wrongness with this stranger.

"Welcome to the Crystal Palace," Gavin announced, waving his hands in a royal welcome. "I suspect you've come here to talk with me. However, I sense that you are from another world. Who are you, and why have you come here to Terra-Quenlist?"

"My name is Helius Rue, Emperor of Chaos," announced the man, turning around and staring at the now-terrified cabinet, then back at Gavin. "I rule a world of darkness and destruction, where evil exists everywhere. I've come to destroy you and take your world from you. I think this world will do good to have evil wreak havoc upon it."

Gavin, who had been sitting calmly, sat a little straighter, but his face revealed nothing. "Perhaps you are mistaken, Rue," he said, frowning and stepping off his throne. He walked up to the menacing man, stopping right in front of him to meet him face-to-face. "Terra is a world of light, immune to evil powers. Destroying me and trying to overtake it will only result in your demise. It cannot be changed because of how it was created." Gavin turned and walked back to his throne, then sat down and announced, "I suggest that you leave here now."

"You dare to speak to me in that manner?!" Helius roared, making the entire cabinet jump as his face flushed a shade of crimson. "I can crush you with my little finger, you pathetic fool!"

"Perhaps I am a fool," Gavin smirked, still calm and collected in comparison to the red-faced, wheezing Helius. "But I am a fool who at least has the common sense not to threaten people in their own element."

Helius drew his wand and pointed it at Gavin. "You're going to be a dead fool!" he screeched. A beam of darkness shot out of the wand and headed straight for Gavin. Gavin calmly held up a hand and the beam turned into spring water, splashing him in the face. Helius stood there sputtering, shocked that his dark magic had not even come close to affecting the other ruler.

Gavin again stood up, a smile now forming on his youthful face. "Emperor Rue, my suggestion to you would be to leave Terra and never return. Go back to your dark world and stay there for all eternity. But lay one finger on my world or my people, and you will suffer the consequences of my wrath." Gavin started to glow a bright white color. Helius backed up, and just in time. A bolt of lightning struck the floor where he had been standing only a second earlier.

"How dare you! You don't know who you're dealing with!" Helius shouted, backing toward the doors leading out of the throne room. "I can crush you easily! You'll pay for daring to strike at me!" His face turned from crimson to purple with all of his rage.

"Now your face matches your robe," Gavin snorted, returning to his normal self. "What you say is rubbish. Be gone, you have no power here." With a dismissive gesture from the emperor of Terra-Quenlist, Helius was sent flying out one of the open windows of the throne room, landing on the soft grass some miles below. Hitting the ground with a cushioned thump, Helius lay on the warm grass a minute, screaming with rage at the top of his lungs. His terrible voice could be heard echoing throughout Terra.

"Mark my words, Moonstone!" he shrieked, jumping up and stomping his feet. "I'll make you and your disgustingly happy little planet pay for what you've done! You haven't heard the last of Helius Rue!" Exploding from the ground in a cloud of black fire, Helius raced back toward the looming darkness of the Onyx Castle, his mind already forming a terrible plan with an even more terrible purpose.

*****

CHAPTER II: KEEPERS AND KEYBEARERS

"YOUR MAJESTY," SQUEAKED THE FRAIL-LOOKING OLD man kneeling before Gavin. "The royal cabinet of Terra is very ashamed of its actions, or lack thereof. We should have taken better action against Emperor Rue, rather than hiding from him."

"Please, Rodaine, you need not kneel to me," the ruler spoke, rising and helping the old man to his feet. "I do not blame any of you for your actions in response to Helius," he continued, smiling and sitting back down after helping Rodaine regain his balance.

"With all due respect to you, we are here to protect you with our lives. On behalf of the royal cabinet of Terra, we hereby submit our resignations. We think that with the recent happenings, you do not need a cabinet, but a council. Helius is a very evil and very dangerous man, capable of destroying this world. We fear that he will return. A council of highly-skilled keepers would most likely be more effective than a frail old cabinet. The most skilled of magical people should be the protectors of your great magic and the magics of this world, not us. We have taken the liberty of selecting the twelve most skilled witches and wizards this planet possesses. However, there are some problems. Aside from the fact that their locations are mostly unknown, some of the most skilled beings have some disciplinary problems, so to speak."

"What do you mean by that, Rodaine?" the emperor inquired, sitting straighter.

"We've noticed that these twelve are skilled in magic but have no concept of respect or interest in rules," Rodaine shuddered, his face reddening with embarrassment.

"I sense," Gavin smirked, "that the cabinet is correct in their reasoning." He rose at last, snapping his fingers and grinning. His clothes changed form, from royal, imperial robes to a purple velvet shirt and black leather pants. His jeweled crown disappeared, letting his white-blonde hair shine in the sun. His velvet shoes shimmered and changed into matching leather shoes.

"Your Majesty, what..." Rodaine started, silenced when Gavin raised a hand.

"I think that the future keepers will need some diplomatic persuasion, but not from an emperor." He grinned, walking toward a large mirror behind his throne. "That is why I am going myself, but traveling incognito. If, at any time, anyone asks who I am, my name is Aleister. No one at the palace, save for you, is to know that I am gone unless the circumstances are dire."

"But, Your Majesty," protested Rodaine.

"Rodaine, you can't call me that anymore," Gavin sighed. "I'm not a ruler for the time being. You can't give away my cover."

"Forgive me, Aleister," Rodaine chuckled, producing a piece of parchment and handing it over. Immediately afterward, he bowed and exited the throne room.

Gavin waved his hand at the large mirror and it disappeared, revealing a small door with intricate designs carved upon it. He tapped on the door three times and clapped twice, then laughed. The door opened, and he stepped through. It closed behind him and disappeared, only to be replaced by the large mirror.

"It's been a while since I was last down here," mumbled Gavin, walking swiftly down the marble stairs into a large, well-lit chamber. "I must say that I was unprepared for this day. I knew that a great and powerful evil would invade Terra once again, yet I never found out how to stop it." He walked across the room to a small table full of magical tools. He picked up a clear crystal ball and muttered, *"Appeara."*

The crystal expanded into a thin, glowing sheet. The glowing surface soon was replaced by the image of a beautiful woman. "You have called, oh Great One?" she asked, her voice echoing in the large chamber.

"Yes, Oracle, I have," Gavin replied, bowing to her. "I am in need of your assistance. The day has come at last. The evil I feared has finally re-emerged on Terra."

"Evil, indeed, this man is," the Oracle replied.

"What can I do to stop him from destroying this world?" Gavin inquired.

"You must gather your army for the coming battle," the Oracle responded. "The Royal Army of Terra-Quenlist must again be called together. Also, seek out the names of those whom your cabinet has chosen. Their magics, when combined, can conquer all evil. You must act quickly though, or all will be in vain."

"What else?" Gavin asked.

"There is a traitor within the walls of your palace," the Oracle cautioned. "He is the Duke of Terra. He will kill you unless you expel him from your midst."

"It's not possible!" Gavin stammered, dumbfounded at the fact that one of his own trusted officials had turned evil. "It isn't possible because there was no evil before Helius came!"

"Nay, wise emperor," the Oracle replied. "Evil can never be completely eradicated. Such is the balance of things. The duke is lost to you. He cannot be returned to the light because he chose his path." The Oracle paused.

"I have not the power to fight Helius!" Gavin protested. "My true power was lost ages ago! I was severely drained after using white lightning against Helius! I had to keep myself from collapsing after I threw him out the window!"

"The answer to your problem is simpler than you may know," the Oracle responded. "Your power lies in your happiness."

"What do you mean?" Gavin asked.

"I must leave you, wise emperor, for your time grows short," the Oracle responded, smiling. "Remember what I have told you. Gather all of your magical tools and artifacts together to aid you and your new council. The magicians you are setting out to find shall need training. Farewell." The crystal mirror shattered, and the pieces flew together and neatly formed the white crystal, which floated gently back onto the table. The soft glow from the ball dimmed, then disappeared completely.

"If the Oracle was worried that time was running out, I should do my best not to waste the time that I do have," Gavin whispered. He pointed at a small black bag and shouted, *"Salimarsa!"*

The bag opened and started to pack, by itself, all the magical tools in the room. It bounced up and down the length of the table, tapping the artifacts and urging them into it. When the bag had finished packing, it bounced back off the table and over to Gavin, where it immediately stopped.

"Excellent. Thank you very much!" Gavin said, bending over and patting the bag. He then stood up and turned to the farthest corner of the chamber. "Only a couple things left to take," he stated, walking over to the marble wall and pressing his hands against it.

The wall shivered and split, revealing a small closet with a few shelves of powerful magical artifacts. Gavin packed these artifacts but stopped when he reached the stone wall on the other end. Symbols had been carved into its base, and he immediately knew what the prophecy meant.

"Evil will triumph," Gavin whispered. "The prophecy said that evil will triumph and crush the forces of good." He turned around to exit and grabbed a broom that had been propped up against the wall.

"Just because the prophecy says that evil will win doesn't mean that I can't try to beat it," Gavin growled defiantly. He picked up his bag, snapped his fingers at the broom, and the broom sprang to life. It jumped out of his hands and zoomed around him, then zoomed underneath him and took off, exploding through the ceiling and into the throne room. The broom sped up and smashed through one of the throne room's great stained glass windows, speeding off toward the dense forests to the west, Gavin laughing all the way.

CHAPTER III: GINGER MOLLOY, KEEPER OF LOVE AND BEAUTY

GAVIN INSTRUCTED HIS BLACK BAG TO PROP ITSELF on the bristles of his broom while he examined his list of names. The very first name on the list was Ginger Molloy. The location wasn't definite, but her residence was suspected to be near or in the dense woods that lined the western part of Terra. Gavin tucked the list back into his pocket and steered his broom in the direction of the Forest of the Mystics.

*****

Calvin Moocher, Duke of Terra, ran through the glistening halls of the Crystal Palace toward the double doors that led to his freedom. Five of the emperor's royal guards were in close pursuit, attempting to capture the duke. They were, however, too late. The duke changed his direction sharply and burst through the doors into the throne room. Finally seeing his chance for escape, Moocher ran to one of the large windows in the room and dove through. The guards were showered by colored glass as they watched the slowly shrinking form of the former duke of Terra.

"What in the holy name of Zeus was that?!" Rodaine shouted as he burst into the throne room. "What are you doing?! Explain yourselves!"

"My Lord, we were patrolling the castle as we usually do," explained the head guard, "when we noticed a door in the north hall ajar. This door had previously been locked for the longest time, so we went inside to investigate. When we entered, we were surprised to see the duke sitting inside a circle of lit candles."

"What's so suspicious about that?" snorted Rodaine. "A lot of people on Terra use candles while praying or meditating."

"Sir, he was talking to the astral form of a man named Helius Rue, discussing how and when to assassinate Emperor Moonstone," the guard protested.

Rodaine's face turned ghostly white, and he held onto the wall to keep himself from shaking. "Helius Rue?" he croaked.

"Yes, My Lord," the guard replied. "He told the duke to wait for the perfect moment, then to kill Moonstone."

"Where is Calvin?" Rodaine choked.

"He dove out the window before we could catch him," the guard said.

"Alert the entire palace to Calvin Moocher's deception!" Rodaine shouted, regaining his composure. "I want magicians from every elemental palace here right now to cast the most powerful protection spells we've got! I think that Helius Rue has just declared war."

The guards saluted and ran off. As they were hurrying out, Rodaine shouted, "Prepare for a complete lockdown of the palace and all of Terra-Quenlist! Allow no one to pass except Gavin Moonstone himself! Gather the Royal Army of Terra! I want the entire army assembled at this palace now! Helius wants to start a war; we'll be ready for him!"

*****

"Please, Your Evilness!" Victoria Bloodmoon screeched as Helius Rue stormed into his throne room at the Castle of Souls.

"Shut up, you stupid twit!" Helius roared, grabbing the table nearest him and throwing it across the room with one hand. The table collided with a bookshelf and smashed, overturning the shelf as well.

Victoria Bloodmoon was the Keeper of Despair under Helius's rule. She had jet-black hair that came to her shoulders, perfectly straight, which matched her impeccable figure. Victoria prided herself on her appearance, which was nothing short of amazing. She wore a dark burgundy dress that came to her knees but allowed her slender figure to bend. Her eyes changed colors with her moods, from a shocking dark blue to a blood red, thus giving her the last name of Bloodmoon. Her perfect white teeth were hidden behind a constantly depressed look, giving her the powers of despair and depression.

"I left here to conquer a world!" Helius shouted at the top of his lungs, shattering various glass beakers standing on a different table. "I was humiliated in front of my arch-nemesis! He nullified my evil magic as if it were a fly being crushed by an anvil!" He roared with anger again, grabbing a bowl sitting on one of the tables and flinging it into the air, then pointing his wand at it and melting it.

"Your Evilness! I came here specifically to tell you something!" Victoria protested. "It's Emeralda! Emeralda Creatan, the Keeper of Dishonesty! She's dead!"

Helius immediately stopped his rant and turned to glare at Victoria, who immediately started backing toward the door. "Emeralda's dead?" he asked, his voice deadly quiet.

"Yes, Your Majesty!" Victoria squeaked. "She died while you were away. We're not even sure why! A couple of us were walking away from the Hall of Records when she just clutched her throat like she was choking on something, then fell over and exploded in flames!"

"Did you try to resurrect her?" Helius asked, his voice now barely audible. "Did you use one of her personal items to bring her BACK?"

"N…no," Victoria stammered. "We couldn't find anything…or…I mean…we didn't have time…wait…I mean…"

"Shut up," Helius said quietly. For the first time in his entire evil history, he was scared now. "Victoria," he started, stumbling to his throne and falling into it, "assemble the rest of the keepers immediately. This requires an emergency meeting."

*****

Gavin steered his broom downward and instructed it to land. The broom gently touched down right outside the Forest of the Mystics. Jumping off, Gavin grabbed his black bag and walked into the dense forest, his broom hopping along behind him.

The forest had no path; no one ever went into it. It was called the Forest of the Mystics because it was believed that some powerful spells were trapped somewhere inside the forest, waiting to be unleashed. As Gavin came to a small clearing in the thick forest, he was attacked. A spear missed his face by inches, sinking deeply into the tree next to him. He turned to see who, or what for that matter, had thrown it.

He was shocked to see a beautiful woman seated on a wolf, staring at him. She had long brown hair that reached to her knees. It was uncombed and wild-looking. She had dark brown eyes and wore various necklaces and bracelets, and she was clothed in a rawhide skirt and vest, with rawhide boots covered in sap to keep them stiff. In all respects, she resembled an Amazon. The wolf she was seated on had black-and-white fur with sky-blue eyes.

"Get outta this forest at once!" she shouted, nudging her wolf toward Gavin. "It's not a place for anyone! Leave now!"

"I'm terribly sorry," Gavin replied. "I was looking for someone named Ginger Molloy. I was told she might reside around this area."

"Who's askin'?" the woman snapped, jumping off her wolf and walking up to stare into Gavin's face.

"I am," he replied, meeting her gaze.

"Ginger Molloy doesn't live here," the woman stated abruptly, walking past Gavin and trying to pull her spear out of the tree. Failing, she walked back to her wolf and patted it on the head, adding, "She's farther south, at the southern edge o'the forest."

"You may have been able to fool others, Ginger, but you can't fool me," Gavin said, leaning against a tree and smirking.

"Who're you?" Ginger asked, so shocked at his last statement that she forgot to disagree.

"My name is Aleister, the emperor's advisor," Gavin replied. "I have come on behalf of the emperor of Terra to offer you something."

"If it's money, I don't want it," Ginger snarled.

"How would you like to be gifted with a special ability, an ability so powerful that you could literally alter reality?" Gavin replied.

"I'm listenin'," Ginger said, pretending not to be interested in his offer but unable to effectively hide her excitement.

"The emperor is in need of twelve gifted people who are powerful enough to harness ancient magic. Your name was first on the list."

"What would I have to do?" Ginger asked, scratching her wolf behind its ears.

"The power would be given to you, for you to protect. You would be able to use it to battle the forces of darkness. I'm sure that even if you haven't met a dark being, you would have learned about them in school."

"What kinda power?" Ginger inquired, ignoring Gavin's speech.

"I think the powers of love and beauty would suit your personality fine," Gavin replied, smirking again.

"Woo hoo!" Ginger suddenly yelled, running back over to Gavin. "Give it to me! Count me in!"

Gavin nodded and held out is hands, palms facing Ginger. Closing his eyes and mumbling under his breath, pink beams exploded from his hands, hitting Ginger in the stomach and knocking her flying across the small clearing. She landed softly on a patch of grass, her body glowing the pink color of the beams, the new power coursing through her. Gavin's hands returned to their normal color, as did Ginger's body.

"That was so awesome!" she exclaimed, jumping up and running over to Gavin, who had fallen over and was sitting cross-legged.

"There," Gavin sighed, smiling. "You are now Ginger Molloy, Keeper of Love and Beauty."

"I can feel the energy!" Ginger said, looking at her hands.

"Why don't you try practicing your power?" Gavin suggested.

"How?" Ginger asked.

"That's why I'm here, to train you," Gavin said, getting to his feet. "I'm going to throw some spells at you. Try to block them or alter them."

Without warning, Ginger's spear sprung to life, pulled itself out of the tree, and flung itself at her. Ginger shrieked and held out her hands in a defensive position. The spear shimmered into a bouquet of roses, which gently landed at her feet.

"Bravo!" Gavin cried, clapping as Ginger stared at him, openmouthed.

"How'd I do that?" she asked, appalled.

"I told you to do something, either defend yourself or change the spear, and you did," Gavin replied.

"But I dunno how I did it!" Ginger cried in frustration.

"Love is a powerful emotion. Work with your emotions and you'll have no trouble at all with your powers," Gavin said.

He snapped his fingers and a flower appeared in front of him. It was a carnation. Wilted and dying, it looked like the flower had been greatly neglected.

"Do you see this flower?" he replied, motioning to it. "It has been neglected, starved of the nutrients it needs to be beautiful. Help it be beautiful." Ginger knelt down next to the little flower, touching it. The flower exploded, leaving only a stem.

"Careful! Too much of something can only destroy," Gavin said, also kneeling down. "Try it again, but regulate the flow of magic into the plant. Feel the power and work from it."

Ginger nodded and touched the stem where the flower had been. Slowly, a bud grew, and a beautiful pink carnation emerged from the end of the stem to replace the one lost. "I did it!" Ginger exclaimed, standing back up.

"It's a start," Gavin said, nodding. "But remember that this was only a flower. The forces of evil are much stronger."

Gavin stood up as well. "We'd best be on our way," he said, whistling for his broom.

"But I need to practice!" Ginger said, standing next to him.

"You'll have to practice on the way," Gavin told her as his broom bounced toward him. "We still need to find eleven more individuals like yourself."

"Okay, so who's next?" Ginger asked as Gavin straddled his broom, black bag now perched on its bristles.

"We're going to Somnus Town," Gavin replied. "We're looking for someone named Cody Bell. Follow me."

Gavin hovered on his broom as Ginger called, "Storm!" Her wolf ran to her side and stood still. She mounted him and they took off through the forest, following Gavin in the direction of Somnus Town, to the north.

*****

CHAPTER IV: CODY BELL, KEEPER OF MUSIC AND DREAMS

THE SLEEPY LITTLE TOWN OF SOMNUS WAS SUDDENLY rocked by loud drumming and cymbal crashes. "Confound it Bell, you hooligan!" shouted the village headman, banging on the door of the thumping house. "Quit that racket or I'll be forced to kick you out of town!"

From inside the small house, laughing could be heard. The drumming stopped and the door opened. "What's the matter, Pops?" Cody Bell said, leaning against his doorway.

"That racket you're making is disturbing the entire town!" shouted the headman, his face turning scarlet. "No one can ever get any rest!"

"All everyone ever does is rest!" Bell exclaimed, a large grin crossing his face.

"Don't you smirk at me, you brat!" the headman shouted. "I'll have you escorted from this town for good if you don't stop your noisemaking!"

"Blah, blah, blah," Cody blurted out, yawning. "Tell me something I haven't heard before."

"That does it!" the headman shrieked, advancing toward Cody. Cody slammed his door in the headman's face, then locked it and went back to playing on his drums, drowning out the yells of the village headman.

"I'll have you arrested and brought before the emperor! He'll find a fit judgment to pass on you!" the headman vowed as he walked away from the trembling house.

*****

"How much farther until we reach Somnus?" shouted Ginger from below Gavin as they sped across Terra's vast landscape.

"We should be there in a few minutes," Gavin shouted back as his broom dodged trees and hills.

"How'll we know who we're lookin' for?" she asked, stopping for a while to let Storm rest.

"I'm not sure," Gavin replied, halting his broom as it gently floated to the ground. "All we can really do is ask around."

"So how exactly did my name happen to pop up on this list o'yours?" Ginger inquired, dismounting from Storm, who lay down on the cool grass.

"The emperor's former cabinet compiled a list of the most powerful beings on Terra," Gavin replied.

"I already know that, Aleister," Ginger said, snorting and lying down next to her wolf. "I wanna know how they got my name when I live in a forest that's untouched by civilization."

"The cabinet had its ways of getting certain information if the need arose," Gavin said, smirking.

"Spill! Tell me how!" Ginger demanded, sitting up and crossing her arms petulantly.

"Each member of the cabinet possessed a special ability, much like all of you will," Gavin responded. "The head of the cabinet, Rodaine, could access anything he so desired through means of a large crystal he used. Most likely, he called upon higher forces to give him a list of the names of those with the true power."

"Why'd he do that in the first place? Why couldn't the cabinet just help the emperor?" Ginger inquired.

"The cabinet decided that replacements must be attained because they felt they were unable to harness the great powers at such a late stage in their lives," Gavin replied.

"Have you ever met the emperor?" Ginger asked.

"Upon occasion, yes," Gavin said, smirking.

"What's he like?" Ginger inquired.

"Well…he's compassionate and fair to all," Gavin finally said, after thinking long and hard.

"Well, what's the palace like?" she asked.

"The Crystal Palace?" Gavin said.

"Yeah! You live there, don't you?" she asked excitedly.

"What makes you think I live at the palace?" Gavin inquired.

"By the clothes you're wearing," Ginger replied, pointing at Gavin's pants. "I may've lived in the forest, but I'm not stupid. Leather's an expensive commodity, and purple velvet's something worn by very rich people."

"How do you know that?" he asked.

"I'd heard rumors many times that my mother and father were nobles who lived in the palace," she responded. "I never knew my parents. A wise woman who lived near the forest found me when I was a baby and adopted me. She told me one day that she knew who my real parents were. She was an extremely gifted psychic."

"So did she tell you who your parents were?" Gavin inquired.

"She told me that my mother was Lady Rowena, who died giving birth to me, and that my father, Calvin Moocher, was the duke of Terra."

"No one ever said a word," Gavin breathed, sitting abruptly on the ground. "I was told that Lady Rowena's child was still-born. I never knew…"

"So what the wise woman told me was true, then?" Ginger said.

"I should have recognized you sooner," Gavin replied, shaking himself out of his confusion. "You look just like your mother. Rowena was a wonderful woman."

"D'you know my father, too?" Ginger asked eagerly, jumping to her feet.

"Your father has fled the palace," Gavin said sadly, shaking his head.

"When?" Ginger asked, the smile disappearing from her face.

"Just a little while ago," Gavin responded, standing up.

"How d'you know? You've been with me the whole time!" Ginger replied quickly. "You'd have to be a psychic to…"

"Of course I am," Gavin replied. "I happen to be highly gifted in the Sight. Why do you think I've been to the palace so many times?"

"But the wise woman told me that mostly only women were gifted in the Sight unless…"

All the pieces finally came together. Ginger dropped to her knees and bowed. "Your Majesty," she said, her head bowed. "I'm sorry I didn't know it was you sooner. Forgive me for my rudeness."

"Ginger, get up!" Gavin commanded. "You need not bow to me! I'm as normal as everyone else!"

*****

High atop the Black Tower at the Castle of Souls, Helius Rue called council with his eleven most powerful minions. They were seated at a large table made of black marble, with thirteen tall, marble armchairs. The armchairs were intricately carved, with large spikes at each of their tips. One of the total thirteen chairs stood empty.

"I assume," Helius started, sitting forward in his large chair and drumming his fingers on the table, "that all of you are aware of the unfortunate demise of one of our own." All seated nodded in agreement.

"I saw it happen!" Burgundy Alabastor, Keeper of Insanity, spoke up, a crazed look in his eyes. Alabastor was a short man, his brown hair always unkempt and wild-looking. He smiled constantly, though out of madness rather than happiness, and his green eyes were always devoid of sense. He wore various heavy chains around his neck and clothed himself in gray garments.

"Well then, Alabastor, tell us what happened," Helius retorted, leaning back into his chair.

"It happened right after you left," Burgundy stated, looking around wildly. "Victoria, Morpheus, Emeralda, and I had visited the Hall of Records to research how many different species of ghouls there actually were, and how vampires reproduced. Emeralda opened the doors and stepped outside, then burst into flames!"

"YES, Burgundy, we've already established that!" Helius snarled, slamming his fists on the arms of his chair. "I want to know HOW it happened!"

"I saw the whole thing, even though I was inside the Hall of Records," spoke another voice. It was Morpheus Eternia, the Keeper of Death.

Morpheus was a very tall and slender man who wore a black robe that covered all of his body. Only his mouth could be seen moving; the rest of his face was cloaked in shadow. "Emeralda was laughing about how many minions she had under her control when a bright light suddenly appeared. It was the brightest light any of us had ever seen. It was so…"

"Pure and welcoming?" Helius finished, sitting forward again.

"Yes," Morpheus responded, shivering. "It was disgusting. The light hit Emeralda with full force. Everyone covered their faces to keep the light from touching them. When it disappeared, Emeralda looked at us, shrieked, and burst into flames."

Helius leaned back in his chair for a moment, examining his eleven remaining keepers with curiosity. Victoria, Morpheus, and Burgundy you've already met, as well as Emeralda. There were eight others.

Callus Nightshade was the Keeper of Destruction. His long black hair hid most of his face from view, except for his mismatched eyes. His right eye was a brilliant red, glowing all the time, while his left eye was bright blue, contrasting greatly with his red eye and pale skin. Strapped to his right side was his great sword with which he worked his evil abilities. He wore black armor with silver embroidery. A band of black leather was fastened around each of his wrists. He rarely spoke because his words brought forth earthquakes and tornados.

Next to Callus sat Regina Zeal, Keeper of Confusion. Her white-blonde hair always looked as if it had greatly interacted with static, constantly standing on end. She wore a dress of silver, with many rings on her fingers. Her beautiful face contrasted greatly with her personality—she frequently forgot who she was or what she was doing and sat on the ground, trying to remember. Her odd powers fittingly dubbed her Keeper of Confusion.

Across from Regina sat Charity Moonshadow, Keeper of Nightmares. She constantly had black clouds circling around her head, little nightmares waiting for her commands. Her tall and slender figure was clothed in a dress of silver and gray with gold embroidering stitched into it. Her purple eyes flashed constantly, stopping only when she blinked or slept. A leather band tied back her purple hair, which resembled small snakes. Charity carried a small silver wand with which she commanded her spirits.

Next to Charity sat Bracchus Moonshine, Keeper of Deception. He wore many expensive pieces of jewelry, having stolen them from his minions and even from his colleagues. Rings of gold and silver lined his short fingers, and gold was stitched into his brown velvet robe. He wore a small crown on his head, hiding what little hair he had left. His short figure was often laughed at, but his powers of intimidation were great. His gray eyes added to his powers of deception, along with the terrible false smile he could muster up in an instant. He turned and grinned at Victoria and Burgundy, who sat next to each other.

Across from Callus sat Shane Shadowstrife, Keeper of Hatred. It was easy to recognize this particular man because he constantly had a scowl on his face. His red hair was short and dark, and his complexion was fair. His eyes glowed red with hatred. He wore a crimson uniform with a black belt and a spiked earring in his left ear. Next to him rested his dark staff, which he used to cause hatred among all.

Next to Regina sat Matthew Hexus, Keeper of Shadows. His short, silver hair glowed under any light, matching his soulless dark eyes. He wore a silver band around his head with silver wristbands fastened tightly around his wrists. His silver robe with black, etched designs looked like the light of the full moon cloaked with shadows, thus giving him his name. He carried a large black book, which kept all of his most powerful magic.

To the left of Hexus resided Morpheus, and next to Morpheus sat Maximus Altair, Keeper of War. Altair wore heavy silver armor and carried a sword and a shield. His short black hair was neat and tidy, as well as his trimmed mustache and goatee. He wore a silver chain around his neck, which reflected the glow of his sapphire-blue eyes. He wore large, black boots and had his helmet resting in his lap.

At the very end of the table sat Torizar Fairplay, Keeper of Injustice. His short, gray hair had small streaks of black still running through it, matching his neatly trimmed mustache and goatee. He wore a gold robe with orange symbols, and a small gold band that was fastened around his head. His emerald-green eyes were his most powerful weapons. When working magic, his eyes would flash wildly. All who witnessed this spectacle—save for the other keepers—were immediately transformed into greedy, selfish people. Across from Torizar was the empty chair where Emeralda had once conversed.

At long last, after a prolonged and decidedly uncomfortable silence, Helius spoke. "Even though this is a tragedy to our council and there is currently no means of resurrecting Emeralda, there is a replacement. I assume he is on his way here as we speak. His name is Calvin Moocher. He was the duke of the planet Terra-Quenlist until a couple of the emperor's bumbling royal guards caught him talking to my astral self. They ran and told the emperor's advisor about the plot to assassinate Moonstone, then drove Moocher out of the palace. He will be a perfect replacement as Keeper of Dishonesty."

All nodded in acceptance. "Now," Helius continued, "as my magic is limited at the moment, I have not the power to resurrect any of you morons if you get killed. And I have a feeling that our adversary, Emperor Moonstone, is preparing for a defensive. I vowed to him before he so bluntly threw me out a window that I would return to crush his planet and enslave his people. What say you?" All cheered and clapped in agreement with Helius's last statement.

"All right, shut up!" he snarled, jumping up and immediately quieting all who were seated. "A simple 'yes' would have been just fine."

All were deadly silent now as Helius sat back down, calming himself. "I believe that some research and preparation is in order," he stated. "As of right now, I want everyone to stay away from the Hall of Records. I will personally be investigating and researching there. I want the rest of you to split up and gather every evil force on this world together that will aid us. Vampires, demons, sorcerers, ghouls—I want all of them."

All keepers rose, bowed, and exited. As they were exiting, Helius yelled, "See if some of you can convince the legion of dark dragons to join us as well!"

*****

"So why didn't you just tell me you were the emperor?" Ginger asked, sitting next to Gavin on the soft grass.

"It would have been twice as hard to convince you to join in my cause, I believe," Gavin replied, snapping his fingers and making a picnic basket appear. He distributed its contents to Ginger, who began eating immediately. She unwrapped a sandwich and gave it to Storm, who also started eating immediately.

"Why would it have been twice as hard?" she asked in-between chewing her food.

"Think realistically about the whole situation," Gavin responded, standing up and climbing onto a nearby tree branch. "If I had told you I was the emperor, would you really have believed me?"

"Nope," Ginger admitted, unwrapping another sandwich and eating thoughtfully.

“Aside from Rodaine, you are the only other person who knows my true identity and where I’m from, let alone the fact that I am not at the Crystal Palace. Everyone else still thinks I’m somewhere in the palace,” Gavin told her.

“Maybe people might feel safer if they knew you were out and about,” Ginger suggested.

“Perhaps,” Gavin replied as he swung himself out of the tree, landing softly on the ground. “Maybe you’re right in thinking this.”

“‘Course I am!” Ginger exclaimed, giggling. The ground suddenly changed as flowers burst from its depths. Pinks, blues, yellows, purples, oranges, and reds filled the area around Ginger, Gavin, and Storm. Storm yelped and jumped up, trying to hide his enormous bulk behind the still-giggling Ginger.

“I see your powers are growing, but you still need to restrict your energy flow and control it more,” Gavin responded, laughing as more flowers erupted around him.

“If anyone messes with you, Your Majesty, I’ll take care of ‘em,” Ginger snickered.

“Call me Gavin,” he replied, helping the laughing Ginger to her feet. “I suppose we should continue on our way as quickly as possible.” Ginger, finally over her giggling fit, nodded and patted Storm, who sat at attention once more.

“On to Somnus Town!” Gavin shouted, pointing ahead of him. He grabbed his black bag as his broom swept him off the ground, propping it on the broom’s bristles as he climbed higher into the sky. Ginger jumped on Storm, who immediately dashed after the speeding broom. Somnus Town lay straight ahead, and it looked as if something was stirring.

*****

“Bell! Get out here now!” bellowed the headman, once again banging on the door of the vibrating house. Gathered around the headman were four others, all bleary-eyed. Two were men; the other two were women. All, save for the headman, were dressed in the uniforms of the Royal Army.

The door opened and Cody emerged, loud music blaring from somewhere inside the house. "What now?" he groaned, leaning against the door's frame. The guards grabbed him and dragged him out of his house.

"Hey! What're y'doing?!" Cody shouted as the guards' grips tightened.

"I asked some of the guards who were stationed in this town to escort you from it. I am hereby banishing you from Somnus Town forever! Finally, we'll be rid of the ridiculous noise you make every day!" The headman seemed overjoyed.

"Hey Pops, guess what?" Cody asked as the guards walked him toward the town's entrance. "JUMP UP!" With this last phrase, the volume of music resonating from the house increased significantly. Unseen speakers exploded with sound throughout the town.

"You hooligan! Turn them off!" the headman shrieked, covering his ears.

"What is going on?!" yelled a different voice. Cody, despite his extreme satisfaction at seeing the headman suffering, turned to see who had spoken. A man in velvet stood at the entrance of the town, a broomstick in one hand and a black bag in the other. A beautiful woman riding a wolf was next to him. He had never seen these visitors before.

*****

The boy just stared at Gavin and Ginger. He was dressed in a black shirt and ripped jeans, and he sported an eyebrow ring and neatly combed dark brown hair. Four guards stood around him as if to escort him somewhere. The boy continued staring, then mumbled something. The blaring music immediately stopped.

"What's going on here?" Gavin asked, stepping forward.

"Who's asking?" sneered the headman, walking forward and addressing Gavin.

"Gavin Moonstone, Emperor of Terra-Quenlist," Ginger snapped back, jumping off the growling Storm.

The sneer on the headman's face was replaced by immediate fear and utter embarrassment. He bowed awkwardly then stood back, shaking. The guards also bowed.

"The emperor is looking for someone named Cody Bell," Ginger announced. "He was told that Bell lived here in Somnus Town."

"I'm Cody Bell!" the boy spoke up, slapping the guards off him and stepping forward.

"Excellent! You're just the person I'm looking for!" Gavin exclaimed, stepping forward and shaking Cody's hand.

"Y-Your Majesty, I must protest!" the headman stammered, stepping forward. "This boy is the most undisciplined person to walk the face of Terra-Quenlist! He's done nothing but disturb the entire town with his blaring music!"

"Good. He's perfect," Gavin responded, smirking. The headman looked as if he were going to have a heart attack. After several seconds, he performed another shaky bow and motioned to the guards to follow him. They exited the street, leaving Gavin, Ginger, and Cody alone together.

"So, you're the emperor?" Cody asked, breaking the silence.

"Indeed, I am," Gavin chuckled, kneeling on the ground and opening up his black bag. He then stood back up and turned to Cody. "I am here for a specific purpose," he stated, looking Cody straight in the eyes.

"And that would involve me how?" Cody questioned, leaning against the nearest building.

"A great evil has threatened the well-being of Terra-Quenlist and its inhabitants," Gavin continued, unphased. "I require twelve of the most magical people on Terra to help me beat back this evil. I already have one," he finished, motioning to Ginger, who nodded.

"Wait…so you're sayin' thatcha think I'm one of these twelve people?" Cody erupted in uncontrollable laughter. Ginger and Gavin just stood there staring at him, their expressions unchanged. After several minutes, Cody's laughing fit passed and he returned to leaning against the wall, his eyes tear-streaked and face very red.

"What exactly was so funny about that?!" Ginger finally burst out, losing her composure and clenching her fists. She stomped up to Cody and grabbed him, lifting him from the ground. "The most powerful person on this planet just offered you the chance t'help save this world and you LAUGH AT HIM?!" Cody's expression turned to immediate fear and confusion as his feet dangled several inches from the ground.

"Ginger, please," Gavin calmly interrupted. Ginger's grip around Cody's neck loosened, and she let go. Cody fell to the ground and stayed there, looking up in awe.

"We need to work together and be able to trust one another," Gavin continued, helping Cody to his feet and addressing Ginger. "In order to do that, we can't have you choking everyone who disagrees with our statements." He laughed out loud, turning back to Cody, who was still in awe. "This matter is of the utmost importance. Are you willing to work under the command of an emperor?"

"What do I have to do?" Cody asked at last, apparently so appalled at Ginger's strength that he decided to accept the offer for the time being.

"Do you like music?" Gavin asked, already knowing the answer.

"You bet! I love playin' music, too!" Cody answered excitedly. "I even listen to music while I'm sleeping!"

"Excellent!" Gavin exclaimed, clasping his hands together. "How would you like to be the Keeper of Music and Dreams?"

"Well, what'd I have to do?" Cody asked eagerly.

"You would have the ability to bring wonderful music to this world and stop nightmares from entering people's dreams," Gavin responded.

"Sounds like quite a power to me," Ginger cut in, crossing her arms and pouting.

"By the way, you two haven't been properly introduced," Gavin said thoughtfully. "Cody Bell, this is Ginger Molloy, the Keeper of Love and Beauty."

"Nice t'have been choked by you," Cody stammered, taking a step backward.

"Nice to have choked you," Ginger replied, snickering.

"Cody, do you agree to use your power for good and never for evil purposes?" Gavin interrupted.

"Sure," Cody replied.

"Very well," Gavin answered. He clapped his hands together and brought them apart quickly. They emanated a light blue color. He crossed his hands, then pointed them at Cody and chanted something.

The light blue energy erupted from Gavin's fingertips and engulfed Cody in its light. After a few seconds the light faded, leaving a normal-looking Cody standing in front of the other two. "That was really weird," Cody murmured, walking up to Gavin. "What'd you do to me?"

"I gave you the powers I told you of," he replied, smiling warmly. "You are now the Keeper of Music and Dreams."

*****

CHAPTER V: MJ HOLMES, KEEPER OF STRENGTH AND WISDOM

SITTING UPON HIS ONYX THRONE, HELIUS SCOWLED, muttering to himself. What could be powerful enough to kill one of his strongest keepers in the blink of an eye? It just didn't make sense. Worse yet, he hadn't the power to resurrect his fallen – at least not at the current time. A dangerous chance to take, as they added to his power source. Helius stood up and yawned. He'd better get going and investigate the area around the Hall of Records to see if he could find the source of his late keeper's demise.

*****

"So now what's my job?" Cody asked as he, Gavin, Ginger, and Storm gazed toward the setting sun.

"Your job, among what I told you, is to protect the power bestowed upon you," Gavin answered, shrinking Cody's house and its contents into his black bag.

"Hey! How'd you do that?" Cody demanded.

"My secret," Gavin replied, chuckling. "This bag never becomes full. It's sort of like a black hole, except that I can take out whatever I need."

"Sorry to interrupt," Ginger spoke up, "but we'd better find the other keepers soon."

"Quite right, Ginger," Gavin answered, taking Cody by the arm and exiting the town. Ginger followed behind on top of Storm.

"How fortunate it is that we found the keeper with night powers before the sun set," Gavin said out loud as they followed the road away from Somnus Town. "It's also fortunate that none of you fell asleep while we were in Somnus," he added after a moment.

"Why?" Ginger and Cody asked at the same time.

"When Somnus Town was first built, it was meant to be a resort. I wanted people who vacationed there to get the sleep and relaxation they needed, so I cast a spell on the town. It worked extremely well. So well, in fact, that some tourists became permanent residents, making Somnus the town of slumber."

Gavin paused a moment, then whistled for his broom. It came zooming toward him from the direction of Somnus Town. He caught it and leaned against it, then continued.

"No one ever goes to Somnus Town anymore because of the powerful spell. It catches all visitors and ensnares them in a deep sleep. I'm amazed that you two remained unaffected. To deflect a spell of that magnitude takes great power indeed."

Ginger blushed and Cody grinned. They continued walking south for a while, Gavin using his broom as a staff. After walking slowly for several hours, Gavin steered them to the left, onto yet another road.

"Where's this lead?" Ginger asked.

"It leads to Chrysocolla Pass," Gavin replied.

"Chrysocolla Pass?" Cody cut in, speeding up to walk beside Gavin.

"Chrysocolla Pass is a safe haven for travelers," Gavin explained. "Some members of my army guard it and protect the travelers. We will be able to rest there."

"What about helping Cody practice his powers?" Ginger asked.

"I think I'll let you handle that for the time being," Gavin answered without turning around. "It will teach you responsibility, patience, leadership, and control." Ginger, surprisingly, complied without an argument. While the party continued toward Chrysocolla Pass, Ginger had Cody practice producing music out of nowhere and projecting dreams to conquer people's nightmares. Surprisingly, he also possessed the power to create illusions.

At long last, they reached their destination. A small castle made of green stone stood in front of them. Many carvings lined its cool surfaces. Several torches were attached to the outside walls, lighting themselves when the sun set. Two imperial guards were posted at the gate. They brandished their swords when Gavin and the others arrived.

"State your purpose!" one of the guards barked, tensing when Gavin walked closer.

"What is the meaning of this?" Gavin asked the guard as he put his broom into his bag.

"By the orders of Rodaine, the emperor's advisor, we are not allowed to let anyone travel beyond this pass," the guard responded.

"I am the emperor," Gavin replied, smirking. Both guards bowed lowly, stepping aside.

"Why did Rodaine order you not to let anyone past this point?" Gavin questioned.

"All that we were told was to block passersby from continuing on this road," the first guard responded. "Master Rodaine issued a worldwide lockdown this morning."

"His orders were to keep everyone but the emperor himself from passing," the second guard added.

"Rodaine must have issued the order after I left," Gavin mumbled, frowning.

"He also issued a call to arms for the Royal Army of Terra," the first guard stated, faltering.

"He did?" Gavin stammered, losing his composure for a couple seconds, then quickly regaining it.

"Yes, Your Majesty," the guard continued. "He instructed some of the royal guards to protect the cities and passes, and the rest to report to the Crystal Palace immediately."

"Thank you," Gavin replied, sounding distant. "We would like to stay at Chrysocolla Pass for the night."

"Of course, Your Majesty," the guards answered simultaneously, pulling open the heavy stone doors and admitting them.

Inside stretched a large foyer. A double stone staircase led to the second, third, and fourth floors of the pass. Few pieces of furniture were in the foyer, but there were many wooden doors.

"Ginger, take that door nearest to the left staircase. You can sleep in that room with Storm. Cody, you take the door nearest the right staircase. I'll see you in the morning. Get some sleep. Goodnight." Gavin smiled enigmatically.

The other two nodded and proceeded into their designated rooms. Gavin lay down on the sofa in the foyer and pulled a blanket out of his bag. Tomorrow, unbeknownst to his colleagues, was going to be an eventful day.

*****

"Of all the idiotic things in the world, I get the most idiotic," Maximus Altair snarled, sitting on the ground and looking at the list Hexus had given him. His duty was to recruit the necromancers, gremlins, and the harpies. He'd already recruited the first two. His job was almost over; he just had to convince the queen of the harpies to join them. Maximus remembered what Hexus had told him. He had warned him to beware of Queen Jasmine. She was a tricky character. He should be careful not to fall under her enchantments.

"I'll be wary all right," Maximus growled, brandishing his fiery sword. "If Jasmine gives me any trouble, she's going to have a meeting with Cosmo." His sword flashed when its name was mentioned. He chuckled, sheathing it. "Helius wouldn't be happy if I killed her, though. I'd better be as diplomatic as possible. She commands a gigantic army of her own."

Maximus reached down to his boot and pulled out the dagger Hexus had given him as an offering for the queen. The blade was made of white diamond and was extremely sharp. The handle was made of silver and gold, inlaid with pearls, rubies, and emeralds.

"Fancy little toy," Maximus murmured, turning the dagger around and examining it further, then putting it back into his boot.

Stretching, he stood up and looked around him. He'd already visited Midnight Village and the Marsh of the Fallen. He wasn't far away from Hell's Gate, where the harpies resided. He turned around and instructed the necromancers to keep the rest of the creatures there until he got back. They nodded, and he turned around.

Maximus took a few deep breaths, concentrated, and continued along the rocky path at an incredible speed, passing Rueful Vista and the Keep of Eternal Darkness at a lightning pace. He slowed to a walk, after many minutes, as he neared the looming castle. Hell's Gate blocked out what little sunlight filtered onto Chaos's landscape. Though Maximus was extremely warm because of the armor he wore, he shuddered nonetheless.

"Even in the day, this thing gives me the creeps," he muttered, walking up to its heavy front doors and kicking them open. "I'm going to get this over with as quickly as possible," he stated, nodding and cautiously stepping inside, sword drawn.

He became immediately confused when he stepped inside, not even noticing the doors when they closed behind him. Though he was evil, he was standing in a beautiful paradise and enjoying it. In front of him stood a large fountain made of white marble. Water spouted from the mouths of five angels standing on its central base. Five smaller angels stood between the larger angels, trumpets pressed against their lips. At the very top of the fountain stood a woman made of crystal. Her hand was open, palm pressed against her chin and making her appear to be blowing a kiss. Water flowed from her mouth to her hand, cascading into the pool below.

Maximus continued to gaze at the other spectacles around him. Long white staircases rested behind the fountain, along with large marble pillars that lined the room. Various vines and ivy wound around the pillars, reaching all the way to the large domed ceiling. Jewels were embedded in the fountain, pillars, and the floor. The four large crystal chandeliers made the gems sparkle brilliantly.

Maximus quickly shook off his awe and clenched his teeth, pressing forward. Hexus had told him that Queen Jasmine used many illusions. This room could perhaps be one of those illusions. He reached the door at the opposite end and kicked it in as well. Subtlety was not Maximus Altair's style.

The Keeper of War walked into the elaborately decorated throne room, glancing around cautiously. The most beautiful women he had ever seen were reclining on large silk pillows and sofas, eating various fruits. At the very back of the room stood a large silk throne. Upon it sat the most beautiful woman of all.

She had long blonde hair that cascaded down her back and around her shoulders like a waterfall. She was clothed in garments of silk and wore jeweled shoes that twinkled under the light. Her emerald-green eyes resembled the cool depths of the sea. Atop her head rested a crown of gold, inlaid with emeralds and sapphires. Perhaps the most glorious sight of all, though, was the pair of large white wings that grew from her back. None of the other women possessed wings as large or as beautiful as hers. The queen truly resembled an angel.

All the other women had stopped what they were doing now, their attention drawn to Maximus as he knelt before the queen. "How dare you enter the realm of the harpies, foolish man!" the queen bellowed, rising from her lavish throne and floating down to stand in front of Maximus.

"I am here on the orders of Emperor Helius Rue," Maximus announced, standing and trying not to lose his warrior-like composure at the sight of the beautiful creature.

"What does that old fruitcake want?" Jasmine chuckled, relaxing a bit.

"The emperor wishes to enlist you and your harpies to destroy a world of light, Queen Jasmine," Maximus continued.

"Really? What's it worth to you?" Jasmine's voice sounded like melting honey. She stood so close to Maximus that he could feel her soft breath on his face. She rubbed up against him and wrapped her arms around his waist.

"Don't do that," Maximus said sharply. "I'm immune to your seductive power."

"Ha! No man can resist me!" Jasmine cackled, releasing Maximus and floating back to her throne. She sat gracefully upon it and crossed her legs. Smirking, she purposely shifted her dress so part of her leg was exposed. She was amused with the look on Maximus's face.

"What have you to offer me?" Jasmine finally asked, carefully observing the handsome man in front of her.

"Twelve inches, that's all I've got," Maximus responded, producing the glamorous dagger. He was met with cackles and wild laughter from all of the harpies, including Jasmine. He felt his face slowly redden. After several minutes, Jasmine finally caught her breath.

"Very well. We will join you, brave warrior," she responded as she took the dagger. "When do you need my army?"

"Immediately," Maximus replied.

"So be it. We will follow you," Jasmine replied, lounging lazily on her throne. "Wait for me outside. I must change." Maximus nodded, bowed, and then exited. As soon as he was out of sight and the door closed behind him, one of Jasmine's handmaidens rushed to her side.

Penelope was a slender, beautiful woman, shorter than most but strong. Her long blonde hair flowed down her back in one large braid, clasped with gold bands. Her bright green eyes sparkled in perfect synchronization with her porcelain-like face and slightly blushed cheeks. Her velvet green dress sparkled, etched with gold. Gold bands were fastened around her wrists and ankles, matching the gold buckles on her emerald-studded slippers.

"My lady, have you lost your mind?!" Penelope exclaimed.

"Quiet!" Jasmine snapped.

"But my lady, you can't possibly be in love with a human!" the flustered handmaiden sputtered.

"This harpy wants to fall in love. End of story," Jasmine said.

"My lady, I know you've been observing this man for a while, but you're breaking rules! You're not supposed to fall in love!"

"Penelope, I have made my decision. He will be mine," Jasmine finished with a dismissive wave. "Now get my traveling clothes." Penelope, finally giving up, went to find Jasmine's clothes.

"I have to tell him. There's no point in denying it anymore. I have watched him for a long while, seen his strength and his power. He has long held my fascination. Rules or not, I love Maximus Altair. I will have him, even if I have to sacrifice everything," Jasmine whispered to herself.

*****

The warm sun stretched itself through the windowpanes to rest on Ginger's face. For the first time in as long as she could remember, she was happy. Ever since Eden Starglass—the woman who had adopted her—mysteriously vanished, she had been frightened and angry. Now that she had spent some time with Gavin, she felt as if she was needed, her purpose in life clear once more.

After Eden had left, Ginger had gone through an introverted phase, running into the Forest of the Mystics to be alone. There, she had found a pack of wolves that had taken her in and helped her survive. Though they could not speak, they were extremely intelligent. That was how she had come across Storm, her loyal friend and companion. They, together, had hunted and enjoyed life. Now, she was entering a new phase of her existence.

The smell of breakfast wafted through the door of Ginger's bedroom, beckoning her to get up. She groaned and rolled off her bed onto Storm. He grunted and growled with disapproval.

"Sorry, Storm," Ginger muttered, standing up and stumbling sleepily toward the door. Yawning, she pushed it open and stepped into the foyer.

She was met with an empty room. Several plates of food rested on a table in the middle of the room, steaming. Only two chairs were set at the table, as well as two places. Gavin was nowhere to be seen.

Ginger's throat started to close and she began gasping for breath, panicking. Gavin wouldn't just leave her, would he? She couldn't handle having someone else leave her again. Ginger fell to her knees, sobbing in frustration. She tried to regain control but failed. It was then that she saw Cody rush to her side.

"Ginger, what's wrong? What happened?" he said, shaking her slightly.

"Cody…Gavin's not here…" Ginger gasped.

"Ginger, why would he just leave?" Cody asked. "Did y'even check to see if he stepped outside for a minute?" Ginger looked up, finally able to breathe again. She managed to stand up with Cody's help, then propped herself against the staircase.

Cody walked over to the table and picked up a piece of paper. "Ginger, it's a note from Gavin," he said, reading it out loud. "'My two keepers…I have left for a while in search of another. I would like the two of you to stay where you are and practice your abilities. I will be back soon.'"

"Why didn't he take us with him?" Ginger asked.

"He said he wanted us to stay here and practice our powers," Cody said, shrugging and reading the note again. "He prob'ly had a good reason for keeping us here. Besides, he said he'd be back soon. Let's just do what he says until he gets back."

"You're probably right," Ginger said, nodding. "I s'pose we should eat, then start practicing."

"Sounds like a good idea to me," Cody agreed.

*****

Across the landscape Gavin raced, his broom shaking slightly under his grip. He was nearing Sunrise Village; he could tell because the town looked like a giant mirror as the sun was rising. He had seen it glittering as he left Chrysocolla Pass.

He took a bite of the toast he was holding, chewing thoughtfully. If he couldn't train all the keepers before Helius came back, Terra would be in grave danger. The five palaces could set up defenses, but they would not last long against the powers of the evil man.

"I know that Helius will return," Gavin said to himself, finishing his toast. "I just hope we're ready." He steered his broom downward toward the brightly shining town.

*****

"Come one, come all, and experience the wonder!" the woman yelled, sitting at a large orange table in the center of Sunrise Village. "See the great MJ Holmes! She has advice for every trouble that you could ever have! Gifted in the Sight, she can solve any problem imaginable!"

No one seemed to pay attention to the woman. She had short brown hair with streaks of blonde running through it and wore thin-rimmed black glasses, which hid her bright blue eyes. She was wearing large earrings to match her glasses, and a bright pink shirt and jeans. Atop her head sat a large gypsy's turban, making her look like a hilarious mocking of a fortuneteller. In height, she rated average; her figure was slender.

Though no one seemed to be paying attention to her, the woman continued yelling. "You sir!" she called, motioning to a man in an expensive-looking suit. "You look troubled! How would you like me to solve a problem of yours?"

The man walked over to the table and sat down nervously. "I'm running a bit late, but I suppose I have time enough to listen to what you have to say."

"Well, what is troubling you today?" the woman asked, sitting on the edge of her own chair.

“For some reason, my wife is angry at me,” the man started.

“I already know the solution to your problem!” the woman exclaimed, making the man jump. “I sense that you are either a woman trapped in a man’s body or you have a childhood obsession with your mother’s shoes.”

The man stood up abruptly, his face very red. “You’re all alike, liars,” he spat. Several people who were watching chuckled as the man turned and started to stomp away.

“Charlie,” the woman said, making the man stop, “your wife isn’t mad at you! She’s going to have a baby!” The man turned and smiled, then tipped his hat and walked away. The people standing and watching clapped, and the woman bowed.

“Thank you everyone! MJ Holmes is grateful!” she said.

“Does MJ always refer to herself in the third person?” a man’s voice said. MJ, startled, turned around to see who had spoken.

*****

“Well, I think everything is working out quite well,” Matthew Hexus said to Callus Nightshade as they walked across the bridge, away from the Isle of Demons. Callus nodded in agreement, his features unchanged. “We’ve managed to ally ourselves with the griffins, the hyppogriffs, and the manticores. We should also recruit the three legions of dragons and the giants.”

Hexus paused for a moment, turning to Callus. “Perhaps it might be a good idea to see how the others have faired with their recruiting.”

“I can check in with the others. You continue with your recruiting. I will report back,” Callus whispered, making the wind swirl lightly and the ground around them tremble. “Even though you gave them lists, they may not have been able to recruit some of the creatures.”

“Very good, Callus,” Hexus replied coolly. “You do that. Meet me at the Fire Hills.”

Callus nodded, whistling. A large bird made of stone came quickly into view, its enormous wings flapping slowly. The "Roc," as it was called, landed next to Callus, bowing its head until it touched the ground. Callus nodded to Hexus once again and stepped onto the bird's head, walking down its neck and standing on its large back. The Roc lifted its head and departed quickly. Hexus watched as Callus and his bird disappeared almost instantly.

"I think I'll visit the giants," Hexus said to himself, opening his black book and flipping through its pages. He executed a symbol with his hand and mumbled something under his breath. In a blast of fire, Hexus disappeared, leaving a large scorch mark on the ground.

*****

The large creature roared, its three heads quivering dangerously. Its serpentine tail twitched furiously as it advanced toward Regina Zeal and Burgundy Alabastor.

"Burgundy, what do we do?" squeaked Regina, backing up against the wall of the large cave they were in.

"I don't know. He'll probably eat us," Burgundy replied, giggling insanely as he also backed up.

"Stay away, beast!" Regina yelled, picking up a rock and throwing it at the Chimera. The rock impacted with the goat head. The other heads, those of a lion and a serpent, and its lion body, tensed and prepared to attack.

"Why did Hexus have to put me with you?" Regina cried, throwing another rock. "You're a nutball and have already almost gotten me killed twice!"

"Because you LIKE me!" Burgundy cackled, his eyes shifting crazily from Regina to the Chimera and back multiple times. The creature roared again, scaring Burgundy into another laughing fit and causing Regina to jump. The room suddenly became very warm, and Regina's hair stood straight on end. She pointed at the Chimera and released a ray of green energy. The energy hit the Chimera in the chest and it stumbled backward.

The beast sat down on the ground and stared curiously at Regina and Burgundy. Regina's hair no longer stood on end, and the room had cooled down considerably. Her hair had now fallen perfectly still against her back. She looked around as well.

"Regina, you are brilliant!" clucked Burgundy, patting her on the back.

"Is that my name?" Regina asked, looking at Burgundy curiously. "Where am I? Who are you? Why is my house so cold?"

Burgundy raised an eyebrow and took Regina by the hand. "I think we have a lot to talk about. Take your pet and let's get out of this cave."

Regina walked over to the dazed Chimera and sat on its back. It turned its heads around and looked at her. She patted one of the heads and said, "Okay, puppy. Let's go with the funny-looking man wearing the straightjacket there."

Burgundy giggled crazily again as he led a confused Regina and the Chimera out of the cave. He pulled the list that Hexus had given him out of his pocket.

"This was our last creature to find!" he said excitedly. "We just have to pick up the cockatrices, dire wolves, wyvern, and barghests that we left in the Forest of Confusion. Guess we'll just round up our recruits and report back to the castle." He laughed again as he and Regina headed toward the Forest of Confusion to retrieve the other creatures.

*****

Calvin Moocher arrived at the Onyx Castle, completely out of breath. He tried to tell himself that the robes he was wearing were far too heavy, but he knew that it was a lie. He was a short, plump man with a red face and thinning brown hair. He had a graying mustache and beard, and his beady black eyes gave him an advantage over lesser beings. The long cloak that he was wearing was fastened around his neck with a gold chain.

Calvin leaned against the large doors, gasping and thinking to himself. He had been dishonest for many years now.

There was no doubt that Helius wanted his great ability as an aid. He had been the one who'd gotten rid of his infant daughter after his wife had died. She had reminded him of Rowena, and he hated her for it. He told the emperor that she was still-born and smuggled her away from the castle, hoping to drown her. But that cursed wise woman had found her and saved her. There was nothing more he could do about that situation and the wise woman's meddling—yet. He'd just have to have help finishing her off when he returned with Helius, because the wise woman had disappeared. His daughter had also vanished, yet another problem that he would also have to deal with at a later time, when Helius could help locate her as well.

After catching his breath, Calvin shook his head, putting aside his plans for the moment, and stepped inside the Onyx Castle. He was met with immediate shock as he was lifted from the ground in the dark room and sent spinning through a portal at the room's opposite end. Through the portal Calvin whizzed, spinning so fast that he became nauseous quickly. Finally, he stopped spinning and regained his senses long enough to notice the ground rushing toward his face.

*****

Gavin sped down toward Sunrise Village, observing all the people. It was easy to recognize the permanent residents of Sunrise Village. All of them wore orange, red, or yellow. The visitors wore different colors.

The town itself was a peculiarity. The houses were made of wood as any normal houses would be, but they were all painted red, yellow, or orange. All of the roofs had red shingles and red chimneys. No one in the town seemed to mind, though. Large buildings that produced the unique paint for artwork had been built in Sunrise. These factories produced the three rich colors of the sun in many different shades and hues.

Gavin landed gently on the red cobblestone street in the middle of the town. Luckily, everyone was so busy with their own affairs that they took no notice of the emperor. He looked around, trying to find a place to start looking for MJ. She had to be around somewhere.

He picked up his bag and opened it, putting his broom inside. Closing the bag, he walked slowly along the street, observing some of the vendors while keeping his senses alert for a sign that would point him to MJ. Some women were selling various pieces of jewelry, displaying it fashionably. A man was selling scarves and carpets in brilliant shades of red, orange, and yellow. "Sir, would you like to buy a carpet?" the man asked, addressing Gavin. "They are hand-crafted right here in Sunrise Village!"

"I suppose I could buy one," Gavin said, reaching into his bag and pulling out a small leather pouch. He gave it to the man, who emptied its contents into his hand and gasped.

Twenty pieces of gold rested in the vendor's hand, shimmering in the bright sunlight. "How many carpets do you want?" the man stammered.

Gavin was suddenly struck with a brilliant idea. "I think I'll take them all," he said. "Twenty pieces of gold for twenty carpets. Does that sound reasonable?"

The man, appalled at this large amount of gold, nodded and put the gold in his pocket. Gavin picked up each rug, one by one, and put it into his bag. The man became even more appalled as he did this and managed to mumble "Thank you!" as Gavin walked away.

The rest of the vendors sold general items, such as kitchenware, clothes, and shoes. The very last vendor, however, caught Gavin's eye. This woman was dressed differently from all of Sunrise's residents. She wore a pink shirt and jeans, with black glasses and black earrings. A brightly-colored turban sat on her head, hiding most of her brown-blonde hair. She was yelling something that Gavin couldn't quite hear, so he came closer.

A man in a business suit had been sitting in a chair across an orange table from the woman. She was chuckling as the man stood up, his face very red. He said something to her that Gavin couldn't make out, then stomped away. She yelled, "Charlie! Your wife isn't mad at you! She's going to have a baby!" The man tipped his hat and walked away smiling. Some other onlookers clapped. "Thank you everyone!" the woman replied. "MJ Holmes is grateful!"

"Does MJ always refer to herself in the third person?" Gavin spoke up, smirking slightly as he realized the woman was undoubtedly MJ. The woman turned around and looked at him, her face lighting up.

"Are you a customer?" she asked, hurrying over to Gavin and leading him to the chair the man had just been sitting in. She sat him down and hurried around the table to sit in her chair.

"What can I help you with?" she asked eagerly.

"I am actually here to see you," Gavin said, leaning forward.

"Yes, I figured," MJ replied, snorting.

"I'm not sure if you know who I am," Gavin continued, unaffected, "but I am Emperor Gavin Moonstone. I need your help."

MJ's smile disappeared from her face, and she became very serious. "I'm sorry, Your Majesty. What can I do for you?"

"The planet is in great danger. I need your help to save it," he replied shortly.

"What can I do to help?" she asked uncertainly, sitting on the edge of her chair.

"I am giving great power to the twelve most gifted individuals on Terra," Gavin responded.

"How does that involve me?" MJ asked.

"Your name was one of the twelve that showed up on my list," Gavin answered.

MJ's eyes widened. "Me? I was on your list?"

"Yes," Gavin said, nodding. "I need you to come with me."

"But no one's allowed to leave the city," MJ protested. "Plus, I've lived here all my life."

"Not a problem. We'll take everything with you," Gavin said.

"No," MJ said after a moment, shaking her head. "I don't need anything. I just think I'll miss this place a little." She stood up when Gavin did. "Sure, let's go. I'd like to see new places." Without further discussion, Gavin and MJ hurried along the road to the edge of town.

"I get the impression that you're different from the rest of the people here," Gavin said as they neared the town's entrance.

"Why do you think that?" MJ asked, stopping.

"Well, your clothes are clearly different, for one thing," Gavin said, indicating the pink shirt that she was wearing.

MJ grinned. "I guess I enjoy being different."

"Being different isn't always a bad thing," Gavin said, referring to himself as he said this. "Sometimes, it's a relief to be yourself and not the person most people see you as."

They continued until they reached the town's front gates. Two guards stopped them as they reached the city's entrance, barring their way. "No one's allowed to exit the town, by orders of the emperor," one of the guards said.

"I am the emperor," Gavin replied.

"Yeah, and my aunt has a beard," the second guard cut in.

"Your aunt DOES have a beard," MJ answered, snickering with delight.

"Never mind, MJ," Gavin interrupted, ignoring the reddening guard and the grin on MJ's face. "If they won't let us walk out, we'll fly out."

He pulled his broom and a scarlet carpet from the bag, rolling out the carpet on the ground. Reaching into the bag again, Gavin produced a small wand made from a willow branch. Pointing it at the carpet, he said, "Hover, hover, with restless might, I give this carpet the gift of flight!"

The carpet shuddered and lifted a few inches off the ground. Gavin pointed his wand inside his bag and repeated the spell. The bag shuddered, indicating that the other carpets had been activated as well.

"Climb on," Gavin said to MJ, motioning to the carpet. "This is a gift from me to you for being so cooperative."

"Thanks!" MJ said excitedly, climbing onto the carpet and sitting cross-legged. "Uh…what do I do now?" she asked, her brow furrowing.

"It will follow your instructions," Gavin said, straddling his broom and lifting off the ground airily.

"Follow Gavin," MJ instructed, gripping tightly to the edges of the carpet.

Gavin put his wand back into the bag and propped it on the broom's bristles once again. He then kicked off the cobblestone pathway and sped upward, right over the speechless guards. MJ's carpet rose also, chasing after the shrinking figure of Gavin.

"Bye, boys!" MJ shouted as the carpet climbed higher. She blew a kiss to the befuddled guards, then turned around and instructed the carpet to go faster. The guards heard MJ's cries of joy for several seconds, and then all was silent, except for the softly blowing wind and the happy chirping of the birds.

*****

"Well, what have we here?" Torizar Fairplay asked as he, Morpheus Eternia, and Bracchus Moonshine stumbled across Charity Moonshadow and Victoria Bloodmoon.

"We were just making our way back to the castle," Victoria sneered, motioning behind her. Torizar looked behind the two women at the large army of creatures, immediately recognizing some. He could distinguish the giant crabs, scorpions, and spiders which cowered under Charity's withering glare. He also recognized the army of skeleton warriors. There were two groups, however, that he did not recognize.

"What are those things right behind Charity?" he asked, pointing.

"Nightmares and winged nightmares. They are Charity's minions," Morpheus spoke up. The nightmares were shapeless creatures, molding into whatever form they chose. The winged nightmares were black horses with black wings and red eyes.

"I see," Torizar muttered, stepping backward to stand next to Morpheus.

"And I see you acquired all of your creatures," Charity cackled, observing the battalion of creatures arrayed behind her male companions. There were the vampires, the werecreatures, shadows, the goblins, and the ghouls. All looked eager to fight.

"Ha! Hexus gave you all the lesser creatures to recruit!" Victoria snorted, pointing at the goblins, which glared at her and snarled, their weapons raised.

"That's what you think," Bracchus sneered. He turned to Morpheus, who reached into his robes and brought forth a baby serpent.

"Is that what I think it is?" Charity gasped in sudden awe, stepping forward to get a better look.

"It is the last basilisk on this world," Morpheus said, putting the baby serpent back into his robes. "He'll be a full-grown basilisk by the time we are ready to invade."

"You think you're so special?" Victoria huffed, stomping her feet on the ground and raising her arms to the sky. She screamed, an ear-piercing shriek that echoed throughout Chaos. The ground around the keepers shook as figures began emerging from its depths. Distorted bodies rose and stood at attention, waiting for Victoria's orders.

"Zombies? So what?" Bracchus retorted drawlingly, chuckling and rolling his eyes lazily.

"Enough!" boomed Callus's voice, making the wind pound against the army furiously and the ground tremble, making the keepers feel as if Chaos was going to split in half. They had been so busy bickering that they had not noticed Callus, who had ridden in on his great bird.

"You fight like children," he whispered. "We have work to do. Report back to the castle and wait for Helius and our other comrades." With that said, he left as quickly as he'd come, making the Hills of the Bluebells shudder as his gigantic bird took flight.

"Has anyone seen Shane?" Torizar asked, breaking the silence.

"He's waiting for everyone at the castle," Morpheus answered. "Let's go."

"Very well," Charity said sourly. "Let's go before I get too cranky."

*****

Helius was becoming rather angry. He had spent hours looking for any sort of clue leading to Emeralda's untimely death, and all he had managed to find was her pile of ashes in front of the Hall of Records. If any good energy existed on his planet of darkness, he wanted to find it and eradicate it.

Helius calmed himself. He could worry about this problem after destroying Terra-Quenlist. After the world of light was razed and its people enslaved, Helius would be able to take over the rest of the galaxy unchallenged. No one would be able to stop him. He would be able to construct a galaxy-wide empire of evil without any resistance whatsoever.

He chuckled to himself and took one last look around before disappearing in a flash of black fire, speeding back to the looming darkness of the Castle of Souls. As soon as all of his keepers arrived with his army, he would give the order to attack. Gavin Moonstone would finally meet his end.

*****

Gavin and MJ landed outside Chrysocolla Pass. Gavin put both the broom and the carpet back into his bag. "Call it when you need it," he instructed her. MJ nodded and looked around curiously.

"Well, let's introduce you to the others, shall we?" Gavin said as the guards opened the doors once again. Gavin escorted MJ inside to see Ginger throwing bouquets of flowers at Cody and Cody throwing what looked like dust at Ginger.

"What's going on?" Gavin asked loudly. Ginger and Cody both stopped and looked at Gavin, grinning.

"I told you two to practice, not try to kill each other," Gavin said. Turning to MJ, he said, "The woman you see is Ginger Molloy, and the other is Cody Bell." MJ waved and sat down in one of the chairs at the table.

"MJ is going to be the Keeper of Strength and Wisdom," Gavin remarked. Turning his full attention to the woman, he said, "Are you ready to receive your powers?"

"As ready as I'll ever be," she answered.

Gavin clapped his hands, making a noise like thunder. He brought them apart slowly. They glowed a dark blue color. He pointed at MJ and shouted something.

The power exploded from his hands and hit MJ in the forehead, knocking her off her chair. She jumped up quickly, her face glowing bright blue. The glow faded quickly, leaving a flustered-looking MJ standing in front of Gavin. Her turban still lay on the floor in a heap.

"What did you do?!" she shouted, slamming her fist on the table in anger and confusion. The table exploded into a cloud of splinters when MJ's fist impacted. She gasped and put her hands over her mouth.

"I gave you your powers," Gavin said, trying to hold back a laugh. "You should get a little more acquainted with your fellow keepers. They can help you develop your new abilities. I'm sorry that I have to rush off so quickly, but we're running out of time."

CHAPTER VI: THE INVASION BEGINS

"MAYBE WE CAN HELP," GINGER CUT IN, WALKING over to Gavin. "What if we could round up some of the other keepers and bring 'em back here? It'd take less time!"

"That's not a bad idea. I'll speak to Rodaine and have him issue two more orders," Gavin said, opening his bag and extracting his crystal ball. He threw it in the air and it expanded into a mirror, floating back down slowly and resting on the floor. The figure of an old man came into shape in the mirror. He bowed gracefully.

"Yes, Your Majesty?" Rodaine asked.

"Rodaine, I need you to issue two more worldwide orders," Gavin said. "I need you to allow free passage to all of the keepers. I also need you to tell the five palaces to prepare the most powerful spellwork they can acquire."

"Yes, Majesty," Rodaine answered. "Do you require the Royal Army?"

"Send them to Twilight Pass, along with some of the five palaces' strongest mages," Gavin replied. "I want the entire army to encircle the Onyx Castle. I want its doors sealed, both physically and magically. If anything tries to break through, I want it destroyed immediately."

"Yes, Your Majesty," Rodaine said, bowing once again. His figure faded, and the mirror molded back into a ball. The ball floated back over to Gavin, who put it in his bag once again.

"Okay. I want the three of you to stick together and get to know each other better. Also, I can't stress enough the fact that you should all practice your powers," Gavin said to the three, giving Ginger a list. "It is imperative that you be able to defend yourselves." He began walking toward the door, then turned around and added, "Ginger will be in charge."

"As long as she is responsible, I don't care," MJ said, nodding at Ginger, who smiled back at her.

"Whatever," Cody said, shrugging and shooting Ginger a malicious grin.

"Obey her as you would me," Gavin said.

"How are we gonna be able to get to everyone in time?" Ginger asked. "It'll go faster with us helping, but some of these people are a long way away."

"I almost forgot!" Gavin said, opening his bag once again and producing two more carpets, as well as extracting MJ's and tossing it to her. "I knew that we'd need these. Use the carpets! They'll take you to the places you tell them to. They can even find people!"

"Storm's afraid of heights!" Ginger said, motioning to the wolf that was sleeping next to the right flight of stairs.

"I'll tell you what," Gavin said. "I'll transport Storm to my palace and have Rodaine look after him for you. That way, you won't have to worry about him."

Ginger nodded reluctantly. Gavin nodded back at her and pulled out his crystal ball once again, throwing it in the air. It expanded into the mirror for a second time, and again Rodaine appeared.

"Yes, Majesty?" he asked.

"I'm going to be sending a wolf named Storm. He belongs to Ginger Molloy. Would you look after him for the time being?" Gavin asked, motioning to the sleeping wolf.

"Of course," Rodaine replied, nodding. "Send him over."

Gavin walked over to Storm and gently picked the enormous wolf up, being careful not to disturb him. Then, miraculously, he walked into the mirror and set the wolf at Rodaine's feet.

"Thank you, Rodaine," Gavin said, stepping back out of the mirror.

"Anything for the emperor," Rodaine said, chuckling as his figure disappeared. The crystal mirror turned back into a ball and flew back into Gavin's open bag.

"Very well," Gavin said, turning around to face his three keepers, whose mouths were all hanging open.

"How did you do that?" MJ asked, appalled.

"You'll find that there are many things I am capable of doing," Gavin said, grinning.

"So Storm's safe now?" Ginger asked anxiously.

"He'll be perfectly fine. He's in the safest place on Terra," Gavin assured her. "I'm going to find Serenity Hall. You three find Tasha Magnolia and Daniella Borealis. Meet me at the Mystic Gardens." Gavin once again turned for the door and said, "Be careful. Even with our defenses, I suspect Helius will break through anyway. Stay away from the area around the Onyx Castle."

He waved and closed the door behind him, his broom in one hand and his bag in the other. As soon as he left, Ginger and Cody unrolled their carpets. Ginger's was a golden-yellow; Cody's was orange.

"How exactly do we use these?" Ginger inquired.

"I'll teach you!" MJ responded. She unrolled her carpet as well and sat on it. "Hover," she instructed. The carpet lifted gracefully off the ground a few inches and stopped, waiting for its next command.

"See? It's easy!" MJ said, laughing and sitting in a comfortable position on her carpet.

"Okay, I can do that," Ginger said, sitting on her carpet. "Hover," she said. Her carpet lifted as well. "All right!" Ginger yelled.

"That's nothin'," Cody remarked, standing on his carpet. "Hover," he instructed. His carpet lifted and he bent his knees, resembling a surfer or a skateboarder.

"Showoff," Ginger grunted, adjusting herself into a cross-legged position. "Let's just go." She gripped tightly to her carpet and said, "Take us to Tasha Magnolia."

The carpet glided lazily to the door and paused, waiting for Ginger to open it. Cody and MJ instructed their carpets to follow Ginger. Ginger pushed open the door and the carpet glided outward at a slow pace.

"Can't we go any faster?" Ginger asked impatiently. The carpet shuddered and shot straight upward, taking Ginger's sarcasm offensively. "Stop! I didn't mean it! Go slowerrrrrrrrrrrrrr!" Ginger screeched as her carpet flew like a rocket across the landscape.

"Go right!" Ginger shouted, panicking. Her carpet turned sharply, almost throwing her off. She screamed, clinging to its fibers for dear life. "No, I mean go left!" Trees and fields blurred by below, as well as one of the elemental palaces.

"I'm going in the wrong direction!" Ginger yelled, her hair blowing crazily in the wind. "Stop!" she shouted.

The carpet immediately stopped in mid-flight. It was only too late that Ginger realized she was falling downward at a rapid pace. She couldn't issue an order because her breath caught in her throat due to the air pressure. She plummeted into a forest and hit something hard. She looked up to see large trees enclosing her. The rest became darkness.

*****

As soon as Maximus stepped out of the throne room, he was met with a terrible sight. The beautiful room that he had seen before was no more, replaced with horror. The elegant staircases he had seen earlier were made of gray stone and crumbling. A large piece was missing from the middle of one. The chandeliers were rusted and full of cobwebs, swinging slightly and creaking as if they were about to break.

The walls were covered with thorns, thick and menacing. The thorns stretched onto the broken and cracked pillars, trailing all the way up to the damaged ceiling as if to claw their way toward the heavens in defiance. Many large holes were embedded in the domed ceiling, exposing the dark clouds and weak sunlight of the outside world. Instead of jewels on the floor, there lay bugs. Many large, black beetles were scattered across the floor, long since dead. The marble floor was nothing more than gray stone, cracked and half-covered with moss.

The most horrifying sight of all, though, was the fountain in the center of the room. What Maximus had once viewed as a work of art was not at all what it had appeared to be. In place of angels stood horned demons, growling and bearing large teeth, forever trapped in menacing positions. Smaller demons stood next to them, holding what looked like human bones. The statue of the glass woman was in reality the figure of a human with a goat's head, sitting cross-legged atop a bronze pillar. It appeared to be reading from a large book, also made of bronze. No water spouted from the fountain. The empty pool was stained and cracked, as were the figures of some of the statues.

"It's lovely, isn't it?" Jasmine said, touching Maximus on the shoulder and making him jump. "What's the matter?" she asked silkily. "Are you afraid of me?"

"You just startled me, that's all," Maximus said gruffly, turning around to face Jasmine. She was now dressed in a violet gown with gold embroidery.

"You look as though you never saw this room before," Jasmine said.

"It was beautiful when I walked through it the first time," Maximus remarked, touching the cool statue.

"My best illusion," Jasmine said, smiling coldly. "You see, we use it on the people we ensnare. It makes them want to stay. It also makes it easier to enslave and torture them."

"So they're your slaves?" Maximus asked, looking around and expecting to see prisoners.

"No, they're all dead!" Jasmine cackled. "We merely break their spirits. Once their spirits are broken, their souls become extractable, and they are extracted and stored in Helius's castle. That's why it's called the Castle of Souls. You are one of his keepers and you didn't know that?"

Jasmine snorted, sitting on the edge of the fountain. "How do you think Helius gets his power? All of the humans who once lived on this planet at the time of its creation were held as slaves in the castle's dungeon. They were then brought to me and I extracted their souls, returning them to the castle. Helius took in the souls and turned them into power. The problem is—all of the humans have been eradicated from Chaos. This breaks the cycle that has always been concrete. Why do you think Helius wants to invade this other world?"

"I thought he wanted revenge," Maximus said, trailing off.

"That's probably a reason too, but his biggest reason is the fact that he needs more human souls to maintain his absolute power and to survive," Jasmine finished. "He must have finally run out of energy to utilize and now needs more to sustain himself."

"Well, either way, we get to fight," Maximus said, grinning.

"You men and your war," Jasmine replied, shaking her head in disgust. "That's really all you care about, isn't it?"

"It's not the only thing we care about," Maximus said defensively. "There are other things."

"Such as?" Jasmine said, stretching herself across the fountain.

"Women," Maximus replied without thinking. "And weapons," he added quickly.

"I'll bet," Jasmine cackled, sitting back up and beckoning Maximus to sit next to her. He complied without argument.

"Maximus," Jasmine started, putting her hand on his leg, "I want to tell you a story." Maximus nodded and turned his full attention to the beautiful queen expectantly.

"A long time ago, when this planet was first created, I was among one of the first great powers here. I ruled using fear and oppression, under Helius, of course. I was a ruthless ruler, bound by countless laws and rules." She paused, turning to face Maximus completely.

"Then along came a man. Not just any man; a human endowed with great powers. I observed him for a long time, watching his strength flourish, and I broke the biggest rule of all." She paused again, her eyes sparkling.

"What rule?" Maximus inquired, listening closely.

"The golden rule of the harpies," Jasmine continued. "We are not allowed to fall in love, but I broke that rule. And I'd do it again if I had to. I fell in love with a human, with a warrior. You," she finished, visibly trembling.

"You're in love with me?" Maximus asked in disbelief.

"Yes. I have been for a while," Jasmine said, her lips quivering. "There's no point in trying to hide it anymore, at least not from you."

Maximus leaned close to Jasmine, his face inches from hers. "Helius would have us both killed for falling in love," he said. Jasmine looked away, tears forming in her eyes. Maximus put his hands on her cheeks, turning her head to face him. "But I would rather love you in death than be without you in life." His lips met with hers, his hands holding her gently. She wrapped her arms around Maximus's waist, pulling herself closer to him.

*****

Penelope gasped as she watched Maximus kiss Jasmine, their figures locking in a tight embrace. "This is bad…" she whispered, shrinking into the shadows. "This is very bad. If the emperor finds out, he'll kill them both." She paused for a moment, an idea suddenly forming. "On the other hand, that may be an intriguing option." She smiled enigmatically and slowly turned around, taking one last look at the two lovers before disappearing.

*****

Callus and his large bird landed in front of Hexus, who held a large jar with tiny creatures inside. Dragons, to be exact.

"It's one of my best transformation spells," Hexus said with pride. "As soon as the jar is opened, they will return to their normal size." He turned behind him to the empty space, then looked back at Callus. "The giants are all dead, at least as far as I can tell. The dumb beasts fought over which would be leader and killed each other, or so it would appear. However, I did manage to find these beautiful little dragons."

A loud rumble could be heard as fire exploded from out of the ground. Callus nodded with approval and motioned in the direction of the castle.

"I assume that I am to return to the castle?" Hexus inquired, shaking the jar and making the tiny creatures inside hiss with rage. Callus nodded and his bird took off once again, headed for the Castle of Souls.

"Let's go, shall we?" Hexus said to the tiny dragons, floating off the ground and speeding toward the castle.

*****

Back at the Castle of Souls, the keepers assembled. All were present, save for Maximus and Calvin. An army of evil creatures was assembled outside the castle, waiting for Helius's orders.

Helius looked around at his loyal keepers, a dark frown crossing his face. "Where is Altair?" he shouted, his keepers jumping in their chairs. "He should have been back by now!"

"Helius, he had to reason with the harpy queen. He has every right to be detained. Give him some time," Hexus interjected.

"Time is something I don't have!" Helius roared, slamming his fists on the table. "And where is that blasted oaf, Calvin Moocher?!"

"We have no idea!" Regina shrieked, having regained her senses after the encounter with the Chimera. Her lips quivered furiously as she shifted in her chair.

Helius roared with fury, shattering all the windows of the tower. "Forget about those two, then!" he screamed. "I am declaring war against Terra-Quenlist and my patience is at an end! March to the portal at the Onyx Falls and invade Terra!" He paused, gasping.

"Helius, what if Terra has defenses set up to keep us from invading?" Shane asked, his scowl worsening with every word he spoke.

"You leave that little problem to me," Helius retorted. "I'll ensure you safe passage." He paused once again, then said, "After arriving on Terra, wait for my orders. Stay inside the Onyx Castle until I arrive. Go!"

The keepers nodded and stood up in unison. "One more thing!" Helius added quickly. "If any of you come across Maximus or Calvin, send them to me immediately." Once again, the keepers nodded; they headed for the door and exited, making their way down to the waiting army.

Upon arriving, Hexus stood on a large mound and spoke up. "Loyal Army of Chaos," he boomed, raising his arms. "Prepare to attack!"

Loud cheers and roars erupted from the army. Hexus smiled and spoke once again. "March to the Onyx Falls. There, we will divide you into separate groups, or waves. The invasion of Terra has begun!" he shouted, met once again with an uproar from the army.

"Move out!" he shouted. The ground shook as the army marched across the landscape, heading for the Helio River.

"Cross the bridge and head north!" bellowed Hexus, jumping off the mound and motioning to the other keepers, who followed him.

"What about Helius?" Victoria yelled over the roar of the army.

"You heard him. He's working on a spell to enable us to enter Terra unharmed!" Hexus yelled back.

"I just hope that Maximus comes soon, for his own sake!" Charity yelled. "Helius was furious! Plus, we will probably need all the reinforcements we can get!"

*****

CHAPTER VII: SERENITY HALL, KEEPER OF PEACE AND PROSPERITY

GAVIN WAS FLYING OVER TOPAZ LAKE WHEN THE vision hit him. He saw Ginger and her carpet plummet into a forest…then all went dark. He lost his balance on his broom and slipped off, plunging into the deep waters of the still lake below him.

*****

The woman was gazing out the window of her house, observing the calm waters of Topaz Lake, when a man fell from the sky and hit the water, shattering the peace around her. She jumped out of her chair and burst out of her house, running to the water's edge. The man swam toward her, a black bag in one hand and a broken broomstick in the other. She grabbed him by the arm and helped him onto shore. He gasped and sat on the ground for a minute, water streaming off his face.

"That looked like quite a fall," the woman said quickly, helping Gavin to his feet. "Are you all right?"

"I'm fine, thanks to you," Gavin replied, wringing out his shirt. He looked around at the small island he was on. Many plants and trees grew around him, and a small house was the only indication of human inhabitance.

Gavin turned back to the woman. She wore a sky-blue dress and had her dark brown hair tied in a neat bun. A symbol of the peace figure was around her neck. Her dark brown eyes gave off a soothing feeling, and her slender figure made her graceful as well as beautiful.

"Are you lost?" she asked, looking at Gavin's bag, then turning and looking at the snapped broom lying on the ground.

"I'm not sure," Gavin replied, rubbing his head. "I was on my way to find a woman named Serenity Hall when I was struck with a vision."

"I am Serenity," the woman said, sitting on the grass. "You must be the great emperor. Only men of royalty or power are gifted with the Sight."

"Correct," Gavin said, wringing his shirt out once again. "I'm incredibly glad that I was able to find you. You see, I am in need of your help. A great evil is threatening Terra and its inhabitants, and I fear that all are in danger. I need your help to destroy the evil that is undoubtedly preparing to attack."

"I am a peaceful person and do not believe in violence," Serenity answered, standing up abruptly and heading for her house. "I'm sorry, Your Majesty, but I cannot help you."

"You have to!" Gavin protested, biting his lower lip and following Serenity to her front door. "If you don't, many innocent people are going to die!"

Serenity paused as she opened her door, her face etched with worry and sadness. "I can't help you. It would break the vow of peace that I have taken. I'm sorry." She closed the door behind her, and Gavin heard a bolt lock in place.

"Sometimes," Gavin said softly, "even though we do not want to fight, we are given no choice." He opened his bag and took out a red carpet. Setting it on the doorstep, he said, "If you change your mind, use the carpet. It will find me. I trust that whatever decision you make will be the right one. Please."

"Your Majesty," came Serenity's voice from the other side of the door, "I don't think you understand exactly why I have taken the vow of peace. My childhood was very chaotic; my parents fought constantly, and I never knew what it was like to experience peace and tranquility. I was never given the opportunity to be taught that. After my parents died, I took a vow to uphold peace and tranquility so that I would never again be forced to re-live the chaotic life I had as a child."

Gavin paused for a moment, sighing lightly and closing his eyes in a gesture of empathy. He knew that nothing he could say would be able to influence the woman's decision; Serenity was a strong woman, no doubts there. But free will was something that not even his magic had control over.

Gavin decided at last to merely say nothing. He'd extended the request for assistance. The best he could hope for was that Serenity would change her mind. Taking one last look backward, he stepped away from the house, frowning slightly. Then, closing his eyes and raising his arms to the sky, he exploded off the ground and flew upward, the rushing wind quickly drying him. He looked down to see the island slowly shrinking, along with the small house at its center.

Turning his attention toward Ginger and what had happened to her, Gavin flew toward the nearest forest. Ginger had fallen into a large forest, but it was not the Forest of the Mystics. He had to find her; she might be badly hurt and need help.

"Gavin!" someone yelled, making him stop and turn around in mid-air. He was so absorbed in his thoughts that he hadn't noticed Cody and MJ. They sped toward him on their carpets, their faces ghostly white.

"She fell into the forest!" MJ cried, pointing downward to the large trees below. "The carpet acted really oddly and took all of her sarcasm seriously! It stopped in mid-air and dropped into the forest!"

"Did you see where she fell?" Gavin asked quickly, shooting a glance downward.

"She fell somewhere right in front of us!" Cody answered, pointing ahead of him.

"Well, we have to find her!" Gavin exclaimed, floating downward.

"Gavin!" yelled another voice from behind him. Serenity came zooming toward him on her carpet, waving. She stopped in front of him, hovering. "I thought about what you said and got here as quickly as possible. You were right. Sometimes things can't be avoided. I'll fight if it means that I'm saving innocent people." She stopped and smiled.

"I knew you would change your mind," Gavin remarked, grinning. "Besides, technically, saving innocent lives fulfills your vow to uphold peace." He inwardly sighed with relief at Serenity's decision. As he turned back to begin looking for Ginger, one thought echoed in his mind. *Thank the gods.*

*****

Ginger opened her eyes, dazed and confused. Her head throbbed, and every one of her bones felt like it was broken. She tried to sit up and winced, her chest exploding in pain. One or more of her ribs was either cracked or broken.

It was then that Ginger noticed something different. She was not lying on the ground as before, but was now lying on a soft bed. Trying to focus her eyes, Ginger blinked. When her vision came into focus, she couldn't believe what she saw.

The room she was in was made completely of ice. Small crystals formed on the ceiling and walls. The windows that lined the room had frost crystals dancing across them. Amazingly, the room was not a bit cold; quite the contrary, it was cozy and warm.

The door at the opposite side of the room opened, and a beautiful woman stepped in, carrying a small tray with food and drink. The woman's appearance stunned Ginger. She wore a light pink dress that sparkled all over, matching her pink slippers. Her icy blue eyes contrasted with her dress, but were in perfect harmony with her shining silver hair. A medallion of quartz hung around her neck, and a diamond tiara rested atop her head.

"You're awake!" she exclaimed, hurrying to Ginger's side and setting the tray on the table next to the bed. The woman pulled the chair that sat next to the bed closer, sitting in it.

"Am I dreaming?" Ginger asked, gazing at the woman.

"Heavens, no!" the woman laughed, taking a small vial off the tray and opening it. "You are in the realm of the fairies. I am Princess Mae Snowfall."

"Nice t'meet you. I'd bow t'you, but I can't move," Ginger said, blinking.

"Well, I have something here that will remedy that," Mae replied, opening Ginger's mouth and pouring in the vial's contents.

"Gah! What IS that?!" Ginger asked, sitting up and surprising herself when her pain suddenly disappeared.

"It's an old-fashioned elixir designed to quickly heal any wound," Mae replied, closing the empty vial and setting it on the table. "An old family recipe that has been around for generations."

"Wow, that works pretty well!" Ginger said, getting up quickly and stretching. "I gotta go. Thanks for your help!"

"Go? Why?" Mae asked, laughing.

"Because my friends need my help!" Ginger replied, grabbing her tattered carpet that hung on the bed and rushing through the door.

She stumbled through the long icy hallway, which had many doors. Heading for the door at the end, Ginger heard Mae yell, "Wait! Don't go through that!"

Ginger reached the door and yanked it open, stumbling into the bright sunlight. Something was wrong, though. Everything seemed…bigger than normal. She hadn't remembered the trees being so tall. She turned around and almost screamed. The lavish palace that she had just stepped out of stood half as tall as one of the gigantic trees that stood behind it. She finally realized that she was, well, less than life-size.

"I was going to tell you," Mae said, touching her gently on the shoulder. "The only way to stay in Fairyland is to become small."

"It can be reversed, right?" Ginger said wildly, turning around and shaking Mae.

"Only my mother can reverse it," Mae responded, visibly flustered.

"I have to see her!" Ginger said, running back to the castle's door and opening it.

"Why? Don't you like it here?" Mae called, chasing after her.

"My friends need me!" Ginger cried, running back down the icy hallway.

Mae caught up to Ginger and stopped her. "Don't worry, I'll take you to my mother. She'll know what to do."

She guided Ginger to a door next to the room Ginger had been in. They opened it and proceeded through into a large dining hall. Mae took Ginger by the hand and led her through another door into the throne room.

The room completely astounded Ginger. Its walls, ceiling, and floor were all as icy as the rest of the castle, but great gardens grew all around. These gardens, however, grew unique plants, all made of crystal and ice. The only normal-looking plant in the room was the elegant ivy that seemed to grow everywhere.

The throne sat against the back wall of the room, atop a crystal dais. It was carved in a lavish fashion, made of blue topaz. Two large rosebushes grew on both sides of the throne, covered with frost. The roses themselves were light blue, sparkling from the frost that rested on their petals. Gently falling snow throughout the entire room added the final touch. Two fairy guards stood next to each rosebush, protecting the illustrious queen.

The queen was an object of splendor in herself. She wore a large ballroom dress, purely white with a tint of blue to it. The crystal slippers on her dainty feet were also tinted a light blue. The queen's lips were painted a dark blue color, matching her purple eyes perfectly. Her snow-white hair flowed magnificently across her shoulders and back, resting with not one hair out of place. She wore icicle earrings and carried a long wand with the tip of a snowflake. Her crown was made of silver with gold tips. A large sapphire was embedded at its center.

"Mother, this is the stranger I found," Mae stated, curtseying and stepping backward to reveal Ginger.

"Welcome," the queen spoke. "I am Queen Ivy Snowfall of Fairyland." She waved her hand gracefully in the direction of her daughter. "You have already met my daughter, Mae."

"Please, Your Majesty," Ginger said, trying a curtsey and failing, then moving closer to Ivy. "I need you to return me to my normal size. I have to find my friends. They need my help."

"My dear child, it's all right. Slow down. What is your name, first of all?" Queen Ivy asked, smiling warmly.

"Ginger Molloy, Keeper of Love and Beauty," Ginger replied. "I need to find Emperor Gavin Moonstone! He needs my assistance!"

"The emperor is not in the palace?" Ivy asked, sitting forward. "Something must be very wrong."

"A lotta things are very wrong," Ginger responded.

"Why don't you tell me everything that's happened?" Ivy asked. "It might help."

*****

Gavin and the others landed in the forest, searching for some sign of Ginger. Gavin frowned as he touched down on the soft grass, his brow furrowed due to deep thought. "Perhaps I should give Serenity her powers right now," he said aloud. "That way, she can practice whilst we look." Cody and MJ nodded, as did Serenity.

Once again, Gavin put his hands together, making them glow a soft green. He closed his eyes and pointed at Serenity, and the energy flowed gracefully toward her, entering her eyes and making them glow. Serenity smiled and nodded.

"Huh! Wish it'd been that easy for me!" Cody huffed, crossing his arms.

"It's different for everyone, Cody," Gavin said, his voice gathering a hint of sympathy for the Keeper of Music and Dreams. "But think of it this way. Either way, you've received something fantastic. So in the end, you've never really lost anything or been somehow treated in a different way."

Cody blinked, absorbing Gavin's words, then slowly nodded. "I never thoughta that. Guess you're right. Yeah!"

*****

Helius stormed along the dark hallway that led to his observatory. Kicking open the door, he walked over to a tall wooden cupboard that stood in one corner of the room. Various bottles rested on the floor, as well as a large telescope and many charts. A large oak desk was pushed against one wall, cracked and rotting. The chair that corresponded with it was broken in two pieces, its jagged splinters brandished dangerously. The large glass dome that covered the observatory was closed, giving the room a darker shade of gloom. A control panel was attached to another wall, some of its wires running up the wall to the dome; others attached themselves to the large telescope.

Helius threw open the cupboard's doors and observed the contents within. More bottles sat on the many shelves, dusty and oddly shaped. Old spell books occupied another shelf, their pages yellowed and weather-worn. Powders, potions, and amulets sat on the bottom shelf, some glowing and others dark.

The topmost shelf, however, held the prize Helius was seeking. A large black bottle with a cork resided there, the bottle emblazoned with many ancient markings and warnings. Helius pulled the large bottle off the shelf and popped open the cork. A cloud of dark mist poured out, encircling Helius.

"Azrael's Veil," Helius murmured, putting out a hand and touching the dark cloud. "Enter the portal to Terra-Quenlist," he hissed, pointing out the large window that occupied the last wall. "Block out the sun and put a damper on the happiness. Make the world vulnerable to my evil."

The mist whirled itself into a small tornado and sped quickly out the window, Helius flying behind. Across the darkened landscape they raced, quickly reaching Onyx Falls. Helius landed on the ground with a tremendous crash, standing still and observing the mist as it passed through the waterfall to the portal beyond.

"Yes," Helius whispered, clenching his hands into fists and smiling cruelly, his lips curling back into a sneer.

From behind Helius, someone groaned. He whirled around to see a disgruntled Calvin Moocher stand up. Calvin rubbed his head and back, groaning again. His hair was windblown and his face was red.

"Moocher! Where were you?!" Helius bellowed, his eyes flashing wildly.

"Sorry Helius," Calvin wheezed, brushing himself off and standing straight. "I had a bit of trouble with the guards. To top it off, I then had issues with the portal."

"Ah! No time for that!" Helius huffed, producing a vial from his pocket and opening it. "Drink this to receive your power!"

Calvin grabbed the vial and drank its contents greedily, glowing as the liquid traveled down his throat. He grinned and winked, obviously showing that he had received his power.

"Very good," Helius said, sneering as he stalked toward the waterfall and stood in front of it. "You will not need training because you are already an expert at dishonest acts," Helius continued, motioning for Calvin to follow him. "Very soon," he said, clasping his hands, "Terra will be mine."

*****

MJ shrieked and pointed to the sky, one hand over her mouth. A large, dark veil stretched itself across the sky, blocking out the sun. Within seconds, all of Terra was covered in darkness.

"It has begun," Gavin whispered, his eyes changing from a purple to a green color. "Helius is preparing to attack."

*****

CHAPTER VIII: TASHA MAGNOLIA, KEEPER OF LIFE AND YOUTHFULNESS

"ARE WE READY?" JASMINE ASKED, COMBING HER ruffled hair with her fingers.

"You bet," Maximus answered, standing and adjusting his weapons belt, then helping Jasmine to her feet.

"My harpies, to me!" Jasmine shouted, making the entrance room quiver. From every door in the room emerged a group of harpies. These harpies, however, differed from Jasmine and her handmaidens. These were old and ugly, winged and hag-like in appearance.

"These are your harpies?" Maximus inquired, frowning.

"Yes," Jasmine answered with a grin. "Only my handmaidens are beautiful."

"I see," Maximus replied, heading for the entranceway.

Jasmine whistled, and a great beast burst through a door nearest the crumbling staircases. It looked like an overgrown Rottweiler, with glowing red eyes. Its teeth were large and sharp. And it stood there, baring them at Maximus.

"Come here, Max," Jasmine called. The hellhound obeyed, sitting at Jasmine's feet after being beckoned to her.

"Your hellhound's name is Max?" Maximus said, looking quizzically at Jasmine.

"I happen to like the name Max," she replied playfully, grinning. "It just has a certain…hmmm…something…to it."

"Uh huh," Maximus snorted, heading for the door and shaking his head. "Let's just go. Helius is probably waiting impatiently for us."

They pushed open the large doors of Hell's Gate and stepped out. Jasmine held Maximus tightly around the waist and lifted from the ground, her harpies following suit. One grabbed her hellhound as it took off. First, they stopped and gathered the other creatures Maximus had recruited, some of the harpies carrying them. Then, they flew quickly toward the castle, only to see a large army in the distance, heading toward the Onyx Falls.

"They must have left without us!" Maximus shouted over the wind. "We have to catch up to them!"

*****

"Gavin, what do we do?" MJ squeaked, shaking. "What is that cloud?"

"An evil spell," Gavin replied. "Project your powers to protect yourselves. I'm not sure what this spell can do."

"What about the other keepers?" Cody asked, looking at Serenity.

"We have to find Ginger first!" MJ commented, looking around the dense woods as if Ginger was nearby.

"We've already looked everywhere, MJ!" Cody replied in frustration, punching a tree.

"Maybe we aren't looking in the right place," Gavin said suddenly, an idea springing to mind. He turned his attention away from his keepers, instead knocking on the trees until he found one that sounded hollow. "Aha!" he cried, running his fingers over its trunk. Without warning, he pushed the tree and it turned to dust, revealing a large clearing with an enormous dollhouse-like castle at its center.

"What…" MJ started, looking around, then back at the crystalline castle.

"The Realm of the Fairies," Gavin answered, stepping closer to the castle. "I forgot about it completely. My guess is that Ginger is here, in Fairyland."

The tree behind them returned to its normal form, blocking them in. "Now what?" Serenity asked, laying her carpet on the ground. MJ and Cody followed suit as well, looking tired.

"Well, I guess we'll just have to go in," Gavin replied, smiling. He took out his wand and smacked Cody on the head with it.

"Ouch! What the heck?!" Cody yelled, suddenly feeling shorter than everyone. Within seconds, he was small enough to enter the castle with ease.

"Stay right there," Gavin's voice boomed from above. "We'll be joining you in a minute." He repeated the process with MJ and Serenity, then finally himself. He was the last to shrink, rubbing the top of his head as he became small.

"Let's go," he said, heading for the castle. He reached the elegant front door and grabbed the knocker, releasing it and letting it hit the door. A guard with gossamer wings opened the door and immediately stepped aside, bowing. Gavin nodded and stepped inside, the others following him.

The guard, after entering and closing the door, led them down a long blue hallway to a door nearest its opposite end. He opened it for them and said, "Her Majesty is through the door at the end, Your Imperial Majesty."

"Thank you," Gavin said to the guard, proceeding through the door into a large dining hall. Icy chandeliers hung from the ceiling, and a long wooden table stretched from one end of the room to the other, where a door stood. Gavin led the others to the door and opened it, stepping into the glamorous throne room. Ginger was on the other side of the room, talking with the queen and the queen's daughter.

"Ginger!" MJ yelled, running across the room and almost knocking Ginger over when she hugged her.

"Hi!" Ginger remarked, patting MJ on the back and giggling.

"Gavin Moonstone!" Ivy roared, jumping out of her throne and meeting Gavin in the middle of the room. She shook his hand and smiled.

"Ivy Snowfall, it's been a long time," Gavin replied, hugging her gently.

"Indeed," she agreed, turning and facing Gavin's friends.

"Thank you for caring for one of my keepers," Gavin added, gesturing toward Ginger.

"Mae took care of her," Ivy answered, turning to her daughter, who was now talking with Ginger and the others.

"I remember when she was a child. How she has grown," Gavin murmured, observing the princess.

"So tell me," Ivy said casually, walking over to her throne and sitting back down. Gavin followed, standing in front of her. "What's going on?" she continued. "You have never left your castle for this long unless something has gone terribly wrong."

Gavin leaned close to Ivy and whispered, "It's here. The Great Evil from the prophecy."

Ivy gasped and shuddered, suddenly feeling chilled. "So the prophecy is true?" Gavin nodded solemnly as she continued. "What can we do? The evil is destined to destroy us all!"

"Not all prophecies have come to pass. All we can do is fight back and hope to vanquish it," Gavin replied.

"Have you spoken with the Oracle?" Ivy asked, dreading the answer.

"Yes," Gavin replied, shaking his head. "She told me what I feared—that good would lose."

"The Oracle is never wrong," Ivy whispered, her face suddenly turning deathly white.

"Just because she's never been wrong doesn't mean she is infallible," Gavin remarked stubbornly. "We will do what we can. It's my job as emperor to protect my people."

"As is it mine as queen," Ivy agreed, standing up. "If this is indeed the dreaded prophecy, then my fairies will join you. This evil threatens the existence of all."

"Thank you, Ivy," Gavin said, bowing. "You are a true queen."

"Gavin!" Ginger yelled, making him jump. "We still gotta find the rest o'the keepers!"

"Right," Gavin said, turning to Ginger and nodding. "We have to be very quick."

"Mae," Ivy instructed, "assemble all of the fairies. We're going to help the emperor fight." Mae nodded and ran for the door. "Mae!" Ivy called. "Get some weapons for Gavin and his keepers!"

*****

Tasha Magnolia stepped out of her house, her jaw dropping when she saw the abomination that filled the skies. It was blocking out the sun! In her opinion, anything that blocked out the sun completely was evil. She shivered. The dark veil had cooled the air and had given a great feeling of sadness.

Sighing and trying to think positive, Tasha turned to the large garden she had been caring for and picked up a watering can, sprinkling water lightly across the small plants that grew. The veil emitted a terrifying sound, and bolts of lightning suddenly erupted from it. They struck the ground near Tasha and her garden. She yelped as a bolt hit close and missed her, striking the garden's foliage and setting it ablaze.

*****

The army arrived at the Onyx Falls, meeting Helius and Calvin. Close behind the army came another army, led by Queen Jasmine and Maximus. They set down behind the larger army and stopped, Jasmine and Maximus stepping forward.

"It's about time," Charity chided, shaking a finger at Maximus and frowning as she emerged from the gathered army.

"Negotiations take time, stupid woman," Jasmine growled, her eyes staying on the fuming Charity.

"There you are!" a voice roared over the rest of the army. Helius waded through the crowd to meet Maximus. "Excellent! You're late, but your tardiness does not deter my plans one bit!"

Helius chuckled, wading back over to the dark waterfall and standing on a large, mossy rock.

"Army of Chaos! We will be invading in waves!" He paused as the army quickly silenced, all attention on him. Once he was satisfied he had everyone's attention, Helius continued. "I want the first wave to go with Callus, Regina, Charity, and Burgundy. The second wave will go with Bracchus, Calvin, Victoria, and Shane. The final wave will be with Maximus, Matthew, Morpheus, Torizar, and me. The second wave will provide support for the first wave, and the third wave will split into two groups. One group will fight with the rest, and the other group will guard the Onyx Castle." Roars and cheers erupted from the army, eager creatures waiting to fight. They quieted down quickly, waiting for Helius to speak once more.

"First wave, move out now!" he roared. A large portion of the army stepped forward and followed Callus, Regina, Charity, and Burgundy through the waterfall.

*****

Equipped with magical weapons, Gavin, Ivy, and the others exited the castle. Gavin pulled his wand out of the bag once more and pointed it into the air. A beam of light erupted from it, exploding when it was high in the air and showering everyone. Within seconds, all had returned to normal human size, including the fairies gathered with them.

"Mystic!" Ivy called over the crowd. From the depths of the forest emerged a unicorn, its horn shining and sparkling. Its mane and coat were pure white, the purest white ever to exist. Its hooves were white as well. Its eyes, like Ivy's, were icy-blue. The unicorn trotted over to Ivy, who stroked its head, then swung herself onto its back. She clicked her tongue and the unicorn started forward at a fast trot.

"My fairies," Ivy spoke, quieting everyone as she turned the unicorn around to face them. "Report to Twilight Pass and join the Royal Army. We will report to all of you as soon as possible." The ground shook, and lightning erupted from the black veil above, shattering the cool air with an electric crack. Mae shivered, her tiara reflecting the lightning's image.

"Warriors," Gavin suddenly cut in. "Every town that you pass, order evacuation to the Crystal Palace. I want everyone to be safe. Those who are not fighting, evacuate as well. Those fighting, evacuate refugees and report to Twilight Pass."

"Heed the emperor's words," Ivy boomed, raising her arms. All of the fairies nodded and proceeded through the woods at a rapid pace, leaving Gavin, his keepers, Mae, and Ivy alone.

Gavin turned to Ivy as the keepers picked up their carpets. Ginger's carpet, which had been ripped and tattered from her fall, was now repaired, thanks to the great magic of the fairies. "Ivy," Gavin said, "I'm going to continue locating my keepers."

"I will gather the pixies and the nymphs, then the brownies and the dryads," Ivy said. She grabbed Mae and hoisted her onto the unicorn.

"We must hurry," Gavin said quickly. "We haven't much time. Helius approaches."

"Mother," Mae spoke, "what about blocking the portal with fairy magic? It might not hold them for long, but it may give us a little extra time."

"Excellent idea!" Ivy answered, pointing her wand at the sky. She muttered something, and an icy beam sped upward, heading in the direction of the Onyx Castle.

"The spell should take effect quickly," Ivy said, patting Mystic on the head. "It won't hold for long, I'm afraid. But it should lend a bit of aid. And now I'll be on my way."

"We'll meet at the Mystic Gardens," Gavin said, nodding to Ivy and Mae and bowing slightly.

"We shouldn't all travel together!" Ginger suddenly protested. "Some of us should protect Ivy and Mae; the others should go with Gavin."

"Right," Cody added, smirking.

"Very well," Gavin answered, after receiving an affirming nod from Ivy. "Ginger, Cody, and MJ—go with the royals and protect them. Fairy magic is powerful, but it has its limitations."

The three nodded and readied their carpets, sitting on them in consistency with each other. Waving to Gavin, they hovered in flight, then followed the swiftly moving unicorn. Within seconds they had disappeared, leaving Gavin and Serenity alone.

"Well, Serenity," Gavin sighed, sitting on his black bag for a moment, "we'd better hurry. Things are going to get complicated very soon."

*****

Helius was furious. Though his magical veil had seeped Terra in darkness, a strong magical seal prevented him and his army from exiting the Onyx Castle. They were officially stuck. He had arrived to see everyone crammed into the entrance hall; over half of his army had been expelled back to Chaos. His plans, he felt, had just been sabotaged.

"Hexus!" Helius roared over the noise, wading through the crowd to meet a flustered Hexus. "What's preventing us from getting through, and why?!"

"The emperor must have anticipated this attack!" Hexus bellowed back. "It's some kind of fairy magic! There is also an elemental net as well! All five elements are intertwined!"

"Can you break them?!" Helius shouted.

"It may take some time, but I think I remember a certain spell from my book," Hexus shouted.

"Just hurry!" Helius screamed in rage, his voice echoing over the overwhelming noise of the crowd. "I want this seal broken in less than an hour!"

*****

Tasha emptied buckets upon buckets of water from Moonlight Marsh onto the inferno that used to be her garden. If she couldn't put the fire out, it would engulf her house in a matter of minutes. She loved her house and would do anything to protect it.

Her great-grandmother, who had raised her, had left the house and its belongings to her in her will. Though it was an older house, Tasha adored it.

Its structure was modeled after old architecture, a large elegant-style house made of special oak. A balcony had been built on the house's second floor, attaching to the master bedroom. A small patio with a garden was constructed in the center of the house; all of the first floor rooms connected to it. A small fountain sat in the patio's center, the surface of its water always still, unless birds decided to bathe in it.

The fire inside the garden grew larger and more intense, its flames already engulfing the small fence around the garden's perimeter. Tasha frantically ran for more water, hoping she could at least hold the fire at bay until it burned out.

The fire crept ever closer to the large trees that encircled the house. Tasha scooped up another bucket of water and ran toward the garden, noticing immediately that the heat of the fire had intensified. It was then that she realized she was fighting a losing battle. Without help, she would lose everything. She sat on the ground, dropping the bucket and sobbing in frustration. It wasn't fair! What had she ever done to deserve this?!

"Help me, please!" Tasha cried, her voice carrying on the wind, barely audible to her over the raging inferno.

"Hold on!" someone cried. A man with blonde hair rushed to her aid, brandishing a willow wand. He raised the wand and shouted, "Frigid be the air o'er yonder, come now swift with blowing snow!"

A whirlwind of a blizzard exploded from the wand, shattering the barrier of heat that seemed to be everywhere. The snow smothered the blazing fire, putting it out almost immediately. In a matter of seconds, the air cooled, leaving a charred and smoking garden, only remotely similar to the lush foliage that had grown so abundantly only minutes before.

"You saved my house and my life! Thank you!" Tasha breathed, lying on the ground with sweet relief.

"It's no problem!" the man said, helping her up and steadying her before continuing. "What happened?"

"A lightning bolt shot out of that cloud and hit my garden!" Tasha exclaimed, pointing upward at the menacing anomaly.

"So the lightning just erupted out of the cloud?" the man asked, his brow furrowing when Tasha nodded.

"It seemed like the lightning purposely targeted me!" Tasha continued. She paused when she noticed a woman on a flying carpet behind the man. She was puzzled and afraid for a moment, but relaxed when the woman smiled warmly and waved. "One minute, I was watering my garden. The next minute…" she trailed off, motioning to the charred area that had once been a garden.

"Interesting…" the man said with a hint of distance, rubbing his chin.

"Who are you? You look so familiar," Tasha suddenly said, aware that this man was someone she had seen somewhere before.

"Gavin Moonstone," Gavin replied. "I've actually come seeking Tasha Magnolia."

"You can't be the emperor," Tasha said in disbelief. "Why would the emperor want my help? I'm just plain old Tasha!"

"Well, 'plain old Tasha,'" Gavin continued, "you have a certain gift, do you not?"

"I dunno," Tasha replied, stopping a minute to think. Her mind was suddenly racing with so many thoughts. Did she have a special talent? What about her would make the emperor insist upon her help? And WHY?

"The flowers in my house never die," Tasha said, suddenly feeling stupid for opening her mouth and voicing the first thing that came to mind. Why did the emperor care about some stupid flowers?

"Very interesting," Gavin mumbled, mentally checking the powers he had yet to distribute. "How do you manage that?"

"Well, I talk to them," Tasha added, feeling even stupider than before. Quickly, she added, "They belonged to my great-grandmother. I loved her very much and kept them after she died. They remind me of her."

"Ah…I see," Gavin said slowly.

"You probably think I'm insane," Tasha said, shaking her head and cringing at the answer she knew was to come. But it did not. The woman behind Gavin smiled with slight amusement and trust.

Gavin looked at Tasha for a moment, a hint of amusement in his features also. "I don't think you are insane, my dear. Quite the contrary, I think you have a special ability called Creative Visualization. Have you ever heard of it?"

Tasha searched her memory, trying to remember. So many jumbled thoughts. She had never been to one of the palaces of magic—she had only gone to a normal school. She finally gave up and shook her head, unable to recall any sort of subject.

"Okay," Gavin started. "Have you ever wanted something to happen so badly that it actually did? For example, you said that the flowers in your house remind you of your great-grandmother, whom you loved very much. Perhaps you wanted these plants to live so badly because they were your great-grandmother's that you made them immune to death." Tasha finally realized where the wizard was going with his thoughts and nodded.

"Creative Visualization is based upon putting thoughts into powerful energies," the woman cut in. "If it is needed badly enough, the thought can actually be transformed into a reality."

"Thank you, Serenity," Gavin said, smiling. "Tasha, this is Serenity Hall, Keeper of Peace and Prosperity."

Serenity smiled once again and winked at Tasha, who smiled back and laughed, despite the cold and the dampened mood the cloud created. When at last understanding, Tasha asked, "So…you think I have this ability?"

"Without a doubt," Gavin immediately responded, "which brings me to my original purpose. I require your help to fight a great evil and am willing to give you a lot of power to help." He paused, nodding as if to confirm a disputed argument's conclusion.

"I am willing to give you the powers of Life and Youthfulness." He paused again, noting the glimmer of interest in Tasha's eyes.

"Life and Youthfulness?" she repeated, slowly emphasizing the words' syllables.

"Yes," Gavin said, grinning ever so slightly. "You could restore organisms to life and keep them from ever growing old."

"What's the catch?" Tasha asked warily.

"Discretion and better judgement must be used with these two particular powers," Gavin warned. "Misuse of these two can have disastrous consequences."

"So I could bring back people from the dead?" Tasha asked hopefully.

"No," Gavin said firmly. "Doing that tampers with the balance of nature. They would come back…differently…than you remembered them."

"How so?" Tasha asked.

"Their souls have transcended to a higher realm," Gavin explained. "Trying to bring them back from a higher enlightenment would be futile. Their bodies would come back, but not their souls, leaving nothing but evil zombies. Then you're dealing with the reanimation of the dead, called necromancy. It's an extremely dark type of magic used for vengeful purposes."

Tasha shuddered, deciding against the idea at reviving any people. "I happen to be very good at using the right type of judgement," she said proudly, dismissing the previous thought.

"Very well," Gavin said, shrugging. "Do you accept?"

"What exactly am I helping you with?" Tasha asked, suddenly smothered with a cloud of confusion once again.

"That cloud above us is no cloud at all," Gavin said gravely as he pointed upward. "It is a shroud of evil, summoned by a powerful, decimating force."

Tasha felt a cold shiver run up her spine. Though she had never been to one of the palaces of magic, she had heard about a 'Great Evil,' a terrifying force destined to swallow the world she loved. She shuddered.

"If we defeat the evil, will the spell go away?" She felt a wave of relief when Gavin nodded in confirmation.

"Once the Great Evil is vanquished, its presence will be lifted from Terra forever," Gavin replied.

"Count me in," Tasha responded, nervously running her fingers through her hair.

Gavin clasped his hands together, muttering, "Spirit of Life, flee from me to she who is intended free. Entwine with your jubilant Youth."

A shock wave of white light erupted from Gavin's silhouette, encasing Tasha in a glowing orb. The light faded instantly, absorbed by Tasha's figure. She sighed with content, feeling immense power coursing through her being.

The new magic within her made her tingle, but in a warm and comforting way. It offered an unseen protection as if say, *"You are not alone."*

"Are you all right?" Gavin asked, looking visibly drained and, somehow…older than normal.

"I've never been better," Tasha replied, still feeling the absolute energy drifting smoothly through her veins.

Gavin opened his mouth to reply, but a shock wave suddenly sent both of them toppling to the ground. The wave rippled across the landscape, shaking all of Terra. Serenity, who was sitting on her carpet, watched smaller trees crash to the ground as the earth beneath them broke apart.

*****

"Well?" Helius asked impatiently, one of his black boots clicking against the cold stone floor. Hexus stood in front of the door, his large book open. Its pages revealed letters of gold, words glowing as he chanted and recited them.

"The spell went through, but a few barriers remain," Hexus replied, annoyed that he had been interrupted. "The first few barriers must have caused a shock wave when they shattered. Undoubtedly, this has alerted the emperor."

"Who cares?" Helius snapped, his face purpling. "Hurry up and break through already! I'm getting impatient!"

"Just calm down. Destruction will come swiftly once the final spell is uttered," Hexus replied coolly, shifting the weight of his book from one arm to the other. "Don't worry. Releasure will promise complete takeover."

Hexus turned his attention back to his beloved book, his lips forming a terrible sneer. He was the most powerful force aside from Helius, and he intended to use that power. A couple of puny white magic containment spells cast by imbeciles would not be nearly enough to stop him, the great Matthew Hexus. He'd show those do-gooders what true power could really do!

*****

"Mother, I'm worried," Mae whispered, clinging tightly to Ivy's waist as the ground beneath them shook from the shock wave. "We looked for the pixies and the nymphs at Sapphire Falls, Topaz Falls, and Ruby Falls. We haven't found a thing!"

True enough, the three waterfalls were wonders of nature. Each was unique in its own special way. Sapphire Falls had beautiful water, sparkling and cool, perfect for drinking. It flowed from a small reservoir over a smooth cliff and pooled in a shallow indentation of rock. Embedded in the cliff and also in the pool were hundreds of sapphires, gathered and carefully placed by the nymphs.

The same held true with Topaz Falls. A larger, more jagged cliff shaped and molded the cold water as it fell to a larger, more indented pool. The pool sparkled as the many pieces of topaz reflected the sunlight. It was a true wonder of nature.

And then there was Ruby Falls. Its cliff was shorter than all the others, but in no way was it of less value. The precious rubies at the bottom of its deep pool tinted the water red instead of a clear blue. Ruby Falls was Mae's favorite spot for relaxation.

"I assume that the pixies and the nymphs sought shelter at either Emerald Falls or Diamond Falls," Ivy answered, shattering Mae's daydream and bringing her back to reality.

Oh, how Mae wished everything were back to normal. Her memories were of beautiful, bright places and a world of purity, where darkness could not exist. Now that she had been robbed of her daydream, the darkness of reality shocked and angered her.

Something took sudden hold of her and she clenched her fists, a fire of intense hatred welling deep inside. Her face contorted into an ugly snarl, and she felt compelled to unleash an unseen fury upon the first person closest to her…her mother.

Unaware of what she was doing and overtaken by a sudden haze of red-hot menace, Mae brought her hand up swiftly, slapping Ivy upside the head with a powerful blow that knocked the queen toppling right off the unicorn. Completely dazed, Ivy looked up at Mae. But this was not her daughter, the sweet girl she had raised. An evil creature had taken possession of her, body and mind.

Mae's eyes glowed red with fury. She gnashed her perfect teeth as white fists clenched and unclenched. One perfect arm raised, a finger outstretched. Electricity sparked from the end of it, waiting to pounce upon the disgruntled queen.

Quick as a flash, MJ jumped in front of Ivy, bearing the silver shield she had been given. Cody uttered a wave of sound in Mae's direction, slowing the princess. MJ, nodding to the others, signaled to Ginger, who unleashed a pink beam from the palm of her right hand. The beam struck Mae in the abdomen and knocked her backward off Mystic. The possessed princess landed on the ground with a crash, then lay still.

Ivy, now fully recovered, pulled out her wand and shouted, *"Expellara!"* The princess shrieked in a terrifying, double voice as the offending shadow was expelled. Trapped in a magical web more powerful than itself, the shadow floated helplessly in mid-air.

"My magic isn't strong enough to destroy this creature!" Ivy yelled, obviously asking for assistance.

"MJ, do you know what to do?" Ginger asked, frantic to destroy the horrid creature before it was released.

"Try a blessed weapon!" MJ replied as the shadow howled with rage.

"We don't have a blessed weapon!" Ginger shrieked, panicking as the magical web ensnaring the creature weakened.

"Gavin!" MJ shouted to the wind. "Help!"

In a flash of light, the wizard stood next to her, his face whitening as he caught sight of the terrifying shadow. A girl, obviously Tasha Magnolia, stood with him, terror apparent in her eyes at the sight of the monster. Serenity's face paled as she hovered on her carpet, next to the girl.

Gavin quickly opened his bag and produced his wand. Pointing it at the shadow, he shouted, "Light of day, expel dismay!"

Light shattered the darkness, and the shadow's cries were cut short by its inability to utter another shriek. In terror, it struggled to escape the beam that shot toward it, but to no avail. The light impacted with the anomaly, vaporizing it in an instant. A small explosion lit up the sky, causing Azrael's Veil to shrink upon itself momentarily.

Ivy collapsed, her strength drained. The shadow had been powerful. If Gavin had not come when he had… Ivy shuddered, suddenly feeling cold. She noticed that Gavin looked worn out as well.

The wizard helped the queen to her feet, turning his attention to Mae, who was now quite silent. "The shadow possessed her, didn't it?" he asked. Ginger was appalled at the sound of his voice. It seemed weary, devoid of its usual jovial tone.

Ivy nodded shakily, tears streaming silently down her cheeks. Gavin released his grip on her, allowing Ginger and Cody to catch her as she collapsed from fatigue. He motioned for Tasha and Serenity, who followed him to the fallen princess.

Kneeling down, Gavin produced a small plant out of thin air. He turned to Tasha, his voice quiet. "Tasha, please wake her. Be gentle and soft." Serenity hopped off her carpet and shifted her weight from one foot to the other, biting her lip as she uneasily waited for her orders.

"Serenity," Gavin continued, "let your peace flow into her when she awakens. We want her to be calm so stress does not further drain her."

Serenity nodded, kneeling on one side of Mae. Tasha knelt on the other, rubbing her hands together vigorously. She had no experience with her new powers, and she wondered if Gavin knew that. Or perhaps he was testing her? She had no idea what to do.

Placing her hands above Mae's head, Tasha whispered, "Awaken."

Serenity, sensing Tasha's magic and somehow knowing exactly what to do, touched Mae's arm and whispered, "Be one with peace, princess."

Mae's eyes fluttered open as she felt a sudden surge of awesome power. It felt as though she had just drunk a thousand cups of fairy wine. Her fingers twitched as she shakily sat up with the help of Serenity and Tasha.

What had happened? One minute she had been sitting on Mystic with her mother, daydreaming, and the next... The shocking event became clear at once to Mae. Something had made her angry. Yes, that was it. Then a terrible darkness had suppressed her abilities to move, to think. She remembered seeing her own arm lift and hit her mother, but had no control to stop it.

She cried out in fear when she saw Ginger and Cody cradling the figure of her mother, MJ quietly talking to them. What had she done?! She quickly tried to get up to check her mother.

Gavin's strong hands came swiftly, firmly holding her. "Mae, it's all right! Calm down! Your mother will be fine; she's just fainted!"

Mae relaxed, but only a little. "Gavin, what have I done?! I could have killed her!"

"Mae!" Gavin said sharply, shaking her lightly. "You know as well as I that there was no controlling what happened! Thank the gods that the shadow didn't kill you!"

Sensing that he had frightened the princess, Gavin softened his tone. "Understand that this was not your fault. You could not have stopped what happened." He held up the plant for Mae. "Now eat this. It's peppermint. It works wonders at calming and soothing an individual."

Mae accepted it gratefully, gnawing on it and savoring its wonderful taste. Somehow suddenly feeling exhausted, Mae's eyelids became heavy. The peppermint made her sleepy. Losing the battle with fatigue, Mae immediately slipped into a dreamless slumber.

CHAPTER IX: DANIELLA BOREALIS, KEEPER OF TRUTH AND HONESTY

GINGER SAW THE FIGURE OF MAE SLUMP AND STOOD up, allowing MJ and Cody to care for the queen. She walked briskly over to the standing Gavin and stood close, gently touching his shoulder. Serenity and Tasha sensed that Ginger needed to speak to him privately, so they stepped away from the slumbering Mae to aid Cody and MJ.

"Gavin…" Ginger started.

"Ginger, she almost died," Gavin said, turning to face her. "If the shadow had not been pulled out when it was…" He paused, silently cursing himself for not casting protection charms over everyone.

"Gavin, she's fine," Ginger said softly. "She's asleep, regaining energy."

"The point is—why did I not protect all of you with my magic?" Gavin said miserably. "I knew that this sort of creature would undoubtedly appear, but I refused to think that it was capable of inflicting harm!"

"The point is that you saved Mae and destroyed the shadow," Ginger said, becoming impatient. "Everything's fine; you still can cast protection charms upon us."

"You're right, as always," Gavin said, smiling weakly. "I am confident that you will be an excellent leader." Ginger had noticed an immediate change while Gavin was talking to her. He looked as though he had begun to age. A couple wrinkles had formed on his face, and he now had permanent dimples.

"They will both sleep for a while," Gavin said, indicating Mae and Ivy. "Make sure to explain everything to them that has occurred. Continue on the journey to find the magical beings Ivy was searching for. Then meet me at the Mystic Gardens."

He pointed his wand to the sky and muttered an incantation. Seven bubbles of white light spouted from it, each encasing its own individual. Within seconds, the entire party was under the protection of the purest light.

"What about you?" Ginger asked quietly.

"Don't worry," Gavin said, smirking. "I'll be fine." He turned away, depositing the wand back into his bag. He then pulled out another carpet, this one pink.

"Show Tasha how to use this and get acquainted with everyone," he said firmly. "If any more creatures like the shadow appear, fight them with your powers or a blessed weapon. Do not try to use the incantation that brings light."

"Gavin, we don't have any blessed weapons!" Ginger protested.

Gavin laughed out loud, causing Ginger to redden. "Ginger, all fairy weapons are blessed. Of course you do!" Yet again he paused, then added, "I must emphasize the importance of your getting to know one another. Take Tasha and Serenity with you. You may need all the help you can get."

"What if we need you again?" Ginger asked, not ready to accept defeat.

"You must learn to be independent but also rely on each other," Gavin answered. "I will not always be able to rush to your aid. But if you do need me, do as MJ did. Call me. As you saw, I am quite able to appear whenever I'm needed."

"But…" Ginger started, then shrugged. It would be no use to argue, and questioning Gavin's ability to teleport might just aggravate him.

Sensing her hesitation, Gavin reached into his bag and pulled out an amulet, attached to a silver chain. An amethyst was fastened to the center of the small medallion, glowing a bit. "Wear this talisman," Gavin said, fastening it around Ginger's neck. "It works with your feelings. In times of trouble, it can work wonders."

"Thank you!" Ginger burst out, hugging the emperor as her emotions were suddenly let go.

Gently, Gavin patted her on the back, his good nature returning despite his fatigue. "Don't worry, Ginger. I know that everything will be fine. Now, I must locate Daniella Borealis. I will see you at the Mystic Gardens."

She released him and he evaporated in a flash of color. Gently trailing her fingers over the talisman, Ginger prepared to give everyone their orders. She smiled as her fingers touched the gentle surface of the amethyst.

*****

Asterel Sunfire, queen of the high elves, paced back and forth in worry. She had been observing the good emperor and his friends for a while. If Gavin could not succeed in locating the rest of the keepers, then…

Asterel shuddered, remembering the hideous image of the shadow. She had first looked in on the emperor when one of her guards had informed her of Rodaine's call to arms. Immediately sensing that something terrible was brewing, Asterel had looked into her Pool of Sight and seen what she had been dreading. A horrid man the likes of which none had ever seen whizzed through the air like a projectile, speeding toward a dark castle that had previously not existed on Terra.

Asterel had remembered a little of the prophecy. *"The Great Evil shall then come seeking his token, and at last in ruin shall Terra be broken."* That was all that Asterel could remember of the ancient rhyme.

So the prophecy was true and coming to pass. The Great Evil had come at last. Asterel bit her lip while thinking. Did she dare to intervene and help the emperor? She had known Gavin for the longest time, and also Ivy and Mae Snowfall. The royals of

Terra, including Gavin, were all good friends and looked out for each other. At last making her decision, Asterel nodded in silent confirmation and waved a hand over the pool, calling for a glimpse of the future.

The sight she observed made her utter a cry of terror. A burned landscape, devoid of life, stood in the pool's image. No birds sang. The water was tinted black. Bodies were strewn across the ground, faces contorted in absolute terror. At the center of the world stood the evil man, his cruel laugh echoing in Asterel's ears. She waved her hand over the pool, nullifying the monstrous image. If there was any way to change the future, she had to see to it immediately.

Rushing to her throne, she thrust a hand under its cushioned seat, grabbing a diamond sword. She called it "Luna." The blade was made of white diamond, unmatched by all other weapons. The hilt was silver, inlaid with opals and garnets. A gold band wrapped itself around the hilt, intertwining perfectly with the silver.

Asterel turned to the large mirror adjacent to her throne and looked carefully at her image. Her white-blonde hair and blue eyes were her favorite traits, as well as her dainty pointed ears. Her smooth, fair face stared back at her, a small smile forming and giving her an elegant appearance.

Asterel moved down to her clothes. Actually they weren't clothes, but armor. The armor was made of mythril, the hardest and most impenetrable metal of all. Gold also glittered on the armor, flitting across it to form the seal of the high elves. A necklace with a peridot glittered, dangling around her neck. The bright green color of the gem had always fascinated Asterel. The scabbard for her sword was attached to her right hip; she returned Luna to its place. Her armor traveled all the way down, even forming armored boots.

Asterel turned her attention to the crown that sat on her head. Though it was not as exclusive as the crowns of the other royals, it suited her liking. The crown she wore was merely a crown of laurels, fitting snugly around her head.

Asterel took a look around. Her eyes sparkled with unshed tears as she thought of the prophecy. If it came to pass, Pristine Vista—her home—would be destroyed.

Pristine Vista was more of a large town than a palace or castle. The throne room was at its heart, the very epicenter of the high elves' realm. Pristine Vista's buildings had quartz windows and were made of white stone. The town had rare trees and plants growing throughout, cared for by the queen herself. The magic she used protected the rarities from outside forces.

The beauty of Pristine Vista caused Asterel to lose her train of thought for a moment. Quickly snapping herself back to reality, Asterel summoned her maid. "Fauna!" she called, her silky voice carrying on the wind through the large town. Fauna, a young woman with black hair, quickly shuffled into the throne room. She was clothed in a yellow dress.

"Yes, Your Majesty?" Fauna asked, aware of the queen's distress.

"Summon Veronica Narcissus and my son, Thistle," Asterel said, her voice brisk. Fauna quickly nodded and hurried away.

Asterel sat in her throne, taking a final look around. She loved her throne room. It had high open windows that allowed bright sunlight to filter through unperturbed. The large yellow carpet that ran in a strip along the length of the room gave it a certain type of elegance. Planted trees stretched along each wall, towering to reach the windows. Delicious fruit grew on some, flowers on others. The high ceiling gave the room a lofty feel, making even the largest creature feel comfortable.

Fauna returned almost immediately with Thistle and Veronica. Asterel stood up and smiled as both bowed, awaiting her commands.

Veronica Narcissus was Asterel's commander. She always wore light, durable armor and a helmet, which hid her brown hair and pointy ears. Her beautiful face was in perfect synchronization with her hazel eyes. A heavy sword and shield resided in each hand.

Thistle Sunfire, prince of the high elves, was also a marvel to behold. He had short white-blonde hair like his mother's, but did not have her blue eyes. Instead, he had green eyes. Upon looking into them, one would notice a resemblance to the calm ocean. He wore mythril armor as well, almost the same as Asterel's. A sword was attached to his side, polished and ready. His fair features made all the women attracted to him.

"Commander," Asterel said after clearing her throat. "Take the army and assist the Royal Army of Terra at Twilight Pass. Ensure that no evil passes through to the rest of Terra."

"Yes, My Queen," Veronica said, bowing once again.

"Evacuate all beings to the Crystal Palace," Asterel continued. "The strongest protection rests at the emperor's palace."

Veronica nodded, saluted, and exited briskly. She must have anticipated Asterel's decision, for Asterel heard the marching of her army almost immediately. Her people were very efficient and loyal.

Turning to her son, she said, "Thistle, we must join forces with the emperor. The Great Evil approaches." Thistle's eyes widened with shock at her last statement, but he recovered quickly and nodded.

"Your Grace, what about me?" Fauna squeaked. Asterel couldn't help but smile. Fauna had been loyal to her for at least a century, carefully looking out for her wellbeing.

"Things are going to get dangerous. I wish for you to evacuate with the rest," Asterel replied warmly. "I don't want anything to happen to you, Fauna. You are family."

The maid nodded reluctantly. "At least allow me to ready your horses." Thistle chuckled as Asterel nodded in confirmation. Fauna hurried out of the room, leaving the royals to wait.

*****

"Gavin," crackled a voice. The crystal ball had unexpectedly flown out of the bag, transforming into the mirror. Rodaine's figure appeared, looking very worried.

"What's the matter, Rodaine?" Gavin asked quickly.

"An order of evacuation was issued," Rodaine began.

"I issued the order," Gavin answered. "What's the problem?"

"It seems as if magic is starting to fade," Rodaine said at last. "Good magic, that is. Only here in the palace does it function at its best."

"What's the status report?" Gavin asked.

"The palace is filling up with refugees quickly," Rodaine said, sighing. "I have cast what expansion spells I know to accommodate for the planetary exodus. Every magical race, including the five elemental palaces, has put up their strongest defenses around the palace."

He was cut short when a wolf pounced on him and knocked him over. "Ow! Stop that, you oversized mongrel!" Storm whimpered, plopping to the floor next to Rodaine. He wagged his tail like a puppy when he saw Gavin, but quickly sat still when Rodaine threw him a sharp glance.

"Many are still unaccounted for, including a great portion of the elves, fairies, and the whole Royal Army, of course. Also, we are missing refugees from quite a large number of towns. The five towers refused to evacuate, staying at their grounds to use their magic to protect themselves." Rodaine's voice sounded strained.

"Don't worry," Gavin said. "I'm sure that many are not aware of the order of evacuation. I'll make sure everyone gets there, or maybe to one of the other palaces." Rodaine nodded, and his image disappeared. The crystal mirror shifted, returning itself to the depths of the bag.

Gavin held tightly to his bag as he sped across Terra, toward Sunset Village. He could tell even before he landed that there was a big commotion. Perhaps another creature had slipped through the barriers around the Onyx Castle? No. The first shadow had been an unexpected accident. It must have somehow managed to slip through the magical webs. No other evil creatures were present, not even Helius! The shadow's appearance must have been accidental.

Gavin steeled himself, speeding downward to witness the total uproar occurring at Sunset Village. Hopefully, Daniella Borealis was still down there. He gritted his teeth and quickened his speed.

*****

"Mae…" Ivy whispered, finally stirring after what seemed like an eternity. Her head hurt, probably from the tremendous slap she had taken. Or maybe it was from falling down? She couldn't quite remember.

Finally seeing the queen stir, Ginger stopped the unicorn, which had two carpets attached to it. Ivy was on one carpet, Mae on the other. Mae still slept peacefully.

"How long have I been asleep?" Ivy asked drowsily as she sat up. She looked around, expecting to discern the time, but Azrael's Veil kept the time from her.

"At least an hour," Ginger answered, helping the queen off the carpet.

"And Mae?" Ivy asked hopefully. Ginger shook her head, indicating that Mae had not stirred. Ivy wobbled shakily to the other carpet, cursing her body for being so weak.

Gently, she caressed her daughter's forehead, speaking softly. "Mae, darling…wake up."

The princess emitted a soft sigh and opened one of her eyes. Seeing her mother, the other eye opened and she tried to sit up. However, she failed, wincing at the head rush it gave her. Opening her mouth to speak, Mae could somehow not utter any syllables. Cody, Tasha, Serenity, and MJ gathered behind the queen, relieved that both had finally awakened.

"Darling, please do not apologize," Ivy said softly. "It was an unfortunate event that should not have happened, but everything is fine now. The shadow is vanquished and Gavin put enchantments around us all." Ivy smiled warmly as her daughter finally managed to sit up.

"Mother, have we found the pixies and the nymphs?" Mae asked, finally able to speak. She groaned, sliding off her carpet.

"I don't know," Ivy said, puzzled. She turned to Gavin's keepers and asked, "Where are we?"

"We passed Sunrise Village a while ago," Ginger answered, helping the royals back onto Mystic.

"We're near Diamond Falls," Ivy murmured.

*****

Daniella Borealis sat inside her house, in front of her mirror. She brushed her curly light brown hair, observing her reflection and the long curls that flowed to her shoulders. She liked her dark blue eyes. In terms of height and weight, she measured average. She wore a light blue dress, covered by a long dark blue cloak with fur stitched around the outside of the hood, even though she was attempting to stay as plain as possible.

Finally finished brushing her silky hair, Daniella tied it in a tight ponytail. She stood up and stretched, looking around. Chaos had erupted in Sunset immediately after the dark cloud had arrived. People talked frantically of an apocalypse, a prophecy that was destined to come true. She had attended a non-magical school and had been told of a prophecy, but she refused to believe it.

The people were still trying to evacuate, pushing and shoving each other out of the way to exit. All had the same idea—flee to the safety of the Crystal Palace. Daniella, realizing that she would be trampled if she tried to escape, sat in her house, alone.

The commotion started to quiet down as more people managed to escape. After a small amount of time, the entire town was completely quiet. Daniella decided that she would go outside to take a look around.

*****

"Almost!" Hexus yelled, his book shivering tremendously. The doors of the Onyx Castle gleamed wildly as the magical webs came down. One last chant from Hexus and they exploded outward, showering the waiting army with debris.

"Go!" Helius shouted. The first wave poured out like an army of ants. Swords immediately met as army clashed with army.

"Defense!" yelled Bracken Pennyroyal, Commander of the Royal Army. Bracken was a younger man, with short brown hair and a mustache. His eyes were gray, matching his gray uniform. He rode a brown horse named Spark and carried a large broadsword and shield. His job was to protect the rest of Terra from invasion. Unfortunately, the opposing army outnumbered his, at least ten to one, and they just kept coming. Plus, he could not block the shadows that escaped his army so easily.

As if his prayers had suddenly been answered, an army of fairy warriors emerged from the west, brandishing silver weapons and shields. Leading them was the legendary Ross Hepatica.

Bracken had heard countless stories of the great Ross Hepatica, Commander of the Fairies. Ross was a tall man with silver gossamer wings. He had long black hair and a goatee. Sharp purple eyes were his most famous characteristic. He wore silver armor with the royal seal of the fairies embroidered on his breastplate. Bracken had idolized Hepatica ever since he was a child, hearing numerous tales of how valiant a warrior Hepatica was.

Now, seeing him in person…it was a dream come true. Bracken shook his head as the army of fairies approached swiftly, their weapons ready. He could reminisce later! Right now, he had to be a commander!

"The fairies are here to aid!" Hepatica bellowed, his warriors jumping into the battle, supporting the soldiers of the Royal Army. Rather than riding a horse, Hepatica sped around on foot, destroying any creature that crossed his path.

*****

Helius stood inside the Onyx Castle's entrance, observing the war that raged outside. Humans and fairies had combined forces to fight the forces of evil. Their efforts would be all in vain.

Helius's lips curled into an evil smile, and he chuckled. The hope that survived in the opposing army was too strong for even Azrael's Veil to destroy. He gave them credit—they were bold, fighting a losing battle. His second wave would be back through the Onyx Castle's portal any moment, followed by his third.

Helius remembered the book that he had catalogued in the Hall of Records. The book had a prophecy in it that spoke of him. However, it seemed almost as if a part of the prophecy was missing. Helius had no idea if it was a complete prophecy, nor if anyone knew for certain. Even so, the part of the prophecy he did possess stated that he would crush Terra-Quenlist for good. Undoubtedly, Terra knew of the prophecy as well. Helius wondered if someone on Terra possessed the seemingly missing part of the prophecy, but immediately shook off the idea. There had been no portal that connected the two worlds before he had created one. It was impossibly hard to create a magical tie between worlds.

"Now what?" Torizar asked as Helius turned and signaled to the arriving second wave of his army.

"We wait for the opportune moment," Helius replied, carefully observing the crowded battlefield. "When good and evil are fully locked in battle, we will cut through the middle. A path shall become clear."

Torizar shrugged, confused as to how a path could just appear. He turned to Maximus, who stood next to Jasmine. Torizar had destroyed many justices in his lifetime, but the justice that resided within the man standing next to him was too strong for even him to break. How could it be possible that Maximus had fallen in love with Jasmine? Even more unbelievable, how could Jasmine return his love?

Torizar silently yelled at himself to keep quiet. He knew that Helius would kill both Maximus and Jasmine if he ever found out. Technically, it was impossible for evil beings to love, since love was an element of a good nature. Besides, Maximus was his friend.

Torizar's thoughts were suddenly shattered when Hexus spoke up. "Helius, a path has formed! Look!"

Torizar spun around, his mouth dropping open in utter disbelief. At the very center of the battle, a small path had formed. Helius smiled and proceeded forward, ignoring the warring creatures around him. Torizar, Maximus, Hexus, Morpheus, and Jasmine followed. Helius reached into the crowd and pulled out Charity. She stopped struggling and stood at attention when she realized who had snatched her.

"Charity, gather the rest of the keepers and follow me. Start moving some of the troops through the fighting. We'll wreak havoc upon the whole planet!"

Charity grinned at Helius's words and jumped back into the battle, shouting for the rest of the keepers. While she continued shouting, Jasmine signaled her harpies to follow. They immediately proceeded down the path.

"Where are we going, Helius?" Hexus asked as they hurried down the narrowing path.

"All of us, save for Jasmine and her harpies, will launch an offensive on the Crystal Palace," Helius said, sneering evilly. "Jasmine and her harpies will invade all the towns and take people back to Chaos. Their souls will be most useful." All nodded as they continued down the ever-narrowing path. Helius headed west, all following him in silence.

*****

Gavin felt the shields shatter as he landed in Sunset Village. It would only be a matter of time before the Army of Chaos swept across Terra. Hopefully, all had evacuated to the safety of the palace.

A woman stepped out of one of the houses in the otherwise empty town. She saw Gavin and immediately walked over to him. "Your Majesty, what's going on? I heard people yelling of a prophecy and an apocalypse as they were evacuating!"

"I'm not sure if this is the apocalypse, but it is the feared prophecy," Gavin said.

"I don't believe in prophecies and fate," the woman stated adamantly.

"Excellent! I like the way you think!" Gavin said, a smile playing across his face as if he already knew the answer to the next question. "What is your name?"

"Daniella Borealis," the woman said, nodding slightly. "I'd take you to our village headman, but he evacuated with everyone else."

"Actually," Gavin said with a grin, "I was looking for you. I was hoping that you had stayed, and I was right."

"What would you, the emperor, want my help for?" Daniella asked in disbelief.

"I am compiling a council of the twelve most-skilled magical forces on the face of Terra-Quenlist. Of course, your name was one of them." Gavin paused, smiling.

"But I never attended any of the palaces of magic, Majesty," Daniella said, fidgeting as she tried to think.

"Daniella, just because you didn't learn magical techniques doesn't mean you don't possess magic," Gavin said. "True magic exists in your heart. It is something that no evil can ever defeat. Magic, whether people choose to admit it or not, is alive everywhere and in everyone."

At long last, Daniella stopped fidgeting and spoke. "What does the prophecy that I heard of say?"

"The full prophecy was lost ages ago," Gavin explained. "I don't even know the rest of it. I did, however, receive a part of the missing prophecy. It said that a dark castle and a great evil would appear, thus bringing Terra to ruin."

"The prophecy has to be wrong!" Daniella spat with rage. She set her jaw and continued. "I'll prove it! What do you need me to do?"

"I will give you the powers of Truth and Honesty," Gavin answered. "You would have the power to bring about feelings that are good and true."

"All right! Give them to me and I'll stomp that evil!" Daniella said confidently, her fists clenching with both anticipation and anger toward all forces of evil.

Gavin clenched his right hand into a fist. It glowed a light purple color. He opened his hand, releasing a small purple butterfly. It fluttered over to Daniella and landed on her nose, flexing its wings. Then, it exploded into purple dust, covering Daniella. She sneezed, backing up a little.

Rubbing her watery eyes, Daniella blinked away tears. She nodded again to Gavin and said, "Ready to kick some evil, boss. Let's go."

Gavin laughed lightly and opened his bag, pulling out a dark yellow carpet and laying it on the ground. "Just get on and give it instructions," he said as he motioned to the carpet.

"Take me to the evil!" Daniella shouted suddenly, jumping on. The carpet shot off the ground and sped toward Twilight Pass.

"Daniella, wait! Stop! Don't!" Gavin yelled, quickly closing his bag and chasing after the stealthy carpet.

*****

They had walked right onto the battlefield purely by accident. Ginger quickly jumped in front of the royals, acting as a human shield. Serenity almost fainted when she saw the war being waged. Horrifying creatures littered the battleground, locked in conflict with fairies and humans.

"Great! This is just what we needed!" MJ shouted over the clanging of weapons. "We were just trying to get to Emerald Falls!"

Though Diamond Falls had been an object to behold, it had also been devoid of creatures. MJ remembered looking into the shallow pool at the base of the towering waterfall and seeing her reflection in hundreds of perfectly shaped diamonds. They been cut by nature's hands, carved into flawless objects of splendor.

Ivy had remembered a small cave behind the green waterfall that was Emerald Falls and figured that the beings they sought were hiding there. However, they were now blocked from Emerald Falls by the warring armies in front of them. No path was visible.

"Well, don't just stand there!" MJ shouted to her colleagues. "Ginger, retreat with Ivy and Mae! Tasha, Serenity, and Cody, follow her! You can take shelter at Sunrise Village!"

MJ's words froze in her throat when an icy laugh echoed from behind her. It seemed to chill everything. Mae's face contorted into an expression of fear and horror as she looked past MJ at the man who had laughed.

MJ turned around, finally coming face to face with the man who had terrorized her dreams ever since she had learned of the feared prophecy. In an effort to hide her fear, MJ said, "Hm…you're uglier than I imagined."

Emperor Helius Rue's face curled into a snarl. "Hold your tongue, brat!" he said sharply, quieting MJ immediately. He looked around briefly, then turned back to MJ. "Where is your emperor, wench? Was he too afraid to fight? I'll bet that the freak is hiding somewhere!"

"I'll kill you!" Ginger screamed suddenly, lunging at Helius with her spear. Helius grabbed Ginger with one hand and tossed her away like a rag doll.

"That was fun," Helius said cruelly, his eyes narrowing as he observed the good group in front of him. "I would wager a bet that the pathetic little wretch has feelings for him!"

"Helius, would you like us to dispose of them?" Charity asked, stepping next to him. The other keepers and Jasmine seemed to advance as well.

"Keeper against keeper? Well now, that is an idea," Helius said, grinning. "I believe it would be quite enjoyable to see just how well these fools match up to my own keepers. Charity, take out that snotty boy. Victoria, you've got the wench I threw. Regina, take the brat with the ugly hair in a bun." He motioned to Serenity as he said this, then continued. "Calvin, you take the trollop in front of me. Torizar, you can have the one with the blonde hair."

Ivy and Mae backed off with Mystic as the keepers faced each other. Charity acted first. She waved her wand in a spiraling motion, summoning her nightmares. They arrived immediately, in conjunction with black-winged horses, also referred to as winged nightmares. She pointed at Cody and yelled to the nightmares. They charged at him, fire blazing from the nostrils of the horses.

With a mighty yell, Cody threw the fairy sword he had been given. It sliced across the barrage of nightmares, producing a pure white light. The remaining nightmares backed up, afraid of the blessed sword. Like a boomerang, it returned to Cody's hand.

Tasha ducked as Torizar's fist flew past. She darted behind him and gave him a mighty kick, knocking him to the ground. He jumped up and swung his hand around, administering a mighty blow to Tasha's face, knocking her off her feet.

Victoria jumped on Ginger, slapping her wildly. Ginger bit her on the hand and Victoria screamed, "Yuck! You're foaming at the mouth! Rabies!!!"

"So what if I foam at the mouth?! I was raised by wolves!" Ginger shouted, bringing up her closed fist and smashing it into Victoria's chin, then pushing the dazed keeper off her. Victoria recovered quickly, jumping up and brandishing a gold ring with a ruby at its center. She pointed it at Ginger, laughing wildly. A beam shot out of it, knocking Ginger head over heels.

Serenity looked at Regina in amazement as the keeper sat on the ground, scratching her head. "Where am I?" she asked, looking around. Turning to Serenity, she said, "Hello. I'd tell you my name, but I don't remember it. Come to think of it, I don't remember anything. Are we having a picnic?" Hexus jumped in with a roar and hauled away the amnesiac Regina, disappearing into the crowd of onlookers. Serenity, now free of an opponent, jumped in to help Ginger.

"You IDIOT!" Helius roared at Regina, who smiled stupidly at him. He turned away and yelled, "Morons! Why are you fighting without your magic? I gave you powers for a REASON!"

"Don't be afraid of me," Calvin said sappily to MJ, putting up his hands and walking toward her. MJ dropped to the ground and swept her foot across it, kicking Calvin's legs out from under him. She stepped onto the fallen Calvin, who grunted.

"My mother once told me something," MJ said angrily. "She said 'never trust a stranger.'" Her pressure on Calvin's chest increased as she put more weight on her foot. "Guess what? I'm not stupid! I'm the Keeper of Strength and Wisdom! So get out of my face, you traitorous bloated walrus!" She stepped off Calvin and gave him a hard kick in the side. He was sent rolling into the crowd of keepers, knocking them over like bowling pins.

Tasha threw her shield at Torizar, hitting him in the face. When his face became visible again, blood trickled from one corner of his mouth and from one of his nostrils. He angrily wiped it away, retreating back into the fallen crowd to help his colleagues up.

Serenity and Ginger grabbed Victoria by the arms and legs and threw her as hard as they could into the crowd of gathered harpies. They hissed and moved as Victoria careened past, landing on the ground with a thud. She stayed still as soon as she hit the ground.

"Get OFF me, you great oaf!" Helius roared, emerging from beneath Calvin. He stood up, brushing himself off furiously. His face had purpled with rage. All of the keepers he had sent to fight had been temporarily defeated, aside from Charity. He had underestimated the power of Moonstone's stupid minions. Curses!

"Finish him, Charity! Use your magic!" Helius yelled, indicating to Charity that the battle was no longer fun and games. Charity was winning. She had knocked the boy to the ground; his face was bruised from her punches. His bottom lip was swollen and bleeding. His sword had been dropped and was laying several feet away. He seemed to have given up.

Charity turned to Helius and nodded, her eyes flashing with pleasure. She raised her wand and pointed it at Cody, grinning. "I am really going to enjoy this," she said, starting to chant.

"My parents always told me not to hit girls," Cody said shakily, reaching into his pocket and producing a small leather bag. "So I guess I'll just have to improvise." He opened the bag and threw the powder that was inside in Charity's face.

Charity dropped her wand, sputtering and screeching. The dream powder all over her suddenly glowed, and she burst into flames. Helius's mouth dropped open as his Keeper of Nightmares exploded in a flash of fire. Her wand still lay on the ground; its silvery glow had faded to black.

"You'll pay!" Helius screamed, pointing his wand at Cody. From above, a ray of light emerged, hitting Helius and knocking him backward, once again toppling over the rest of the keepers. Victoria, who had just managed to stand, was sent flying once again. Gavin, along with Daniella, landed in front of their fallen adversaries. Gavin's wand sparkled, a trace of light still evident.

Helius jumped up, sputtering and fuming. "This is far from over! You may have won the first round, but you will not be so lucky next time!" Helius stomped against the ground and exploded upward in a blast of flames. Hexus opened his book and chanted something. He, the other keepers, Jasmine, and her harpies disappeared in a flash of smoke. Cody lay on the ground, sighing with relief. His empty bag was in one hand, and Charity's wand was now firmly gripped in the other.

"What were you doing?!" Gavin exploded, his eyes flashing amber. "Helius could have killed you! If I hadn't stepped in, you'd be a smoking pile of ash!"

"Gavin, it was an accident!" Ivy cut in quickly. "We were just trying to get to Emerald Falls! Helius and his keepers ran into us!" Gavin's eyes changed to blue, and he relaxed a little.

"Besides," MJ said calmly, "one of Helius's keepers has been vanquished."

"That is not the point! You were lucky this time!" Gavin said. He paused for a moment, the realization finally sinking in. Helius had twelve keepers, the same number Gavin would have. Now, Helius only had eleven. One, whom Helius had called Charity, had evaporated in an explosion of flame because of Cody's dream powder. Gavin now praised his keeper for his ingenious creation of the magical powder.

"Very well," Gavin said at last, rubbing his temples as the war behind him raged on. Unable to think clearly because of the noise close by, Gavin turned around and shouted, *"Obturare!"*

It seemed as if the entire battlefield was slowing to a stop. Creatures stopped in mid-blow. Weapons and shields were raised, frozen in the positions they had taken. The entire war had ceased in the blink of an eye.

"Wow..." Serenity breathed, sitting next to the bruised Ginger, who cradled her left leg. "What kind of power is that?"

"It's called the 'Time Freeze' ability," Gavin said, kneeling next to Ginger and mending her leg with an ancient magic. "We don't have much time. The spell doesn't last very long, so I have to be quick. It seems as if we are now winning, thanks to Cody's victory. Helius's power must have weakened from the loss of one of his keepers."

He paused as Cody handed him Charity's wand. Gavin examined it for a few seconds, looking at the name inscribed on it, then continued. "There are a couple of problems, though. First, we do not know what kind of powers Charity Moonshadow possessed."

"I do!" Mae cut in excitedly. "I was watching her fight with Cody. She was commanding some type of horses. They were black with black wings."

"I've read about those," Ginger added. "My adoptive mother, Eden Starglass, taught me to read. She had me study this odd book often. It was very old, and it carried a lotta information."

When Gavin gave her an encouraging nod, Ginger continued. "The book dealt strictly with evil creatures, and a whole section was devoted to studying the undead. One particular creature that I read about was the winged nightmare. It was a horse resurrected by a necromancer. It had large black wings and glowing red eyes. Sometimes it breathed fire from its nostrils!"

"What's a necromancer again?" Tasha interrupted.

"A necromancer is a dark sorcerer," Gavin answered, frowning. "They can command creatures of the undead. Their powers are even strong enough to resurrect. We want to avoid them at all costs. In some aspects, they can be worse opponents than even Helius's keepers."

"Anyway," Ginger continued, "they correspond with regular nightmares. Nightmares themselves are shapeless. They only take on a form when one has a great fear of them. Otherwise, they're just black clouds or humanlike silhouettes."

"Call me crazy, but none of this seems to make sense," Ivy commented. "We still don't know why that woman exploded when Cody threw a bit of powder in her face."

"Of course!" Gavin said suddenly, his eyes twinkling a bit. "Now it all makes perfect sense! Cosmic order states that good and evil must remain equal yet opposite!"

"And that means?" Serenity asked.

"It means," Gavin continued, shoving Charity's wand into his bag, "that for every good, there is an evil. Cody is the Keeper of Dreams. Ginger and Mae recognized the nightmares and winged nightmares. That means…"

"Charity was the Keeper of Nightmares!" MJ finished, her eyes flickering with excitement.

"Exactly," Gavin said. "It would explain why Cody's powder destroyed her." He paused briefly, chewing on one of his fingernails. "However, we are still left with two problems. We do not know anything about the other keepers, so we don't know what we're up against."

"If it helps, we know the names of some of them," Serenity added. "I remember Torizar, Charity, Regina, Victoria, and Calvin."

"Calvin was here?" Gavin asked. "He's one of Helius's keepers?"

"I guess," MJ cut in, snorting. "Fat old blob."

"Regina was very strange, Gavin," Serenity continued. "I didn't even fight her. She couldn't remember who she was. She just sat on the ground and scratched her head. One of the keepers who wasn't fighting had to carry her away!"

"That is interesting. I'll have to think about that. Perhaps we may be able to find out what type of power Regina has," Gavin commented. Turning to Ginger, he said, "Now back to business. Do you know where the book you read is?"

"The last place I remember seeing it was at Ivory Pass, where Eden lived," Ginger replied. "The pass has been deserted for some time. It's probably falling apart."

"I'll take my chances," Gavin said, smirking.

"Well, now what?" Daniella, who had remained silent the whole time, finally spoke, confusion currently keeping her from understanding anything that had just occurred.

CHAPTER X: THE CRY OF TERRA

"I WILL TRAVEL TO IVORY PASS AND LOOK FOR THE book," Gavin said briskly. "The rest of you should get to Emerald Falls. With Helius and his creatures on the loose, we should try to evacuate as many as possible. If you do manage to find the pixies and the nymphs, usher them swiftly to the safety of the Crystal Palace."

He turned to leave, but was stopped by Daniella. "What about me?" she said sharply. "This is way too much for me to absorb! You aren't even going to be here to explain it to me!"

Gavin's expression turned to one of deep sympathy. "Forgive me, Daniella," he said. "Other issues tend to ensnare me so much in thought that I sometimes forget the things that are most important."

He rubbed his eyes, pushing away the fatigue that gripped at him. "I wish for so many things, but I cannot be in two places at once. Ginger is my substitute here. I only hope that you can follow her with the courage and inspiration you did for me."

Gavin motioned to Ginger, who smiled and gave a small wave. "My job is not always easy. It is mostly very trying, and I am doing the best I can. In my one thousand years of rule, I have never had to deal with a threat of this magnitude. Please, just for the time being, stay strong for me."

"I will, Your Majesty," Daniella agreed at last, bowing slightly. Gavin smiled weakly, bowed as well, and then turned to the rest of his colleagues.

"I strongly advise against any more encounters with Helius until we know more about his keepers. I also assume that Helius will try to resurrect Charity. In order to do that, he needs her wand. I have it, so I will protect it from him. After analyzing it, it will be destroyed. Lastly, remember—stand as one and you shall conquer; fight alone and you shall fall." With that said, he soared into the air, his bag tightly clutched in one hand.

"Try to meet at the Mystic Gardens," he yelled as he slowly shrank into the distance.

"Now what do we do?" Serenity moaned, leaning against a nearby tree.

"First, we should help Cody," Ivy responded, taking out her wand and producing a silver strand from its tip. She touched it to Cody's bleeding arm and the strand wrapped around it, making the wound glow a silvery color. The strand moved up to Cody's face and healed his bloody lip, as well as his bleeding nostril. Then the strand faded as quickly as it had appeared.

"I'm sorry, Cody," Ivy said apologetically, "but Damiana's Strand can't heal bruises or black eyes—it can only heal cuts and bleeding areas."

"Thanks, Ivy," Cody said, sitting up. "It's no problem. I'll wear my first war wounds with pride." He grinned boyishly at this last statement.

"I'm sure we all will, to an extent," Ivy said, laughing and shaking her head. "Come. Let's get to Emerald Falls before the Time Freeze spell wears off."

*****

Rodaine was ready to rip his hair out. What little hair he had left, that is. He was in the final stage of his life but refused to openly acknowledge it. The hair on his head was the least of his problems. The palace was crawling with a great number of Terra's inhabitants, and more were still arriving. It was a good thing that

Terranians could pass through the magical webs encasing the palace; it would be dangerous to continually tear down and rebuild the protective barriers.

Aside from the large amount of refugees, an overly hyper wolf had been placed in his care. He silently cursed himself for being so kind. One of these days, his kindness would eventually kill him.

Storm huddled closer to Rodaine as the volume in the throne room continually increased. Finally, Rodaine could stand it no longer. He stood in front of all the beings and shouted, "QUIET!"

All faces, human and non-human, turned to gaze upon him as the room became deathly quiet. "I know that it has been a long day for all of you," Rodaine started. "For that reason, I think it best for everyone to get some rest. The grand staircase is through the entrance hall to the right. Floors two through nine are guest floors. Please proceed there. Any who cannot fit in the rooms on the floors stated should report back to the throne room, where sleeping arrangements shall be made. The palace will continue to grow as needed to accommodate all of you."

All started to gradually filter out. Rodaine called, "Good night!" as they left. Finally free of his burden of leadership, he collapsed into Gavin's throne, immediately drifting to sleep. Storm lay next to him, quiet.

*****

Trees all around the Plateau of Kindness were set ablaze with Helius's fury. It had not even crossed his mind; the possibility of any of his keepers dying by the hands of some puny magic users had never occurred to him. Now, with Charity gone, that left a hole in his powers…and he still wasn't strong enough to resurrect any of his keepers yet. Helius screamed again with rage, fire erupting from his eyes. Another tree was engulfed.

Hexus, who was chanting from his book, turned around impatiently. "Helius, we can't worry about Charity right now! We have to concentrate on healing our wounded! Then we have to direct firepower on the palace! Stop interrupting!"

Helius gasped and wheezed, realizing he had over-exerted himself, using much of his magic to torch the greenery. He leaned against a scorched tree, wheezing. "Hexus," he croaked, "I need to replenish myself. I exerted too much power in my rage."

Hexus spun around angrily, finished with healing his wounded comrades. "You should have known better in the first place. We need your power to break down the immense magic surrounding the palace. Now we'll have to wait."

"Jasmine," Helius crackled, "send some of your harpies out to find some humans. Have your winged beasts bring them back here."

"Helius, maybe we should hide out," Burgundy said suddenly, giggling idiotically.

"Shut up, you insane little man," Helius snapped.

"Actually, that's not a bad idea," Torizar cut in. "You could use a structure on this world other than the Onyx Castle as a base of operation. And if it were close to the Crystal Palace, all the better for us!"

"Come to think of it, I have an idea for the perfect place," Calvin agreed sappily. "It's just a little way down this road to the left."

"Hm, the insane twit may have a point," Helius said, indicating Burgundy, who was now gnawing on a piece of burned wood.

"Disgusting," Hexus said repulsively. "Someone get that out of his mouth!"

"Bad dog!" Regina yelled, grabbing Burgundy by the hair and slamming his head against a tree. "Don't chew on that bone!"

"I'm surrounded by morons," Helius said exasperatedly as Burgundy started crying.

"Helius, should we leave now?" Maximus asked, indicating Jasmine and her harpies. Immediately, he knew he had slipped up.

"Who said you were going with her?" Helius growled, his face reddening.

Torizar quickly cut in, breaking the stress Maximus was trying to endure. "I think what Altair is trying to say is that Jasmine may need a bodyguard in case Moonstone and his fruity gang show up again. After all, who would deliver your souls with Jasmine gone?"

"Oh, for Hades' sake, go!" Helius croaked at last. Torizar gave Maximus a little wink, indicating that his secret was perfectly safe. Maximus nodded back and smiled with acknowledgment.

Torizar was a great friend, one of the only close friends Maximus had. Now, he was gladder than ever that someone else knew of his affair with the harpy queen. It felt as if a huge boulder had been lifted from Maximus's shoulders. He was safe for the moment. Maximus, Jasmine, and her harpies departed, leaving the rest to talk.

"Would someone please get these two psychotic idiots away from me?" Helius moaned. "They are giving me a headache." Bracchus and Shane stepped forward, restraining the sobbing Regina and now-giggling Burgundy. Shane's cold stare silenced them both almost immediately.

"Can we just get to this place as quickly as possible?" Victoria whined. "The sickening feeling of good still lingers, especially around the palace."

"I agree with Victoria," Morpheus said. "Even with Azrael's Veil above us, it cannot choke out all of this overwhelming good."

"What is the name of this place we are going to?" Hexus asked, rubbing one of his temples with his free hand.

"Chrysocolla Pass," Calvin replied, pointing a chubby digit in the direction of the dirt path. "It's usually unguarded and abandoned. Not many travelers go there nowadays."

"Very well," Hexus said. He opened his book and chanted, *"Circumdare nos!"*

A large pentagram appeared beneath the entire party, glowing a blood red color. Hexus took a deep breath and spoke again. The ancient words that emerged from his mouth were spoken perfectly, demonstrating his great intelligence and skills with magic. *"Capere nos ad Chrysocolla Pass!"*

Beams of red light exploded from each of the five points of the star, forming a central point where they met above the keepers. The beams expanded, forming a large red casing above everyone. Then, all went dark as Helius and his keepers went spinning through a dimensional warp to Chrysocolla Pass.

*****

Gavin paused for a minute outside Ivory Pass. The air had cooled; he could feel it. The entire atmosphere of Terra-Quenlist was changing to become more dismal. He shivered from the cold, realizing that the clothes he wore would no longer be sufficient. He snapped his fingers, making his leather pants change to heavy jeans. He chuckled lightly, knowing that Rodaine would never approve. He snapped his fingers again, and his shoes changed to durable walking shoes. One more snap and his velvet shirt changed to a woolen sweater.

"Much better," Gavin said to himself. From above, the veil murmured unnatural sounds of thunder. It belched another shower of lightning bolts, this time followed by heavy rain. Gavin quickly pulled open the doors of Ivory Pass and stepped inside.

*****

"We've finally found them!" Mae exclaimed with delight. She looked around her, trying to ignore the noise of the once more fully mobile battlefield far in the distance.

Emerald Falls was an excellent spot for a picnic on any given day. The dark green emeralds at the bottom of its pool glittered when any amount of light grazed them. The waterfall was tinted green from the emeralds embedded in the wall behind. Behind the large waterfall was a small cave, protected and used as a safe haven for stranded creatures. The pixies and the nymphs were indeed hiding in the cave, as Ivy had hoped. They immediately reacted with grace when they saw the fairy queen.

"My children," Ivy said to them, "I require your help. A great evil is threatening the entire world, and certain places must be protected. I need all of you to use your magic to form a protective barrier around the Crystal Palace. After that task is done, I want all of you to flee there. The palace is heavily guarded against evil and offers the best protection."

Ginger marveled at these little creatures. The pixies resembled the fairies but had wild-looking hair and were a bit smaller in size. Also, they could not talk as humans do, nor could they transform to a larger size.

The nymphs, though, were a bigger curiosity. They resembled tiny humans, fragile and delicate. Their bodies were made of water, giving them a sparkling, dreamy look. All of them were blue, and all were woman-like.

All the tiny beings nodded in compliance to agree with Ivy. They glowed as a magical web of protection was constructed around the palace, joining and merging with the many other webs that already existed. After complying with Ivy's request, they quickly exited the cave, escaping toward the safety of the Crystal Palace.

"Now where do we go?" MJ asked the queen.

"The brownies and the dryads are located somewhere in either the Forest of Light or the Forest of Visions," Ivy said, "although I can't remember which."

They stepped out of the cave and passed through the waterfall without a drop of water touching them. Immediately after all had exited, the black veil above them rumbled and erupted into a blaze of lightning bolts. A gigantic torrent of rain shot downward.

"Great! Now what?" Daniella shouted over the pounding rain.

"Head for that tower!" Ivy yelled back, pointing ahead of everyone to a large structure. "We passed it on the way here! It's one of the five elemental towers! We'll be safe there!" She put her hand on Mystic, petting him softly and speaking quickly. "Mystic, I think it might be best if you departed for the Crystal Palace as well. Things are getting very dangerous, and I don't want anything to happen to you."

The unicorn snorted with distaste. "Please," Ivy begged. "I don't want to leave you either, but I would rather do that and return than never be able to see you again!" Mystic huffed, wiggling his ears and shaking his head. Without another sound, he turned and galloped off to follow the pixies and the nymphs across Starlight River.

"Goodbye for now, my friend," Ivy whispered. "I hope that you and the others will be safe." Turning to the rest who stood in awe, she said, "Let's go!"

"This rain's messin' up my hair!" Cody yelled as they all ran for the tower. Their carpets were rolled up and tucked under their arms. No one wanted to take a chance riding a carpet in the terrible storm.

"You have short hair! Try working with wet hair when it's as long as mine!" Ginger shouted back.

"You don't do anything with your hair anyway!" Cody complained.

"True…" Ginger snickered.

Ivy reached the doors of the Tower of Torrent first, yanking on their handles, to no avail. "I can't get them open!" she cried in dismay.

"There's an inscription," MJ said, reading the words etched onto the doors. "It says, 'By water or by none…speak the name of water and enter the haven of Torrent.'"

"What does that mean?" Serenity asked.

"It's a riddle," Tasha answered. "It says to speak the name of water."

"Well duh, we just heard that," Cody snorted.

Tasha stuck her tongue out at him and continued nonchalantly, despite the pouring rain. "Remember class at school? There were gods associated with each element. The one for the element of water was Torrent! The answer to the riddle was in the question! The name of water is Torrent!"

The doors shuddered and swung open, revealing the inside of the tower. "Wow…that was pretty cool. I thought I was the only one who paid attention in school," Daniella said, smirking.

"Excellent work, Tasha," Ivy said, patting her on the back as they stepped inside. As soon as they had all entered, the doors closed behind them, locking the downpour of rain out.

"Wowzers!" MJ said, her voice echoing in the vast room. The room stretched upward to end in a large ceiling. A vast depiction of an ocean was painted across it, the white waves cresting and rolling. It almost looked as if the painting were alive.

The rest of the room was extremely large, with a marble floor spanning across its base. Large statues of gods were erected on either side, forming a long hallway. All looked valiant and good, poised in actions of superiority. At the end of the hall was a large shrine. Candles were lit around it and the smell of burning incense filled the air. An even larger statue was at the center of the shrine, a depiction of the Elder God of Water, Torrent.

Tasha was explaining all of the statues to everyone. "The first on the left is Poseidon, with his mighty trident. Across from him is Venus. Next to her is Damiana, Queen of the Sirens. Across from her is the final god, Leviathan."

"That one looks scary," Serenity commented, looking at the statue of Leviathan. "What is it?"

"Leviathan's a great serpent," Ginger replied. "He has great power over the element of water. He's a very powerful god. Legend says that he was supposed to be the Elder God of Water instead of Torrent, but he wasn't allowed because he was a serpent and not an image of a man."

"Yeah! Where did you learn that?" Tasha asked in awe.

"Leviathan's catalogued in the book Gavin's lookin' for. You'd be surprised what's in that book," Ginger answered. "It not only had every evil creature imaginable, but it had chapters on gods and other magical beings."

Between the four great statues were small pools of water with purple flowers at their centers. Small lily pads were placed in each of the pools, giving the entire scene a feeling of calm. "What are those purple flowers?" Daniella asked with curiosity.

"I can answer that because I lived on a lake," Serenity responded. "Those purple flowers are very rare. I thought they had gone extinct a long time ago. They are purple water lilies, the rarest and most beautiful of all of Terra's flowers."

"Well, it seems to me like each of you has a certain area of expertise," Ivy said with a smirk.

They reached the large shrine and marveled at the gigantic statue that stood in front of them. Torrent was an Elder God. The statue showed him sitting on a throne of water. He wore a crown of purple water lilies. His hair was wavy, the same as his beard and mustache. A flowing robe clothed him, and the Seal of Torrent was suspended on a silver chain around his neck. A staff of gold sat next to Torrent's throne. Torrent's hands were cupped in front of him, holding a blue orb. A blue mist swirled inside of it.

"That is Torrent, the Elder God of Water," a voice said from behind them. Everyone turned around to face the old man who had spoken. He wore a blue toga with gold edges. The Seal of Torrent was etched into the front of his outfit. Nine others stood behind him, clothed in the same robes, except that theirs lacked the gold edges.

"We know that, sir," Serenity said, immediately thinking that she sounded rude.

The old man chuckled and nodded. "Of course you know. This is the Tower of Torrent, after all."

"Sorry, but who are you?" Serenity asked, trying not to sound impatient.

The old man smiled and replied, "I am Carthon, High Priest of the Tower of Torrent. I oversee everything here and make sure that all is in order."

"We are the keepers of Emperor Gavin Moonstone," Ginger started, faltering when the priests bowed. "We came here seeking shelter from the storm that's raging outside."

"All of you are most welcome here," Carthon replied. "The tower is a holy place and is protected from outside influences."

"I am Queen Ivy Snowfall, and this is my daughter, Mae," Ivy said, introducing the two of them.

"Welcome, Majesties," Carthon said, bowing once again. After a moment's silence, Carthon said, "Things, I gather, have gotten out of hand."

"A battle between good and evil is raging not far from here," Daniella replied.

"Then the time has come at last," Carthon whispered, walking to the shrine and kneeling at its base.

"The time has come for what?" Cody asked, confused once again.

"Boy, read the inscription on the base of the Great Torrent's throne," Carthon commanded. "Read it out loud for all to hear."

Cody cleared his throat and knelt down. "'He who is destined to part the waters shall hold the Eye of Torrent in his grasp.'"

"What does it mean?" Tasha asked.

"It means," MJ said, "that a person who is highly skilled with the element of Water can take that globe thing in the statue's hands."

"That is not just a 'globe thing!'" Carthon sputtered, shocked by MJ's words. "It is the Eye of Torrent! It is a powerful artifact, capable of controlling all within the element of Water!"

"We will definitely need it. It will help us fight Helius," Mae murmured.

"But none of us has a power associated with water!" Daniella argued. "If an unsuited person grabs it, terrible things might happen!"

"Let's think about this logically," MJ said, taking on a professional tone. "I have the answer all figured out. Ginger will be the one to take the orb."

"WHAT?!" Ginger yelled, making everyone jump. "If what Daniella said is right and I'm the wrong person, my eyeballs might get fried outta my head!"

"Don't be a twit!" MJ said sharply. "Just grab the dumb ball and be done with it!" She gave Ginger a shove, pushing her into the statue. But when the ground didn't shake and her eyeballs didn't get fried out of her head, Ginger gained more courage and took the orb from its cradle.

"Praise Torrent, our savior has come!" Carthon announced, dropping to his knees and bowing. The rest of the priests followed suit.

"Please, get up!" Ginger insisted. The priests obeyed, standing at attention. Ginger turned to MJ and said, "How'd you know I was the one who could carry the orb?"

"It was easy!" MJ answered, giggling. "All it took was some common sense. Your powers come from Venus, who was born inside a shell that emerged from the ocean!"

"No wonder you're the Keeper of Strength and Wisdom," Ginger breathed, impressed by MJ's awesome intelligence.

"Sorry to cut this short, but the rain burst needs some controlling," Ivy said.

"That storm outside cannot be controlled," Carthon cut in. "It is an evil influence that is not bound to Terra. Trying to control it is futile."

"So now how do we get out of here?" Daniella said exasperatedly.

"Well, if you are searching for the rest of the orbs, we may be able to help," Carthon replied. "All five of the elemental towers are connected by teleportation devices, secrets that only the priests are entitled to. In this case, however, I think you will be able to use them."

"We were trying to get to the Forest of Visions," Ivy answered.

"Why don't you retrieve the other orbs and come back here? By then, the rain may cease," Carthon suggested.

"If all of the other orbs have as much power as the Eye of Torrent, perhaps we can beat Helius without Gavin's help!" Mae spoke up. "Where is the device?"

"Over there in the corner of the room," Carthon replied, pointing to the left of Torrent's throne. The Seal of Torrent was etched into the floor, covering that whole corner of the room.

"Everyone, step onto the seal," Carthon instructed, motioning.

"Hey, what's this?" MJ asked, stepping onto the seal and leaning close to it. She read out loud, "'When night is day and day is night…'"

Carthon's eyes widened and he stuttered, "How are you able to read that?"

"When I attended an academy, I craved knowledge," MJ explained. "I spent most of my free time in the academy's library, wading through all the books. One day, I came across a book that had been hidden, tucked inside an old historical novel. I suppose it was no coincidence that I came across it, as it contained many of the things I'd been searching for."

"Such as?" Carthon inquired, failing to see MJ's point.

"Many different languages, including Drusilla's Runes," MJ answered, indicating the runes etched inside the seal. "It also included backgrounds and the significance of each language."

"What academy did you say you found this book in?" Carthon asked, his voice cold.

"Gwendolyn's Academy of Knowledge," MJ replied.

Carthon turned to one of the other priests and said, "Locate the book and make sure it is filed with the others, away from the people of Terra."

"WHAT???" MJ burst out, confused.

"My dear," Carthon said, turning back to her, "it is the duty of all the priests to ensure that languages dead to the outside world stay that way. We will take this ancient book to file away, just as we did the others."

"You are confiscating information that is as ancient as this world itself!" MJ argued as three of the priests vanished.

"Drusilla's Runes are only used by enlightened beings because they are linked to a powerful magic," Carthon replied. "They are for no one else to utilize."

"How are people to know where they came from if you hide their ancient ancestry?" MJ shot back heatedly.

"You do not understand!" Carthon insisted, his pleasant personality suddenly taking a dramatic turn for the worse. He shook his head and sighed.

"As it happens, Carthon, I have the ancient book you sent your priests to retrieve," MJ said. "I believe that you are in the wrong. I do not have time to fight about this now, but I will return later. Please open the portal. We will be on our way."

"The secrets of the book are not to be revealed!" Carthon shouted, raising his voice and advancing toward MJ. Quickly, he was restrained by the suddenly-active priests.

"Carthon, she won't tell anyone. Aside from her and the priests, no one else can read Drusilla's Runes," one of the priests insisted.

"The orb activates the portal," another priest spoke. "Just activate it and go. Carthon will be fine. We'll calm him."

"Everyone onto the seal!" Ivy said hurriedly.

As soon as everyone had stepped on, Ginger shrugged and said to the orb, "Open the portal."

The tower shook as the large seal glowed. "Everybody hold on!" Ivy shouted.

"To what?" Daniella cried. The room shook harder and glowed a blinding white. In a blur, the entire company, save for the priests and the struggling Carthon, disappeared.

*****

The weakened structure shuddered as Gavin closed the heavy doors behind him. All of the windows in the foyer were boarded up, allowing rainwater to trickle through cracks. Gavin looked around carefully. The stairs that led to the upper floors were smashed by a large beam that had fallen. Cobwebs were everywhere, woven intricately on the broken furniture and ceilings. Water marks stained the once-ornate floor. The only thing that seemed untouched was a small table stationed at the center of the room. A small chair sat in front of it.

Gavin paused, a small and mysterious smile forming on his face. "It's all right, Eden. You can come out."

Behind Gavin, Eden Starglass emerged from the shadows she had been standing in. Clutched tightly in her hands was a large, leather-bound book. "Your Majesty," she said, smiling equally as mysteriously and bowing slightly as Gavin helped her into the chair. "Still as powerful as ever. It's been too long."

"I know," Gavin said solemnly. "I wish that our meeting could have been under better circumstances. Doubtless you know why I'm here."

"Absolutely," Eden replied, handing Gavin the book. "The one and only copy of *Saint Benedict's Book of Light*."

"Thank you," Gavin said, taking the book and putting it into his bag. "I don't mean to seem rude, but due to the change of events, I must be on my way."

"Not at all," Eden replied. "Just don't mention to Ginger that you saw me."

"Of course not," Gavin said. "But you do realize that you must explain everything to her soon."

"The time grows near," Eden replied. "Upon your next encounter with Ginger, send her to the Village of Prophecies. Then, and only then, shall I explain everything."

*****

Maximus and Jasmine stood in the middle of utter chaos. The harpies filled the skies, carrying screaming people toward Chrysocolla Pass. Jasmine looked around, a smile skimming across her face. Fire engulfed houses and greenery everywhere. Mountains of ash indicated places where flames had already eaten.

Jasmine turned to Maximus, who had removed most of his armor due to the heat. "I think they have everything pretty much covered," she said, trailing a finger across his chest. "Why don't we rest for a while?"

Maximus turned and saw the vacated house Jasmine indicated. It seemed to be the only object untouched by flames. "I suppose," he said with mock exasperation, a small grin etched on his face. He scooped Jasmine into his arms and carried her into the house. She clung tightly to him, listening to the soft beating of his heart.

Maximus closed his eyes, feeling the soft breaths of his lover, who caressed his exposed chest ever so slightly. A thought had continually occurred, nagging, pulling at the back of his mind. He shrugged it off yet again and entered the bedroom, setting Jasmine on the soft bed and gently closing the door.

Soon, he would have to address the thought that terrorized him—he had been evil all of his life. Was he really changing into a good soul?

Jasmine's sultry voice beckoned, and he forgot the thought for the moment.

*****

CHAPTER XI: THE VISIONS BEGIN

A BLAST OF SOOTHING AIR HIT GINGER AND THE others as the teleporter shut off. They glanced around at their surroundings. Yet again, the décor was very elaborate. Much like the Tower of Torrent, this tower had the same basic design, except for the color. Rather than different shades of blue, various shades of gold lined the hall. Also different from the previous tower were the centerpieces. Instead of small pools, small whirlwinds churned, tiny sparks emitted from them.

Statues were also set up in the same fashion, as well as the large shrine at the end of the elaborate hallway. Small whirlwinds rotated around the shrine as well. Several priests knelt in front of the shrine, chanting softly.

"Where are we?" Daniella inquired.

"The Tower of Zephyr," MJ answered, walking over to one of the statues and touching its smooth marble surface. "This tower worships the element of Air. Like the Tower of Torrent, they set up statues to honor their deities."

"Who are all of the deities?" Tasha inquired, walking over and standing next to MJ.

"The one in front of us is Hermes," MJ replied, smiling slightly. "Next to him is Iris, Goddess of the Rainbow. Across from her is Circe, the White Sorceress. Behind us is Zeus, supposed king of the gods in some religions."

"And the large statue is a representation of the Elder God of Air, Zephyr," a voice from behind them said. They turned to see the high priest. Or rather, priestess. She was extremely beautiful, wearing a dark gold robe etched with orange. Large gold earrings dangled from her ears, and a gold band was tightly fastened around her head. Her hazel eyes and short chestnut-brown hair shone jovially, matching her ruby lips and slightly rosy cheeks.

"Sorry if I frightened you," she said with a gentle tone. "I am High Priestess Cordelia of the Tower of Zephyr. Welcome."

"We came from the Tower of Torrent," Ivy replied from behind Cordelia. "We are representatives of Emperor Gavin Moonstone."

"Of course," Cordelia replied, bowing. "I assume you are here for the Eye of Zephyr?"

"Correct, Priestess," Ivy responded, smiling and nodding.

"Follow me," Cordelia said, motioning to the large shrine.

"'He who is destined to purify the air shall hold the Eye of Zephyr in his grasp,'" Cordelia announced, remembering the statue's inscription perfectly. "Only the chosen may touch the incredible power of the orb."

"No one here is linked with Air," Mae said quietly.

"You do not necessarily need someone directly linked to an element," Cordelia added.

"According to my books and knowledge, Air is associated with balance and honesty," Serenity responded.

"Daniella, it's yours," MJ said quickly. "Hurry and take it so we can help Gavin."

Daniella nodded with uncertainty and stepped up to the statue. Zephyr was a wizened-looking old man, holding a large sword in one hand and the orb in the other. He wore a gold robe and a gold crown.

Wincing, Daniella wrapped her hands around the orb and pulled it from its cradle. While she was doing this, MJ noticed another message etched onto a second portal, in the same corner of the room as that of the previous tower. She read it silently, and her eyes widened. A scream from behind everyone made Daniella jump and almost drop the orb. All spun around to see MJ clutching her head, her eyes tightly shut.

"'Our powers we combine to fight!'" she shouted, collapsing to the floor and lying still. Ivy rushed to her side and knelt, checking her.

"She's fainted," Ivy said, looking up at the flustered party.

"What happened?!" Ginger exclaimed frantically.

"I don't know!" Ivy said angrily. "How am I supposed to know?!"

"Enough," a voice chimed in, kind but firm. Gavin stood behind them, his arms wrapped around a large book.

"Gavin, do something!" Ginger said.

"Your Majesty," Cordelia breathed, bowing. Gavin patted her on the shoulder as he walked past. He walked up to the fallen warrior, smiling briefly and nodding.

"Everyone, step back," he instructed, kneeling in front of MJ. "Fallen hero, breathe in deep the light of life."

MJ gasped and sat up abruptly. "I saw terror everywhere!" she cried, tears streaming down her cheeks. "People who didn't have time to get to the palace were being carried off by horrible creatures with wings!"

"Harpies," Gavin said simply. "They carry off people and extract their souls for containment."

"All those people…" MJ gasped in between sobs.

"I felt it too," Gavin said sorrowfully. "But there is nothing we can do now."

"Where?" MJ asked, her voice cold.

"Somnus Town," Gavin answered. "They destroyed Somnus Town."

"What?" Cody shouted in confusion. "No! They can't! They couldn't!"

"They did," Gavin replied blankly.

"They're goin' down!" Cody roared, storming down the hall and crashing through the heavy front doors.

"Wait!" Serenity called. "Gavin, do something!"

"Everyone, let's go! High Priestess, we shall return! Thank you!" Gavin cried as he and the rest of the party rushed out into the pouring rain.

*****

It appeared that the defending army was winning. The elves, fairies, and humans had concentrated most of their armies into one space. However, the evil leaders had escaped. Bracken had been knocked off his horse—Spark was nowhere to be found. He was fighting on foot, next to Ross. He felt proud and honored.

Side by side they fought, vanquishing wave after wave of creatures. Never in his entire life had Bracken ever dreamed of a battle such as this, but now it was happening…and he was winning. He was doing himself proud.

*****

Hexus rubbed his throbbing temples as the screaming finally stopped. Apparently, two guards had taken shelter at Chrysocolla Pass. Helius had made short work of one, extracting his soul immediately. The other he had decided to torture for information. After the torture, he had extracted the second guard's soul as well.

Helius emerged from one of the rooms, a grin spreading across his face. "I haven't tortured someone in so long. It felt good to do it again."

"I see you've returned to yourself," Hexus replied distantly. "Now what?"

"That bratty boy will pay for killing Charity," Helius snarled through gritted teeth. "I may have my strength back, but my powers are still not strong enough to resurrect. And we don't have time for that right now." His face screwed itself up into a terrible sneer. "All of the fires of the earth cannot match the fury that rages inside of me."

He paused a moment, silently calming himself. "I will send some of you back to Chaos, including the harpies. Ensure that all is kept under order. You are in charge of Chaos temporarily."

Hexus's eyes flashed with delight. Finally, he would show everyone what true power could do. "I will take Morpheus with me, as well as Maximus and Torizar," Hexus replied boldly. He turned to Calvin and said, "The harpies will be here shortly. I assume they've captured people from the closest town. Go to that town and send Maximus and Jasmine here."

Calvin grinned and replied, "Of course. They'll be here shortly." With that said, he slithered out through the front doors.

Hexus turned to Morpheus and Torizar, who both stood silently. "Are the two of you ready to go?"

"As ready as we'll ever be," Torizar responded, yawning and stretching.

Burgundy looked out one of the front windows and giggled with delight. "Look, Helius! The harpies have returned with prisoners!"

Regina, who had finally remembered who she was, walked over to Burgundy and said, "You are a bizarre little twit, do you know that?"

"I may be bizarre," Burgundy retorted, "but at least I can remember that."

"I can see where this is heading," Victoria said loudly. "I'll end it now by telling the two of you that you are both idiots."

Before another word could be said, the harpies burst through the front doors, people clutched tightly in their arms. Like a colony of ants, they filled the lofty room. They were everywhere, hissing and growling at the terrified prisoners they held.

"No, no, no! Stop, you hags!" Helius shrieked. The noises and movements ceased, allowing him to speak without shouting. "Return to the Onyx Castle under the command of Matthew Hexus. Take the prisoners to Hell's Gate. Then stay there to await further orders."

The harpies stood silently, waiting for Hexus. "MOVE!" Hexus bellowed, signaling to Torizar and Morpheus. The entire party exited, save for Hexus.

"I will send Maximus and the queen to Chaos as soon as they arrive," Helius said. Hexus nodded and retreated, closing the doors behind him.

Helius turned to his remaining keepers. "We have a new target. That feeble Moonstone has a keeper who killed Charity. He is our new target."

"He'll pay," Victoria snarled. "They'll all pay."

*****

Cody's carpet darted past Gavin and the keepers, scooping Cody up and soaring into the sky, obeying the orders he shouted at it.

"Gavin!" Ivy cried. "Do something! He'll be killed if he doesn't stop this rage!"

Gavin turned and looked at Ivy. The pouring rain had drenched them all. "If I try to stop him, he will be."

The other carpets exploded back to life, a couple springing out of Gavin's bag, and scooped all the others up. "Follow Cody!" Gavin shouted over the pouring rain and rushing wind.

The carpets, now fully mobile, careened toward Cody's lightning fast carpet. "I think I'm gonna be sick," Ginger mumbled to herself as she clung tightly to the edges of her carpet.

The party climbed higher and higher, the fierce conditions spiraling and rocking their carpets. Ivy was worried. A rage such as Cody's led to uncontrolled bursts of power. It could kill him. And unless someone was able to calm him, the rage would be his end.

*****

Jasmine rolled her eyes as the fat, stupid man babbled. Calvin blabbed something about reporting to Helius at Christmas Pass, or something similar. She and Maximus were to report there immediately.

"Very well, goodbye," Jasmine said, eagerly dismissing the disgusting man. Calvin attempted a bow and stumbled, then retreated into the shadows.

"I suppose…" Maximus started. He was cut short when a blur slammed into him, knocking him sprawling across the remnants of the town. He lay still for a moment, then jumped to his feet and drew his sword.

"Get him, baby!" Jasmine growled when she saw who had impacted with Maximus. Cody hovered above the ground, his eyes ablaze with fury.

"You destroyed my home!" he shouted, charging once again at Maximus. Maximus drew back his sword and swung it at Cody.

The evil keeper was thrown backward before his sword could touch Cody. Cody was thrown backward as well. Gavin landed in front of the fallen Maximus. "You will not touch him!" Gavin shouted.

Maximus jumped up and limped over to Jasmine, who put her arms around him and lifted off the ground. "Your emperor won't always be there to save you!" he shouted. "Mark my words, boy! When Moonstone is dead, you're going down!"

"Savor your victory, because it won't last long! This isn't over!" Jasmine hollered as they soared away.

"Before this's over, I'll kill you!" Cody screamed with rage.

"Gavin…" MJ said. They looked at the burning pile of rubble that used to be Somnus Town. One house still stood intact. The rest had been burned beyond recognition or leveled to smoking heaps of rock. Fires still burned all over the ruined city, eagerly lurking for something to engulf.

"All is not lost," Gavin replied. "The people are alive. There are no bodies here. They must have been taken as prisoners by the harpies."

"Where have they been taken?" Serenity asked softly.

"Undoubtedly to Chaos," Gavin answered. "We need more assistance. The rest of the keepers must be located. Head to the Palace of Gaia. Find a woman named Tinuviel Seren. Then use *Saint Benedict's Book of Light* to research all the evil creatures that you can. I must pay a visit to the gnomes."

Gavin handed the book to Ginger and whispered, "Take good care of them."

"I will," she replied, nodding in affirmation. With that said, Gavin waved to everyone and nodded to Ginger, who nodded back. He looked to the sky and shot through the rain, disappearing quickly behind the veil of mist that was forming.

Ginger closed her eyes and concentrated, replaying what Gavin had just told her through her mind. He had said, "Calm them by using love." With a parting word, he had also told her he had something extremely important to relay to her when he returned.

She concentrated on her powers, glowing a bright pink and encircling her comrades with a pink bubble. Almost immediately it disappeared, leaving a calmed party.

"What did you do?" Serenity inquired.

"I used my power to calm everyone's nerves," Ginger replied. "We need to stay strong so we can all pull through. Now, let's find Tinuviel Seren."

"Where exactly is the Palace of Gaia?" MJ asked.

"To the north," Cody replied unhappily.

"Then, let's go!" Tasha exclaimed. "The more people we get to help, the harder we can whip Helius and his cronies!"

"Hey!" Mae chirped. "Where did Daniella go?" Everyone looked around for her, but it was no use. Daniella had vanished.

CHAPTER XII: TINUVIEL SEREN, KEEPER OF SANITY AND HOPE

WHILE EVERYONE HAD BEEN BUSY TALKING, Daniella had decided to inspect the single remaining house. A shadow had crossed one of the windows from the inside. Perhaps someone in the town had survived the attack!

Opening the door, Daniella saw a larger man standing in a corner of the room. She recognized him immediately. "Duke Moocher! What are you doing here? You should be safe at the castle!"

"My dear," the former duke replied, "thank you for your kindness in caring for a sick old man."

"You're sick?" Daniella said, awed and completely oblivious to the duke's treachery—while he had been with Helius's keepers at the time of Charity's demise, Daniella had not noticed his presence among them. "Well, it's no wonder you couldn't make it to the castle! Let me help you!"

"Thank you, my dear," Moocher said with extreme emphasis. Daniella helped the faking duke to the door. As they neared the open doorway, Moocher sprang to action and slammed the door, locking Daniella in.

"What's going on?" she demanded.

"You stupid girl!" Moocher laughed, a low growl that made Daniella shiver. "I was expelled from the castle because I am evil! Now I have you by yourself! I'll kill you so Helius can sap Moonstone's power!"

Moocher lunged at Daniella, who ducked behind him and gave him a kick. He flew forward and smashed through the front door. A shower of splinters exploded outward as the ex-duke's rotund figure shattered the fragile mahogany wood.

*****

Ginger and the others whipped around when they heard the crash. Calvin Moocher exploded through the front door of the vacant house, Daniella emerging after. The ex-duke stumbled and charged at her again, his face red. Daniella dodged the fat keeper and kneed him in the abdomen.

Moocher fell to the ground, coughing and wheezing. He looked as if he was choking. His face was purple, and his eyes were bulging. His wheezing became gasps, then gurgles. After a couple seconds, the duke was still.

"What was that?" Daniella shouted, glaring at the open-mouthed crowd. "What's the matter with all of you? And what was the duke's problem?"

"No one told you?" MJ answered cautiously. "The duke was in league with Helius Rue. He was going to kill Gavin. He's one of Helius's keepers."

"Was…" Serenity said softly. She bent down and checked the duke. "There's no pulse. He's dead."

"I didn't kill him!" Daniella cried, bursting into tears. "He attacked me when I went in the house to check for citizens! I didn't even hit him that hard!"

"Quiet, everyone!" Ginger shouted. She knelt next to her father and put her ear to his chest. She looked back up at her comrades with tears in her eyes. "He had a heart attack."

"This's great!" Cody exclaimed jubilantly. "That's one less evil power to worry about!"

"He was my father," Ginger said bitterly.

"I'm sorry…" Daniella gasped. "I didn't know…"

"It's all right," Ginger said, wiping her eyes. "The man who died here wasn't my father. My father's soul died when he abandoned me."

"We're all sorry," Serenity said gently, placing a hand on Ginger's shoulder.

"It doesn't matter now," Ginger replied, standing and observing her friends. "What matters is stopping Helius from taking over. The only way t'do that is to find the rest of the keepers. Let's find Tinuviel Seren and report back to Gavin." All nodded in agreement and hopped back onto their carpets, speeding toward the Mountains of Hope, the location of the Palace of Gaia.

*****

Maximus burst through the doors of Chrysocolla Pass, Jasmine following behind. "I'm going to kill that little idiot!" he shouted, slamming his fist on the table.

"Calm yourself, Altair," Helius said coolly, stepping in front of the enraged keeper. "All in good time."

"But…" Maximus started angrily.

"Those do-gooders will all pay," Helius replied. "Now, where is Calvin?"

"Don't know," Maximus answered. "He gave us the message and disappeared. We were attacked by that psychotic keeper of Moonstone's. We don't know where Calvin went."

Helius frowned, darkening the atmosphere of the room. Addressing Maximus and Jasmine, he said, "Report back to Chaos. Hexus, Morpheus, and Torizar are there waiting. Make sure no one except prisoners is allowed passage to get there."

Maximus and Jasmine exited, and Helius turned to the rest of his keepers. "We need to get Calvin back here immediately. Shane, Victoria, and Callus—go out there and find him. I'll send a sign as well."

Helius raised his arms and shouted, *"Incine!"* The pouring rain ceased outside, replaced with comets of fire raining from the sky. Azrael's veil shuddered and disappeared, leaving a clear night sky. Clear, that is, except for the fireballs. The small cloud of mist that had stretched itself across the sky returned to the Onyx Castle.

"Now go!" Helius roared. His three keepers exited, leaving him with Bracchus, Burgundy, and Regina.

"Now what?" Bracchus drolled, lazing on the couch.

"Prepare for an all-out offensive on the Crystal Palace," Helius barked.

"What do you want us to do?" Regina asked.

"Prepare for the biggest surge of power ever released," Helius said, his lips curling into an evil smile. "I'll show Moonstone who holds the power."

*****

At the Palace of Gaia, Tinuviel Seren paced in her room, occasionally looking out the window at the fireballs falling from the sky. It hurt to see the landscape ravaged by war. All of those people, all of those trees…

Tinuviel turned away from the window, her fists clenching. The ground around her shook and wavered. She breathed deeply, calming herself. She had to learn to control her power. It was extremely dangerous for her to lose her composure.

Tinuviel was a tall girl, in her very early twenties. She had short brown hair that curled slightly upward. Rather than wearing the robes of her palace, she wore suspenders and a white shirt, deciding that it matched better with her dark brown eyes. Her powers of Earth were great, even greater than the headmaster of the Palace of Gaia.

"I have to do something," she said aloud. "There must be a way to end the pain." She grabbed a cloak that hung over the chair in her room and opened the door.

*****

"Well, this's just peachy," Ginger growled, standing in front of the large mountain range.

"Why don't we just fly over them?" Tasha suggested.

"We've already tried that," MJ said with exasperation. "There's a force field preventing us from doing that."

"What about the inscription?" Serenity asked softly.

"We dunno what it means!" Cody shouted, stomping his feet.

The mountains shook and a piece of the rock surface vanished, revealing a doorway. The force field vanished around the doorway, leaving it open.

"What happened?" Ginger asked, completely confused.

"Of course!" MJ said, mentally slapping herself. "The inscription read, 'When the earth doth tremble, quiver, and shake, the mountains shall part and reveal the gate!'"

"I get it!" Daniella piped up, latching herself onto MJ's train of thought. "When Cody stomped his foot, the earth shook! It opened the gate!"

"Exactly!" MJ answered. "Now let's find Tinuviel!" They proceeded through the doorway, which closed behind them, sealing tightly.

*****

The beautiful Hills of Undar, famous for their rare plants and animals, were no more. The raw beauty of the near-extinct life of Terra-Quenlist was wiped out in an instant. No longer would the Lotus Butterfly rest its tired wings in the bushy trees, nor the white squirrels play in the meadows filled with Angel's Trumpets. All of that had been taken away brutally and quickly by an evil that none was prepared for.

The Hills of Undar were ablaze, due to the falling fire. Gavin dodged the blazing orbs as he found the entrance to the underground. He slipped inside and sealed it tightly. There was nothing he could do to stop the chaos outside, save for trying to contain its wickedness—to attempt containment, however, seemed futile at this point. The destruction was far beyond his control.

A long, winding tunnel led down to the center of the gnome kingdom. The gnomes normally did not associate with the outside world, keeping to themselves. These gnomes weren't all smiles like the small gnome statues that people put in their gardens. They were gruff, grumpy, moody, and became irritated quickly with the few visitors they had.

The gnomes were miners by trade. They dug tunnels under the earth, creating a honeycomb-like effect all around. Precious metals and gemstones were unearthed, making the gnomes the richest beings in the world.

They glared at the emperor as he came past, working faster to keep their minds off him. Gavin smiled pleasantly and continued to the palace, entering through the very small doorway. He shrank himself to the size of a gnome and continued through to the throne room.

The gnome king was planting seeds on either side of his throne. Except, he wasn't planting them in the ground. He was planting them in the ceiling of his large room. He pushed the seeds in and stood back, pointing at them. Roots curled out of the ceiling, extending downward into the soft earthy clay of the floor.

"Better than sunlight," Gavin said, making the small man whip around.

"Confound it, Moonstone!" he shouted, stomping his feet. "First of all, my powers are no substitute for sunlight. Second of all, why sneak up on me?"

Taran Demetrius, the gnome king, was a small man—average for the size of a normal gnome. He wore a gold crown embedded with various gems, and brown and green clothing. A brown belt was wrapped tightly around his pudgy waist. He was older, with white hair and a wizened-looking face. He had a very short temper.

"Do I really need a reason to be here?" Gavin asked. "You know what's happening on the surface."

"It does not concern me!" the gnome king said angrily, turning around and stomping to his throne.

"Taran Demetrius, I can't believe I heard you say that!" Gavin bellowed menacingly, making the underground city shiver. "Like it or not, this war affects you! If you don't do something, you will be destroyed as well!"

"Gavin," Taran started, his features loosening, "the last time we came to the surface…"

"The Great Evil didn't have a form," Gavin finished. "The time has come at last. The humans, fairies, and elves have joined forces. It's time for the gnomes to complete the elemental circle."

Taran shook his head, rubbing his temples as he finally gave in. "I will assist you. I'm not happy about it, but I will assist you, as will my gnomes."

"We must hurry," Gavin urged, listening to the rumbling above. "I fear that Helius is concocting a horrible plan."

*****

By this time, the falling fire had changed to hot ash. The ash bounced off the protective shields around the Crystal Palace.

Rodaine paced around inside, Storm following. "This is bad," he said to himself. "Even with the shields, it won't be long before the rest of the planet is destroyed."

He paced over to the large mirror that hung behind the throne and touched it. The surface of the mirror rippled, changing to reveal the wispy form of Gavin. Next to him stood Taran Demetrius, the gnome king.

"What's the matter, Rodaine?" Gavin asked.

"Sire, the falling fire has turned to falling ash!" Rodaine exclaimed, unconsciously patting Storm on the head. "I fear that the planet's defenses are dangerously low, even about to fall!"

"I believe you are right," Gavin replied, worry etched into his features. "We must hurry."

He nodded to Taran, who yelled, "Commander Periwinkle!"

"Yes, Sire!" A woman cried, running into the throne room and saluting.

"Assemble the army and take them to the surface. Join the allies on the battlefield."

"Yes, sir!" Aster Periwinkle replied, rushing out of view.

"It will all work out, Rodaine," Gavin said. "You'll see."

The image faded, and the mirror returned to normal. Rodaine slowly walked over to the throne and sat, closing his eyes. This was, by far, the worst week of his long life.

*****

Ginger collided with a woman halfway through the tunnel. She fell backward into the rest of the party, knocking them all over. The woman, who had fallen also, jumped to her feet and took a fighting stance.

"Go ahead," she snarled. "Just try to get past me."

"What's the matter with you?" Ginger retorted angrily, getting to her feet. "We're trying to walk here!"

"You shall not pass!" the woman yelled, picking up a nearby rock and throwing it at Ginger. MJ jumped in front of Ginger and punched the rock, reducing it to powder.

"I've had enough," MJ said loudly. "We were sent here for Tinuviel Seren, and we're going to get her!"

"Why?" the woman snarled.

"Emperor Gavin Moonstone needs her help," Serenity chimed in.

The woman relaxed, standing silently. After several seconds, she spoke again. "I am Tinuviel," she said, her eyes flashing. "What am I needed for?"

"The emperor believes you to be capable of helping us to stop the apocalypse outside," Daniella said, stepping forward.

"He must be a mind-reader," she said over-enthusiastically. "I was just on my way out to do something."

"Come with us," Tasha said eagerly. "We could use your help."

"Fine," Tinuviel said at last. "But someone had better fill me in on everything."

*****

Taran and Gavin waited until the entire army had exited. Turning to the rest of the gnomes, Taran said, "Tunnel your way to the Crystal Palace. If you find any civilians, take them with you to safety. Seal the tunnel after you are all safe."

The remaining gnomes nodded and rushed off immediately. Gavin turned to Taran. "I think we should get going as well," he stated. Taran shrugged indifferently.

They climbed out of the ground after following the tunnel back. Gavin waved his hand and encased both of them in two bubbles. The ash bounced off easily.

Gavin grew to his normal size and grabbed the smaller man, exploding from the ground. Taran screamed until Gavin landed in front of the Mountains of Hope. He put down the struggling king.

"You crazy moron!" Taran shouted angrily. "You above all others should know that gnomes have a very big problem with heights!"

"You're right. I'm sorry," Gavin said, chuckling. "Next time I'll just teleport."

"Teleporting takes longer!" Taran protested.

"Then don't complain," Gavin replied, chuckling once again. The doorway leading inside the mountain opened once again, revealing Ginger and the others. Along with them was a new person who was undoubtedly Tinuviel Seren.

"Ah, there you are," Gavin said to her.

"Emperor Moonstone," Tinuviel replied. "I heard you needed me for something."

"Yes!" Gavin said, his features brightening as the subject was brought to light. "Upon you I will bestow two great powers, which you will use to fight."

"Helius?" Tinuviel hissed.

"Not…exactly," Gavin replied, smiling slightly at Tinuviel's response to the evil man's name. "You'll be with the others, protecting everyone."

"Bummer," Tinuviel muttered, her fists clenching. "I was really looking forward to introducing my fist to his face."

"I like her," Taran said loudly. "She's got spunk!"

"Indeed," Gavin replied, smiling. "Everyone, this is Taran Demetrius, king of the gnomes." All in attendance bowed to the small king, who blushed crimson. Ivy stepped forward with Mae.

"Now that the apocalypse has temporarily halted, I think it best for Mae and me to gather the remaining creatures." Ivy smiled slightly.

"Good idea!" Taran squeaked. "As will I!"

"We shall join you, friends!" echoed a woman's voice. Like the rising sun, the queen of the high elves rode in on a horse, her son close behind.

"At last we are all here," Gavin breathed. "I present to everyone Queen Asterel Sunfire of the high elves and her son, Prince Thistle Sunfire."

"Greetings!" Asterel said. "Though we haven't had a very good chance to meet, there will be time later. For now, we must concentrate on protecting the world we love."

"Well spoken," Gavin answered. "Go and do just that."

Ivy, Mae, Asterel, Thistle, and Taran exited quickly, heading toward the Forest of Visions, which resided near the Tower of Torrent. Ivy and Mae flew, gently carrying the squirming gnome king. Asterel and Thistle followed closely, their horses whinnying softly.

Gavin turned back to Tinuviel, who looked extremely overwhelmed. "Don't worry about them. They'll be fine. Are you ready to receive your power?"

Finally shaking off her confusion and the overwhelming series of events that had just occurred, Tinuviel said, "Of course! No one wrecks my world and gets away with it!"

Gavin stood absolutely still, then stomped on the ground. Cracks appeared, spreading and forming a circle around Tinuviel. A large bubble encased her, oozing out of the cracks. Her eyes flashed green, then returned to brown. The bubble, as well as the cracks, disappeared.

"Welcome back," Gavin said. "You are now and forever Tinuviel Seren, Keeper of Sanity and Hope."

CHAPTER XIII: ADAM ZIRCONIA, KEEPER OF JUSTICE AND REASON

"I HAVE A QUESTION," MJ SAID, BREAKING THE silence. "I thought you could answer it, Gavin."

"Okay, go ahead," Gavin replied.

"At the two towers we visited, there were pieces of a phrase. They were, 'When night is day and day is night' and 'Our powers we combine to fight.' What do they mean?"

"They are two parts of an ancient incantation," Gavin replied, frowning. "Written in Drusilla's Runes, they have been around for as long as I can remember. To protect the incantation from outside influences, it was split into five parts, one part inscribed inside of each elemental tower. Up until now, I didn't think anyone but I and the priests could read Drusilla's Runes."

"That great oaf Carthon tried to steal my book!" MJ said defiantly, snarling.

"As he was instructed to," Gavin replied. "I believed that it was a terrible incantation, so I instructed him to confiscate any books that dealt with Drusilla's Runes for the safety and stability of the people of Terra-Quenlist."

"What does the incantation do?" MJ asked eagerly.

"I don't really know, to tell you the truth," Gavin said, shrugging. "It's supposed to summon something called Oblivion, but I don't quite remember what happened. I used the incantation only once. It sounded evil, so I locked it away to protect everyone, just in case."

"What about the elemental orbs?" MJ inquired.

"Each of the five contains the life force of the planet in different aspects," Gavin said. "Using those taps into the planet. That is why they were meant only for chosen individuals."

"Ginger has the Eye of Torrent, and Daniella has the Eye of Zephyr," MJ added.

Tinuviel, who had been quietly listening, chimed in. "I know where another orb is. It is easily accessible."

Gavin turned and looked at her, surprised that she had not a bit of surprise on her facial features. "How are you so calm?"

"Well, I am the Keeper of Sanity," Tinuviel said simply. "Why should I go crazy about getting new abilities when I've dealt with magic my whole life?"

"Excellent point," Gavin replied, grinning. "Now, which orb?"

"At the Tower of Gaia," Tinuviel responded, pointing southwest. "It's not far from here."

"Well, we must retrieve it then," Gavin replied. "Tinuviel—take MJ, Daniella, and Serenity with you. Ginger—you, Cody, and Tasha go to the Palace of Zephyr. Find a man named Adam Zirconia. He is yet another keeper we must acquire."

"You got it," Ginger said. "But what about you?"

"I'm going to continue my search for civilians," Gavin replied. He waved as his party split into two groups and departed. Ginger, however, stood for a minute, waiting.

"You said you had something important to tell me," she said.

"Yes, I do," Gavin replied, frowning. "You have a very interesting journey ahead of you. I'll fill you in on the details as soon as you return with Adam. I promise."

Ginger nodded reluctantly, then turned and sped off on her carpet after the rest of her party. As soon as she had gone, her figure no longer visible in the distance, Gavin raised his arms to the sky and shouted, *"Conligere!"*

*****

The Hills of Thunder were aglow. Lightning bugs filled the atmosphere. No other creatures resided there, save for the tiny Air Elementals that liked to ride on the sparks of lightning that etched the sky. They were floating through the air when they heard the emperor's call. Instantly, they sprang to life and sped across the sky toward the voice.

*****

Torchlit Vista had been deserted for a while, now housing only the small, human-like Fire Elementals. They liked to gather near the large torches placed around the town. These were sources of energy for them.

That was exactly what they were doing too, until they heard the emperor calling to them. Immediately, they melted together, forming a fireball that sped toward the direction of Gavin's voice. They could tell by the tone of the voice exactly why they were needed.

*****

All the lakes were calm and peaceful, giving shelter to the fairy-like Water Elementals. The tiny creatures lazed about on the numerous lily pads that sat in the middle of the lake. Upon occasion, one elemental would splash another with droplets of clear water.

They sat up when they heard the noise. A voice like thunder called out to them from out of nowhere, and yet from everywhere. The emperor was calling them to him. They had to go. It was important. Forming a large ball of water, they flew through the sky, heading toward the Mountains of Hope.

*****

High atop the frozen peaks of the Mountains of Prudence, the Earth Elementals sat. They created small designs on rocks, and they helped to shape the beautiful mountains. It was what they had always liked to do.

A voice they had not heard for a long time echoed through the valleys and crevices up to the highest mountaintops. It called them. The emperor was calling to them. They merged together to form a large boulder and cascaded down the mountains, heading quickly toward the voice that called them home.

*****

Gavin waited as the elementals began to arrive. First came Air, then Water, then Fire, then Earth. United again at last were the elements. As if attached to magnets, the elementals merged with each other to form a whole. Gavin held out his hand, releasing a small purple orb of light that joined the others. The result was a spirit in the form of a white mist. It was the spirit of the planet itself. The spirit of Terra-Quenlist had been called upon.

"Spirit of Terra-Quenlist, I have conjured you to protect you," Gavin said loudly. He produced a large glass bottle and opened the cork. "It's just for a short while," he added. "I fear that you will be damaged by the physical pain Helius Rue has wreaked."

Seemingly from the bowels of the earth, the voice spoke, its words crisp and clear, thunderous and rich. *"My creator. You have given me life and helped to preserve it. I shall follow your reasoning. Keep me safe."*

The mist sealed itself inside the bottle, frosting the glass with ice. Gavin put the cork firmly in place and set the bottle inside his bottomless bag. Closing the bag, he picked it up and sighed.

What if this war never ended? Was he really sure that he could release this powerful spirit soon? He could never be sure of anything, and looking into the future would not help much. For everything changes in the future. Nothing is ever concrete.

"I'll gather the dragons at the Mystic Gardens, seeing as we can never seem to meet there at one time," Gavin said aloud. Turning and raising his arms to the sky, he lifted off the ground.

*****

"Please help us," Ivy pleaded to the large centaur that stood in front of her. "We can't get across the river without your help, and the battle blocks the only way by land!"

"Your Majesty," the centaur replied in a flowing, honey-like voice. "It is illegal for anyone to ride upon the back of a centaur. We are beings of great intelligence. To have another upon one's back makes one feel like an animal."

"Please! It's an emergency!" Mae said with exasperation. "The lives of many depend on this!"

"In this certain instance," the centaur continued, "we will help you." He turned and whistled. From within the small hills emerged the whole centaur race.

"Help these kind beings across the river," the leader of the centaurs instructed. "Assist them anywhere else if it is required." The centaurs obeyed, carrying the royals across the swift current of Starlight River to the safety of the land on the other side. Unfortunately, Asterel and Thistle had to leave their horses.

"We'll have to somehow get to the Gospel Marshes to rescue the salamanders," Asterel commented with worry. "The wood elves at the Hills of Content and the dwarves at Twilight Vista must be rescued as well."

"Madam," the centaur replied, "we shall rescue them and take them safely to the Crystal Palace, where we will also take refuge."

"Bless you, kind sir," Ivy said.

"Mother, what about the dryads and the brownies at the Forest of Light?" Mae asked.

The chief centaur turned and looked at Mae. "My lady, fear not. I shall personally rescue them."

"Oh, thank you, thank you!" Mae cried as the centaurs galloped off.

"I don't mean to break up the happy fest," Taran interrupted, "but shouldn't we get the creatures to safety as quickly as possible?"

"Quite right," Asterel replied. Quickly, the royals vanished into the dense woods called the Forest of Visions.

*****

"He's dead," Victoria breathed, examining the lifeless figure in front of her. "Calvin's dead."

"Revenge must be sought for this outrage," Shane growled, his fingers curling tightly around the dark staff he held.

"Helius will be furious," Victoria replied, quivering with fear but also smiling slightly. "I want to see him level this disgusting planet!"

"Then go tell him that," Shane snarled. "Callus and I are going hunting."

*****

Morpheus stood silently outside the entrance to the Onyx Castle, observing the battle that was raging. The gnomes had now entered the battle, on the side of the humans. It appeared that good was winning.

"Morpheus," said Hexus, emerging from inside, "let's go."

"I believe we need to even the odds a bit," Morpheus replied, reaching into his robes and pulling out the tiny basilisk. He set it on the ground, and it slithered toward the warring armies, magically growing to its full size.

"Ah! I'd almost forgotten!" Hexus responded, pulling out the jar with the tiny dragons. Winding up, he threw the jar as far as he could, right into the middle of the battlefield. It shattered, and an army of full-size dragons exploded seemingly out of the ground.

"Now that's more like it!" Torizar chimed in, having emerged from the darkness. "Those dragons will devour everything in no time!"

Maximus, carried by Jasmine, drifted down from the sky. She gently set him on the ground, holding him to keep him balanced.

"What happened to you?" Hexus inquired.

"We were attacked by one of Moonstone's loopy keepers," Jasmine replied. "I think he hurt Maximus pretty badly."

"Probably just a couple of bruised ribs," Maximus answered, limping to the entrance.

"I'm sure we'll get it all taken care of when we get back to Chaos," Torizar said, rushing to Maximus's aid and helping him through the entrance. Jasmine followed.

"Come, Morpheus," Hexus said. "Leave these fools to their fate."

*****

The winds were incredible, almost knocking Ginger off her feet. They had gone through the Forest of Antiquity, observing the very old trees and sparkling, petrified wood. Now, they were crossing a bridge over Scarlet Desert that led to the great Palace of Zephyr. The wind that blew across the bridge acted as a shield for the palace, trying to repel the outside world. They realized immediately that their carpets were useless against the winds, bucking and twisting. They dismounted, each with one hand gripped to his or her own carpet and the other clinging tightly to the railing of the bridge.

"I think I'm going to fall into the desert!" Tasha yelled, gripping the edge of the bridge and inching herself along.

"Don't you dare!" Ginger cried back, pushing both Cody and Tasha forward.

The wind suddenly stopped, making Tasha, Cody, and Ginger tumble and roll the rest of the way across the bridge. They landed in a pile in front of the palace doors. The doors opened, and a blonde-haired man stepped out.

"Terribly sorry!" he stammered, helping them to their feet. "I thought you were invaders!"

"Well, as you can see, we aren't," Ginger snorted, brushing herself off. "We're here for Adam Zirconia, by orders of Emperor Moonstone."

"I'm Adam, the gatekeeper," he said proudly. "I use the power of wind to repel invading forces."

Ginger carefully eyed the man, up and down. He was tall, with sandy-blonde hair and glasses. Behind the glasses were clear blue eyes, matching perfectly with the freckles that covered his boyish face. He wore a pair of faded jeans and a bright yellow shirt.

"What does the emperor need me for?" he asked, his eyes darting nervously back and forth.

"The emperor believes that you are capable of helping him stop the evil that has invaded our world," Tasha explained.

"Me?" Adam asked in disbelief.

"Oh, just come with us!" Ginger exclaimed, throwing her hands in the air. "We'll explain everything to you on the way!"

"Well…I suppose," Adam said with uncertainty, closing the palace doors behind him.

"Woo hoo! Let's go!" Ginger whooped, grabbing the flustered man and throwing him onto her now-mobile carpet.

"Hey!" he cried, sitting up. Ginger jumped onto the carpet as Tasha and Cody sat on their carpets.

"Take us to Gavin!" she cried, "and step on it!" Her carpet rocketed off the ground, Tasha and Cody's following.

"Wait! We're going too fast! Wahhh!" Adam's voice echoed across the sky as the carpets sank into the distance.

*****

Bracken fell to the ground, closing his eyes. He had been wounded by something, but he couldn't seem to focus to remember what it was. He knew it was the end. He just laid there, waiting for his end to come. He had fought bravely, protecting many.

Before he had closed his eyes, he swore that he had seen an army of dragons erupt from the earth. A snake-like creature had entered the battlefield as well, turning people to stone. Perhaps this was just a delusion, though.

He rolled onto his side, feeling a sharp pain. He opened his eyes, staring at the lifeless figure of Ross Hepatica. The commander of the fairies was dead, his eyes closed and his body resting in a peaceful position. Bracken's idol had fallen. There was nothing left to live for. Once again, Bracken's eyes grew heavy with delirious slumber.

Bracken was pulled violently off the ground by something. A dark dragon had picked him up in its talons, claws tightening around him. Bracken couldn't breathe. His vision was blurring, though it was hard to tell whether it was from lack of oxygen or blood in his eyes. He was suffocating. The pain that he felt was unbearable.

A light embraced him, warm and gentle. He felt good, feeling its warmth. Suddenly, he was falling, falling... He was caught by a soft force and silently drifted into slumber.

*****

Gavin had arrived too late. He had managed to rally the blue, white, and green dragons from the Mystic Gardens. Together, they had headed to the battlefield. A terrifying sight had met his eyes. An army of dark dragons had joined the battle, as well as the feared basilisk. It was calmly slithering around the field, either devouring people or turning them to stone with its glare.

"Armies!" Gavin cried, "take down the basilisk! Aim for its heart! Do not look it in the eyes!"

The leader of the white dragons blew a gust of fire, targeted at the basilisk's face. The fire hit the beast in the eyes, blinding it. Gavin saw a dark dragon carrying a man in its claws—Bracken Pennyroyal.

With a mighty cry, light erupted from the tip of Gavin's wand, engulfing the dragon. The creature screeched and dropped the commander. A green dragon, at Gavin's command, gently caught Bracken and took him out of the heat of battle. Warriors attacked the blinded basilisk, smashing at it with every sharp object they could find. It shrieked and screeched, finally falling dead on the ground.

"Champions of Terra, take cover!" Gavin shouted. He glowed a bright white, then erupted into a wave of sunlight. The human emperor had turned into a wave of sunshine, flowing across the battlefield and annihilating a large portion of the remaining evil army. The dragons shrank back and scurried into the Onyx Castle. The few evil beings that remained followed the dragons, closing the damaged doors to protect themselves from the light.

Gavin returned to himself, hearing a wave of cheers erupt from the victorious army. He drifted to the ground, his strength sapped almost entirely. He had not wanted to use that ability because it was so draining and could leave everyone in danger, but he had resorted to it as a last minute decision. Not only was he trying to protect his people, he was also trying to help them to learn that he would not always be there for them. It might have been because he sensed a change in the winds.

"We are not yet victorious!" Gavin cried, trying to conserve his remaining strength as best as possible without collapsing. The crowd quieted. "Many creatures are still wreaking havoc throughout our world. They must be destroyed."

The crowd cheered and yelled once again, supporting Gavin. He held up his hands to once more silence them. "The wounded must be taken to the safety of the palace. The dragons shall assist in this. The rest of you must round up and destroy the lingering evil."

*****

"H-Helius?" Victoria squeaked, slinking through the doors of the pass into the foyer.

"You bring news?" Helius said impatiently, tapping his foot.

"Yes, Sire," she said quietly. "We found Calvin."

"Well, where is he?" Helius demanded, his bony hands clasped behind his back.

"Dead," Victoria replied, cringing.

Helius was silent, his brow furrowed deeply as he processed what Victoria had just told him. "Dead, is he?"

"Y-yes, S-Sire," Victoria sniffled.

"Quit your sniffling, you stupid twit," Helius commanded sharply, his eyes like daggers. "He's dead. Nothing can be done about it now. Except for the fact that this world will die."

*****

Daniella marveled at the interior of the Tower of Gaia. Set up in similar fashion to the other two, it had the long hallway and statues, as well as the large shrine at the end of the hall.

"Who are all of these gods?" MJ asked with curiosity.

"These four are Artemis, Hera, Bacchus, and Medea," Tinuviel explained. Artemis and Hera were beautiful goddesses. One was a warrior; the second, a queen. The third was a powerful sorceress, mother of Circe. Bacchus was a jolly-looking fat man, drunken-looking and holding a bottle of wine. A crown of laurels rested atop his head. Between each of the deities were small planters with beautiful orange and purple flowers. Between each of the planters were earthen dishes with balls of green fire at the center of each.

"Welcome to the Tower of Gaia," the high priestess said, emerging seemingly from nowhere. "I am High Priestess Lavinia of the Tower of Gaia. High Priestess Cordelia informed me of your imminent arrival. You are the keepers of Emperor Gavin Moonstone, are you not?"

"We are," MJ said, stepping forward and curtseying.

"Doubtless you are here for the Eye of Gaia," Lavinia responded.

She was quite a beautiful woman, with creamy skin and light green eyes. Her long, light brown hair was braided tightly. She wore a dark green velvet robe with gold symbols embroidered on it, and brown shoes with gold clasps. A small crown of laurels rested on her head.

"We are here for the Eye of Gaia and the missing part of the incantation," MJ said.

"Incantation?" Lavinia asked.

"Written in Drusilla's Runes," MJ replied. "By orders of the emperor. He requires the incantation."

"Then who am I to argue with the emperor?" Lavinia responded, stepping aside and motioning to the large shrine.

"Tinuviel," MJ said, "the orb is yours to take."

The shrine was much the same as the others, except that a woman sat upon the large, golden throne. Gaia was a young woman, to represent the youth of the planet. She had long dark hair and wore a robe of green, brown, and silver. An emerald crown was perched upon her head. Her hands stretched in front of her, a shining green orb resting on her palms. Tinuviel approached cautiously, observing the orb. Then, she reached up and plucked it out of the Great Gaia's hands.

"Bravo!" Serenity cried, clapping her hands. MJ, who had wandered over to the runic symbols, turned around.

"'The evil that has brought us down,'" she recited. Smiling when she saw the expression on Lavinia's face, she explained, "I found a manuscript that catalogued Drusilla's Runes. I learned to read them."

Lavinia nodded, closing her mouth and blinking her eyes. With another wave, she activated the portal in the corner of the room. "You will need to retrieve the other orbs. It is better to retrieve them as soon as possible than to wait. Sometimes, options can disappear more swiftly than quicksand."

MJ nodded, turning to everyone. "Let's go!"

*****

Gavin turned to see Ginger, Cody, and Tasha speeding toward him, a sick-looking man clinging tightly to Ginger's waist. The carpets slowed, stopping and hovering in front of the emperor. "Ah, you're here," Gavin spoke, smiling weakly. His power had almost been completely sapped from his usage of magic. He hoped he had the strength to transfer the necessary magic to his new keeper.

"Get me…off this…carpet," Adam croaked.

"Mr. Zirconia, I presume?" Gavin said, a firmer smile playing across his weary face.

"Yes," Adam said, hiccupping and covering his mouth.

"Is the battle over?" Cody asked, looking around at the empty battlefield.

"This battle, yes," Gavin replied. "Our combined armies are combing Terra, searching for remaining creatures and refugees."

"Is this good?" Tasha asked.

"Yes, and no," Gavin answered. "It's good that we won the battle, but I believe the war is far from over. It's bad because I used a great deal of my energy to destroy and drive back the attacking creatures. It was something that I had never intended to do. I did it as a last minute decision. I believe I have enough strength left to give Adam his powers."

"Then what?" Ginger asked.

"We'll worry about that when it happens," Gavin replied. "For now, we must be careful. Helius, if he knows what has happened, will be beyond furious. His next move will be unpredictable. We have to be alert."

"Anyway," Ginger continued, yawning, "as you can see, we brought Adam Zirconia. We told him everything on the way. He agreed to help."

"Wonderful," Gavin breathed, immediately releasing a yellow beam from his eyes. The beam encircled Adam, making him glow. He raised his eyebrows, feeling the surge of energy. He was powerful now, more powerful than he had felt in a long time. The glow faded, but the new power he had acquired did not.

Gavin fell to the ground, no longer able to stand. His strength was sapped. He was at the point of exhaustion.

"Gavin!" Ginger gasped.

Gavin chuckled as he lay on the ground. "That was nifty."

"What happened?" Adam asked.

"I have made you Adam Zirconia, Keeper of Justice and Reason," Gavin replied. "Ginger, you remember what I was supposed to tell you?"

"Sort of," Ginger answered.

"I'm telling you now," Gavin said. "You must go to the Village of Prophecies. Your quest will begin there."

"Right, the quest!" Ginger replied.

"Can we go with her?" Tasha asked.

"Regrettably, no," Gavin replied. "This quest is for Ginger alone."

"I understand," Ginger said, climbing onto her carpet. "I'll be back as soon as possible." She and her carpet flew toward the village, quickly disappearing from view.

"The rest of you must go to the Palace of Apollo to rejoin the others," Gavin continued. He snapped his fingers, and a carpet appeared out of his bag. "This is for Adam," he said. "Now go. I'll be all right."

*****

CHAPTER XIV: AUTUMN FIRESTORM, KEEPER OF THE ELEMENTS AND THE SEASONS

CLOUDS WHIRLED AROUND MAE INSIDE THE FOREST of Visions. She could see misty images inside of them.

"Mae, darling, don't touch them," Ivy cautioned gently. "These visions weren't meant to be seen by any of us."

Mae lowered her outstretched arm, refraining from touching a crystal-like cloud.

"This place gives me the creeps," Taran grunted, inching around a motionless cloud. "Let's just find the blasted creatures and get out of here!"

A cloud suddenly charged at Mae, slamming into her and disappearing as she fell down. She gasped, her eyes wide with fear. "That was no accident," Asterel cautioned, helping Mae to her feet. "What did you see?"

"I saw a terrible beast jumping upon us!" Mae shrieked, covering her eyes. "It was horrible, with red eyes and dark fur! It looked like a wolf!"

"A hellhound," Asterel replied, her face deep with worry. "One of the most dangerous of all evil creatures. It can kill in an instant."

"Where did you see this beast, girl?" Taran inquired, looking around.

"Right there!" she screamed, pointing. The hellhound lunged at them from the deep bushes, knocking over Taran and heading for the screaming Mae. Thistle stepped in and drew his sword, splitting the beast in twain with expert accuracy. The dead hellhound fell at his feet, the glow in its eyes gone.

"You saved me!" Mae cried, flinging her arms around Thistle and hugging him tightly. He returned the embrace when he heard her soft sobs of relief.

"Ha," Taran chuckled, standing up and brushing himself off. "Should we continue our search and leave you two alone?"

"Of course not!" Mae sniffled, pulling away from Thistle. He smiled at her and wiped away the tears that remained on her cheeks. She smiled back at him and gave him a kiss on the cheek. "You are my hero. I will never forget it."

*****

"Well, this is a big surprise," MJ grunted, looking around at the interior of the Tower of Apollo. Statues of the gods were set up much like the other towers. They included Ra, Ares, Tyche, and Hephaestus.

On each side of every god were small fires, burning endlessly inside golden chalices. At the very end of the hall was the shrine where the Great Apollo sat. He held a fiery sword in one hand and a red orb in the other. He wore a battle helmet and red armor. Strapped to his feet were golden sandals. The Seal of Apollo hung from his neck.

"I see that you are observing our spacious surroundings," a voice from behind them said. They turned to see a man, obviously the high priest, standing behind them. He wore an orange and red robe, matching his fiery red hair and bright green eyes.

"I am High Priest Ignatius of the Tower of Apollo," he stated, bowing. "Welcome. I was told of your arrival."

"Guess what?" MJ said loudly and with great annoyance.

"What?" Daniella replied, equally annoyed.

"None of us can take the orb," MJ answered. "If Ginger, Tasha, and Cody found Adam, though, maybe he could take it."

"Why should he be so lucky?" Tinuviel snapped.

"Haven't you ever heard the expression, 'The fires of Justice shall scorch the wicked?'" MJ asked. "When I read, I acquired great knowledge. When I received my powers, I also gained Gavin's knowledge, including his expansive list of magical abilities. He was planning on giving the powers of Justice and Reason to Adam Zirconia."

"So what do we do now?" Serenity asked quietly.

"We wait and hope that they come here," MJ answered.

*****

"Callus, what say we cause a bit of damage?" Shane snarled, tapping the ground with his staff and causing large fissures to appear.

"Good idea," Callus said loudly, his voice knocking over trees and causing the wind to blow violently.

"We'll search this world until we find Calvin's murderers," Shane snarled, his eyes flashing violently. "They're all going to die! I'll maim them first; then I'll kill them!"

*****

Maximus lay on Jasmine's bed, resting. She had treated his wounds and ordered him to rest. She and Torizar sat silently on either side of the bed, watching over the warrior. Torizar, however, finally broke the silence.

"I know about the two of you," he said, causing Jasmine to jump.

"Know what?" she replied, trying unsuccessfully to regain her composure.

"There's no need to hide it from me," Torizar continued. "I'm Maximus's best friend. I would never betray him."

"You know of our affair, then?" Jasmine said, a hint of fear in her voice.

"You need not worry," Torizar answered. "Sometimes, these things just happen. It is the power of Fate."

"Torizar..." Maximus said, stirring. "Does it really mean I'm not evil anymore?"

Torizar was silent until Maximus asked him again. He then replied, "I cannot tell, Maximus. But what I can promise is that I will still be your friend, no matter what you become."

*****

"We don't know the incantation to open this door," Adam said sullenly to Cody and Tasha, looking at the entrance to the Tower of Apollo.

"We're not giving up that easily!" Tasha said, jumping onto her carpet.

"What are you doing?" Adam asked, climbing onto his carpet as well.

"Finding someone who knows how to open the door," Tasha replied. She flew toward the wall of fire to the west, the barrier that protected the Palace of Apollo.

"Tasha! Stop! You'll be burned alive!" Cody shouted.

"Puh-leese!" Tasha groaned back. "I'm the Keeper of Life! How can I die?" She exploded through the fiery barrier, realizing that it was a mere illusion. She landed in front of the palace doors and banged on them.

A young woman opened the door, her brow furrowed with curiosity. "Yes?" she asked.

"Is there anyone who knows the incantation to open the doors of the Tower of Apollo?" Tasha asked.

"No, sorry," the woman said, trying to close the door.

Tasha stopped it quickly. "We are the keepers of Gavin Moonstone. By his command, open these doors!"

"Terribly sorry, Miss," the woman said, shrinking back a little and reopening the door. "I was instructed to turn away all inquiries. But when it is the concern of the emperor, of course. I'll come and open the doors."

The woman came into full view from behind the door, her plain dress showing. It was a dull orange, flowing to her ankles. She had green eyes and ruby lips, matching her pale complexion. Her shocking red hair stood out greatly.

"I am Tasha," Tasha said, holding out her hand. The woman shook it.

"My name's Autumn," the woman replied. "I keep up the defenses at the Palace of Apollo."

"Pleasure to meet you," Adam said, stepping forward. "I'm Adam."

"The name's Cody," Cody said, grinning and waving.

"We're kind of in a hurry, so we'll have to go quickly," Tasha commented.

"No problem," Autumn replied.

"Just hop on one of our carpets and we'll be there in no time!" Adam said.

*****

"What are you going to do, Helius?" Victoria asked nervously.

Helius stared at her blankly. "I'm going to dance around in a tutu."

"Really?" Victoria asked with surprise. "I didn't think…"

"Oh, shut up, you twit," Helius snorted. "I'm going to attack the Crystal Palace. With my powers restored, I'll bring it crashing to the ground, plateau and all!"

"What should we do?" Burgundy giggled excitedly.

"Victoria—take Burgundy, Bracchus, and Regina back to the Castle of Souls. Wait there for further orders. I don't think this will take too long."

Victoria bowed and exited with the others, Regina babbling incoherently once more. As soon as the doors closed, Helius sat in one of the chairs. "I must center myself so I can tap into my darkest magic." He laughed, closing his eyes and concentrating. "Soon, I will destroy all."

*****

Ginger landed in the strange village. It was devoid of all life, yet there was life all around. She could feel a presence all around her, but she could not decipher what it was. The village itself seemed to be alive, having a soul of its own. Ginger saw a solitary light coming from one of the houses, and she went inside.

"Eden?" she gasped, her breath catching in her throat. It was true. Eden Starglass, her adoptive mother and savior, sat at the table, in the center of the room.

"Yes, my dear," Eden replied, standing and walking over to her. She touched Ginger's face, smiling warmly. "You have grown up beautifully. I am so very proud of you."

"Why did you leave me?" Ginger felt betrayed by her own voice. There had been so many things she had wanted to say to Eden, and all she could do was choke out a stupid question.

Eden laughed, motioning to one of the two chairs that sat at the table. "Sit, child. The time has come to explain everything to you."

Ginger sat immediately, waiting patiently as Eden sat as well. She looked at her mentor with confusion, not understanding anything.

"I left for a good reason, Ginger," Eden said. "I knew that the war with Helius would occur, and I knew that you would be needed. I didn't want you to depend upon anyone but yourself."

"I suppose I understand," Ginger said, crossing her arms. "But why are we here?"

"For many reasons," Eden replied. "Mainly because of a prophecy that was hidden a long time ago."

"What prophecy?" Ginger asked.

"Long ago, when this world was created, a prophecy appeared," Eden commented. "It was strange, really. The prophecy was conveyed by three mystical creatures. They were a Phoenix, a Firebird, and a Pegasus. Only put together did they speak the complete prophecy."

"Does Gavin know it?" Ginger asked.

"He and the other rulers only know part of the prophecy," Eden replied. "I, however, was there. I alone know the true prophecy."

"What did it say?" Ginger urged.

"Go to the Village of Memory," Eden said, her figure disappearing, "and your remaining questions will finally be answered."

*****

Gavin sat up abruptly, feeling the chill in the air. It seemed that he had fallen asleep. At least his strength had returned. He stood and stretched, shaking off the remnants of slumber.

How long had he been asleep? He didn't know. Ever since Helius had invaded, time had become lost somewhere in endless translation. Days and nights became one endless stretch.

"I have to get to the Tower of Apollo," he mumbled, brushing himself off and picking up his bag. He lifted off the ground and sped toward the red tower barely visible in the distance.

He landed in front of the doors, noticing they had just been opened and were closing fast. With lightning speed, he slipped through. Tasha, Adam, Cody, and an unfamiliar woman were walking quickly toward the rest of the keepers. MJ waved when she saw Gavin walking behind them.

"Sire!" the unfamiliar woman cried when she turned around. She dropped to her knees and bowed.

"Please, get up," Gavin said. "What is your name?"

"Autumn Firestorm," the woman replied.

"Ah! Excellent! I didn't even have to find you!" Gavin exclaimed, overcome with excitement and enthrallment that one of the needed keepers had emerged seemingly accidentally.

"What…" Autumn started, stopping when she heard a strange sound. Adam had been beckoned to the orb by MJ, who instructed him to take it. Upon taking the orb, a strange sound was heard.

The red orb glowed, lifting off Adam's palms and floating in mid-air. Ginger, Daniella, and Tinuviel's orbs followed suit, glowing and floating. They came together all at once, forming a blindingly white light. The light catapulted itself at Autumn, hitting her square in the abdomen. The force knocked her to the floor, skidding her across the hall. She slammed into the wall and gasped frantically.

"What happened?" MJ cried, rushing to Autumn's aid and helping her to her feet. "Are you all right?"

"I…" Autumn started.

"She will be fine," Gavin replied calmly, wearing a small smile.

"Fine? She was hit with the essence of four elements!" MJ retorted angrily.

"Exactly," Gavin answered. "And in doing so, she received her powers. In this rare instance, I didn't even have to do anything."

"P…powers?" Autumn stammered, trying desperately to regain her balance. "But I just got here. How do I tie in with all of you?"

"The essence of the four elements is now within you," Gavin responded. "Great power courses through your veins. You may now call yourself Autumn Firestorm, Keeper of the Elements and the Seasons."

MJ, finding perfect sense in Gavin's words, left Autumn and busied herself translating the piece of the incantation. Her smile indicated that she had deciphered the message. "'We summon you,'" she said aloud. Turning to Gavin, a puzzled look on her face, she said, "That's it? It seems like there's still a piece missing."

"That's because there is," Gavin said. "There are five elemental towers. One tower remains unvisited."

CHAPTER XV: THE HIGH COUNCIL

"WHAT TOWER MIGHT THAT BE?" TINUVIEL ASKED.

"The Tower of Heaven," Gavin replied.

"The Tower of Heaven?" MJ asked. "Impossible. There's no way in. It's protected by strong magic. There aren't even any windows!"

"The spell of protection gives false appearances to the tower," Gavin answered. "There is, in fact, a door to get in, and there are stained glass windows. There is, however, no portal."

"Why?" Tasha asked.

"I believe I can answer that," High Priest Ignatius cut in. "A long time ago, the four elements were constantly at war. The fifth and most powerful element was made to center and balance all powers. It is, essentially, the most powerful element of all."

"Thank you, Ignatius," Gavin said, smiling.

"Excuse me, Gavin," Serenity said quietly, "but where is Ginger?"

"Ginger is on a quest to find an answer to a long-asked question," Gavin said. When he was met with looks of confusion from everyone, he added, "It's complicated. Perhaps Ginger can explain it to you when she returns."

Autumn, who had been silent the whole time, finally spoke. "I can't take this! I'm going home!"

*****

Ginger landed softly in the ghost town. She looked around, her eyes filled with wonder. The town, in an odd way, was beautiful. It seemed to have been deserted a long time ago, because many of the buildings were overgrown with lush foliage. The cobblestone streets were cracked and ruined, various plants and flowers growing out of the cracks. There were no longer windows in the houses, and the doors creaked on broken, rusty hinges when the wind blew. Ivy clung to the broken shingles and warped wooden structures lining the cracked and shambled street. Some houses had large trees protruding from within them, spreading their branches out like a mother's protective embrace.

"Over here, child," Eden called. Ginger turned to see her motioning to a large stone house. Ginger got off her carpet and followed Eden into the house.

"Sit," Eden said, motioning to a large chair that sat next to a table. Upon the table was a large crystal ball.

Ginger sat in the chair and started to speak. "Eden…"

"Questions later," Eden replied, touching the crystal ball. "Ask them, if you have any at all, after you see this."

The crystal ball shuddered, a mist appearing inside of it. Ginger leaned closer to see what was happening. In an instant, the room disappeared, and a field appeared in its place. Gavin stood there with another man who was none other than Helius Rue.

"Brother, why must we fight?" Gavin asked as Helius backed away from him.

"Our ideas differ greatly!" Helius snapped back, his eyes flashing. "You created this world and left my attributes out."

"A world without evil is a blessed world indeed," Gavin replied, readying his wand. "I left you out so your evil could not destroy it."

"A world without evil is nothing!" Helius shouted, raising his wand as well. "No matter how much you fight, evil is everywhere! Such is the cosmic order of things!"

"Gavin!" A young Ivy Snowfall came rushing to Gavin's side, with younger versions of Asterel and Taran following.

"Stay back," Gavin instructed.

"Are they afraid?" Helius rasped, smiling cruelly. "They should be."

"Why do you try to destroy me?" Gavin asked, his facial features pained.

"I seek power," Helius cackled hysterically. "As you plainly witnessed, I defeated Torrent, Zephyr, Gaia, and Apollo. Not even gods can withstand my awesome power!"

"I will teach you a lesson you'll never forget," Gavin whispered. He and the royals began a chant that Ginger recognized immediately.

"When night is day, and day is night," Ivy started.

"Our powers we combine to fight," Asterel continued.

"The evil that has brought us down," Taran spoke.

"We summon you, Oblivion!" Gavin finished. "Water, Air, Earth, Fire, Spirit…such is the order of the incantation."

"Save your words," Helius spat. "I am finished here for now. Mark my words, brother—I will be back."

All at once, Ginger was back in the chair inside the rickety house. She gasped, tightly gripping the edges of the chair. "Oh my…Helius is Gavin's brother…"

"It does not end there, child," Eden replied. "Gaze once again." Ginger did so, and once again did the room disappear.

She was again in the field, immediately after Helius had just spoken. Behind her was the village that she now sat in. Helius and Gavin watched in amazement as a Pegasus, a Phoenix, and a Firebird came together.

"WHEN THE DARK CASTLE DOTH APPEAR," they started in unison.

In a flash, a middle-aged woman appeared, jumping onto the Pegasus and urging it to fly. She grabbed the Phoenix and Firebird by their tails and soared off. Their voices could still be distantly heard.

"ALL OF TERRA HAS MUCH TO FEAR," they continued. "THE GREAT EVIL SHALL THEN COME SEEKING HIS TOKEN, AND AT LAST, IN RUIN, SHALL TERRA BE BROKEN."

Helius laughed gleefully, and Gavin and the others stood there in amazement. The words suddenly stopped, and a blinding light blurred Ginger's vision. When the light returned, Helius was gone, and Gavin and the royals sat on the ground, odd expressions on their faces.

"That's odd," Gavin said. "I can't quite remember what I was doing here."

"Neither can I," Ivy commented as the other two royals shook their heads in confusion as well.

The room sprang back, and the crystal ball shattered. "What happened?" Ginger cried.

"You saw what happened," Eden said. "They summoned Oblivion."

"What I mean is why didn't Gavin tell us about this?" Ginger asked.

"His memories, as well as those of the royals, were partially erased by the light of the spell they used on Helius," Eden replied. "They only remember that they were fighting an evil with no form, and they also remember the partial prophecy. They, however, have no memory of Helius and Gavin's relation, nor for that matter does Helius."

"The same thing happened to his memory?" Ginger asked.

"Yes," Eden replied.

"So, how do you have those memories?" Ginger asked.

"You were shown the missing memories," Eden answered. "They stayed at the very location they were lost—the Village of Memory. The event you witnessed occurred only a couple decades after the birth of Terra, one thousand years ago."

"Gavin's older than one thousand years?" Ginger asked.

"I suppose," Eden replied, smiling mysteriously…almost as if she knew more than she was admitting to. "I've never been quite sure of that, myself."

"What about the prophecy?" Ginger asked.

"It is divided among the Ruins of the Pure Ones, the Wise Ones, and the Ancient Ones," Eden said. "Speak nothing of what you have seen. No one remembers or knows, as you and I do.

When the time is right, all shall know. Gavin was led to believe that he split the prophecy. He does not know it as I do. I split it and concealed it."

"What do I do now?" Ginger asked Eden.

"Go to your friends," Eden replied. "Help them. The time will come for their enlightenment, but for now, you must fight."

"What about the ruins?" Ginger asked.

"The prophecy is divided among them. Retrieve the pieces to reveal the true prophecy," Eden answered, fading away.

"But what if I…" Ginger stopped, realizing that she was alone once more. Eden had vanished. "I must help everyone," she whispered, getting to her feet and rushing out the door.

*****

"Autumn, wait!" Cody yelled, rushing in front of her.

"Please get out of my way," she said coldly.

"No," Cody replied flatly, shrugging his shoulders. "I can't let you leave."

Autumn held out her hand and blew Cody away like a dried leaf. She surprised herself by this action, putting her hand over her mouth and gasping. She ran to Cody's side and helped him quickly to his feet.

"Oh my Zeus, are you all right?" she stammered, her face turning bright red.

"Yeah, I'm all right," Cody said, wincing at a sharp pain in his side. "You knocked the wind outta me, though."

"I'm so sorry! I didn't mean to!" Autumn stuttered, her face in a full blush now. I'm such a freak!"

"Well, now ya fit in perfectly with us!" Cody commented, grinning.

"Watch it, Bell, or I'll break a couple of your ribs," Tinuviel growled, her eyes flashing with glee.

"Ahem," Gavin said, clearing his throat loudly. Everyone stopped talking immediately.

"Why don't we split again so we can get things accomplished quicker," Gavin said. He reached into his bottomless bag and pulled out another carpet, this one a fiery red. He handed it to Autumn, who observed it with amazement.

"Obviously, it's a magic carpet," he said, grinning.

"Why didn't I get one of those?" Tinuviel asked indignantly.

"Terribly sorry! I never gave you one, did I?" Gavin asked, pulling out a dark crimson carpet.

"Oh, what a nasty color!" Tinuviel said, snapping her fingers and changing the color of the carpet to velvet green. "That's better," she said with satisfaction.

"Well now…" Gavin started, stopping when Ginger crashed through the front doors and came zooming in on her carpet. "Excellent! You're back just in time!" Gavin said to her as she landed. Ginger didn't look him in the face or reply; she simply nodded.

"Good, then," Gavin said calmly. "Ginger, we were just going to split into groups again."

"I'll pick a group to go with me," she said quickly, still refusing to look directly at Gavin. "The people coming with me will be Cody, MJ, Serenity, and Tasha. Daniella, Tinuviel, Adam, and," she paused to look at Autumn, "you are to go with Gavin."

"Very well spoken," Gavin said reassuringly to Ginger. "Now, where will we head to?"

"I have a suggestion," Daniella cut in. Everyone turned to look at her, and her face reddened. "Why doesn't Ginger's group go to the Tower of Heaven? After all, there is still one orb left, as well as the final piece of the incantation."

"But we need to go to the ruins!" Ginger protested.

"Why doesn't my group head for the ruins?" Gavin said gently.

"Fine," Ginger mumbled. "Let's go, guys." She and her team lifted off the ground and sped out the doors of the tower.

"Let's go, everyone," Gavin said. He turned away from everyone for just a moment, worry crossing his face. Ginger had acted strangely toward him. What in the world had Eden shown her?

"Ginger!" he called suddenly, making everyone jump. Ginger emerged almost immediately from the outside.

"Yes?" she asked.

"I must speak with you a moment. Everyone, please start for the ruins. I'll only be a moment."

Gavin's team left, and Ignatius bowed and backed away as well. Gavin and Ginger were left alone.

"Ginger, what's the matter?" Gavin asked, only a deep seriousness in his voice.

"What d'you mean?" Ginger said, looking away and frowning.

"What happened? What did you see?" Gavin asked.

"It's too hard to explain!" Ginger snapped suddenly, her eyes filling with tears. "I can't even tell you because I can't trust you anymore!"

"Ginger, what…" Gavin started with confusion.

"Here!" she shouted, grabbing his hands and putting them to her temples. In an instant, he was shown the memory that had been lost for so long.

"By the gods…" he whispered, letting his hands drop. "At last, it all makes sense. This memory is the missing piece that completes the puzzle. Everything is so clear now."

"But Helius…" Ginger started.

"Is no longer regarded as my brother," Gavin finished sternly. "I am not in league with him, nor do I support what he does. Do you understand?"

"Yes," Ginger squeaked.

"Ginger, you know me!" Gavin replied. "You know I would never help him! If I was in league with him, why would we be fighting in the first place?"

"To defeat Helius," Ginger replied, mentally slapping herself for even thinking that Gavin was helping Helius. "I'm so sorry I ever doubted you, Gavin."

"Oh no…" Gavin trailed off, suddenly realizing something.

"What is it?" Ginger asked, a hint of fear in her voice.

"If I got my memories back…" Gavin started.

*****

Helius's eyes snapped open, flashing as his long-lost memories came flooding back to him. Now he remembered why destiny had brought him to Terra. He had been teleported by some unknown force to the deep reaches of space. Though it had taken much of his magic, he had created Chaos so he could take revenge upon his good brother.

"At long last, my reason for revenge is clear again," he said, his lips curling into an evil smile. "Don't worry, Gavin. I'm coming for you. This feud will be put to an end once and for all."

*****

"Asterel…" Ivy gasped, seeing what she somehow knew she had been missing for so many years.

"I know, Ivy. I saw it, too," Asterel said, her memories returning as well.

"Well, now," Taran said gruffly, "everything makes a little more sense."

"What's the matter, Mother?" Mae asked, staying close to Thistle.

"We must go to Gavin immediately," Ivy answered. "He may need our help at this very minute."

"It's a good thing we found the great eagles when we did," Taran grunted. "Now we can go straight to Gavin."

"Then, let's go!" Mae said, clinging to Thistle's side.

"No, Mae," Ivy said sternly. "I was a fool for allowing you to come with us this far. I could have gotten you killed. Go to the Crystal Palace, where you will be safe."

"The same goes for you, Thistle," Asterel confirmed.

"But…" Mae started.

"No arguments!" Ivy said sharply. "Please. So we'll all know you're safe."

"Ah, don't worry," Taran cut in. "You two will be alone again." He winked at Mae, who blushed.

"Taran, you dirty little gnome," Asterel commented, slapping his shoulder playfully. "Let's hurry."

*****

"Gavin, what is it?" Ginger asked once again.

"Helius knows," Gavin whispered. "If one memory comes back, they all come back. The spell has been broken."

"Oh no…" Ginger whispered, fear in her voice. "What do we do?"

"Do just as you were going to," Gavin said quickly. "Go to the tower and retrieve the orb. It is also imperative that you train everyone to master their powers. Don't frighten them, or we'll have an even bigger issue to deal with."

"Right," Ginger said, calming down a little. "Then what d'we do?"

"I don't know," Gavin said exasperatedly. Suddenly, an idea struck him. "But I know who will. You know where the Ocean of Peace is, right?"

"Of course," Ginger replied. "It's to the north, right near Sapphire Falls."

"There is a great city on an island in the middle of the Ocean of Peace," Gavin said. "After you retrieve the orb, go there. It is the Temple of the High Council."

"How can a temple be an entire city?" Ginger asked with wonder.

"Questions later!" Gavin said hurriedly. "Hurry!"

"What about you?" Ginger asked.

"We'll skip the ruins for now and go straight to the temple," Gavin said. "That way, you can do whatever you needed to at the ruins. Now hurry!"

"Gavin?" Ginger asked.

"What is it?" he replied.

"You really are a great ruler," Ginger said, smiling.

"Thank you, Ginger Molloy," Gavin replied, blushing slightly. "And you are a wonderful woman."

Ginger bowed and flew back out through the doors. Gavin bit his lip with worry. There was no telling what Helius would do now that he had his memories back.

*****

Maximus was walking around the room, flexing his muscles to work them out. He had his armor and shirt off, and Jasmine was watching his figure hungrily. He walked over to her and grinned.

"You are a goddess," he said, kissing her tenderly.

"Ah…please," Torizar said. "Excuse me. I'll leave you two alone."

He turned for the door and was knocked over when it burst open and hit him in the face. "As if my face doesn't hurt enough!" he yelled, clutching his nose.

"Sorry, sir!" Penelope gasped, her face reddening. Turning to Jasmine, she exclaimed, "Mistress! Max is gone!"

"You didn't take him with you?" Jasmine asked, her voice quivering.

"No! He was with me when we invaded, but not on the way back!"

Jasmine grabbed her mirror resting on the table next to the bed and looked into it. *"Cresta!"* she said, looking closer. The mirror's reflective surface misted over.

"Show me Max!" Jasmine said frantically. The image that appeared made her shriek and drop the mirror. It clattered to the floor, its surface shattering.

"He's dead!" she cried, jumping up. "Split in two by an elf!" She turned toward the door, her eyes ablaze with fury. "I will kill him!"

She collapsed to the floor before anyone could argue with her. She clutched her stomach, breathing heavily. Maximus and Penelope were at her side instantly.

"Mistress!" Penelope cried, dropping to the floor next to Jasmine. "What ails you?"

"Penelope," Jasmine gasped, "I think I am with child."

Penelope gasped, slowly backing away as the surprised Maximus picked Jasmine up and laid her on the bed. "Don't just stand there!" he bellowed. "Get her some water!"

Penelope ran out of the room, her head spinning. Not only was it illegal for a harpy to fall in love, it was dually illegal for a harpy to bear children. Jasmine would be exiled for sure. The harpies would have to choose a new queen. The exiled queen would be relieved of her status and made human.

Penelope suddenly got an astounding idea. A terribly awful, astounding idea. She would poison Jasmine's water and kill the queen, allowing herself to be crowned the new queen. After all, Jasmine had grown weak and pathetic. Besides, she was more beautiful than Jasmine and much more suited to be queen. It was a perfect idea.

*****

Mae walked alongside Thistle over the bridge that spanned Starlight River. She had never quite felt this feeling before toward anyone. Could it perhaps be love? Mae wasn't sure. She had never been in love before.

Thistle turned and smiled at her. At that very moment, Mae knew it was love that she felt. Partly because of the fact that he looked at her the same way she looked at him.

"Thistle?" she said, stopping and turning her whole body to face him.

"Yes, Mae?" he replied, also stopping and facing her.

"Look out!" she shouted, knocking him out of the way and dodging the creature that had lunged at him. It was a vampire, she thought. Human-like with large fangs. Her mother had told her about them. To kill one, you needed to either drive a wooden stake through its heart or cut off its head. The vampire lunged at Mae, and she kicked it in the face, stunning it.

"Thistle, your sword!" Mae cried. Thistle threw his sword to her, and she swung it mightily. The vampire fell to the ground, a pile of ash. It had not the time to attack before she chopped off its head.

"Excellent, indeed," a voice said. Mae turned to see two men standing near a tree, looking at her. The man spoke again. "That was quite impressive for a girl."

Making perhaps the first mistake in her entire life, Mae replied, "I am no mere girl! I am Mae Snowfall, princess of the fairies!"

"Forgive me, Highness," the man said, a smile of maliciousness skimming across his face. "Allow me to introduce myself. I am Shane Shadowstrife, the Keeper of Hatred. This is Callus Nightshade, the Keeper of Destruction."

Mae's eyes filled with fear, and her grip on the sword tightened. "Keep your distance, both of you."

"Well, you see, that's the problem," Shane said venomously. "Charity kept her distance and still managed to burst into flames. We're out to seek revenge on Moonstone's keepers, but I think you two will suffice momentarily."

Mae charged at Shane, swinging the sword. He held up his staff and threw her aside with ease. She landed hard, jumping to her feet quickly to fight. Thistle grabbed her by the arm.

"Mae, run!" he yelled, pulling her by the arm and fleeing.

"I don't think so," Callus spoke, making a small tornado shoot up. He pointed at Mae and Thistle, and the tornado sped toward them like lightning. It engulfed them in a matter of seconds.

"Grow!" Callus commanded, his voice booming throughout the land and causing the tornado to grow in intensity. "GROW!"

Winds swirled furiously around Callus and Shane, uprooting trees and ripping plants and flowers from their earthy residence. The sky blackened further, lightning playing across it. Thunder rumbled loudly, cracking through the cool air. Though the rain and falling fire and ash had ceased, fires started everywhere, and the earth cracked and shuddered.

"Wonderful show, Callus!" Shane shouted, covering his ears due to the whistling winds. "Now finish up and kill them!"

A sword came flying from the depths of the tornado. Neither Callus nor Shane had time to react. The sword hit Callus, piercing him straight through his black heart.

"Good shot!" he gasped, disappearing in a horrendous crash of thunder. In a matter of seconds, the battle was over. Callus had died, fading away. With him died his powers.

The winds stopped, as did the tornado. It dropped Mae and Thistle. Shane could not believe what had just happened. In a rage, he stalked over to Mae and grabbed her around the throat, lifting her off the ground.

"You rotten little wench!" he cried, his fingers tightening. "I'll strangle you for what you did!"

"It was worth it," Mae choked, failing to break Shane's grip. She flailed her arms at him weakly, her legs kicking frantically.

"Wait, I have an idea," Shane said, dropping Mae, who crawled over to the unconscious Thistle. "I'll let Helius deal with you! Prisoners you shall be!"

With a wave of his staff, Shane sent Mae and Thistle spinning into the Onyx Castle. She managed to grab the sword as they were whisked away. "I hope your cells will be accommodating!" he spat. "Helius will torture you for eternity! After all, you killed three of his keepers!"

Shane roared, smashing his staff against a nearby tree. The tree burst into purple flames, crumbling quickly to ash. "Despite my capture and the enraging loss of my best friend, I'm going to continue my search for Moonstone's keepers," he hissed. "And when I find them, things are going to be oh so invigorating!"

*****

"Stand back!" MJ cried as the great doors of the Tower of Heaven opened. She and the others quickly proceeded through the doors into the brightly-lit hall.

The tower was much the same as the others. It had the gods and the elaborate furnishings, except for the fact that everything was decorated with purple and silver. Pentacles were etched into the floor, between each of the gods.

"If I'm not mistaken," MJ said, "I know these gods. They are Maat, Osiris, Anubis, and Horus."

"Very good, indeed," said a woman's voice.

MJ turned and smiled when she saw that the woman was a priestess. However, a man was with her, dressed in the same design of robes. "Who are you?" MJ asked.

"I am High Priestess Adrienne, and this is High Priest Llewellyn," the woman replied.

Adrienne was a very beautiful woman, with pale skin and silver eyes. Her long black hair matched her robes of purple and silver. She wore a silver headband and silver armlets.

Llewellyn was dressed much the same, with armlets, robes, and headband. He, however, differed in human features. He was very handsome; younger, with purple eyes and white hair. His cheeks were as pale as the moon; his lips flushed slightly. They, together, worked in harmony with his snow-white hair.

"Wait a minute," Ginger said. "Two high priests?"

"Yes," Llewellyn commented. "We represent balance and spirituality, knowledge and centering. We are one with our brothers and sisters."

"Sure, okay," Ginger said. "Do y'know why we're here?"

"We know all," Adrienne answered. "Take the Eye."

"Of course you do!" Ginger said overenthusiastically, snorting.

"Even though it's going to be Autumn's orb anyway, why don't you take it?" MJ suggested, nudging Cody forward and stopping cold in her tracks when she saw the statue.

"G-Ginger?" she said in disbelief.

"What's the matter?" Ginger asked, her mouth dropping open when she observed the statue. Cody stood next to them, staring.

"Now that's just freaky, man," he said softly.

In front of them, seated upon a rainbow throne, was a statue of Gavin Moonstone. He wore an outfit suited for a royal, consisting of a purple and silver robe. In one hand was his wand; the other held the purple orb.

"What's wrong?" Adrienne asked. "You came for the Eye of Moonstone, so take it."

"Gavin's a god," Serenity breathed, feeling an overwhelming sense of pride at having been in the presence of a god for such a time.

"That's kind of cool, in a really scary way," Tasha commented.

Cody stepped forward and took the orb. "Did you get the piece of the prophecy, MJ?" he asked thoughtfully.

"You're right!" MJ replied, shaking off her stupor and finding the runic message. It consisted of one word. "'Oblivion,'" MJ said, standing and smiling slightly.

"If it helps you any," Ginger cut in, "the correct order for the incantation is arranged in Water, Air, Earth, Fire, and Spirit. I learned that during my quest."

"It does," MJ said, making a mental note of what Ginger had told her. "Now that we have the incantation, let's get that orb back to Autumn."

"I still don't believe it," Ginger whispered.

"Why not?" Llewellyn cut in.

"After all, Gavin created this world and gave us life," Adrienne finished.

"I guess it shouldn't surprise me," Ginger commented, shrugging her shoulders. Turning to the others, she said, "Let's go. We need to get to Gavin."

They mounted their carpets quickly and started on their journey to the Temple of the High Council. In a matter of time, they were flying over the vast Ocean of Peace, looking out at its shimmering waters. True to its name, it calmed the keepers with its gently swishing waters.

They spotted the temple almost immediately. It was the grandest thing they had ever seen, save for perhaps the Crystal Palace. It was a floating city, with high, sun-colored citadels and towers that seemed to stretch to the heavens. Large walls, buildings, and structures created a honeycomb-like network, more of a grand palace or city than a temple.

"Where do we even begin to start looking for them?" Ginger cried over the rushing wind.

"There they are!" Tasha yelled, seeing a glint of metal near the largest citadel in the entire city.

They landed in front of Gavin, who was holding up his crown. He grinned and put it back into his bag. "I was hoping the shine would catch your attention."

"Here's the orb," Cody said, getting off his carpet and handing the orb to Autumn. As soon as it touched her hands, it melted and was absorbed into her skin.

"Well, that's not something you see every day," Daniella snorted, unable to contain herself.

"Gavin, you are truly enigmatic," MJ said, stepping down from her carpet.

"Enigmatic? He's a curmudgeon," Ginger said flatly, jumping off her carpet and walking right up to Gavin to look him in the eyes. "Why didn't you tell us you were one of the five Elder Gods?"

Everyone looked at Gavin, who simply blinked. "I thought you all knew, so I saw no need to brag to the world. There's no sense making such a big deal out of it."

"A BIG DEAL?" Ginger roared, knocking on Gavin's head. "Hello?! YOU ARE A GOD! G-O-D, GOD!"

"Your point being…?" Gavin said blandly.

"Never mind," Ginger said exasperatedly, turning away and grunting. "My point was obviously lost since, like, forever."

"Gavin!" Ivy cried from above, breaking the trance over everyone. She carried the squirming Taran in her arms. Asterel appeared next to Ginger in a puff of smoke.

"I hate teleporting," she said sourly. "The smoke always makes me cough."

"What are you doing here?" Gavin asked as Ivy touched down.

"Helping you, of course," Taran grunted, looking at everyone.

"Where are Thistle and Mae?" Gavin asked, looking around.

"On their way to the Crystal Palace, where they should have been in the first place," Ivy said, still obviously angry at herself.

"I see," Gavin said.

"Hey!" Ginger said to Asterel, "did you know Gavin is an Elder God?"

"Of course," Asterel replied.

"Fine, I see how it is! Don't tell me anything because I'm a little odd!" Ginger cried angrily.

"Ginger, you're foaming at the mouth," Adam said with disgust.

She turned and looked at him, blinking and wiping her face. "So what if I foam at the mouth?! I was raised by wolves!"

Adam put his hands up in a defensive gesture, backing up a couple steps. Gavin shook his head and spoke.

"We have come here to seek help from my fellow members of the High Council. They alone can help us to decide how to handle Helius correctly."

"Okay, so let's get this over with!" Ginger said crankily. "I'm tired and hungry."

"I need to inform you of some things first," Gavin said. "The High Council, particularly Torrent, does not like disrespectful people. Please show them courtesy and remain silent unless they address you directly."

"Fine, silent it is," Ginger replied. "Let's do this!"

Gavin nodded and pushed open the doors of the large citadel. They climbed stair after stair, following the winding staircase to the very top of the citadel. A large table was positioned in the empty room, with four beings seated at it. A fifth chair sat empty. Gavin sat in it, alongside the other Elder Gods. They included Torrent, Gaia, Apollo, and Zephyr.

"Why have you come before the High Council?" Torrent asked in a menacing voice. MJ, apparently the chosen spokeswoman, stepped forward and bowed.

"We come before the High Council in hopes of finding a way to defeat Helius Rue," she answered. "We are in need of assistance."

"Assistance you shall not receive!" Torrent bellowed, making MJ shrink back.

"Now, Torrent," Gaia said in a kinder voice. "Don't be so rude. This girl was kind and courteous."

"Yes, she was," Apollo added, winking at MJ, who blushed crimson.

"I think that perhaps we can do something," Zephyr added, speaking kindly. The five Elder Gods deliberated. MJ winced when she saw Gavin frown, but regained her composure when the five returned their gazes to her.

"Helius Rue is a powerful god himself," Torrent said crossly.

"Well, he's not exactly a god, per say," Gaia added.

"But he has the powers of a god, as I do," Gavin finished.

"Therefore, he is unbeatable, and we have no solution toward his defeat," Apollo said.

"However," Zephyr cut in, "we do have something to aid you in fighting him." Zephyr nudged Torrent, who finally groaned.

"All right, fine! We, the High Council, give you the aid of Leviathan, the water god." He slid a small, turquoise-colored crystal across the table. "If you need the aid of a god, summon him."

"Thank you, High Council," MJ said, taking the crystal and curtseying.

"Best of luck," Apollo said, disappearing.

"You have my blessings," Gaia added, also disappearing.

"Peace be with you," Zephyr said, nodding and vanishing.

"Use Leviathan wisely," Torrent said roughly, nodding and vanishing as well. Gavin stood and walked over to them.

"I guess we'll have to find our own solution," he said, shrugging. "But at least we have the help of a god."

"You mean ANOTHER god," Ginger said, correcting him.

"Yes, Ginger," Gavin said, yawning. "I suggest that we get some rest here for a while, then eat and continue our quest. Doubtless you are all tired and famished."

For the first time since the war began, everyone realized how fatigued they really were. Gavin snapped his fingers, conjuring blankets and pillows. "Rest well," he said, sitting in his chair and yawning once more.

*****

CHAPTER XVI: THE PURE ONES, THE WISE ONES, AND THE ANCIENT ONES

HELIUS STOOD IN FRONT OF THE CRYSTAL PALACE, laughing insanely. "Now this structure will come crashing to the ground!" He raised his wand and unleashed a purple beam at the palace. The beam impacted with the energy field surrounding the grand structure. The field glowed, dispelling the beam.

"Oho!" Helius laughed with surprise. "So you have a force field. I should have guessed. I suppose I'll just have to double my efforts."

*****

Rodaine stumbled backward as the throne room shuddered. He ran to one of the windows to see Helius firing upon the force fields. "Sweet mother of Zeus!" he shouted, stumbling toward the doors. Storm followed obediently.

"Get the chanters in here immediately!" he bellowed, gripping the edge of one of the doors as another shock wave hit the palace.

A group of chanters hurried down the stairs with books in their hands. "Keep the force fields going!" Rodaine instructed, turning on his heels and heading for the mirror again. The figure of Gavin appeared in no time.

"Gavin!" Rodaine said immediately. "Helius is attacking! We need help!"

Gavin nodded and started to speak, but another jolt on the palace interrupted him. The mirror bounced off the wall and smashed, its glittering surface crushed to powder by the impact of hitting the floor. Communication with the emperor was now cut off.

Rodaine was thrown backward by the last shock wave, falling to the floor and skidding a little. He was knocked unconscious from the fall. The last thing he remembered was seeing Storm curl next to him in a protective position.

*****

Gavin's crystal ball exploded. He covered his face to protect it from the shards that blew outward. He had just finished fixing breakfast for his slumbering comrades when his crystal had popped out of his bag and Rodaine had started talking. Gavin had heard a rumble just before the crystal ball had shattered.

"Sorry, everyone," he said softly, grabbing his bag and heading for the door.

"What's wrong?" Asterel asked as she emerged from behind the door where her room was located.

"Helius is attacking the palace," Gavin said, throwing open the doors and stepping into the cool air of the outside atmosphere. Asterel followed him, looking at the sky.

"Already do I miss the sun," Asterel sighed, her features drooping. "I had hoped that all of this was just a bad dream and that when I woke up, the sun would be shining on me again and all would be as it was."

She sighed again, shaking her head. "It hurt me to take one last look at the home I had. It got me thinking about what might happen if I was never able to come back to that."

"Don't say that!" Gavin said sternly. "We'll find a way to defeat Helius for good. For right now, I have to go. There is trouble afoot."

"We'll go with you," Ivy said shyly, coming from inside the structure. A sleepy-looking Taran followed her.

"I love this world and my home as much as the next being," Ivy continued, stronger than before. "If it means I have to fight to keep it, I will."

"We overheard accidentally," Taran added, shrugging. "You'll need help, I have no doubt."

"After all, you remember what happened last time," Asterel commented, almost angrily. But her anger was not directed at Gavin; it was directed toward Helius.

"I know," Gavin said sympathetically. "We'll just have to beat him without the help of the incantation. We can't afford to lose our memories again."

"I do hope Mae and Thistle got to the palace in time," Ivy said.

"Ivy, carry Taran please," Gavin said. "Asterel, take my hand." The royals all did so, climbing higher into the air and watching the floating city shrink against a sea of blue.

In a matter of several minutes, flashes became visible. Gavin sped toward the beams of magic at a blindingly fast speed, pulling his wand out of his bag. He pointed it at the attacking Helius and unleashed a beam of light. The light hit Helius in the abdomen and knocked him sprawling. Gavin landed with Asterel and the other royals, who had kept his light-speed travel and now stood behind him. He kept his wand raised, frowning as Helius sprang to his feet.

"I wondered when you'd get here!" he spat, grinning and exposing white, shiny teeth. "It's about time, Gavin!"

"Shut your vile mouth!" Gavin shouted, making the earth tremble. "Why couldn't you just stay away?"

"Stay away?! You're joking!" Helius cackled, throwing back his head and laughing. "I am evil! I will never leave! I vowed I would return to smite you, and that is exactly what I intend to do!"

"Then we will expel you," Asterel said venomously, stepping forward next to Gavin.

"Oh, please," Helius snorted, taking a step forward. "You haven't forgotten how I almost succeeded last time, have you?"

"That's right," Ivy said, also stepping forward and raising her wand. "You *almost* succeeded."

"And we beat you," Taran grunted, pushing between Ivy and Asterel.

"I could turn you to ash where you stand, you filthy little gnome," Helius snarled.

"I'd love to see you try," Gavin replied, his defensive stance not faltering.

"Well, I'd love to stay and chat," Helius suddenly replied, "but I still have a world to overtake."

Shane, who had appeared silently behind the royals, grabbed Ivy and held her tightly. She screamed, and Gavin turned around. His defenses lowered, giving Helius a chance to make his move.

"Ha!" he shouted, grabbing a dart from within the depths of his robes and throwing it at Gavin. The dart hit Gavin in the leg and disintegrated.

"Why you foul…" Asterel shouted.

"Thank you," Helius said, bowing as Gavin fell to the ground. "The magic restraints in that dart should take effect in a little while."

"What do you want me to do with her?" Shane growled, indicating the struggling Ivy.

"Take her prisoner or kill her, I don't care which," Helius replied.

"I'll add her to my collection," Shane said, grinning and stroking Ivy's hair. "A queen will complete my collection. I now have two royal fairies and a royal elf." Shane turned to Asterel, who stood stupefied. "Don't worry, cutie," he said. "I'll be back for you." He disappeared with the screaming and struggling Ivy.

"No…" Asterel said weakly. "Mae and Thistle. He's got Mae and Thistle."

"Aw, boohoo," Helius said mockingly. "Cry about it. They belong to me now."

Taran charged at Helius, his fury overcoming all logic and reason. He head-butted Helius, knocking the wind out of the evil ruler. Helius stumbled backward and fell to the ground, motionless.

"I got him!" Taran shouted, jumping up and down. "A filthy little gnome, am I? Well, look who showed him!"

Helius's hand shot out and grabbed Taran by the throat. "I win," Helius breathed, standing and grinning with horrid glee. "You'll be a nice addition to my garden."

Taran suddenly stopped struggling, going completely motionless. His features literally hardened. The gnome king had been turned to stone.

"Taran, no!" Asterel screamed, taking a step forward.

"I wouldn't do that if I were you," Helius rasped, "unless you want to be a statue as well."

*****

Ginger had been the first to wake, the smell of food making her open her eyes. She had eaten nothing since Gavin had made breakfast for her and Cody, which seemed to have been eons ago. She felt as if her stomach was starting to digest itself.

She shuffled into the main room, seeing the plates of steaming food on the table. Her stomach grumbled ferociously, beckoning her toward the food. She ignored its pleas as she searched for Gavin.

"Ginger?" said a voice behind her. MJ had awoken as well, called by the food. "Where is everyone?"

"Sleepin', most likely," Ginger said, rubbing her eyes. "Gavin prob'ly had to rush off somewhere."

"So what do we do?" MJ asked. "Wait for Gavin?"

"No," Ginger replied. "He put me in charge of everyone in case he wasn't around. I know exactly what we gotta do."

"What?" MJ asked, yawning.

"Wake the others. We'll have breakfast, then we'll head to our new destination."

*****

Maximus stroked Jasmine's hair gently as he sat next to her. She was sleeping now, dreaming of an empty world. He frowned, deep lines forming across his forehead. She was going to have a child. His child. But how was she so certain? Maximus knew that if Helius found out about anything, they would both be executed immediately. It frightened him, because he did not know how to be anything but evil.

Torizar stood silently next to Maximus, thinking. Though he was evil, he was not without a heart. Maximus was his friend, and he would not betray or abandon him to Helius, even if Helius was the emperor.

Torizar put a hand on Maximus's shoulder, and Maximus turned to look at him. "Don't worry, Maximus. Everything will be fine."

"I can't face him, Torizar," Maximus said, turning away. "He'll know. Even if I don't say anything, Helius will know."

"Then stay here," Torizar protested. "Don't go back to the castle. I'll even stay here with you if I have to."

"I don't know how to be a father," Maximus said softly. Torizar sighed heavily and walked away as Penelope came in with Jasmine's water.

*****

The good keepers sat at the table, staring at Ginger with disgust. She was sitting on top of the table, shoving food into her face ravenously. Every so often, she would stop to breathe.

"Ginger, that's just nasty," Cody said, standing and backing away from the table.

"Well…you're…nasty," Ginger said between mouthfuls.

Serenity sat quietly, picking out what Ginger hadn't touched. She stood up with her plate and walked away. A look of disgust was evident in her facial features.

"Ginger, get off the table and let us eat something, you slob," Tinuviel muttered, quickly grabbing an apple.

"Yeah, come on," Adam agreed. "You're our leader, or something. You're supposed to be setting a good example."

Ginger grunted, wiping her mouth and getting off the table. "I can't help how hungry I get," she retorted, wiping off her hands.

"Well, the rest of us will have to go hungry for a while," Daniella said angrily. "I hope you're full."

"I am," Ginger said indignantly, opening her mouth to say something else.

"So Ginger," MJ interrupted loudly, "where are we going?"

"Right," Ginger said, turning away from the angry Daniella. "We're goin' to the ruins."

"Which ruins?" MJ asked. "There are three different ones, and they're all protected by magical spells."

"There're ruins not far from where Somnus Town usedta be," Cody added helpfully.

"I believe those are the Ruins of the Pure Ones," Tinuviel continued. "They've been there as long as I can remember."

"No one's ever been there?" Adam asked.

"I don't seem to remember there ever being any records of anyone living at the ruins," MJ said thoughtfully.

"There were some ruins near the Forest of the Mystics," Ginger said, her brow furrowing. "No one ever lived there, either."

"So, if no one lived at these ruins," Serenity cut in, "why are they here?"

MJ spoke before Ginger could say anything. "Perhaps they are here for the gods. If they are so protected by magic, there must be worthwhile secrets concealed within."

"Exactly," Ginger agreed, mentally sighing. "By the way, did that sequence I gave you help at all with the incantation?"

"I forgot!" MJ said, laughing and stopping to think for a moment. "Actually, it does help. If you put it all together, it makes perfect sense."

"So what is it?" Tasha asked eagerly.

MJ cleared her throat and spoke. "When night is day and day is night, our powers we combine to fight, the evil that has brought us down, we summon you, Oblivion!"

Every person in the room stood quietly, waiting to see what would happen. But after several moments of absolute silence, everyone stirred uneasily.

"What was supposed to happen?" Autumn asked, licking her lips and shifting uneasily on her feet.

"I don't know," MJ said with confusion. "I guess we'll just have to find out later."

"On to the Ruins of the Pure Ones!" Ginger cried.

*****

"Look, Regina," someone giggled insanely, "the prisoner is waking up!"

Mae opened her eyes to see a wild-looking man standing over her. She gasped and tried to sit up but realized that she was restrained by something. Her hands and feet were restrained by large iron shackles.

"There's no point in struggling, dear," a woman's voice said from behind Mae. The woman moved into view, smiling wickedly. "Those shackles were handcrafted by gremlins. They are exceptionally strong."

"Who are you?" Mae asked, trying to hide her fear. Her voice came out shaky, causing the woman to laugh cruelly.

"I am Victoria Bloodmoon, Keeper of Despair under Helius Rue," the woman replied, turning to look at the giggling man. "That giggling moron is Burgundy Alabastor, Keeper of Insanity."

"Who am I?" said another woman next to Burgundy, looking at Victoria with a blank, stupid expression.

"You, Regina Zeal, are an idiot," Victoria snorted, turning back to Mae. "Now who are you?"

"Mae Snowfall, princess of the fairies," Mae said indignantly, struggling in her bonds.

"Oh, we have a royal here!" Victoria said with a mocking tone.

"I demand that you release me!" Mae said forcefully.

"How about not?" Victoria replied viciously.

"Where's Thistle?" Mae demanded.

"Your pretty boy?" Regina giggled. "Bracchus took him to Nightmare Keep."

Mae struggled furiously, trying to free herself. "When I get one hand, just one hand, free…"

Regina took a step back, giggling once more. "Those shackles will never break! They are magically sealed! The strongest shackles ever to exist, and I'm proud to say that they are only used at the Keep of Liars!"

"Release me!" Mae shrieked furiously, tears falling from her eyes.

"All in good time," Victoria said forcefully. "We're only here to keep an eye on you."

"You're my prisoner," Shane said, stepping out of the shadows he had been standing in. "I separated you from your boyfriend so you wouldn't be able to pull any funny business. After all, we can't afford you killing another of our comrades."

Regina shrank back next to Burgundy, who had ceased his insane giggling when Shane spoke. Both Regina and Burgundy bowed their heads, staring blankly at the ground. They knew about Callus's death. Shane had told them when he had brought the beautiful fairy queen.

Victoria, Regina, Burgundy, and Bracchus had stumbled upon the two royals as they entered the portal into Chaos. Suspecting that they were escaped prisoners, the evil keepers had taken them captive. Bracchus had summoned Hexus, who took Thistle to Nightmare Keep. Regina, Burgundy, and Victoria had taken Mae to the Keep of Liars.

Shane had appeared shortly after, tightly clutching an unconscious fairy. He had told them of Mae and Thistle, and how Mae had slain Callus. Shane had then taken Ivy to the Village of Hatred, where she was being held captive. He had returned to the Keep of Liars in time to see Mae awaken.

Shane pushed the cruel memory of Callus's demise out of his head, smirking cruelly. He walked up to Mae and brushed her cheek with the back of his hand. She shivered, trying to pull away from his cold touch. "When Gavin finds you, he will destroy you."

"Quite the contrary," Shane replied, his smirk fading, "your ruler has no power here on Chaos. You, your boyfriend, and your mother are now mine."

Mae's eyes widened with fear as she fought to keep her voice in control. "My mother?"

"Oh, I forgot to tell you, didn't I?" Shane said, chuckling and leaning on his staff. "I captured your mother as well. She's back at my domain."

"No!" Mae screamed, pulling angrily at the chains that held her.

"There's no point in struggling," Shane said gruffly. "If you're a good girl, maybe Helius will let you live and give you to me." The insane laughter from the gathered keepers drowned out Mae's screaming and the furious rattling of her shackles.

*****

Thistle's eyes opened slowly and without ease. He blinked, clearing his blurry vision. The room came into focus, and Thistle at once wished he had not opened his eyes.

Not only was he bound by chains, he was in a terrible place. The room was done over in black, and cobwebs lined its cracked walls. Various writings were inscribed around the walls, creating a sort of pattern.

"Fascinating, aren't they?" a man said, walking up to Thistle and standing next to him. The man wore a black and silver robe and carried a large, leather-bound book.

He turned to face Thistle. "You are a royal, are you not?" he asked.

"I am," Thistle said, turning his wrists to try to release them from the grip of the heavy shackles.

"I would not suggest struggling," the man said. "Even if you managed to escape the diamond shackles that hold you captive, where would you go?"

Thistle realized at once what the man was talking about. He must have been transported to the world of Chaos while he was unconscious. He mentally kicked himself for not realizing his unfortunate predicament at once.

"Who are you?" he demanded, fighting back the urge to shout.

"Matthew Hexus," the man replied, sitting in a chair close to Thistle. He gazed again at the writing on the walls.

"Where am I?" Thistle persisted.

"Nightmare Keep, on the world of Chaos," Hexus replied, keeping his voice cool and controlled. "Charity Moonshadow's house." He stood and touched the cool surface of one of the stone walls. "She was a brilliant woman, you know. These writings were summoning spells of hers. Each was for a different nightmare."

Hexus sighed and rubbed his temples. "Of course, it doesn't matter now. She's dead."

"What are you going to do with me?" Thistle asked, giving up on trying to free himself.

"Well, that is for Helius to decide," Hexus said. "I'm just here to supervise."

"Hexus," another man said. Thistle craned his neck to see a man lounging on a couch in one corner of the room.

"What, Bracchus?" Hexus replied irritably.

"You can leave. I'll stay here and watch him."

"Excellent," Hexus said, turning away from the wall of writing. "Wait here for Helius. I'll be about."

In an unexplainable attempt to anger the keepers, Thistle blurted out, "Mae killed Callus."

Hexus, who had opened his book and was leafing through the pages, shut it immediately and turned to face the elven prince. "What did you say?" he asked quietly.

"Mae killed Callus Nightshade," Thistle repeated. "She thrust a sword through his black heart."

Bracchus sat up, his eyes glittering. "What proof do you have of this foolish talk?"

"Ask Shane Shadowstrife," Thistle replied loudly. "He was there. He's the man who captured us."

Hexus was deathly quiet, standing silently. His fingers tightened around his book until the knuckles turned white. "Very well," he said at last. He turned to Bracchus. "If the prince speaks one more syllable, slap him senseless."

"What about Shane?" Bracchus asked.

"Undoubtedly he is on his way back to Terra-Quenlist to seek revenge," Hexus commented. "I'd better find him before he does anything stupid."

Hexus tucked his book under his arm and shouted, *"Estuans!"* In a flash of fire, the Keeper of Shadows disappeared, leaving Thistle and Bracchus alone.

*****

"Ginger," MJ said quietly as they stood in front of the Ruins of the Pure Ones, "perhaps it would be better for us to split up and explore the three ruins in groups. That way, we could cover more ground."

"That's something I shoulda thought of straight away," Ginger said, sighing and nodding in agreement. "I'm no leader."

"Of course you are!" MJ said cheerfully. "You just need some practice!"

Ginger smiled and turned to face the others. "We'll be splittin' into three groups so we can explore the ruins faster. If there's anythin' relevant at any of the ruins, take it with you. We'll meet back at these ruins."

"So, who goes where?" Tasha asked.

"Serenity and Autumn can stay here with me," Ginger said. "MJ'll take Cody and Tasha. Daniella will take Tinuviel and Adam."

"Where are the other ruins located?" Adam asked.

"There're ruins t'the southa the Forest of the Mystics," Ginger replied.

"There are also ruins east of the Mountains of Hope," Tinuviel added.

"Good," Ginger replied. "Daniella, Tinuviel, and Adam can take the northeastern ruins. MJ, Cody, and Tasha can go to the southwestern ruins." The keepers nodded and split up, leaving Ginger, Serenity, and Autumn alone.

"So this place is magically sealed, huh?" Autumn asked, stepping up to the door and touching it. An electric shock sent her flying backward, knocking over Ginger.

"Goodness!" Serenity cried. "Are you all right?"

"Fine," Autumn mumbled, getting to her feet and helping the stunned Ginger up. "If it's lightning they want, it's lightning they'll get." She raised her arms and sent two bolts of lightning straight through the door. The door blew inward, shattering the magical seal and allowing entry.

"Wow…" Autumn breathed, looking at her hands. "I guess I figured out how to use my powers."

"Uh huh," Ginger replied, stepping through the doorway. "That puzzle didn't seem too hard t'solve."

Serenity and Autumn stepped in behind Ginger. "Nice work," Serenity said quietly to Autumn.

The interior of the building was nothing but spectacular. Large pillars lined the walls, arches spanning across them. The room was made of marble, plain yet elegant. An altar of silver stood on a platform on the opposite side of the room.

"There's nothing here!" Autumn protested grumpily, walking slowly to the other side of the room. "The altar looks like the only worthwhile possession, but we can't take it. It's too big."

"Wait a minute," Serenity said, walking up to the altar and brushing the dust off the top of it. "There are words here."

"Well, what do they say?" Autumn asked.

"They say, 'Power electricity, melt the silver and you'll see.'"

"What the heck does that mean?" Autumn asked.

"Why don't you try usin' your lightning on the altar?" Ginger suggested. "After all, this's the only silver here."

Autumn nodded and stepped back. Serenity hurried out of the way and joined Ginger, who stood behind Autumn. With another flash, lightning erupted from Autumn's fingertips and struck the silver altar.

"Nothing's happening!" Autumn protested.

"Increase the voltage!" Ginger insisted.

Autumn shrugged and squinted her eyes. The lightning intensified, liquefying the silver altar. The altar melted to a silvery puddle on the floor, disappearing through a large hole that was cut in the otherwise-impeccable marble surface.

"What's that?" Autumn asked, inspecting the hole.

"The answer," Serenity responded. "Whatever was hidden is down there."

"I'll go first," Ginger said, slipping down into the hole. Serenity and Autumn followed.

Ginger had expected to see the great bird of fire in the secret room, but was quite surprised when she did not. A small orb of light hovered above a minute platform in the little room they had entered. Behind the light, words were etched into the wall, along with a large, blood red garnet.

"Read the words!" Ginger urged Serenity.

Serenity stepped past the orb and up to the wall. "It says, 'The healing flame of immortality holds Phoenix.'"

"Is it referring to the gem?" Autumn asked.

"It must be," Ginger said, frowning and thinking. If Eden had hidden the Phoenix down here, maybe it had changed into a gemstone. Or maybe it was inside the gemstone. Ginger shook her head, releasing her frown. "Take the gem, and we'll get outta here."

Serenity tugged at the garnet, but to no avail. "It's stuck tight," she grunted, yanking on the embedded garnet. Finally giving up, she stepped back.

"I give up!" she cried, thrusting her hand out, palm facing the gem. A piece of the wall cracked and fell to the ground, smashing. Serenity stood there, confused. "What was that?"

"You tell us!" Ginger retorted, equally surprised.

"I didn't do that!" Serenity insisted.

"Of course you did!" Autumn replied. "You have telekinetic abilities."

"Unless it had somethin' t'do with the gem," Ginger said, "which'd make sense. With prosperity oftentimes comes wealth."

"Why don't you try to pry the garnet out telekinetically?" Autumn suggested, ignoring Ginger.

"I'll try," Serenity said doubtfully, reaching out her hand once again. She closed her eyes, concentrating on the jewel. With a great rumbling, the wall crumbled, and the garnet flew into Serenity's outstretched hand.

"I did it!" Serenity cried, holding tightly to the gem.

"Now, let's get outta here," Ginger said.

*****

CHAPTER XVII: MICHELLE HARMONIUM, KEEPER OF UNITY AND FAITH

"I'M REALLY SORRY ABOUT YOUR LITTLE FRIEND," Helius said, tucking the statue of Taran under his arm. "Look at it this way. He'll be an excellent centerpiece at the castle."

"You horrible creature!" Asterel screamed, lunging at Helius. A wave of his hand sent her flying backward into Gavin.

"I remember now what I came here to do," Helius said cruelly, clenching his hand into a fist. When he opened it, a dark blue ball of energy sat in his palm. He dropped it, and it plummeted right through the ground like a weighted block of lead.

"No!" Gavin cried, crawling across the ground.

"It's too late!" Helius cried, laughing wildly. "In a very short time, the core of this planet will freeze, and the planet will go into a supernova! There's nothing you can do to stop it! Even your magic can't save you now!" With an explosion of black flames, Helius disappeared, taking Taran with him.

"Gavin, what do we do?" Asterel asked frantically.

"We can do nothing," Gavin replied, tears in his eyes. A large tremor wavered throughout Terra-Quenlist, knocking the already-sprawled Gavin and Asterel flat on the ground.

*****

The Palace of Torrent shivered and creaked, its structure cracking. A young woman sat in her room, eyes closed. She opened her eyes when the tremor struck, rolling off her bed onto the floor. She landed on all fours, trying to steady herself.

The tremor passed as quickly as it had come, and the woman got to her feet. She looked in her mirror, combing her short black hair quickly to perfect it. She smoothed her sky blue dress, adjusted her matching shoes and bracelet, and quickly applied a light blush to her creamy white cheeks, smiling slightly and making her dark brown eyes twinkle. Her perfect, white teeth were exposed ever so slightly by her smile.

"My dear child," Torrent said from behind her.

"Yes, Uncle Torrent?" the woman asked, turning to face the Elder God of Water.

"Gavin Moonstone needs your help," he said. "Go to him quickly."

"As you suggest, so I will," the woman replied, grabbing her cloak and throwing it on as Torrent waved his hand. The woman evaporated, such as bubbles carried away by the briny sea.

"Hurry, child," Torrent whispered, bowing and fading. "Time grows short for us all."

*****

"What in Zeus's name…" MJ cried as she fell to the ground. The tremor passed quickly, and the land was silent once again.

"What was that?" Tasha asked, sitting up and rubbing her head.

"Whatever it was, it was not good," MJ replied. "Let's get this over with and get back to Ginger as quickly as possible."

"So, how is this place magically sealed?" Cody asked, getting to his feet.

"I don't know," MJ replied. She walked up to the stone door and pushed. Nothing happened.

"It won't budge," MJ said, shaking her head. She noticed some faded writing on the stone and read it aloud. "'Even stone can soften now, when I hear that heavenly sound.'"

"The only thing that sounds heavenly would be an angel's voice or an angel's trumpet," Tasha said.

"Of course!" Cody piped up. "It's music!" With that, he started humming. The door shattered, breaking the seal. MJ raised her eyebrows, nodding with approval. Tasha smiled and clapped lightly.

"Let's get this done," MJ said, stepping inside.

The room had large pillars lining the walls and was done over in marble. There was nothing in the marble room, save for a bronze altar at the other end.

MJ shrugged and walked over to the altar. "There's an inscription," she said. "It says, 'Atlas doth move the world. Shiver and shake for secrets revealed.'"

"According to legend, Atlas held the world on his shoulders," Tasha said thoughtfully.

"Well, this is quite a quandary," MJ said, sitting on the floor. "It's definitely a tough riddle to crack."

*****

Daniella did not even have to try to solve the riddle that would break the magical seal over the entryway. The tremor that shook the earth ground the stone door into powder and knocked Daniella to the ground. "Ow," Daniella groaned, standing and rubbing her tailbone. "That kinda hurt."

Adam scrambled to his feet, raising an eyebrow when he noticed that Tinuviel was still standing. "How come you didn't fall?"

"I'm used to earthquakes," Tinuviel replied, "because I generally cause them." Daniella opened her mouth to say something, but Tinuviel quickly said, "I didn't cause this one, though. Something else did. And I don't think it was something good."

"Let's hurry and find what we need to," Daniella cut in, "so we can get back to the others."

They stepped inside the ancient structure, marveling at its interior. Though it seemed bland, it was indeed elegant. Large marble pillars lined the walls, matching the marble floor. The room was devoid of furniture or upholstery, save for a large golden altar at the opposite end.

"Wow, an empty room," Daniella said with mock enthusiasm. She strolled across the floor to the gold altar, her shoes clicking daintily against the cold marble.

"There's writing," she said, motioning for Adam and Tinuviel to join her.

"What does the writing say?" Adam inquired.

Daniella cleared her throat loudly. "Well…the writing says, 'A heart of gold, intentions true, find you heart, to see you through.'"

"And that means?" Tinuviel said irritably.

"It's a riddle," Adam said thoughtfully. He touched the altar, feeling the cool metal under his fingertips. "And a very difficult riddle, to be sure."

"Do you know what it means?" Daniella asked.

"I think so," Adam replied, frowning. "We came here to find something of value, but it wasn't gold. We came here to find information. That is our true intention."

The gold altar evaporated. Adam, who had been leaning on it, fell into the hole that it left behind. He yelped as he hit the floor of the room below.

"Adam!" Daniella cried, crawling into the hole after him. Tinuviel followed wearily.

The room they had found was small and well-hidden under the marble floor of the grand, empty room above. A small orb of light hovered above the ground at the other end of the tiny room. Behind the orb was a wall of writing, with a dark blue sapphire embedded in its center.

"Read!" Tinuviel urged Daniella, who stumbled forward. She passed the orb and squinted at the writing on the wall. "Okay,

okay, sheesh. It says, 'Silvery blood, I am immortal. Take my essence to set the winged horse free.'"

"A Pegasus?" Tinuviel asked in disbelief. "Where?"

"I think the writing refers to this gem," Daniella said, tapping the sapphire with a fingernail.

"I always wanted a Pegasus," Tinuviel said, looking starry-eyed.

"Okay, so how do we get the gem?" Adam asked. "Can you pry it out, Daniella?" Daniella tugged on the jewel, grunting and gritting her teeth. After several seconds of pulling, she gave up, her face reddening.

"Oh, get out of the way," Tinuviel groaned, walking past Daniella and kicking the wall. "If you want…something done right…you have to do it…yourself!"

A well-placed kick cracked the wall. Tinuviel grinned and kicked again, for the last time. The wall crumbled, releasing the blue gem from its imprisonment. Tinuviel picked it up and handed it to the flustered Daniella.

"That wasn't very lady-like!" Daniella sputtered, putting the sapphire in her pocket.

"Since when have I been lady-like?" Tinuviel asked. "I threaten to beat people up, and I cause earthquakes. Plus, I like blowing things up."

"Enough said," Daniella chuckled, shaking her head. "Let's get back to Ginger."

*****

The shock waves had stopped after the large but brief earthquake. Rodaine opened his eyes, feeling Storm stir. His whole body hurt. It ached worse than he had ever thought possible. Was he dead?

"A silly question, you old fogy," Rodaine moaned out loud, rolling over and slowly climbing to his feet. Storm stood obediently by his side and followed him when he limped over to one of the broken windows.

"Helius is gone," Rodaine breathed, sinking against the wall. He closed his eyes and inhaled the crisp air of the outside through his nostrils.

"Ah, Storm," Rodaine said, patting the wolf on the head, "I'm too old for this."

*****

Gavin sat up slowly, helplessly. It was too late. Helius had won. The core of the planet would freeze soon, and the planet would wither and die. There was nothing he could do. He voiced his thoughts out loud, not even realizing he was speaking.

"What do you mean there's nothing you can do?" Asterel said frantically, shaking him. "What about the people?"

"It's too late!" Gavin exploded. "That orb will attack the core of the planet! It will kill it from the inside out! Once the core dies, so too does the planet! It will supernova! Once the core crystallizes, the planet will explode!"

"There must be something we can do," Asterel breathed desperately.

"There is nothing," Gavin replied sourly. "Aside from moving everyone to Chaos…" He stopped, looking at Asterel's expression.

"Oh, no," he said, shaking his head furiously. "We can't evacuate them to Chaos. They wouldn't last – it's a world of darkness! I don't even know if we have the power to do it."

"Gavin," Asterel said softly, "there is no other way."

*****

"Heave!" MJ grunted as she and Cody pushed on the bronze altar. The second the altar moved, it disappeared. MJ squeaked and fell forward through the hole that had been exposed in the floor.

"MJ!" Cody yelled, jumping in after her.

"You two are the clumsiest people I know," Tasha said irritably, climbing in after them.

The room they had entered was small and plain, save for a small orb of light and some writing on the opposite wall. A light yellow topaz sat embedded at the center of the writing on the wall.

"Get off me!" MJ cried, rolling the grinning Cody off her. She stood up, brushing herself off.

"Sorry," Cody said sarcastically, standing and brushing himself off as well. "I didn't know you were so shy around people."

MJ turned away from him in a huff, walking up to the wall and skimming over the words. "'From the depths of the great volcano shall I rise, reanimate and summoned forth, the Bird of Fire.'"

"What is it referring to?" Cody asked anxiously.

"The gemstone," MJ snorted. Tasha walked up to the stone and touched it lightly.

"How do we get it out, MJ?" she asked.

"I dunno," MJ said, frowning. "It looks like it's stuck pretty tight. There's nothing in here to pry it out with, either."

Tasha closed her eyes, thinking. The gemstone kept sticking in her mind. It was beautiful, a brilliant vermillion. It reminded her of the sun. She had not seen the sun in so long. She had not felt its warmth or seen its brilliance in so long.

The wall bent and twisted in place, wringing the topaz out of its grip. The small jewel fell to the ground, making a slight tinkling sound as it hit. Tasha opened her eyes, amazed and confused. Somehow, she had distorted space to pry the gem from its cradle. But how had she done it?

MJ bent down and picked up the precious stone, shoving it into her pocket. "Didn't know you had it in you," she said with amazement. Turning back to Cody, MJ continued. "We have what we came for. Let's get back to Ginger."

*****

Ginger, Serenity, and Autumn stepped back into the cool air of the endless night. Somehow, it seemed as if the air had chilled even further. "What now?" Serenity asked.

"You die!" a voice shouted from behind. Ginger tackled Serenity as Shane's staff whizzed by. It missed them by inches, attacking the dead air. Autumn jumped out of the way as it came flying past again.

Ginger jerked her head up. The angry keeper glared down at her, his eyes ablaze with fury. A purple flame exploded from the end of his dark staff, aimed at Ginger. She closed her eyes and put up her arms, waiting for the fire to scorch her. When it did not come, she slowly lowered her arms, wondering why it hadn't hit her.

The fireball hung inches from her face, suspended motionlessly. Ginger looked over to see Serenity with her hand outstretched. "That's just rude," Serenity said, flicking her wrist. The flame flew backward, hitting the astounded Shane in the chest. He yelled and dropped his staff, flying backward and rolling across the ground.

He jumped to his feet and scurried for his staff. It rolled out of his reach, Serenity telekinetically skidding it away. Autumn sprang to action. She twirled her fingers, creating a small whirlwind. The whirlwind engulfed the staff, carrying it to Autumn. She grabbed it and broke it effortlessly over her knee.

"No!" Shane howled, running forward. His magic wisped out, disappearing.

"Too late!" Autumn shouted, throwing down the broken staff. "You lose!"

Shane roared with cruel laughter, standing and staring straight into Autumn's eyes. "I'd be dead if all my power was in my staff." A sword appeared in his hand, gleaming when he turned it slightly.

"The sword is indeed mightier than the pen, you fools!" Shane cried, swinging the sword. Serenity swung her arm and slapped Shane in the back of the head before his sword could touch Autumn. He turned around and charged at the peaceful keeper.

"Stay away from her!" Autumn shouted. The sword in Shane's hands burst into flames. He yelled and dropped it on the ground where it exploded in a blaze of fury.

"Now you die!" Shane shouted in a terrifying voice. Ginger stepped in front of him, having risen from the ground to face him.

"You have been defeated," she said. "Surrender or you will be destroyed."

"Never!" Shane screamed, lunging at Ginger. The keeper closed her eyes and held up her hands.

"Grow from love," she whispered.

Shane stopped dead in his tracks, an odd expression crossing his face. He clutched his throat and fell to his knees, the glow fading from his eyes. He sat motionless and changed. Not into a monster, but into something beautiful. His arms became great branches, his body a trunk. His feet turned to roots and planted themselves firmly into the ground. Shane Shadowstrife was no more. Instead, a beautiful Mulberry tree had sprung to life, its branches abundant with fruit. Shane, in an instant of Ginger's glory, was defeated.

The keepers stood silently for a moment. Serenity finally said, "Peace must grow for prosperity to flower."

"That was astounding," Autumn breathed, looking at Ginger with admiration.

"I didn't do everything," Ginger said, a little astounded herself. "You guys weakened him."

"I suppose it doesn't matter," Serenity said, shrugging and smiling slightly. "The point is that we beat him together."

*****

The woman appeared in front of the emperor and the elven queen. She smiled and curtseyed, standing quietly afterward. "Whom do I have the pleasure of addressing?" Gavin asked.

"I am Michelle Harmonium," the woman replied politely. "My uncle is Torrent, the Elder God of Water."

"Ah, yes, of course," Gavin replied. "He sent you to me in hopes of helping, I assume?"

"Yes, Emperor," Michelle responded. "My uncle informed me that you required my assistance. I am here to aid you in whatever way I am able."

"As a matter of fact, I believe you can help," Gavin said, a weary smile forming as he remembered Michelle's name on his list. "How do you stand on the power of Faith?"

"Faith, I believe, is the most powerful magic of all," Michelle replied.

"I was hoping you'd say that," Gavin said with the slightest hint of relief. "You see, the keepers of mine who are trying to help me need someone to keep them together. Would you like to be the Keeper of Unity and Faith?"

"It would be an honor, Your Majesty," Michelle replied, bowing slightly.

Gavin nodded and licked his lips, clasping his hands together. When he released them, a small white orb floated gently in the air. It floated toward Michelle, who held out her hands and caught it. It was absorbed into her skin, into her very being. She had become one with all.

"Welcome, Michelle Harmonium, Keeper of Unity and Faith," Gavin said.

CHAPTER XVIII: TIER SUNDROP, KEEPER OF LIGHT AND HAPPINESS

"WHAT DO YOU NEED ME TO DO?" MICHELLE ASKED.

Gavin reached into his bag and pulled out a carpet. "I need you to go to the Palace of Powers to fetch a woman named Tier Sundrop. Once you have found her, bring her back here."

Michelle nodded and took the carpet. She sat on it and clutched the sides as it rose. "Go," she said simply. The carpet rose higher and flew off lazily.

"She seems so confident," Asterel said with amazement.

"Why not?" Gavin said, shrugging. "After all, she is the Keeper of Unity and Faith, innate powers she possessed long before I made her a keeper."

"I didn't know Torrent had a niece," Asterel said.

"She's not his niece per say," Gavin replied. "She has just known him for so long that she calls him her uncle. You see, Michelle lives at the Palace of Torrent, a palace specializing in water-based magic."

"I see," Asterel murmured, nodding slightly and seeming to be miles away. She snapped back immediately and turned to Gavin, a look of determination on her face. "We have to evacuate everyone to the Onyx Castle, Gavin. I don't care how terrible Helius's world is. They must be saved."

Gavin, knowing that there was no other alternative, sighed. "Ride throughout the land, Asterel. Send everyone who has not evacuated to the Onyx Castle. I must speak with Rodaine." Gavin pulled out a carpet and handed it to Asterel, who nodded and departed quickly. He turned and started toward the great doors of the Crystal Palace, his pace quick.

*****

Hexus had arrived too late. By the time he had found Shane, he had been in time to see the evil keeper transform into a great tree. "Too late," he whispered, shaking his head and opening his book as he felt the change in the air. "My time will come for revenge, but it is not now." With a chant and a clap of thunder, Hexus was gone, speeding back to the Onyx Castle.

*****

Ivy woke up cold and disoriented. She was captive and bound in shackles, completely unable to move. Her head pounded like thousands of bass drums, with a cymbal crash every so often.

There was no sign of her captor, or of Helius. She was alone. The shackles clanked and rattled as Ivy jiggled her wrists furiously. She shook and smashed at them, finally freeing one of her wrists. She had never been as thankful as she was now. The shackle which had freed her wrist had rotted through and broken.

She unhinged the other wrist and released her ankles. Pushing off the chains, Ivy stumbled away from the wall, rubbing her wrists. She looked around, failing to recognize anything that she saw. She was completely alone.

The room she was in was dark, decorated in black and crimson and lit with small candles. Extravagant tapestries hung over the plain walls. Crimson carpets covered the cold cobblestone floor. The room was devoid of furniture, save for a small chair and table. Upon the table sat instruments such as a doctor or a surgeon would use.

"It's so creepy in here," Ivy said, shuddering. "I have to find a way out of here before my captor comes back." Little did the queen know that Shane Shadowstrife, Keeper of Hatred, was never to return to torment her ever again.

*****

Rodaine ushered people aside as the palace doors burst open. He smiled slightly as Gavin emerged. All present bowed as Gavin strode past. He grabbed Rodaine and pulled him into the throne room, closing the heavy doors behind them. Storm slipped inside before the doors closed, slinking next to Rodaine like a serpent.

"We must evacuate everyone to Chaos," Gavin said quickly. "There isn't much time."

"But, Sire…" Rodaine protested.

"There isn't time to argue!" Gavin cried desperately.

"I was just going to suggest using the Transteleportation Spell," Rodaine explained weakly. "It would save much time."

"It requires more power than I currently can use," Gavin said with exasperation.

"What about the chanters?" Rodaine suggested. "There are more than enough to activate the power of the spell."

"Perhaps," Gavin said thoughtfully, walking over to his throne and reaching underneath. He pulled out a large book and opened it, quickly leafing through the pages. He handed the book to Rodaine, who took out his spectacles and examined the spell.

"They can do it—I know they can," Rodaine said, squinting and looking up at Gavin.

"If they can't master the Transteleportation Spell and work it correctly within one hour, evacuate them," Gavin said briefly, turning and opening the doors of the throne room. He pulled open the front doors and exited amid bows and curtseys.

"Gather the chanters in the throne room now," Rodaine called.

*****

Aster walked alongside Veronica, remaining silent. Ross Hepatica was dead, and Bracken Pennyroyal had been badly hurt. The remaining troops had managed to gather a small crowd of refugees. They had not encountered any evil entities since the great battle. They had also been unable to enter the palaces, as magical shields had kept them out.

"Veronica!" called a voice from above. Aster and Veronica looked up to see Asterel Sunfire hovering on a carpet above.

"My Queen!" Veronica cried, bowing graciously.

"Evacuate everyone to the Onyx Castle," Asterel said. "I will accompany you."

"My Queen, what of the sealed palaces?" Aster asked.

"Someone is already taking care to evacuate the palaces," Asterel replied.

"Some people refused to leave their homes," Veronica said with desperation. "We tried to take them with us, but they would not come."

"Who, and where?" Asterel asked.

"All of the priests and priestesses refused to come," Veronica responded.

"They will not come," Asterel said, shaking her head. "Is there anyone else?"

"Many of the people from Morning Star Vista refused to leave," Aster continued. "The headman said he was set on staying to watch the sun rise one last time. I told him that the sun would never again rise, and he just ignored me and kept staring out his window."

"Someone will come to evacuate them," Asterel said in a reassuring tone. "Come, we must go."

*****

The sound of knocking resonated through the halls of the Palace of Powers. The remaining mystics backed away as the knocking continued. "Oh, for Zeus's sake!" a woman cried, rushing to the door and throwing it open.

Michelle was taken aback when the door swung open abruptly and a woman stood there, glaring at her. The woman was shorter, with short blonde hair tied back in a ponytail. Her blue eyes glistened with the soft light. She wore a dress in a lighter shade of purple, with silver bracelets around her wrists and a silver chain around her dainty neck.

"We are not leaving," the woman declared forcefully. "We are staying here until the end."

"What are you talking about?" Michelle asked.

The glare on the woman's face disappeared. "You mean you're not here to evacuate us?"

"Actually, I was looking for someone named Tier Sundrop," Michelle replied. "The emperor requires her presence."

"What does the emperor need me for?" the woman asked.

Michelle smiled inwardly. She should have guessed that Tier would be the one to open the door. Fate could be so ironic sometimes. "He needs your help."

A murmur broke out from the gathered mystics behind Tier. A wave of her hand quieted them, allowing her to speak. "If he needs me, I will be glad to assist."

"What of the others?" Michelle asked, indicating the crowd behind Tier.

"They do not want to leave," Tier said simply.

"And I cannot force them," Michelle replied. She felt a twinge in her stomach and realized that she was tapping into her newfound power. She continued. "But think of the good they can do protecting the evacuated citizens of Terra-Quenlist. Why, with the combined elements of the mystics from each of the five palaces, everyone would be safe from the darkness!"

Her power had an immediate effect. A man stepped forward and spoke. "This woman does have a point, Tier," he said.

Michelle's face reddened as she realized something. "I haven't told you my name. I am Michelle Harmonium."

"It's a pleasure to meet you, Michelle," Tier responded, shaking her hand. Turning to the gathered mystics, she said,

"Perhaps we're being selfish by locking ourselves away. There are innocent lives at stake. I say we gather the mystics from all the palaces and evacuate to help the helpless."

"Here, here!" the man shouted as the crowd murmured in agreement.

"Summon the other mystics," Tier said.

"And gather at the Onyx Castle," Michelle finished happily.

Tier stepped outside next to Michelle, closing the door amid the hustling mystics. "Where are we headed?" she asked anxiously.

"To the Crystal Palace," Michelle replied, helping Tier onto the floating carpet, "where the emperor awaits."

*****

Another tremor hit just as the keepers had gathered back together. This tremor was far more severe than the last one, knocking over all present. Ginger slid Serenity out of the way as the Ruins of the Pure Ones crashed to the ground. Far off in the distance, pieces of the Mountains of Hope tumbled down, causing large avalanches of snow.

The tremor weakened and stopped, leaving destruction in its wake. Ginger helped Serenity to her feet as the other keepers slowly stood up. "They're getting worse," MJ said, rubbing her lower back.

"Something's very wrong," Tinuviel said, listening intently. "These tremors aren't natural. Something's causing them."

"Look!" Tasha cried, pointing at the sky. A carpet sped across it, two distant figures visible on the top side of it.

"It looks like it's headed toward the Crystal Palace," Serenity said.

"Follow it!" Ginger cried.

*****

Gavin stood back as the Crystal Palace vanished, leaving a large, empty space where it used to reside. He sighed and turned around, squinting when he saw something coming toward him. Backing up, he made room for the people on the carpet.

Michelle landed with a woman who was undoubtedly Tier Sundrop. Tier curtseyed slightly and stood silently as Michelle spoke. "This is Tier Sundrop. She's agreed to help."

"That is a relief indeed," Gavin breathed. He observed the young Tier, raising an eyebrow. He could feel the energy she had. It was good, and it was powerful.

"I will give you the powers of Light and Happiness," Gavin said at last, smiling with kindness. Though he was weary and the world around seemed to be coming undone, he couldn't help but be glad that there was yet another kind person to aid. He released a beam of white light from his eyes. The beam entered Tier's eyes and was gone instantly.

"I feel…" Tier gasped, searching for a word.

"Complete?" Gavin asked, already knowing the answer but expressing the question nonetheless.

"Yes…" Tier said, smiling slightly.

"Gavin!" Michelle cried, finally noticing the empty space. "Your palace is gone!"

Gavin chuckled lightly. "The chanters were able to teleport it to the world of Chaos. You see, everyone here must be evacuated as soon as possible."

"Why?" Tier asked.

Gavin turned and looked her in the eyes. When he spoke, his voice was filled with pain and torment. "Because this world is dying."

CHAPTER XIX: AURORA LIGHTLY, THE EMPEROR'S COUNSEL

"WHAT'S THAT?" TIER ASKED IN ASTONISHMENT.

"Helius Rue, an evil from another world, has poisoned the planet," Gavin said sorrowfully. "He drove a ball of dark magic into the earth. It is right now tunneling to the core of the planet. Once it reaches the core, the planet will freeze."

Ginger, who had landed silently with the others behind Gavin, heard the whole conversation. "What?! That's impossible!"

Gavin turned to face the flustered Ginger, his expression unchanged. "Nothing is impossible. But it is true. The planet is dying."

"That would explain the tremors that have been occurring," Tinuviel said, stunned.

"What do we do?" MJ asked. Her eyes widened, and she said, "Where is the palace?"

"The Crystal Palace has been transported to Chaos. Everyone who couldn't make it to the palace in time is now being evacuated to the Onyx Castle," Gavin replied.

"But that's the link to Helius's world!" Tasha cried.

"Why would we go there?" Cody asked, his eyes widening.

"You don't intend to evacuate everyone to Helius's world, do you?" Serenity asked.

"There is no other choice," Gavin replied. "If they stay here, they will die with the planet."

"But Helius's world is pure evil!" Daniella protested.

"It's too late, and there is no other choice," Gavin responded. "The Crystal Palace has already been transported there as a safe haven for the evacuees."

Another tremor confirmed the decision Gavin had made. This tremor shook the earth so fiercely that it splintered it. Large fissures spread across the ground below. The plateau shook and started to slide as the large rock it rested on split in two.

"Gavin!" Ginger screeched as she fell over and slid toward the edge of the plateau.

"Onto the carpets, everyone!" Gavin cried, hoisting Ginger onto her carpet as the others climbed onto theirs. Michelle grabbed Tier and swung her onto her carpet as the plateau collapsed, falling in on itself. The tremor stopped abruptly, leaving the frantic party hovering in mid-air.

"Go to the Onyx Castle," Gavin commanded forcefully. "Get any refugees through to the world of Chaos."

"Gavin, the palaces have been evacuated as well," Michelle said quickly as she and the others nodded in consent.

Silently, the keepers flew away. Gavin watched the large group go and floated quietly. He looked at the destroyed plateau, and it hurt. The plateau upon which his palace had sat was no more.

"Gavin!" Asterel cried desperately as she sped through the air to his side. "One of the towns hasn't been evacuated!"

"Which town?" Gavin said quickly, the thoughts of his destroyed plateau and evacuated palace suddenly vaporizing with Asterel's words.

"Morning Star Vista," Asterel replied.

*****

"Father, we must leave," the woman said, pulling on the sleeve of the old man's shirt. He sat in a chair, looking out the window at the snow that had begun to gently fall.

"Aurora, someday you will learn that there are some things a person cannot do," the man replied, sighing heavily. He turned and looked at his daughter.

She was clothed in a green gown, with matching slippers and bracelets. The tips of her long blonde hair rested comfortably at the tops of her shoulders, in perfect harmony with her blue eyes. Her creamy white skin, slightly flushed cheeks, and rose-red lips made her seem fragile, like a porcelain doll. This was just a disguise, however, because Aurora was a strong and highly intelligent woman.

"The townspeople will not leave without you," Aurora protested. "You are their leader!"

"Lead them where you will," her father, the town headman, replied. "You must escape with them."

"Father…" Aurora replied softly.

The headman turned once again to his daughter, his eyes watery. "My child. My heart aches at this, but I am too old and know no other place than this. I must stay."

"Father…" Aurora started once again.

"Aurora, you were meant for greater things than to stay here with me. Go and live your life. Pursue your dreams, and do what you have always wanted to do. You have had a dream for the longest time…"

"To marry the emperor," Aurora said, blushing slightly. "He is very handsome, and I've heard that he is a wonderful man."

"That he is," the headman agreed. "Go to the emperor. Even if it's not to marry him, perhaps he may need your help. You are a brilliant and headstrong girl. Go to him."

"The people…" Aurora started.

"I will evacuate them," her father said. "Go. Go and fulfill all of your dreams, my daughter. Do what you know in your heart you were meant to."

"I will wait until every single person has been evacuated before I leave this wonderful place," Aurora said, hugging her father. She clasped a cloak around herself and opened the door of the small house, silently watching the snow as it fell.

*****

A large crowd had gathered outside the Onyx Castle. The gentle snowfall had now turned into a violent blizzard, as if to signal the coming of some terrible end. A foreshadowing, a sign of things to come. Snow swirled past fearful faces, biting at the figures of the gathered evacuees.

"Aster!" Veronica cried over the blowing wind, "Open the doors!" Veronica pulled one door, and Aster pulled the other. The broken, splintered doors swung open, and refugees began filtering in to escape the vicious, whipping wind of the snow that swirled outside.

"Gods save us all," Veronica whispered.

*****

Asterel flew toward the Onyx Castle alongside Gavin, both of them fighting against the fierce wind and snow. Gavin broke away from her, heading toward Morning Star Vista. He motioned to Asterel to continue forward while he stayed behind. A nod from the queen was all he needed to indicate that she understood.

The snow whirled around in small tornados. Gavin could faintly see a large group of people far below. They had obviously come from Morning Star Vista. Far behind them was a solitary figure, fighting against the wind. Gavin's eyes widened as the figure collapsed.

Like a shot, the emperor blazed through the air to the ground below. He knelt down and clutched the woman, who lay shivering. He turned his back to the snow and wind, acting as a shield.

"I found you," the woman whispered.

"Hold on," Gavin said, holding tightly to the woman and covering her face against the violent weather. He lifted off the ground with her, feeling her arms tighten around his waist.

Over the Hills of the Saviors they flew, passing Diamond Falls shortly after. The waterfall had stopped, and the pool was now completely frozen, hiding the diamonds embedded deep below the surface. Across Starlight River they went, landing in front of Twilight Pass.

Holding the trembling woman with one arm while she clung tightly to him, Gavin pushed open the heavy doors with his free arm. A blast of warm air hit the two of them as they stumbled in. Ginger and Tinuviel closed the doors behind Gavin and the woman.

Twilight Pass still retained its charm, despite the terrible weather of the now-dying planet. An enormous fireplace was embedded in one wall, a large fire blazing cheerfully inside of it. The orange-colored staircase led to the upper floors of the pass, matching the elaborate décor of the foyer. The foyer was decorated with luxurious furniture, carpets and tapestries polishing off the structure for a perfect look of splendor.

Gavin looked around to see all of his keepers gathered inside the roomy hall of Twilight Pass. "You're all here?" he said with confusion.

"It was too cold to stand outside and wait to enter the Onyx Castle," MJ explained. "We decided it would be better to go somewhere warm to try to thaw from that HORRIBLE weather outside."

"It gets colder outside every moment," Adam said.

"The planet is truly dying," Serenity said in disbelief.

"The core must be freezing," Gavin breathed. "I can't believe how quickly all of this is occurring. How is that possible?"

"At least we are all here and safe," MJ said, attempting to dodge the question.

"No," Gavin remarked in response to MJ's comment. All turned to look at him. He sat in a large chair as Ginger and Tinuviel helped the woman into another chair.

"There was one more person on the list," Gavin said. "We never found her."

"Who?" MJ asked with worry.

Gavin beckoned to his black bag, which bounced over to him. Opening it, he pulled out a copy of the list. "The final person was Aurora Lightly of Morning Star Vista."

"My name is Aurora Lightly," the woman said weakly, sitting a little straighter and gazing at the astounded emperor. "My father is the headman of Morning Star Vista."

"Well, isn't that a coincidence?" Daniella snorted.

"It is," Gavin said, glaring at Daniella, who shrank back defensively. Turning back to Aurora, he said, "You were the final person we sought. We need your help."

"You do?" Aurora said, brightening a little and standing slowly. "Of course I'll help you! You're cute…ah, I mean…wonderful!"

Gavin wore an expression of surprise as he sat there. Ginger covered her face with her arm to hide the laughing fit she had entered. Cody let out a loud chuckle. Serenity, who had quickly fallen asleep in one of the chairs, snorted and awoke. Tinuviel smiled slightly, standing next to a grinning Tasha. Pretty soon, the entire room was engulfed in fits of laughter, including Aurora and Gavin.

"Okay," Gavin said at last, gasping for air and wiping away the tears of laughter. "Aurora must receive her powers."

He stopped suddenly, frowning. It was not an irritated frown he wore, but one of puzzlement. He scratched his head and looked again at the list he held.

"What's wrong?" Autumn asked.

"It seems that Rodaine made a miscalculation," Gavin replied. "I have no other powers left to give."

"That's all right," Aurora said quickly. "I don't need any special powers. I can help in other ways."

"Such as?" Ginger asked.

"Does the emperor have a counsel?" Aurora asked.

"What's a counsel?" Cody replied.

"A counsel is someone who acts as advisor to the emperor," Aurora explained. "They may help him make decisions, and sometimes they can rule in his stead."

"I do not have a counsel," Gavin remarked. "Rodaine may be an advisor, but he's more of a friend and comrade than a counsel. However, I suppose it is time that I appointed someone." He pulled from his bag a silver necklace. Attached to the necklace was a representation of the North Star. Gavin put it around Aurora's neck, smiling slightly.

"What's this?" Aurora asked, fingering the talisman.

"It is a representation of the North Star," Gavin said. "The star guides us in the right direction. It symbolizes balance and strength of will. And it's also been said to help lost souls find their way home. Consider the pendant proof of your inauguration."

"You mean…" Aurora asked.

"Congratulations," Gavin said lightly. You are now Aurora Lightly, the Emperor's Counsel."

*****

CHAPTER XX: THE PROPHECY

HELIUS TURNED AROUND WHEN THE SKY AROUND HIM flashed a brilliant white. He set down the statue of the gnome king. Flashes that bright had never occurred on Chaos since the flash of light that had killed Emeralda. With a grunt of disapproval, Helius continued toward the Castle of Souls, picking up the statue as he left.

After quite a long while, Helius arrived at his castle. He had passed the Desert of Despair and the Mountains of Illusion, his mood worsening with each step, until he was finally wallowing in fury. His original intent had not been to destroy the other planet. He had wanted to enslave it. Instead, he was forced to use a spell that would kill the planet, freezing the core. Once the core was frozen, the spell would cause the core to heat up quickly, causing a fissure that would force the planet to go supernova.

"At least I win," Helius said wryly, setting the statue on a ledge next to the castle steps and opening the castle doors. "I have prisoners to keep my life force sustained for quite a long time, at least until I can reach out and ensnare other worlds. That alone is a victory."

He laughed and shut the doors behind him, walking briskly through the large hallway he had entered. He stopped halfway down the hall, feeling a presence. Morpheus appeared behind him, bowing slightly. "How fares the emperor?" he asked Helius.

"I am dismal, as always," Helius said. "My plans have gone slightly awry."

"You set out to enslave and conquer a world," Morpheus said quietly. "You enslaved many people. Even now they are held prisoner. Some are here, and others are being held at Hell's Gate. Consider the destruction of Terra-Quenlist necessary collateral damage and a blow to Gavin Moonstone's ego. All in all, I'd say you conquered. You should be overjoyed."

"I will not be overjoyed until I see Gavin Moonstone struck dead," Helius snarled. "And very soon, he will be."

*****

Ivy stumbled across the uneven land outside the village she had left, following the direction the light had come from. Like a spear, the explosion of light pierced the silence and blackness of the dark world, stopping not far from where she was.

Ivy ran toward the light, not caring how far away it was so long as she reached it. She stopped when she saw that a large mountain range stood in her way. Past those mountains, on the other side, was the thing that had made the light—the beautiful, pure light of a world she remembered. She desperately wanted to get there.

Flexing her wings, Ivy started upward, flying slowly. As she climbed higher, the mountains shrank farther. Suddenly, she was over, and she was free.

The most beautiful sight she had ever seen was behind the mountain range. The Crystal Palace had made the light when it appeared. Behind the palace was a small chapel made of white marble.

"How…" Ivy started. But she really didn't care how. The best thing she had ever seen on this cruel world stood in front of her now, and she didn't care how or why it was there. It just was.

*****

"Stop struggling, you brat!" Victoria cried. She tried to still Mae by pushing her against the wall, so Mae bit her on the arm.

Victoria howled with pain, and Regina giggled. "You like biting? Me too!"

"Shut up, Regina!" Victoria shrieked, turning and slapping Mae across the face. Mae stopped struggling, her face stinging.

"That'll teach you," Burgundy giggled.

"That made a funny noise!" Regina cackled idiotically. "Do it again, lady, do it again!"

"Shut up, morons!" Victoria yelled at the two. She whipped back around to face Mae. "And YOU will stay there until Helius says otherwise." Victoria's face was flushed with fury. "Make one more move and I'll use a closed fist the next time I hit you."

*****

"Shall we play a game?" Bracchus said overenthusiastically, lounging lazily on the couch. "I spy something black."

"The wall," Thistle said with exasperation.

"Very good! That's ten out of ten!" Bracchus said with false enthusiasm.

An explosion of fire indicated the return of Matthew Hexus. "Bracchus. Shane is dead." Hexus walked over to a chair and sat down, sighing.

"Dead?" Bracchus whispered, sitting up.

"Yes, dead," Hexus replied, setting down his book and rubbing his eyes.

"If Shane is dead, there's no need to keep his prisoners alive!" Bracchus cried angrily, starting toward the captive Thistle.

"Stop," Hexus commanded. "Helius may have some use for him. That is for him to decide."

Bracchus stepped back furiously, dropping back onto the couch and scowling. "If Helius gives us the go-ahead to kill him, I get to do it."

*****

"You can leave the water on the table, Penelope," Maximus said to the handmaiden. "I'll give it to Jasmine when she wakes up."

"Yes, sir," Penelope said, putting the water on the table and exiting the room.

"Idiot harpy," Torizar grumbled, gently touching his nose. "I'll make sure to hit her in the face with a door a couple times to see how she likes it."

Maximus ignored Torizar's rant, gently stroking Jasmine's cheek with his thumb. "Come on, sweetie. Wake up."

Jasmine's eyelids fluttered open, revealing her beautiful eyes. She sighed softly when she saw Maximus sitting next to her. "You must be thirsty," he said, picking up the glass that sat on the table. "Take a drink."

*****

"Well, now that we're all here, I suggest we prepare to leave," Gavin said.

"Oh! That's right," MJ cut in, stretching. She reached into her pocket and pulled out the glittering topaz. Setting it on the small table in front of her, she said, "This is what we found at the ruins."

"I'm going to check on the progress of the refugees," Gavin said quickly, nodding to MJ, opening the door, and slipping outside into the freezing wind and violent snowstorm.

"We found something, too," Daniella said, putting the sapphire she held next to the topaz.

"So did we," Serenity added, setting down the garnet next to the others. The gemstones suddenly started to glow, causing the keepers to step back. In a flash, the gems transformed into the legendary creatures…the Phoenix, the Firebird, and the Pegasus.

"Wow…" MJ said in awe.

"Quiet!" Ginger cried. "They're speaking."

"When the dark castle doth appear, all of Terra has much to fear," the creatures said in unison, their booming voices echoing through the empty halls of Twilight Pass. *"The Great Evil shall then come seeking his token, and at last in ruin shall Terra be broken."*

"By the gods…" Tasha whispered. "The Onyx Castle…Helius…"

"Quiet!" Ginger rasped.

The creatures continued. *"A ray of hope shines soft and bright, to wash away the darkest night."*

"What?" MJ asked.

"Hush!" Ginger cried.

"Though good's chances of victory are rare, love can pierce the dark despair."

MJ gasped.

"When the Savior's part is done, the broken shall at last be one." The three mystical creatures disappeared in a flash of light, leaving the room silent and empty.

"The true prophecy," Ginger breathed.

"Does this mean…" Serenity asked.

"We're going to win!" MJ cried.

The structure bent and creaked as the most massive tremor they had ever felt occurred. The doors smashed open, and Gavin cried, "Everyone out! It's the end!"

*****

CHAPTER XXI: INTO THE DARKNESS

THE LAND SHOOK AND STRUGGLED TO TRY TO KEEP from breaking. It surrendered at last with a final, terrible, heart-wrenching scream as the last tremor tore throughout Terra-Quenlist. The ground shattered. Trees and villages were overtaken by large crevasses and sinkholes that appeared. There was a great rumbling, but it was not from thunder. The earth was crying out, a shrill cry of death at being torn apart as it finally succumbed.

The mountains cracked, reigning avalanche upon avalanche of snow and rock across the ground. Lakes and rivers overflowed, flooding the lands. Towns split apart like large glaciers, some crumbling to rubble, and others sinking either into the water or into the defeated, dying ground.

The elaborate towers honoring the five elements collapsed simultaneously, unable to handle the pressure of the crushing tremor. The Tower of Gaia was first to collapse, crumbling and sinking deep into the earth. It was followed by the Tower of Apollo, which was crushed by the collapsing Mountains of Prudence. The Tower of Torrent sank into the Starlight River, bubbling and breaking apart as it slid beneath the surface of the flooding water. The Tower of Zephyr rocked and shattered apart, crumbling into a pile of rocks and debris. Subdued and broken, it disappeared into a sinkhole. Last to fall was the Tower of Heaven.

Llewellyn and Adrienne, the last two remaining High Priests on Terra-Quenlist, looked sadly out the windows as the room collapsed around them. The tower crumbled and fell into a sinkhole, covered quickly by other debris. Trees from the forests collapsed and fell over, bending, splintering, and cracking. The old and wondrous trees of the ancient forests shattered and splintered, falling to sparkling pieces.

The great palaces were the last to fall. Each exploded to ruin as the earth around disappeared. The tremor did not stop this time. It continued, increasing in intensity and shaking Terra with never-ending severity. The planet, in its final death throes, had finally been broken.

*****

“Go!” Gavin yelled. Across the treacherous landscape the keepers raced. Their carpets shook violently in the wind that had suddenly become unbearably brutal. The whipping snow stung their faces, and the frozen air chilled them to the bone. Aurora clung tightly to Gavin as he flew toward the looming castle. Behind them, Twilight Pass exploded in a wave of fire, crashing to the ground and sinking into the maw of the opening earth.

Ginger and MJ arrived at the Onyx Castle first, zooming through the open doors. They were followed by Tasha, Cody, and Serenity. Autumn skidded through on a shaky carpet, icicles forming on the tip of her nose. She was followed by a shivering Adam and a cursing Tinuviel. Michelle and Tier flew in next, followed by a hysterical Daniella. Gavin and Aurora were the last to come through. Gavin released Aurora and turned to the doors, slamming them shut as quickly as he could in an attempt to shut out the horrible event occurring on their beloved world of Terra.

The world spun as the keepers and the emperor were teleported. Screams and yells were accompanied by dizziness and blurry vision. The spinning finally stopped, as did the protests and the yells. The room, or whatever they were in, was dark. Not a single object could be deciphered, except for the sound of rushing water and light shining from far off in the distance. The ground no longer shook, and the screams of the dying planet of Terra had fallen silent.

"Follow that light," Gavin rasped.

They stumbled along the stone passageway, tripping occasionally on the uneven surface. At long last, the party reached the light. Or lack of light, for that matter. The light was more of a gray refraction, filtering through the waterfall into the entrance of the cave.

"Let's go," Gavin said, his voice devoid of joy and happiness. He jumped through the waterfall, everyone following.

A blast of stale air hit them as they emerged from behind the waterfall, drenched and shivering, into the first glimpse of Chaos. There was nothing around, save for a small sign that said, "Onyx Falls." Far in the distance, Gavin could see a large crowd of refugees, led by the remaining commanders and Asterel.

"Gavin, look!" Ginger cried, pointing at the sky.

*****

"Moonstone has sent his people here," Morpheus said, turning and walking to the doors of the castle. He threw them open and looked around, Helius following cautiously.

"Are you sure?" Helius growled, looking about.

"I am the Keeper of Death," Morpheus replied. "I feel much life, and it's emanating from somewhere near Nightshade Village."

Helius sprang to action at once. "Gather our forces for a surprise attack! Capture who you can and kill the rest! I'll leave this up to you!"

"As you wish, Helius," Morpheus replied, bowing and vanishing.

"I'll supervise Morpheus later. As for right now," Helius said, looking at the sky, "I'm going to sit back and enjoy the show."

*****

Deep beneath the surface of Terra-Quenlist, a little ball of dark magic finally completed its task. It had successfully frozen the core of the planet. Now, it was time to heat it up again.

The ball of magic changed from blue to red, exploding and heating the core quickly. Too quickly. The core cracked in half, exploding. The explosion, a wave of supernova fire, spread upward, engulfing everything in flames.

*****

The good keepers stared. Far off, the people inside the Crystal Palace watched fearfully through the stained glass windows. The gathered army and refugees watched. All eyes, good and evil, had turned to the fireball in the sky. Terra-Quenlist was no longer a beautiful and majestic planet, a glowing jewel of the galaxy. It was now a ball of fire, hot as the sun and burning with a thousand more intensities.

And in an instant, it was gone. A flash and a loud rumbling echoed throughout the universe as the planet went into a supernova. The orange globe of a planet exploded. A wave of fire blew outward, a large ring surrounding the tiny bit of sparkling debris that remained. The good planet, in fiery ruin, was no more.

*****

CHAPTER XXII: THE EMPEROR'S TEARS

GAVIN MOONSTONE DID NOT SPEAK. HE DID NOT YELL. He did not scream, or shout, or cry. He just stood there, staring into the empty space that had once contained his beautiful world. And it was gone.

MJ closed her eyes, tears streaming down her cheeks. She cursed the power of Sight then, for she had seen the deaths of many who had still remained, trapped and defenseless, on the planet.

Ginger sat on the ground, hugging her legs tightly. She would never again see her forest. She could never again drink from the river or go on wild chases and hunts. The time of joy and carefree days was over. When the planet died, so did the fiery, carefree spirit of her soul.

"But the prophecy said…" Serenity started.

"Never mind what the prophecy said!" Tasha exploded. "It was wrong! Terra is gone! Blown to smithereens!"

"You're so negative!" Daniella yelled furiously.

"Shut up, all of you," Gavin said flatly. A bone-chilling silence descended upon the gathered crowd, who were all awestruck at the emperor's comment.

"What?" MJ sputtered.

"I said shut up," Gavin repeated, turning to face them. He had aged a great deal, now retaining the look of a middle-aged man. Wrinkles creased his face, and weariness sketched across his saddened eyes. He was aging.

"You're aging!" MJ gasped, taking a step forward to look closer. "But you can't age! And you're not even crying?"

"Anything can happen to me now," Gavin said bluntly. "I'm aging and I've grown tired. I've really just stopped caring. My world of light is gone, destroyed by an evil, a plague, a disease. Helius has won. And I don't cry because my tears contain powerful healing abilities. Why should I waste them? What do I have left to be joyful about?"

"Us," Ginger replied, standing up. "So what if the planet was destroyed? So what if y'lost your only happiness?"

Everyone stared at her in shock. She continued her speech, growing stronger and shaking with anger. "You're being selfish. What about us and the people who are still alive?" Tears of fury leaked from her eyes, but she continued. "You're supposed to be an infallible force, for cryin' out loud! Our homes were destroyed, too! All we knew and ever cared about's gone! We're managing! Don't wallow in self-pity over what you should've done! Get off your rear and whip Helius senseless!"

Gavin looked at Ginger, blinked, and silently turned and walked away. He had not gone far, however, when a mountain of rocks crashed down upon him. He disappeared as he was swallowed by a deluge of boulders.

"No!" Aurora cried, rushing forward to the mound of rocks as Helius landed behind her and faced the other keepers, grinning triumphantly.

"I win," he said simply.

Aurora, in fury, picked up one of the smaller rocks and threw it at Helius. The rock hit him in the back of the head, knocking him over. "Take that!" she screamed as he fell.

Fits of quiet snickers engulfed the keepers as Helius lifted his face, dripping with mud. "You should laugh!" he screamed, jumping to his feet. "None of you is worth crushing! With Moonstone dead, I don't even need to bother with you! Enjoy your demise on my planet of darkness!" He vanished in a blaze of acrid fire, leaving the great pile of rocks visible to everyone.

The snickers instantly stopped, and insanity broke out. Ginger, who had tried to remain calm, started foaming at the mouth. She turned and bit Cody, who screamed and frantically swung at her to try to detach her from his arm. Tasha started screaming about rabies, and Serenity sat down and cried. Daniella sat and rocked herself, mumbling and putting her hands over her ears.

In the midst of all the chaos, Tinuviel shouted, "Knock it off, you morons!" Everyone froze, eyes turning to her.

"What's the matter with everyone?" MJ shouted furiously. "You all go insane when you see a mound of rocks?"

"Gavin's dead, you idiot!" Ginger yelled, releasing her grip on the frantic Cody so she could speak. "What d'we do now? He was crushed by a mountain of rocks!"

"Why did we get our powers in the first place?" Tinuviel broke in angrily. "Gavin said he gave us powers to protect everyone in case anything ever happened to him. He said we have the power to defeat Helius! Look what we've accomplished so far! We HAVE beaten Helius! We've destroyed some of his most powerful allies! And Gavin put Ginger in charge of us if anything ever happened to him." She turned to Ginger. "So start acting like our leader, because you ARE from here on out!"

"But I can't..." Ginger started angrily.

"I'll help you," Aurora said quietly. "It's what Gavin would have wanted."

"It's settled, then," MJ said with a steely finality. "Our first task should be to find the Crystal Palace."

"How?" Daniella asked. "We have no clue how big the planet Chaos is, nor for that matter, where we are." Far away, screams could be heard, followed by clashing weapons and the sound of battle. It appeared that the war between good and evil was far from over.

*****

Everything had happened so quickly. The creatures had appeared, led by a man shrouded in a black cloak. Aster, Queen

Asterel, and most of the army, including the refugees and the mages, had been captured. Veronica was fighting alongside the remaining mages, knowing that the small group had only an impossible chance of beating back the enclosing darkness. But they had to try.

"Give them everything you've got!" Veronica shouted, swinging her sword at a vampire that lunged toward her.

The dragons appeared swiftly, crushing even the smallest hope of victory that Veronica had. They swooped down in a great flock and carried off half of the remaining mages, who struggled to wriggle free. In addition, the creatures managed to capture all of the remaining evacuees.

"Water mages! Air mages!" Veronica cried, swinging her sword again. "Target the dragons! Bring them down!"

Blasts of funnel clouds and streams of water hurtled through the air at the flying beasts, weakening many of them. They retained their grips of the prisoners, however, and continued their rapid flight. "Don't give up!" Veronica shouted, futilely brandishing her sword at the enclosing creatures. "We have to…"

Her words were cut off as she was hit from behind. She fell to the ground, dropping her sword. Somehow, she could no longer see. Her vision blurred as unconsciousness gripped her and the world began to fade to black. She had lost.

*****

Jasmine reached for the poisoned water, held out by the unknowing Maximus. As she gripped the glass and he released his fingers, hers slipped off the glass. She watched as it hit the ground and shattered, leaving a large, dark spot on the floor.

"Don't worry about it, darling," Maximus said quickly, gripping Jasmine's shaky hand. "I'll call Penelope. She'll bring you another glass."

Maximus called Penelope in. "Penelope, Jasmine dropped the glass of water before she could take a drink. Would you bring her another glass?"

Penelope's face reddened slightly, but she nodded and exited without a word. As she walked away to get another glass, she mentally screamed. She had stupidly used the whole bottle of poison in that glass of water. It was the only bottle she had possessed, and it had been wasted by that wretch Jasmine.

As Penelope fumed, she suddenly had an epiphany. She could just sit back and wait for someone else to dispose of Jasmine. If Helius found out about Jasmine and Maximus, he would kill them. The rest of the harpies would be more than happy to exile her, especially if they knew she was pregnant. Once exiled, she would become human.

Penelope laughed to herself as she filled another glass with water. She could take the throne and become queen. Very soon, she would be ruler of Hell's Gate. It was only a matter of time.

*****

CHAPTER XXIII: THE HALL OF DEMONS

IT WAS EMPTY WITHOUT GAVIN. THE WORLD WAS empty and lonely. Aurora had only just met him, but she was already hurting inside at losing him. Her heart had shattered when Helius had sent the boulders crashing down upon him.

The sadness that overtook her was nearly unbearable, but she tried her best to hide it. She had to stay strong and in control. He would have wanted that. It seemed as if he was the centerpiece to a delicate operation—the lynchpin that held together the chain. Without him, the whole operation fell to ruin.

The screams and clash of battle had ceased, and Aurora didn't really care. The love of her life was gone forever, along with his black bag. His bag!

Aurora saw the bag sitting next to the pile of rocks, motionless. She ran to it and snatched it up, clutching it tightly to protect it. This was all that remained of Gavin. She would treasure it to keep his memory alive.

"What do you have?" MJ asked curiously, standing next to Aurora.

"Gavin's bag," Aurora said sadly. "It escaped the avalanche."

"This is wonderful!" MJ cried, reaching for the bag. Aurora reluctantly gave it to her, unwilling to let go of the last piece of the great ruler.

"This bag is our answer!" MJ continued. "It holds everything he ever had!" She reached inside and frowned, pulling her hand back out.

"What?" Ginger asked, walking up to MJ and Aurora.

"It's empty," MJ said quietly. "There's nothing in it."

"Why don't you think about what you want when you reach inside?" Aurora suggested. MJ shrugged and reached inside again, this time pulling out a large book.

"*St. Benedict's Book of Light*!" Ginger cried, grabbing the book and opening it. "Every evil monster in the galaxy is catalogued within these pages!"

"What's so special about that?" Aurora asked.

"This book can help us defeat darkness!" Ginger said excitedly. "It might hold a key to telling us how to defeat Helius!"

"I see," Aurora said.

"We're going to need two more carpets," MJ said to herself, reaching into the bag again and pulling out a maroon and a vermillion carpet. She handed one to Aurora and walked over to Tier, who took the other.

"Ginger," Aurora said quietly, "where are we even going to start? We've lost. The refugees have been captured, and we're all alone."

For the first time in her life, Ginger needed no help in making a decision. She had the answer, and Gavin hadn't even helped her find it. She was proud of herself and proud that he had been her teacher. She blessed him, wherever he was, and vowed to stay strong for him so she could help everyone else. She had finally changed her outlook of everything, and at last she understood what Gavin had tried to show her. She was slipping quickly into her position as leader.

Turning to face Aurora, Ginger said, "Eden, my mentor, once told me that the smallest creature's assistance to a cause can tip the scale. One person can make all the difference. If we fight together, we can win. I don't care how powerful Helius thinks he is. We've proven our power with the defeat of some of his keepers. I killed one, Daniella killed one, and Cody killed one. He had twelve. We've eliminated some of his power already. Maybe the time to destroy Helius may not be right this second, but it'll come soon."

"You're the leader," Aurora said quietly, nodding. "Lead on."

*****

Ivy had reached the doors of the Crystal Palace when she heard the explosion. Or felt it, rather. Looking up, she saw the planet she had called home explode in fiery destruction. She could not comprehend what had just happened. All she knew was that something which shouldn't have happened did, and a planet that should be there wasn't. There was a hole in the world, and no matter where she turned, she could still see the darkness where only light should have dwelt.

She opened the doors of the palace and walked in slowly. A hush had descended over the gathered beings. Humans, fairies, gnomes, elves, mythical creatures—all were still as Ivy walked past. No one laughed. Many cried. All knew that Terra was gone.

Ivy entered the throne room to see Rodaine standing next to one of the windows, staring blankly outside. A large wolf sat next to him, whimpering softly. He turned and acknowledged Ivy's presence, managing a small bow. "Queen Ivy. It is nice to see you and a relief that you are safe."

"It's nice to see you too, Rodaine," Ivy replied sadly. "I only wish it were under different circumstances."

"Yes," Rodaine said, trailing off and staring blankly into space once again.

"I was relieved to see the Crystal Palace," Ivy said hopefully. "But I don't see Gavin or the others. Were they…"

"No," Rodaine said quickly. "Gavin issued permission to use the Transteleportation Spell, and he and the other keepers escaped through means of the Onyx Castle."

"Where are they?" Ivy asked.

"I have no clue," Rodaine answered, continuing to stare blankly out the window.

"I hope they find us soon, wherever they are," Ivy whispered.

*****

Asterel struggled against the grip of the cloaked man, slapping him and reaching for the wand attached to her hip. He grabbed it first and broke it with one skeletal-like hand. "I don't think so," a raspy voice said from within the depths of the cloak. "If you hurt me, I'll have to kill you, and Helius wouldn't like that very much."

The man opened a set of large oak doors, throwing Asterel inside and slamming them shut. She pushed and pounded on the doors, but they had been sealed from the other side. The man's muffled voice filtered through the hairline cracks in the ancient wood.

"The doors have been magically sealed. You cannot break them. Your attempts are futile." The voice stopped, and Asterel put her ear up to one of the doors to listen. She heard faint footsteps, indicating that the man was leaving.

She slumped against the door, sobbing in frustration. How had everything gone so wrong? Terra had been destroyed, Taran had been turned to stone, Ivy had been kidnapped, Mae and Thistle's whereabouts were still unknown, and now she was being held captive.

She would have to come up with a strategy. Things would definitely be harder without the aid of her wand. And that man's hand…it looked positively bare. It had almost looked as if it were just bone…

Asterel shrugged off the chilling sensation that crept up her spine, along with the thought. Trying to control herself, she stood up and looked around. Perhaps there was something in her prison that could help her.

The room she was trapped in was more of a hallway. A large crimson carpet stretched along, ending at another door on the opposite end of the room. Two other doors sat on opposite sides of the other two walls. Crimson tapestries hung against cold stone, trying to contain the little warmth generated inside the structure itself. The atmosphere—though eerie, dark, and oppressing—was warm, almost humid.

Asterel walked over to the first door and jiggled the handle. The door was locked. She shrugged and turned to the door opposite the locked one, trying it as well. It was also locked.

She had one door left to try. The crimson carpet ended at this door, which sat opposite the entrance of the structure. The latch of this door clicked when Asterel turned the handle. The door opened, creaking greatly upon rusty hinges.

The glow of candlelight reflected off a small mirror in the room she had entered. It was a large room, lavishly decorated with overstuffed armchairs and a hardwood table. More tapestries hung from the walls, absorbing the light of the ancient-looking candelabra that burned on the table.

A small spiral staircase rested in one corner of the room, climbing upward. It was black, made of iron. Asterel touched the cool metal and felt nothing. There were no memories here. There was only nothingness. Clutching the candelabra tightly, Asterel started her ascent.

*****

Michelle saw the refugees far off in the distance but could not help them. She saw them carried off by strange creatures—*dragons*, she thought—and she could not help. And she could feel their faith slipping away as they were carried off. And still, she could not help. She was forced to stand there, helpless, as the people were dragged away as prisoners. And in a matter of minutes, all was silent.

"Michelle," Tier said softly, standing next to her. "We couldn't have helped them. They were too far out of our reach."

"I feel so helpless, Tier," Michelle said softly, looking around at the vast wasteland that was Chaos.

"I think we're all feeling that way," Tier replied. "It's this planet. It's trying to drain us, to take hold of us and never let go. We can't let it!"

A surge of power erupted from deep within Michelle's soul, and she was struck with the sudden realization. She could hear someone's voice talking to her. She heard it say, *"Stand as one and you shall conquer. Fight alone and you shall fall."*

"I have our answer, Tier," Michelle said triumphantly. "I think it is tied in with my powers. If we fight as one, we will be unbeatable. After all, the powers we received came from Gavin. He was the most powerful person we knew."

"So you're saying that we need to stick together?" Tier asked.

"Yes," Michelle replied. "And my abilities are meant to help with that. When I received my powers from Gavin, he told me I would need to keep together the rest of the group. That is exactly what I intend to do."

*****

Helius chuckled to himself, sitting back down in his onyx throne. He had finally done it. Moonstone was dead. He had taken his revenge upon his good brother. He had proven who the stronger sibling was.

"I've beaten him," Helius whispered. "He's dead, and I've won. His planet is gone, his people are captured, and his army has fallen."

"But his keepers remain, strangely, untouched," Hexus replied, stepping in front of the throne. Moments earlier, he had teleported himself to the castle to inform Helius of the bad news.

"So what if they're still alive?" Helius cackled. "They have no power without their precious ruler!"

"Helius, Shane is dead," Hexus replied, bowing slightly.

Helius stopped his gleeful fit and stared at Hexus menacingly. "What do you mean he's dead?"

"He and Callus are dead," Hexus said, cringing for what he knew was undoubtedly to come.

Helius roared with fury, jumping out of his chair and screaming. "Now TWO more are dead?! How does this rate on my scale?! Like a negative zero!!!"

"There's no such thing as a negative zero," Hexus said helpfully.

"GAH!" Helius roared, overturning the table that had just been repaired. "I don't care! How many are dead, Hexus?!"

"Emeralda, Callus, Shane, Calvin, and Charity are dead," Hexus replied flatly.

"Great!" Helius cried. "Just great!"

"I told you the keepers were trouble," Hexus replied. "They are the ones responsible for the deaths, not Moonstone. You killed the wrong person."

Helius was deathly quiet, sitting in his chair and calming himself. "Hexus, send word to the remaining keepers. We won't attack the good keepers until they walk into a trap. Position the remaining keepers and some of the leaders of the creatures at locations throughout Chaos."

"As you wish, Helius," Hexus replied.

"I will remain here until someone brings me word of any action. If the keepers cause a full out attack, alert me immediately."

"Of course," Hexus said, opening his book and chanting. A wind blew through the hallway into the throne room, sweeping up Hexus and carrying him away.

"Perhaps I should have killed those stupid keepers when I had the chance," Helius mused. "I underestimated them."

He sat back in his throne and relaxed, closing his eyes for some well-deserved rest. "I'll let my keepers handle it. Hexus and Morpheus will know what to do, and they cannot fail me."

*****

The keepers had been restored by Michelle's powers of faith and unity. They were whole again, stronger and tied ever closer to each other. Ginger had been forced to split up the group, taking Cody, MJ, Serenity, Michelle, and Aurora with her. Daniella led Adam, Tasha, Tinuviel, Autumn, and Tier. Daniella's group headed toward the small village where the refugees had been taken prisoner to investigate, while Ginger and her group headed toward a larger structure to the west of the village.

Ginger was on guard now. Anything could happen without Gavin and his spells to protect them. She had to keep in control and ready, in case she needed to fight.

They reached the large facility, staring at it in awe. It was a masterpiece, in an incredibly creepy kind of way. Made of black marble, the building stood towering above the gathered group.

"What is it?" Serenity asked in awe.

"I dunno," MJ said curiously, stepping closer to take a look at the doors. Writing was etched into them, and she read quickly. "'Within these walls doth lay the sleeping gates of Lucifer. Awaken them to release suffering upon the earth, for this is the Hall of Demons.'"

"Let us go," Michelle said, shivering. "There are bad things here. We should not try to go in."

"We have to," MJ said confidently. "We don't really have a choice. If we encounter Helius, we'll escape. How bad can it be in there?"

Ginger stepped up to the doors and gave them a great kick, jarring them open. She stepped inside and motioned for the rest of the keepers to follow.

The interior of the Hall of Demons was decorated in red and orange, MJ's favorite colors. But this was not MJ's favorite place. Pictures lined the walls of the long structure, depictions of demons of various shapes and forms. Some involved battles, others involved temples and eternal darkness and damnation.

"I'm beginning to think Michelle was right," Aurora said hesitantly, moving along slowly as they walked down the hallway.

"Come now!" MJ said sharply. "There's nothing here. There's nothing to be…"

"Afraid of?" said a voice in front of them. A man who had been standing in front of a large archway turned around to face them. He was skeletal-like and frightening, with sunken cheeks and eyes. His graying hair was concealed under a hood, which was thrown over the top of his head. He wore a dark robe and carried a small stick.

"Who are you?" Ginger said sternly, stepping in front of the group and shielding them.

"I am Omicron, the necromancer," the man replied, taking another step forward. "You must be the keepers Hexus spoke of. What brings you to this desolate place?"

"We're searchin' for the imprisoned refugees," Ginger said defiantly. "We thought they might be held captive here."

"Oh no," Omicron replied, chuckling with a raspy voice. "They are being held at the Castle of Souls and Hell's Gate. They are not here."

"Where's the Castle of Souls?" Ginger cried angrily.

"Why in Hades' name would I tell you?" Omicron replied, smirking.

"You're not that scary!" Cody cut in defiantly. "I don't think you have any real power!"

"Boy, you have no idea who you are dealing with," Omicron said threateningly. "You don't know what a necromancer is, eh? Well, allow me to demonstrate."

He raised his arms and pointed them at the archway. A rumbling echoed throughout the hall and the archway cracked in half, along with the floor under it. From inside the crack emerged horrible-looking creatures. They were humans once, but now only mindless slaves.

"Zombies!" Michelle squeaked, cringing as they shambled closer.

"A necromancer," Omicron replied, "is a dark sorcerer who can raise the dead to do his bidding. I've commanded the zombies to kill you, under the orders of Matthew Hexus, the Keeper of Shadows."

"Ginger, what do we do?!" Michelle cried.

"We fight," Ginger said, standing stock still and closing her eyes. She opened them and waved her hand, releasing a pink beam. The beam impacted with the first few zombies and turned them to ash.

"Fight!" Ginger cried to the other keepers. "We can beat them! This's nothing!"

Serenity stepped up next to Ginger and waved her hand, throwing back the advancing creatures. Her telekinetic wave temporarily disabled the path of the zombies, who scrabbled across the floor.

Cody pulled out a second bag of dream powder that he had been conserving and blew some of it at the crawling zombies, setting them on fire. MJ stomped her feet, cracking the floor and shattering the precious stone.

"This isn't supposed to happen!" Omicron cried as his army of zombies became smaller and smaller. "They were supposed to be killed by my army!"

He looked to the crack in the floor where the zombies had emerged and pointed once again. From the hole emerged a shadow—but not just a shadow. It was a dead necromancer, Omicron's mentor Zeta. Zeta was a powerful necromancer in life. Now, he would be even more powerful.

Michelle screamed as the new zombie arose from the hole in the ground. But he was not like the others. He resembled the man who had summoned the zombies.

Before she could say anything, the zombie man raised one hand and pointed at her. Her throat started to close. She couldn't breathe. She couldn't feel. Her vision was blurring. She couldn't see. Silently, she cried, *"Someone help me, please!"*

She fell to the ground, gasping as the invisible grip around her throat was finally released. She saw Serenity wave her hand and the zombie man crumple to the ground. Serenity had saved her.

"Ginger!" MJ cried. "The book you were given! Look in it! There's got to be a section on the undead!"

"Right!" Ginger cried, dropping to her knees and opening Gavin's black bag. She had forgotten she was carrying it. Pulling out the book, she leafed quickly through the pages, finding the entry with undead creatures. She found the entry on zombies and read quickly.

"In order for the zombies to disappear, the summoner's magic over them must be dispelled!" Ginger cried, slamming the book shut. "Get Omicron!"

Omicron heard his name shouted by the woman in front. He pointed his wand at her, urging his undead mentor to kill her. The wand suddenly went flying out of his hand as it was summoned by one of the other girls. Curse that brat! She had telekinetic abilities!

Before Omicron could utter another word, the girl broke his wand in two. His mentor, along with the zombies, dissipated with the escaping magic. "No!" Omicron cried, falling to the floor.

"It is done," Ginger said to the fallen man. "We beat you. Your power over the dead's gone."

"Nice work, Serenity," Michelle said.

"There's nothing else here," MJ confirmed.

"We're done here," Ginger said, whipping around and smashing open the doors. The others followed her out, leaving the defeated Omicron behind.

CHAPTER XXIV: THE CAVE OF THE PROPHETS

OMICRON GAZED AT HIS BROKEN WAND, HANDS balled into fists, fingers digging into his palms and drawing blood. The Hall of Demons was ruined. Large fissures lined the floor, some by his own creation, others from that bratty woman. Pieces of the ceiling had fallen in from shaking the structure. The fissure to the Underworld had closed, sealing the servants of Omicron inside.

He crawled forward on his hands and knees, picking up a large sharp rock that had fallen from the ceiling. He would kill the leader with it. He would throw it and kill her. Revenge would be his.

He ran toward the doors, lobbing the large rock as far as he could. He grinned as the woman turned around quickly, her eyes wide. He counted the seconds it took the rock to fly through the air toward her. One…two…three…

"Die!" he screamed, jumping up and down in fury.

"Ginger, look out!" Serenity cried, flicking her wrist and sending the rock spinning sideways, missing Ginger's face by inches.

"Cheap shot!" Michelle cried angrily, starting forward. MJ arrived first. She grabbed the stunned necromancer by the throat and threw him inside like a rag doll, slamming the broken doors. Omicron skidded across the floor, dazed.

With a mighty swing, MJ's fist impacted with the wall of the Hall of Demons, sending the whole structure crashing to the ground. Omicron looked up just in time to scream and see the ceiling collapse on top of him.

"MJ…" Serenity whispered, backing away.

"Tell me he didn't deserve what happened to him!" MJ said angrily. "Just try!"

"You're bleeding," Serenity said softly, pulling a handkerchief out of her pocket and gently wrapping it around MJ's bleeding knuckles. "Keep that on there until the bleeding stops," Serenity instructed forcefully, stepping backward.

"Thank you," MJ said, her anger disappearing. Serenity had only been trying to help her. She was ashamed of herself for immediately jumping all over the poor woman. After all, they were friends now.

"Yes, thank you, Serenity," Ginger said, stepping forward. "If you hadn't flung that rock out of the way, I'd be dead now."

"It's what I do," Serenity said, blushing slightly.

Cody, MJ, Serenity, Michelle, and Aurora looked to Ginger for further instruction. "Where do we go now?" Cody asked.

Aurora, who had been silent the entire time, now spoke. "Omicron spoke of the Castle of Souls. That's got to be our destination."

"I have a bad feeling about this," Michelle said. "If the prisoners are being held captive there, that must be where Helius is. We shouldn't go there without everyone."

"Right," MJ said. "We want to avoid Helius as much as possible, at least until we find the Crystal Palace."

"Speaking of which," Cody cut in, "how do we find it?"

"I dunno," Ginger said. "I just dunno."

*****

Hexus felt the demise of the great necromancer before he saw anything. Omicron had been crushed. Literally, by the ceiling of the Hall of Demons. The hall itself now lay in a pile of rubble. Helius would not be pleased.

Hexus rose from the high-backed chair he had been seated in, looking out one of the frosted windows. He was too far away to see the destruction of the hall, but he knew it was gone. He had been able to see the faint outline of the Hall of Demons before it had been destroyed. The outline was no longer visible. It was truly gone.

"The wise thing to do would be to tell Helius," Hexus said. "However, I'm quite comfortable right here. Helius is probably just relaxing anyway. Why spoil his good mood? I'll deal with the keepers myself when they arrive here. From the looks of things, I'm guessing they will be here soon."

Hexus sat back in his chair, opening the large book that rested on the table. "Just as a precaution, I'm going to cloak this place. The Hall of Spirits will remain invisible for the time being. I think I'll let the others deal with Moonstone's goody-goody keepers." A large bubble encased the Hall of Spirits, causing it to vanish. The structure had become invisible, cloaked by the powerful magic of Matthew Hexus, Keeper of Shadows.

*****

Daniella led Adam, Tasha, Tinuviel, Autumn, and Tier past Nightshade Village. Far in the distance, they heard the splintering of wood and grinding of stone as a structure crashed to the ground.

"Ginger at work?" Daniella snorted, covering her mouth.

"Most likely," Tinuviel agreed cheerfully, turning to see the large cloud that had plumed out far away.

"Where are we headed to?" Adam asked, looking at Daniella.

"I'm not sure," Daniella commented, looking around. The town they had just gone through was devoid of anything, except the remnants of a struggle. Undoubtedly, Nightshade Village had been the site of the struggle between the refugees and Helius's forces.

To the right of the group lay a great river, rushing quickly. Its dark waters looked cold and deep. Who knew what waited beneath the surface of the water?

Daniella shivered, focusing her attention back to the rest of the group. "The river is too wide to cross. Maybe we should follow it. The river has to end somewhere. If we follow the river, maybe we can find a town or someone who can help us."

"All things considered," Tasha said hotly, "I don't think there's anyone here who is willing to help us."

"Be that as it may," Daniella replied quickly, "I say we follow the river. It's bound to lead us in the right direction."

"After you," Tier said, motioning with her hand.

Daniella nodded, starting forward at a quick pace. The others followed her silently. She hoped that her sense of direction hadn't failed her. She didn't want to lead the group into any danger, especially if they came across Helius. Shivering again, she quickened her pace.

*****

Ginger found out why none of the keepers was using his or her carpet. The magic of the carpets was not working on Chaos. The carpets were as lifeless as they had been before Gavin had enchanted them. It seemed as if his magic was slowly coming undone. She had felt the shield around her fading, and it was not a good sensation. With the protection gone, they would be easy targets for dark forces.

"We gotta hurry," Ginger said. "This was a small victory against evil. I fear that the protection around us is waning."

"I felt it too," MJ commented. "So let's go."

"That's the only problem," Ginger retorted. "I dunno know where we're going."

"How about following the road?" Aurora suggested helpfully. "It would be a better idea than tromping through the wilderness, just waiting for something to try to kill us."

"Sounds like a plan to me," Michelle said.

"The road it is, then," Ginger said, shrugging. "I'll lead the way."

The atmosphere seemed to get darker and darker as the keepers followed the small dirt road. Ginger felt cold shivers run up her spine. She wished that she had her spear. It would give her at least a little comfort. She didn't quite remember where she had left it or how it had disappeared. She wondered about Storm. How was he coping without her? She missed him terribly.

"It's getting dark," MJ said fearfully, looking around as if she expected demons to lunge at her from all sides. "I don't like the dark. I've never liked the dark. It's creepy."

"I see a building up ahead," Ginger said, squinting and trying to discern the shape of the structure. It was shaped like a tower, high-walled and menacing. As they neared it, the last remnants of the gray light of Chaos vanished, leaving the stars and three small, pale moons as their only source of light.

"I can't see a thing," Serenity said, sounding panicked. "Does anyone have a light?"

A shuffling footstep nearby stopped everyone dead in their tracks. "Cody, was that you?" Michelle squeaked.

"No. Was it you?" he asked Michelle.

"None of us made that noise," MJ said.

"Then, what did?" Serenity choked out through the lump that had formed in her throat, voicing the question everyone had been dreading. It was then that Serenity felt something touch her face. A cold, clammy hand brushed across her cheek. She screamed, tripping and falling. Something fell on top of her, groaning low in its throat and making an otherworldly sound.

"H…Help!" Serenity choked, feeling the thing reaching for her. She kicked and thrashed, knocking the thing off her.

"Hold on!" Ginger cried. She grabbed the black bag from MJ and opened it, pulling out a small vial. She threw the vial to the ground, creating a flash of white light. The light illuminated the creature that had lunged for Serenity. It was a ghoul, and from the looks of it, an extremely hungry one. The grotesque creature was barely humanoid, shriveled and olive-skinned. It was also not very bright.

"Do something!" Serenity cried in terror as the ghoul came toward her again.

"Autumn!" MJ cried. "Summon a fireball! Give us some light!"

Autumn nodded quickly and cupped her right hand. An explosion of flame erupted from it, a small orange orb blazing in her palm. She threw it in the air, and Serenity weakly held it with her telekinesis, terrified of the creature that was sliding toward her.

Ginger jumped in front of Serenity, giving the crawling ghoul a kick in the face. The creature fell backward, tumbling and rolling. It was on its feet, angry now that it had been prevented from reaching its food. MJ stepped next to Ginger and muttered a protection spell.

At that moment, the ghoul lunged at Serenity. She screamed and covered her face, breaking her concentration on the floating fireball and allowing it to drop. It hit the ground and evaporated.

The ghoul bounced away from the frightened Serenity, repelled by the protection spell MJ had cast. It shook its head, confused for a moment. Then, it started again for Serenity.

"The power of Faith shall destroy you!" Michelle cried, pointing at the ghoul. It froze in its tracks, clutching its throat. It looked at Michelle and shrieked, exploding in a wave of white light.

"Thank you!" Serenity cried, jumping to her feet and trying to hide herself behind Ginger. "I've never been so scared in my entire life!"

"Obviously, Helius knows we're here," Ginger said angrily. "We gotta hurry and find the Crystal Palace. We're in great danger out in the open."

"We're in great danger out of the open!" Cody cried. "You saw what happened at the Hall of Demons! This planet's a death trap for us! We're not gonna live!"

Ginger gave Cody a slap across the face, silencing him. "Shut up. Don't say that! We're all gonna survive, and Helius's gonna pay for what he did to Gavin and our world."

*****

Torizar grumbled to himself as he left Hell's Gate. He didn't want to leave Maximus. If Helius hurt his friend…he didn't know what he'd do. If he turned on Helius, Helius would kill him in an instant. He really had no active power—just the power of the mind.

Torizar grinned. Who was he kidding? He loved to be bad. He would wait for the good keepers' arrival at the Keep of Eternal Darkness. After all, Morpheus wasn't there at the moment. He liked to stay close to the Hall of Records. He was probably there right now, researching something. Or maybe he was even waiting there to snatch up the good keepers.

"All's fair in war," Torizar mumbled, arriving at the Keep of Eternal Darkness. It was not far from Hell's Gate, so if Maximus needed his help, Torizar could get to him easily and quickly. He opened the doors of the keep and stepped inside, shutting them tightly behind him.

*****

Asterel had reached the top of the staircase only to find a single, small room. It was an odd room indeed. There were a few paintings and a tapestry or two, but aside from that there was nothing else. Except for a large, black door. The door had heavy chains around it, which were fastened tightly to the wall. An exquisite brass handle on the door was also chained. The keyhole was guarded by a glowing energy field.

Asterel shrugged. Even if she had wanted to go through the creepy door, she couldn't. It was chained tightly shut, and she didn't have the key or the counter-spell for the energy field.

"Oh well," Asterel said, shrugging again and turning around. She bumped right into a scaly surface, jumping backward. She was astounded and terrified. How had she not seen this creature? It was certainly hard to miss.

The hydra, as she recalled, was a seven-headed snake with a single body. Its teeth were capable of bringing the dead back to life. And all seven of its terrible heads were now facing her, their yellow eyes glinting against the glow of the candlelight.

Asterel was petrified. What could she do? She was without a weapon, and the hydra blocked her only means of escape. Other than throw the candelabra at it, there was nothing she could do.

Except open the door. But she didn't have the key. How could she open a door that she had no key to? It was worth a try. If she was going to die, she was going to die fighting.

Asterel ran to the door and yanked at the chains. Surprisingly, the chains slid off with ease, leaving only the energy field around the keyhole. Asterel muttered a simple chant to open a locked door, and the energy field disappeared. A small click indicated that the door was now open.

Asterel grabbed for the handle and flung open the door. She recoiled when a dark hand reached for her, barely missing her belt. Turning around, she saw that the hydra was inching closer, hissing with delight. She screamed in frustration and futility, flinging the candelabra at the hydra.

*****

Boards and chunks of rubble were cast aside as the decaying figure tossed them carelessly. Its crumbling fingers were cut by the sharp pieces of debris, but it didn't care—it was no longer capable of feeling pain. It was already dead, beyond the limitations of the mortal realm. Somewhere under the catastrophe was the crushed form of Omicron the necromancer.

The figure was finally revealed as the last pieces of boards were removed. Omicron's broken body laid there, eyes closed and face twisted in agony. The zombie knelt next to the crushed body, opening its mouth. A strange noise emerged as the creature tried to speak through cracked lips.

"I am Zzzzeta, the Great Necromancccccccer, mentor of Oooomicron," said a guttural, raspy voice. *"I give my life to resssssssssurrect him."* The dead necromancer reached forward,

touching the cold forehead of his pupil. He disappeared, absorbed by the dead body of Omicron.

Omicron's eyes snapped open. He couldn't understand. He had died, been dragged into the cold waters of death. It suddenly occurred to him. He was still dead. Someone, or something, had restored his power and put him back in his body.

He felt an old presence, melded with the power of his spirit. His mentor had come back, molding and shaping his powers into Omicron's. They were now one.

With the supernatural strength brought about only in death, Omicron jumped to his feet. His eyes were no longer eyes, but small orbs of fire, burning brightly and fiercely with newfound power. He was even stronger dead than when he was alive.

"Come forth!" Omicron shouted, his voice emerging as two simultaneous voices. Omicron and Zeta spoke together, now completely one. The Omicron creature—or Lich, as a dead necromancer is called—summoned out of the debris a small army of the dead. They rose out of the rubble like statues, waiting for their master to give them orders.

"Find the good keepers and kill them," said Omicron through clenched teeth.

*****

Morpheus sifted through the many books catalogued in the great Hall of Records. He was searching for a way to strip the filthy keepers of their powers. He had found nothing, and it annoyed him. The magic of the keepers was of a disgustingly pure source, and it would be hard to block that source.

He closed the book he currently held, replacing it on the shelf. He was going about this completely wrong. Since the power of Moonstone's keepers was of pure magic, they would probably have many protection spells cast on them. He would have to dispel those first, then try to strip them of their powers.

Morpheus considered asking Hexus for assistance. He dismissed the idea immediately. The Great and Powerful Matthew

Hexus was already full of himself. Asking him for help would only add to his conceitedness.

Morpheus quickly sifted through the books on the shelves, looking for one in particular. It was a dark book, normally only used by Helius himself. It held the worst magical formulas imaginable. It would be perfect for the work Morpheus needed.

He found it at last, bound in chains. He stripped them off easily with a Spell of Defense, flipping open the book. Its title, *Darkest Magic*, glittered as it flipped past, revealing the yellowing pages. The book itself was enchanted, having mostly a will of its own, which was why it was so dangerous.

Morpheus grinned. Perhaps this would be easier than he thought. Since he was the Keeper of Death, reading the book would be no hard task. Executing the magic was the trick. He didn't think he would have a problem, though. He started to read, another grin spreading across his hidden face.

*****

Regina and Burgundy had left Victoria to deal with the fairy princess, heading for Fearsome Keep. True, it was a plain-sounding name, but the keep did strike fear into everyone, including those who knew it well. It was a complete mystery, reshaping its walls frequently and changing its rooms around. It shifted itself to confuse those who didn't know it well enough.

"I can't wait," Burgundy giggled nervously. "When we find those fiends, we'll give them what for, won't we, Regina?"

"Whatever you say, you bizarre twit," Regina replied darkly, shaking her head as Burgundy laughed once again.

"But what if we do encounter them?" Burgundy asked, sounding a bit uneasy.

"That is the stupidest question I have ever heard," Regina snorted. "We'll kill them."

*****

Ginger had instructed MJ to break open the doors of the keep when they heard terrified shrieks from somewhere inside. A powerful Spell of Opening did the trick, twisting the doors off their hinges and blowing them inward in a shower of splinters.

Ginger and MJ stormed in, followed by Cody, Aurora, Serenity, and Michelle. They crashed through locked doors until the screaming became louder. Following the noise up a flight of stairs, Ginger ran face-first into the backside of a gigantic, seven-headed snake.

"Ginger!" cried a familiar voice. Ginger, who had stumbled backward due to the great girth of the snake, recognized the voice immediately. Though she could not see her, Ginger knew that Asterel Sunfire was on the other side of the snake.

"What is that thing?" Serenity choked, quivering.

"It's a hydra!" Asterel called frantically. "Now help me!"

"The book!" Ginger and MJ cried together. MJ rummaged through the bag and withdrew the book. She threw the book open and found an entry on the hydra. By this time, three of the heads had turned to face the gathered keepers.

"Either chop off all the heads or impale it through the heart to kill it!" MJ cried, slamming the book.

"I have a better idea!" Asterel yelled. "Get its full attention for a moment!"

Ginger, completely not thinking, grabbed the long tail of the hydra and did what she knew she could do best—sank her teeth in. The gargantuan snake screeched in pain and fury, all heads now turned to face its new opponent. Ginger dropped the tail and backed away as Asterel, on her own side, flung open the door that stood behind her.

"When I tell you, push the hydra!" Asterel yelled, picking up the already-thrown candelabra and throwing it at the hydra's back. The creature turned to her, hissing furiously.

"Now!" Asterel cried, jumping out of the way as the dark hand appeared out of the open doorway once again.

Ginger and MJ grabbed Serenity's hands, channeling their power into her. With a yell and a mighty force, Serenity spiraled the hydra through the doorway and into the clutches of the shadow hand. Asterel slammed the door as the hydra was dragged into what was apparently the gateway to the Shadow Realm.

"Housekeeping, I clean for you," Cody said in a woman-like voice, chuckling.

"That was crude," MJ said, trying to reprimand Cody but smiling nevertheless. She walked over to the door and muttered a charm, sealing the lock. Asterel reattached the chains, once again sealing the dangerous gateway.

"I'm glad that all of you arrived when you did," Asterel breathed with relief. "If you hadn't…"

"We did," Michelle said firmly. "And now you're here with us."

"How did you get here in the first place?" Serenity asked.

"I was taken prisoner by a man in a hooded cloak," Asterel explained. "At least, I think it was a man. He must have been one of Helius's keepers. He was extremely powerful."

"Well, at least we're safe for the moment," MJ commented. Then she added, "I don't believe you've met Aurora Lightly."

"The final keeper," Asterel said softly. "I'm pleased to meet you."

"Well, I'm not exactly a keeper," Aurora said, blushing slightly. "I was appointed the Emperor's Counsel because there were no powers left to give to me."

"I see," Asterel replied, frowning. "Which reminds me, where is Gavin?"

The room, if possible, chilled beyond that of icy waters. Ginger was the first to step forward. "Your Majesty, Gavin's been killed."

*****

Daniella's direction had not failed her. They had, indeed, arrived at a great bridge that spanned across the dark waters of the fast-paced river. It looked to be an ancient bridge, decrepit and rotting. But it was a bridge, nonetheless.

"I'm tired of walking," Tasha complained. "We've been walking forever! How much time do you really think has passed? How many hours upon days have we been here? I wish we could use our carpets!"

"A lot of time couldn't have passed so quickly!" Daniella retorted. "I'm not sure how long we've been here, or how long it will take to travel throughout this planet. From what I can tell, the planet is about the same size as Terra, which is not very big at all. We could probably travel around the entire planet in a few months!"

As an answer to the second question, Daniella replied, "And we can't use the carpets, aside from trying to cast another spell on them. The magic that operated them is useless on this planet."

"Then we should re-spell them!" Tasha answered angrily.

"At least there's a bridge," Adam interjected hopefully. Tinuviel nodded silently in agreement as she frowned, choosing not to stand in between the quarreling keepers.

"Something tells me we should get across this bridge fast," Tier piped up nervously. "I think my powers are growing, because I feel a mass of dark presences not far from here, and they're quickly coming this way."

"How soon do you think they'll be here?" Tasha asked, now turning from angry to fearful.

"A few minutes, at the rate these things are traveling," Tier replied.

"Everyone, get across the bridge!" Daniella instructed quickly. They stepped lightly and carefully across the seemingly fragile planks, fearing that the bridge would collapse at any moment. But apparently, looks were deceiving, for the bridge held fast.

Daniella was last to step off on the opposite side, seeing the first wave of the dead corpses on the other side of the river. They were hard to make out because of the darkness, but she knew what they were, and her thoughts were confirmed when she smelled the overwhelming stench of death. They had already started to cross the bridge when she heard someone shout.

"We have to do something!" Adam cried.

Coming to her senses, Daniella cried, "Autumn! Set fire to the bridge!"

"Wha…" Autumn started.

"Do it!" Daniella screamed harshly. "The dead can't cross moving water if there's no bridge! I read it in a book once! Now do it!"

"But they ARE crossing water!" Autumn replied.

"They are OVER water!" Daniella answered impatiently. "They can't TOUCH the water. Remove the bridge and they won't be able to reach us. They'd have to wade through the water, and that's forbidden! It would send them immediately into true death!"

Autumn nodded reluctantly and unleashed a pillar of fire upon the bridge. The dead on the bridge burned up with it, emitting howls that could curdle milk and wake up a comatose person. The dead beginning to cross the bridge backed away as the ancient bridge crumbled, sizzling as it hit the water and was carried away. Pieces of the bridge still sat in the water, however, and a few of the dead had made it safely across and were heading toward the frightened keepers.

"Step back!" Tier shrieked suddenly, glowing a blinding white. She unleashed an enormous beam of white light, annihilating the dead that had safely crossed and vaporizing the remnants of the bridge. Corpses threw themselves in all directions to escape the light pillar, some plunging themselves into the river and dying immediately.

The beam of light did not stop, however. It continued across the river, scattering the dead and destroying those not quick enough to get out of the way. Omicron himself had to lunge out of the way to narrowly escape the searing pure light. He crawled out of the way and watched it continue.

*****

Hexus saw the destruction through one of the windows. Apparently, Omicron had come back, bringing a large army of the dead with him. And it was a waste. The keepers were smarter than anticipated, and they also held great power.

One had burned the bridge. An incredibly smart move, for it cut off safe passage for the dead. Another had snuffed out many of them with a burst of light, one so powerful that even Hexus had to shield his eyes. They were proving to be more powerful than he had imagined.

He wondered for a moment if he should fight them, then decided once again not to. He would let them have their fun, and then he would kill them when they were drained of their magic. After all, he could spare a few dead creatures. What did it matter?

Hexus chuckled and opened his book, leafing through the pages. He would prepare his magic for the perfect spell. And he would use it when the time was right. Yes, he would do just that.

*****

They had reached a split in the road. The path split in three directions, one going south, from which they had just come, and the other two going northeast and northwest. “We have to split up,” Daniella said apologetically.

“Split up? Are you crazy?” Adam shouted angrily.

“I wish I were!” Daniella shouted back. “I wish I were a mental patient, sitting in the fourth floor of an insane asylum! Anything is better than this! It’s not easy to lead!”

“I’m…I’m sorry,” Adam stammered. “I don’t know what came over me.”

“It’s this world,” Tier answered weakly. Tasha and Tinuviel supported her, and she did not look at all well. Her lips were dry and cracking, indicating that she was severely dehydrated. The large burst of magic had sapped most of her strength.

“Hold on, Tier,” Daniella said under her breath. She didn’t dare give any of the water from the river to Tier. There were dead creatures on the shores, and the water was probably poisoned anyway.

Tier continued. "This world is draining us. We have to fight it. We can't let it win."

"Who's going where?" Tinuviel grunted impatiently.

"Tasha, Tinuviel, and Tier will take the northeastern path," Daniella replied, "and Autumn, Adam, and I will take the northwestern path."

"How will we contact each other?" Adam asked nervously.

"We can't," Daniella said. "But we can act on instinct. Because we're becoming so close to one another, we're beginning to think alike and calculate plans similar to those of our comrades. I say just to follow the paths, and we'll eventually join up again."

"Daniella, be careful," Tasha said.

"The same to all of you," Daniella replied, nodding at Tasha and trying to muster a smile. She managed a grimace. The entire planet was working against them.

Saying goodbye once more, the party split. Daniella led one group, Tasha the other. Both leaders looked back at each other and waved one final time before diverging down the separate roads into the unknown and its hidden dangers.

*****

The road Daniella had chosen seemed much less traveled than the other roads that they had been on. Autumn had conjured a small fireball to light the way. It hovered in front of them, illuminating the path.

The three were silent for a long time as they hurried down the road, afraid that a single sound would alert the creatures of the night to their presence. A wolf howled in the distance, a long, wailing, mournful call that sent shivers up Daniella's spine. She wished more than anything that she was back home, lying on her bed in her room.

Wishful thinking, she told herself sharply. It would do no good to think of the past. She had to concentrate on the present.

Her thoughts were interrupted by a small gasp from Autumn as the road ended. A large, narrow mountain range stood in their way, and there seemed to be no path around or through.

Closer howls prompted Daniella to action. Panicked reaction, but reaction all the same. As the mournful howls grew suddenly closer, Daniella banged her fists against the mountain, crying in desperation, "Open up!"

"Strange how a simple phrase can move a mountain," Adam commented in awe as a large crack appeared, obviously a doorway of some sort. He ran in with Autumn as the howls droned on, sounding as if they were right next to Daniella.

She ran for the door as a creature sprang out of the darkness. A creature she'd seen only in her nightmares. Towering like a large man with fur and a snout, the werewolf scrabbled across the ground, ready to devour her. She heard the scraping of its toenails against the hard earth as it lunged at her.

And the wall closed, locking it out. Daniella didn't realize she was still screaming until Adam shook her. "Daniella, it's all right! We're safe! It's locked out!"

At that moment, Daniella flung her arms around Adam, hugging him tightly and sobbing with fright. She felt his warm arms wrap around her to comfort her, and a sudden feeling emerged, hidden since the demise of Terra. She kissed him, feeling his lips on hers as they locked in a surprisingly passionate embrace. Her arms wrapped around his neck as he wrapped his around her waist. They held the kiss for a few seconds, then broke apart.

"Wow…" Autumn said with astonishment. "That was…ah…sporadic."

Daniella blushed, as did Adam. Suddenly, her loneliness was not so lonely anymore. She was finally with someone who made her feel happy. And she wanted so desperately for it to stay that way. Locking fingers tightly with Adam, the couple, along with Autumn, headed down the long tunnel.

*****

The road had led to a small waterfall near the banks of the dark river. The water here seemed a little bit lighter in color. And they had to give some to Tier, or they would risk losing her.

"Are you sure it's safe?" Tasha asked uneasily as Tinuviel helped Tier take a drink.

"No," Tinuviel said flatly, "but we have no choice. Tier will die without water. She's severely dehydrated."

"It's unusual tasting," Tier commented, seeming to gain a bit more strength. "I've never tasted water quite like this."

"I wonder where we are," Tasha asked to no one in particular.

"Black Falls," Tinuviel replied, helping Tier to her feet.

"How do you know?" Tasha asked indignantly.

"Read the sign," Tinuviel answered, pointing to a small picket sign that said "Black Falls" on it.

"Oh," Tasha replied. A series of howls prompted them to move on quickly up the road, past the bubbling, rushing waters of Black Falls.

*****

Writings of old were inscribed along the walls. They were everywhere, flowing, twisting. Pictographs, runes, symbols, and pictures. Prophecies lined the walls of the tunnel.

"This is amazing," Autumn said in awe, gently touching the wall and feeling the magic concealed within the writing. "I've never seen anything like this before."

"Nor have I," Daniella added, smiling as Adam's thumb gently caressed her hand. In spite of the surrounding dampness, she was warm.

"I wonder what they mean," Autumn marveled, stopping suddenly as the path in front of her ended. It ended at another rock wall, clearly the resolution of their long trek through the tunnel.

"Open up," Autumn commanded, stepping back as the wall split apart to reveal the pale moonlight of the outside world once again.

Terra had had five moons. Daniella remembered them well, as they had lit the night sky of Terra so beautifully. They were Nysha, the Small; Cretar the Powerful; Suvann the Gentile; and Asta, the Savior. She didn't know the name of the fifth moon; all she knew was that it existed. And as far as she knew, it had no name. Chaos only had three moons, none of which resembled any of Terra's, in appearance or brightness.

Stepping out into the moonlight, Daniella realized she had been holding her breath. She released it, never letting go of Adam's hand. She wanted to be close to him forever. He was her source of light.

Deciding that she would mention the prophetic cave to MJ at a later time—for she knew MJ would undoubtedly want to absorb the writings like a sponge—Daniella filed away the information in her mind for later. MJ could decipher the writings for sure. For now, though, they had a longer journey.

CHAPTER XXV: THE HOLY CHAPEL OF TARA

THE ROAD HAD ANOTHER FORK, CAUSING DANIELLA to clench her free hand. She couldn't split the group again; it was far too dangerous. They had to make a choice and follow through with their decision.

"Take the left road," Daniella said to Autumn. "We started out heading northwest, so we'll continue heading northwest."

They continued up the road, slowing down slightly as the first shards of gray daylight pierced the darkness. Though the light was dim and rather dismal, it was a small comfort to the weary keepers. Exhausted and starving, they temporarily paused to embrace the light of a new day.

*****

The journey after Black Falls had become steadily worse. The road was now thickly overgrown with knots and tangles of thorns, twisting and snaking across it. Tinuviel was thankful that Tier could now walk on her own. It would have been too hard to carry her through the overgrowth. Though she was still quite weak, Tier could at least now support herself.

They stepped past the large vines and thorns, careful of their footing. Tinuviel led the way, with Tasha and Tier following closely behind. "Don't step on the thorns," Tinuviel warned. "I've read about these before, and up until now, I thought they were only myths."

"Why shouldn't we touch them?" Tasha asked.

"They're called Sundown Vines," Tinuviel replied. "The thorns contain a poison capable of instantly killing a person. They are extremely lethal, and there's no antidote for the venom."

"Okay then," Tasha gulped, shivering. "No touching of the vines. Got it."

They stepped carefully across the last few strands of vines, emerging once again onto a cleared road. The surroundings had drastically changed. No longer was the land flat and motionless. It was rolling. Great hills carved the landscape, like an intricate painting.

These hills were a work of grotesque art, however. From the ground spurted towers of flame, belching forth from the earth to scorch the air. A flame burst out near Tasha, who squealed.

"As if I didn't have enough problems," Tinuviel ranted, grabbing Tier and pulling her out of the way as flames exploded out of the spot she had just been standing upon. She grabbed Tasha as well and hurried down the path, spinning everyone out of the way as flames shot outward, lashing at them, eager to reach for them.

Tinuviel broke into a run, dragging the other two with her. Across the Fire Hills they raced, ignoring everything but the road and blasts of fire. Had they been paying closer attention, they would have seen that they were being carefully watched. From one of the protective ground caves, a dark dragon glared at them, snorting as it watched them avoid the pillars of fire that erupted around them. The dragon could not touch them yet. Helius had not given it permission. Besides, it only liked to emerge after dark.

The dragon snorted again, steam spurting out of its nose. It would let them pass. For the moment, they were not a threat to it. And it wasn't very hungry anyway. It turned away and laid down its head, closing its large eyes to take a short nap.

The ground was charred, and a few stumps of trees burned long ago lined the explosive hills, causing Tinuviel to run faster. She saw the hills slowly recede and flatten out once again. With a final burst of speed, feeling as if her chest were about to explode, Tinuviel whirled past the final towers of fire and flung Tier and Tasha onto the safety of the smooth, fire-free road. She jumped and tumbled after them, panting and gasping as sulfuric air hit her lungs.

"We made it," Tier breathed, lying on the hard dirt and watching the sky as an extremely pale sun broke the horizon.

"Dawn at last," Tasha whispered, closing her eyes.

*****

Veronica woke up, disoriented and groggy. She had no idea where she was or what had happened. Then she remembered. The last thing she'd remembered was being hit from behind and losing consciousness. The rest was…

She couldn't remember, or didn't know. She closed her eyes and opened them again, trying to clear her blurry vision. It did clear slowly, allowing the room to come into focus.

She was in a prison cell. Aster Periwinkle lay on the floor against the opposite wall, snoring unhappily. A few mages were huddled together on the floor, a small orb of light at the center of their group. Veronica steadied herself as she got to her feet. The mages stopped their quiet talking and watched her as she walked over to them and sat down.

"Milady, you're awake!" one of the younger mages, dressed in a blue robe, said enthusiastically.

"What's the situation?" Veronica asked, nodding slightly to acknowledge the man's concern.

"The bars are impervious to most of the spells we tried," an older mage clothed in a red robe said. "We tried most of the Spells of Opening, but they fizzed out before we could generate enough magic."

"Did anyone escape?" Veronica asked hopefully.

"No, ma'am," another mage in a yellow robe answered. "They were either captured or killed. The remaining mages have been severely drained, save for a few of us."

"The other mages?" Veronica asked, confused.

"Yes, ma'am," the yellow mage replied, pointing. Veronica now noticed that there were hundreds of other prison cells, all of which were occupied.

"I see," Veronica replied unhappily, physically slumping. Remembering at once that she was a commander, she straightened, observing the small crowd of anxious mages.

"We'll formulate a plan," she said at last. "There's no reason a strong spell can't shatter these bars. If we all combined our powers, do you think one of you could cast a spell on the prison bars?"

"I believe it can be done, Milady," said an old mage clothed in green. "The combined powers of many should be able to break the spell."

"Who can combine all the magics?" Veronica asked.

"I am a Weaver," the old mage replied. "I am and have always been able to weave together magics into one single entity. I can do it."

"Thank you," Veronica replied, managing a weak smile. "Now let's get started."

*****

Victoria was red-faced from shouting. Her throat was raw and throbbing, and her voice had long since fled. She sat in a chair now, fanning her face with her hand as the wretched girl slept.

The princess had a surprisingly strong will. She had not given Victoria any valuable information, remaining abnormally silent. The fairy princess was strong of mind indeed.

"She'll crack eventually," Victoria rasped quietly, quivering with rage. "And if she doesn't, I'll kill her."

*****

Omicron was furious. The stupid girl had burned the bridge, denying his army safe passage. To make matters worse, the other group locked inside Shadow Keep had escaped his surrounding army by means of the large beam of white light.

"Not to worry," Omicron reassured himself. "Soon, they'll be trapped."

He whipped around to address the surrounding corpses that composed his army. "Follow the small group that escaped from Shadow Keep to the Isle of Demons. If they destroy the bridge, cut them off at the other side of the island. I want them alive." There was a sound of squishing and crunching as the vast army of the dead moved toward the Lake of Lost Souls and the Isle of Demons that lay at its center.

*****

They had found a narrow wooden bridge spanning across the dark water to the edge of an island, positioned at the center of the lake. "Run!" Ginger screamed, urging the group across the rickety bridge. Asterel crossed last, stumbling on the rotting boards and sliding across the small beach. She ran over to Ginger, panting.

"We have to destroy the bridge," Ginger said quickly, looking at MJ.

"How?" Cody asked fearfully as he watched the distant, approaching army of corpses.

"Serenity can pull off the bridge's boards with her mind," Aurora suggested, "and MJ can break the support beams with her strength."

"I don't know if I have the energy," Serenity said with worry.

"Just do your best," Aurora said reassuringly.

Serenity stepped forward, concentrating on the long wooden bridge. She reached out with her mind, feeling the bridge as a whole, then seeing the individual planks. She could see each individual nail attached from the boards to the main support beams.

Mustering all the strength she could, Serenity started pulling the boards from the main beam. Quickly and nimbly she plucked the boards, finishing in no time at all. She stepped back as MJ stepped forward. She collapsed, her part done as MJ took over.

"Take this!" MJ cried, kicking one of the support pillars of the bridge. The dead had already started inching across the remnants of the bridge, sliding along the support beams. MJ's crushing blow to one of the main pillars crippled the bridge totally, plunging it into the icy lake, along with the dead crawling across the beams.

Splashes and plopping noises indicated the dead falling into the water, along with the blood-curdling screams. They fell screaming, save for those already crushed by shrapnel from the bridge. The screams were choked off as they plummeted into the lake.

MJ stepped back as howls of fury emanated from the other side of the lake. She saw a figure emerge in front of the rows of the dead as they ranted and screeched.

"G…Ginger…" MJ squeaked.

"What's the matter?" Ginger asked as she looked across the lake at the figure.

"It's Omicron," MJ replied fearfully.

"The necromancer?" Cody asked. "But didn't he…"

"Die?" Michelle finished. "I think so. MJ brought a whole building down on top of him."

"I heard stories once in which necromancers were able to become stronger in death," Ginger replied. "That must be what happened."

"I believe it is," Asterel cut in. "I never met this Omicron you speak of before now, but I'm sure his eyes weren't balls of fire when you last saw him. I believe he is still dead, but has come back more powerful than in life."

"I want to get away from here," Serenity said, shivering. "That man, or whatever he is now, is really frightening."

"Well, we only have one way we can go," Ginger answered, turning to face the dark forest behind them. She took a deep breath and looked at Asterel, who nodded.

"I guess we're going into the forest," Ginger continued. "There must be another way to get off this island. And seeing as there's no path, we'll have to make one."

*****

The two smaller groups of keepers met up at the little village. Daniella hugged Tasha as they saw each other. The six were never happier to see one another as they were now. And the shards of morning, though gray and dull, brightened their spirits further.

"I'm glad everyone's safe," Daniella announced, squeezing Adam's hand gently as he stood silently next to her. "And Fate has reunited us once again."

"Which moves us to our next problem," Tinuviel cut in irritably. "We haven't found any clues as to where the prisoners are being held, and we don't even know where we are."

"I saw a sign near the entrance of the town," Autumn responded. "It said, 'Village of Hatred.'"

"It doesn't feel very bad here," Tasha commented.

They looked around the ghost town, carefully inspecting all parts of it to search for captive people. The few houses were drab, done over in a lesser shade of gray. And they were also empty. Only one dwelling differed from the rest.

The house was located at the very center of the village, large and menacing. It was crimson, decorated with tapestries and lavish carpets. The door had been locked, so Daniella had kicked it open with ease.

"I sense a faint presence," Tasha said suddenly. "I've felt it somewhere before. It's very distinct."

"Is it good or bad?" Tier asked anxiously, fearing it was Helius Rue.

"I'm not sure," Tasha said, stopping to think for a moment. "It's good, very good."

Tier breathed a sigh of relief as Tasha spoke. "I wonder if we could follow it."

"I can try to trace it," Tasha replied. "I've never done this before, and this essence is a bit older."

"We don't really have any other plans," Tinuviel cut in, "so it's worth a shot."

"I suppose," Daniella said, shrugging. "It might lead us to something important. Let's follow it."

*****

Ivy had nothing to say to Rodaine. The poor old man just stood there, staring out one of the broken windows at nothing. He still stood there, silent and frail-looking.

"Rodaine," Ivy said at last, clearing her throat as she finally remembered that she had to ask him something. She mentally slapped herself for not thinking of it sooner.

The man turned to look at her, finally broken of his trance. "Yes?"

"Where are Mae and Thistle?" Ivy asked, looking around. She had forgotten about them entirely, until a few seconds ago.

"Who?" the old man asked.

"My daughter and her friend," Ivy answered, a lump of fearing rising in her throat.

"No one's been here since Gavin and Asterel averted Helius's offensive," Rodaine responded, confirming Ivy's worst fears. Mae and Thistle had never made it to the safety of the Crystal Palace.

*****

The faint traces of good magic had ended abruptly at a large mountain range. It had taken what seemed years for Daniella and the others to follow the trail, and it had just ended at some stupid mountains. These mountains, Daniella realized after a few seconds, were not stupid at all. In fact, they made her feel happy. They were not menacing at all, but pleasant, slightly purpled and capped with brilliantly sparkling snow. They most definitely did not match the other horrible surrounding landscape of Chaos.

"The trail just ends," Tasha announced, stepping back to observe the mountains. "It doesn't go into a hidden path or anything. It just ends."

"Is it possible that the trail goes right over the mountains?" Autumn suggested.

"I suppose," Tasha responded thoughtfully, "though it might be difficult to tell because they're so incredibly tall. I can't really see the top of them because of the clouds so high up."

"Maybe I can get us over the mountains," Autumn continued.

"Get us over the mountains? How?" Tinuviel responded skeptically.

"I could conjure a whirlwind," Autumn replied. "I think I know how to control it. I could pick everyone up with it and fly them safely over the mountains."

"What about you?" Tier asked.

"I'll think of something, I'm sure," Autumn answered, smiling slightly. An idea had already crossed her mind.

"If we want to cross the mountains, I don't think we have any other choice," Adam cut in.

With a reassuring nod from Daniella, Autumn began. She closed her eyes and focused on the air. Millions of tiny particles glided around her gently. She reached out, pulling them together and heating them, causing them to spin faster.

In front of her appeared a small whirlwind, growing in size to spin ferociously. Autumn opened her eyes and forced the great wind to spin slowly, smiling with satisfaction at the great magic she had just worked.

"Jump in," she called motioning to the others with one hand and holding the whirlwind with another.

"I don't want to do this," Tinuviel said suddenly. "I hate heights! I can't do this!"

"Sure you can," Tasha said to her soothingly. "We'll be right with you. Autumn's good at what she does."

"No, please!" Tinuviel, now frantic, pleaded as Tasha and Tier dragged her toward the whirlwind. "I'll jump across! I'll face a thousand poisonous Sundown Vines! Don't make me go in there!" Tasha and Tier, ignoring Tinuviel's frantic pleading, dragged her into the whirlwind, followed by Daniella and Adam, who were once again holding hands and walking closely together. They jumped in together, and it was Autumn's turn to act.

Concentrating as hard as she could so as not to jostle the keepers, Autumn slowly moved the whirlwind up the mountains. When it reached the top, she halted it, realizing that it would spin out of control if she lost eye contact with it. She was strong, but she wouldn't be able to control a whirlwind of that magnitude without direct eye contact.

Gathering more magic, Autumn pushed some of her power downward into her feet, lifting herself off the ground and floating up the side of the mountain to join the swirling tornado. Then, she followed it the rest of the way down the other side, landing and dissipating the whirlwind as it touched down on the soft grass on the other side of the mountain. As the whirlwind dissipated, the other keepers hit the ground and rolled, standing up immediately to brush themselves off. No one had been injured; all were untouched.

Autumn, having landed as well, collapsed to the ground. She stayed where she fell, breathing heavily and shivering. Apparently, she had used a bit more power than anticipated, thus exhausting her energy. Tier and Tasha helped her to her feet as a tousle-haired Tinuviel stalked over to her.

"Never again, in a MILLION YEARS, are you putting me through that!" she snapped, spinning around and walking away as Tier and Tasha suppressed laughter at the sight of her wind-combed hair. This laughter was broken, however, by Daniella when she spoke.

"Oh my…" she said in awe, looking up at what lay on the side of the mountains they had just landed on. It was none other than the Crystal Palace, glorious and welcoming despite the weak light of day.

*****

The forest on the island was thick and constricting. Asterel pushed aside vegetation, muttering to herself. She could still not believe it. Gavin, gone? How could this be? As far back as she could remember—which was quite a long time—he had always been there. After all, he had been there since the beginning of life on Terra-Quenlist.

"And the end," she whispered miserably. How could he have been so easily defeated by Helius after all they had worked to fight against? After all, he had defeated the dark emperor before.

It suddenly occurred to Asterel. Gavin's heart and soul had been poured into the making of his planet of light. With that destroyed, perhaps he had not the will to go on and keep fighting. Naturally, then, a mountain of boulders thrown on top of him would have been the last straw in a long chain of unfortunate occurrences.

Asterel's thoughts were temporarily interrupted when she stumbled on a rut in the path. Well, the path that Ginger was creating. Since there was no obvious path, it was hard to get through the forest. Ginger led the group, hacking away at the various offending foliage as she made her way through the dark trees. Aurora followed closely behind her, keeping watch. Cody, Michelle, MJ, and Serenity followed behind Aurora, their defenses at fullest. Asterel held up the end of the group, now making sure that she could prevent an attack from behind.

Howls and animal noises from undisclosed positions sounded sporadically as they continued through the dense forest. The thick vegetation filtered out most of the dim light. Large trees, looming all around like waiting beasts, stretched out their branches to ensnare the keepers.

"I hope this forest clears soon," Ginger snarled as a branch slapped her in the face. She swore that the tree had done it intentionally. "I hate the darkness."

*****

Regina sat on the ground, resting for a moment. Walking took such a great amount of energy. She knew that there must be an easier way. She tried to make excuses for her lack of endurance, finally arriving at the only logical and correct one…she was just plain lazy.

"I've got it!" she shouted at last, making Burgundy jump as she got to her feet. "I'll use the Chimera! It's under my control anyway! It can get us to Fearsome Keep in half the time it would take us to walk!" She let out a wild, monkey-like cry that should have been impossible for a normal human being to emit. Burgundy giggled idiotically, amused by the noise Regina had made.

She turned on him fiercely. "Just you wait!" she cackled, looking around. "The Chimera will be here any minute to help! And if you laugh at me one more time, I'll tie you to its tail and let it drag you to Fearsome Keep!"

Burgundy was silent, surprising Regina. Whether it was because he respected her or feared her, she couldn't tell. Maybe it was a little bit of both. In any case, she'd gotten him to shut up…at least for a little while.

*****

Bracchus was bored. The elven prince was no fun. He couldn't be tortured, and now he refused to acknowledge the evil keeper's presence. Rather than use the strength to get up and punish the prince for his rudeness, Bracchus decided to continue lazing about on the couch and take a nap for a while.

Thistle was left temporarily unguarded by the snoring keeper. For the minute Bracchus's head hit the pillow on the couch, he was wrapped in the blanket of slumber. Perhaps now was Thistle's chance to try another escape. He could try to break his shackles, but his wrists were already fairly sore.

He sat still for a moment, considering his options. He could sit and wait for help, which would probably never arrive. He could continue struggling and hope that his shackles would break, which was also unlikely, except if he was graced by an unexpected stroke of luck. Or he could comply with Bracchus's questions and give valuable information to the slob of a man. In any case, he was left practically helpless.

What to do, what to do? His mind raced. All he could do was try to break his bonds. It seemed the only remotely logical option. He jiggled the chains once again, hoping against hope that one of the links in the chains would give way and secure his path to freedom.

*****

Mystical beings stepped back and bowed as the six keepers entered the Crystal Palace. The beings could feel the power of Gavin Moonstone flowing within the new individuals, an awesome power that would make evil cringe back in fear. They respected this greatly, which was why they bowed to the humans.

Daniella led her friends past the other beings, bowing slightly to them in respect as she passed to stand in front of the large doors that opened into the throne room. It was eerie, in a certain way, because the evacuated beings almost resembled a welcoming committee.

Daniella pushed on one of the large doors, causing it to swing open. The keepers filtered into the throne room to see an older man, a wolf, and Queen Ivy Snowfall. Ivy was here!

"It was you!" Tasha said excitedly, running up to the befuddled, overwhelmed Ivy and giving her a tight hug.

"What was me?" Ivy managed to say.

"We followed a faint trail of magic to the mountain range," Daniella explained. "We figured it continued past the mountains, so we managed to get over them, with help from Autumn of course. We ended up here."

"So where is everyone else?" Ivy asked.

"We split up with the others a while ago," Tasha replied. "We figured it might be better, however not safer, to do because we could broaden our search for missing people."

"Are Mae and Thistle with the other group?" Ivy asked hopefully.

"I don't know. They might be," Daniella answered.

"And where's Gavin?" Rodaine asked, joining the rest of the group and the conversation. Storm followed him, whimpering slightly at the old man's distress.

"Sir..." Daniella choked, tears welling up in her eyes. "Gavin has been killed."

Rodaine stopped, frozen in mid-motion. "That's impossible," he whispered, walking over to the large rainbow-colored throne and sitting down. "Impossible."

"We saw it happen," Adam continued in place of Daniella, who was now trying to suppress choking sobs. "Helius Rue conjured an avalanche of rocks. He threw them on Gavin and crushed him."

"Abomination," Rodaine whispered, closing his eyes. Ivy wept silently, covering her face as silvery tears streamed down her cheeks.

"Helius will pay for what he has done," Rodaine said at last. "He will pay with his life."

Autumn collapsed, no longer held up by anyone or anything, as Tier and Tasha had gone to comfort Daniella. "She's severely drained," Tinuviel announced harshly, helping Autumn to her feet and supporting her.

"Rest here," Rodaine commanded. "All of you. Regain your strength. We will provide fresh necessaries for you. I will have the chanters cast their strongest protection spells." Noticing the pile of carpets that had been tied together and fastened to Adam's back, he added, "And I'll also instruct the chanters to re-spell your carpets."

The keepers, exhausted and drained, settled on the floor, along with Ivy. Rodaine stood and exited the throne room, locating the chanters and taking the book he had supplied back from the leader. He instructed them to re-spell the magic carpets and cast their strongest protection spells upon the queen and the keepers. The chanters, unfortunately, were drained as well from the vast Transteleportation Spell.

"Rest well, and we will finish this later," Rodaine said hastily, paging through the large book of spells. "By that time, I will be of more use as well."

*****

Morpheus finally found the spell he had been looking for. Unfortunately, it required a great deal of items that he did not possess. He assured himself that they could all be found at the Hall of Records. If they couldn't, he would just have to use what he had available.

That would be much simpler than spending hours trying to find a few magical artifacts. Though the spell might not be as strong, it would still have a great effect. Morpheus was sure he would be able to alter it slightly. Either way, the protection over Moonstone's keepers would be dispelled.

Morpheus chuckled. He loved what he did, and he was good at it. This simple spell would be no problem whatsoever. He would cast it and leave the keepers defenseless. Then, when they least expected it, he would kill them.

Morpheus looked at the yellowed page, carefully observing the golden writing that burned like fire when looked upon. Now that he thought about it, the spell wouldn't be that difficult to cast after all. A few words rearranged, and it would be perfect. Morpheus started chanting, feeling the immense power in the ancient words that flowed out of his mouth.

*****

Ginger fell to her knees, doubled over in pain and unaware of what was happening. Something made her feel like a sword had been stuck through her stomach and twisted sideways, tearing at her insides. She felt the bubble of protection around her shatter, finally realizing that she was not the only one afflicted. Everyone except Asterel had fallen to the ground, gasping and crying out in pain. Their protective spells had been shattered as well.

"What's wrong?" Asterel cried, running to Ginger and helping her up as the pain in her stomach subsided.

"Our protection spells were just shattered," Ginger gasped, clutching her stomach. "Something, or someone, just broke them."

*****

Daniella woke up screaming. Something had shattered the spell of protection that had been cast upon her. Apparently, it hadn't affected just her. The other keepers were awake as well, clearly suffering from the pain as much as she was.

"Chanters, get up now!" Rodaine bellowed, jumping to his feet and waking up the sleeping mages in the great hall. "I want evasive protection spells cast this instant!"

Numb fingers executed symbols, and sleepy voices emitted words to match. Symbols whirled around the keepers and Ivy, embedding themselves to create multiple bubbles of protection. Within an instant, the keepers were protected once again. Rodaine waved his hand and muttered something indistinguishable, giving his own form of a protection spell to the keepers.

"We can't stay any longer," Daniella said, urgent but apologetic. "We have to go now. Whatever just attacked us will not fail to do so again. We have to find it and stop it before it tries for a second time."

"There is a small chapel behind the palace," Rodaine replied, nodding. "I noticed it before we landed in front of it. Why don't you explore it? Perhaps there's something worthwhile inside."

"Like what? Holy water?" Tinuviel snorted, apparently still angry. A sharp glance from Daniella silenced any further outbursts.

"Actually, holy water is an effective weapon against vampires and other undead creatures," Ivy replied, oblivious to Tinuviel's sarcasm. "We may need it."

"Let's hurry!" Daniella cried desperately, focusing on the task at hand. Out of the throne room doors they raced, down the corridor and out the front doors of the Crystal Palace. They hurried around the enormous structure to the opposite side, where a small church stood.

"Let's go in," Tier spoke, pushing open the doors and stepping inside fearlessly. The others followed her, not as fearless, and wary of what might lie inside the recesses of the small church. Which raised another question—why was there a church here in the first place, with no village or any other civilization? It didn't make sense.

The chapel matched the exterior of the Crystal Palace, Daniella realized as she stepped inside. It was white, and one of the most gorgeous things she had ever seen. Long wooden pews made of mahogany stretched all the way down the long room, ending at a small set of stairs that led to a white marble altar. Green plants hung in various places, indicating that the chapel was a place of great good, not evil, as Daniella had expected it to be. Large stained glass windows added to the spectacle, catching even the smallest bit of the weak sunlight and throwing it gracefully through into the church.

Behind the white marble altar stood a young woman, clothed in a plain white gown. A gold band was fastened tightly around her head. Her blue eyes and blonde hair gave her an angelic appearance.

"Welcome to the Holy Chapel of Tara," she announced. "I have eagerly awaited your arrival."

"Who are you?" Daniella asked, rather defensively.

"The goddess Tara, of course," the woman replied. "Come forward."

CHAPTER XXVI: THE HALL OF RECORDS

"ARE YOU GOOD OR EVIL?" TASHA ASKED.

"Oh, very good," Tara replied. "You see, I was transported here when Helius Rue distorted time to arrive on Terra-Quenlist. In order for him to distort space from an evil source to a good source, an exchange was in order. My chapel was switched with the Onyx Castle. When it appeared on Terra, my chapel appeared on Chaos. Quite spectacular, really. When I appeared, the light that emanated off the chapel disintegrated a woman who stood out in the open. It started her on fire. She turned to ash as I continued falling, looking out the window of the chapel."

"If you're a good goddess and this is all true, what are you the goddess of?" Tasha asked.

"I am the Goddess of Balance and Centering," Tara replied. "Which is why I know about the nature of evil. I guessed the woman was evil when the light destroyed her, because evil beings fear the light."

"Are you here to help us?" Daniella asked.

"Yes," Tara replied. She stepped away from the altar and proceeded to walk to a corner of the church. A small fountain stood there, its watery surface still.

"Drink," Tara instructed, motioning to the still water in the fountain's basin. Warily, Ivy stepped up to the fountain and took a sip of the water.

She turned to face the others, literally glowing. "It's pure white magic!" she gasped, observing her glowing hands with admiration.

"It can work wonders," Tara said, smiling warmly. "I trust all of you will need it. I saved just enough of my waning magic for everyone." She pulled out a large flask and filled it with the magical water, handing it to Ivy.

"I know of the other keepers," Tara said, "which is why I saved enough for them as well." She turned to the others. "Now everyone else should take a drink."

"What does it do?" Daniella asked.

"It fully restores even the weakest of people, including magically," Tara answered. "When this magic is gone, so too in physical form shall I be. Use it well. It is my gift to you against Helius Rue and the darkness of Chaos."

The goddess Tara faded and disappeared before anyone could muster a thank you. Daniella considered calling for Tara, then decided against it. The goddess had helped enough already.

"Another fountain is on this side of the chapel!" Tier called, pointing. Another identical fountain stood in the opposite corner of the small chapel, bubbling softly as sparkling water tinkled in its basin. Tier took a drink.

"It's holy water!" she called. She could taste the magic and purity of the water on her lips and tongue. Some flasks sat next to the fountain. She began happily filling them as Daniella spoke.

"Drink some of the water, then help Tier fill those flasks," Daniella said to the others. "I have a feeling we're going to need all the help we can get."

*****

Ginger felt a soft presence, surrounding her and warming her. A strong web of protection spells had been cast on her and the others, including Asterel. She felt restored, refreshed. The spell was powerful indeed, though she had no idea who the caster of it was. She could almost see the thick good energy around her.

"Did you feel that?" Ginger asked the others excitedly.

"Yes," Asterel replied. "A very powerful protection spell from an unknown source."

"This is definitely a good thing," Serenity said as they entered a small clearing. "With a strong protection spell helping us, we can keep up the journey, stronger than ever."

And what a journey it had been so far. They had traveled all night, into the next morning. The light was already at its brightest, indicating that they were halfway through a day on Chaos. Ginger's thoughts drifted back to the web of protection. She couldn't help feeling that she'd felt this power before, but where it had come from she didn't know.

They stopped as they all entered the clearing. It was small, and there was a narrow path at the other end, leading to a faraway bridge. A bridge that looked just like the one they had dissembled earlier.

"We've reached the other end of the island!" MJ cried happily.

Her happiness dissipated and her breath caught in her throat when she heard a silvery, singing voice. "Come fly with me, my children. Come fly with me."

A slim, wispy-looking woman stood in front of the path that led to the bridge. She did not appear at all normal, however. She had snakes for hair and slit, glowing eyes. Her long fingernails scraped across a nearby rock, making MJ clench her teeth.

"What is that?" Cody asked, horrified and disgusted.

"It's a gorgon," Ginger replied grimly. "I remember one of Eden's lessons about them. There're only three, all of whom were sisters. Two were slain. Medusa, one of the slain sisters, had the power to turn people to stone just by starin' at 'em. She was cleverly defeated when her opponent killed her by lookin' through a mirror. Each of the three sisters had a different power."

"Hello, children," the gorgon said, interrupting everyone as she smiled at them and showed a mouthful of razor-sharp teeth.

"Ginger," Cody asked, "which one is it, and how do you kill it?"

"Cut off its head," Ginger replied flatly.

"That's not very nice," the gorgon replied. "My name is Euryale, the Far-Roaming. It's not nice to talk of such things as beheading me. I once was an immortal, forever beautiful."

"You got real ugly," Cody answered quickly, looking away when Euryale turned to face him.

"I am no immortal now, but I still hold my power!" she cried as she turned back to Ginger. Immediately she reverted back to her calm and collected self. "But I will humor you, children." She pulled a long sword out of a clump of bushes and threw it to Ginger.

"What?" Ginger said, confused.

"I have instructions not to let the children through, or I will be slain like my sisters," Euryale sang. "Naughty children killed some of Helius's keepers. Naughty, naughty children."

"So in order to continue across the bridge, we have to kill the gorgon?" Michelle asked, only to hear Euryale answer her question.

"Naughty children won't kill the gorgon," she sang sweetly, making Michelle cringe.

"We'll see about that!" Ginger answered, charging and swinging the sword. Euryale grabbed her and tossed her against a rock, knocking her unconscious.

"Ginger!" Michelle cried angrily, running at the gorgon and forming a spell with her fingers. The gorgon hissed before Michelle could finish her spell, and at the hiss Michelle disappeared in a wisp of smoke.

"The naughty child will enjoy Morpheus's company," Euryale cackled, advancing toward the others. "Soon all the naughty children will be joining her."

A strange noise sounded, and Euryale stopped, gurgling for a second as her head fell from her shoulders. Ginger stood behind the decapitated gorgon, still holding the sword she had been given. She rubbed her head, looking at the others and then back at the slain gorgon.

"Go ahead," she said to the dead Euryale, "laugh." She gave the lifeless body a kick and looked again at the others. "Where's Michelle?"

"The gorgon said something about letting her enjoy Morpheus's company," Asterel commented.

"She must have teleported Michelle," MJ said. "Unfortunately, we can't try to look for her now. That might be just what Helius is waiting for. After all, he put the gorgon here to stop us."

Ginger frowned deeply, clearly not about to accept MJ's words. "It's not fair or right to leave her, who knows where, all by herself."

"We have to keep going," MJ said. "We'll probably find her on the way."

"I don't like it," Ginger said, "but I know that we don't have a choice. We gotta move swiftly to escape the things that are tryin' to follow us."

"Let's hurry," Serenity said, worry easily distinguishable on her youthful face. "I still think we're being followed."

*****

Michelle spun through space, whirling, twisting. She had been teleported by the gorgon. What was its name? Oh, yes—Euryale, that was it. She vaguely remembered hearing Ginger say something about the gorgons having different powers. Euryale must have had the power of teleportation.

Michelle skidded across a stone floor, bumping into a table. She turned over and hiccupped loudly, the dizzying effect of spinning through space causing her stomach to turn. She slowly got to her feet as she noticed a dark figure moving swiftly toward her. It appeared to be a human, but due to her dizziness and the lack of light, she couldn't really tell. What she did know was that a dark cloak covered the figure.

It suddenly occurred to Michelle. A man in a black cloak had captured Asterel. The thing moving toward her was Asterel's captor. Whatever it was, she never had a chance to find out. The room suddenly blackened, and a cold wave swept across Michelle as she slipped into unconsciousness.

*****

Armed with spells, charms, and amulets, Daniella and the others hurried away from the mountains, heading back toward the village they had previously visited. Autumn had received a special spell from Rodaine, enabling instant teleportation to the Crystal Palace. It was a one-time-only spell, draining the user greatly. He had strictly told her that it was only to be used in a dire emergency.

"Why are we going back to the Village of Hatred?" Tier asked, shivering.

"Because there's another road that leads out of the village," Daniella replied patiently, holding Adam's hand tightly. "The road is bound to lead somewhere important, and we have no time as it is. We have to follow it in hopes of finding Helius's castle."

"Who knows what Helius is doing to the prisoners," Ivy said uneasily.

Autumn was silent, clutching the small piece of paper that contained the powerful teleportation spell. She studied the paper intently, trying to memorize the intricate writing. She followed Daniella and the others automatically as they exited the town and followed the small road.

Far ahead, a very distant building was visible. Daniella looked at Ivy, who nodded in silent affirmation. The building might hold a clue as to where Helius's castle was located. And they had to find shelter. Their rest at the Crystal Palace had wasted the rest of the previous day and all of the early morning. It was midday now, Daniella thought, and they could probably reach the distant building just as the day was spent.

*****

The ball of magic collided with the cell's bars, smashing through the magical barriers and destroying the steel frame of the cell door. A large, smoking hole appeared in the now-warped bars, allowing for a quick escape.

"Everyone, out!" Veronica cried. The mages filtered out, conjuring spells to defend themselves from the guards, who were all non-human. Veronica charged out with Aster, who had aroused from her slumber as the Weaver finished putting the magics of the various mages together. Veronica and Aster swung their spelled swords, smashing the locks on the many cells. Refugees and mages poured out of their prisons, charging over anything that stood in their way. They headed for a doorway at the top of a flight of stairs—a doorway that led to their freedom.

*****

Hexus was becoming a bit uneasy. He had been searching for the perfect spell and still had come up with nothing. He knew that he had a spell of the right type in the book, but he just couldn't seem to find it.

He leafed through the pages once again, cursing softly. Now he remembered why he couldn't find this particular spell. He had put a magical seal on it, hiding it somewhere in the book so it could remain unseen to prying eyes.

He had cloaked the spell so well that even he couldn't find it. He had done it in case anyone ever read his book. Hexus wasn't sure now why he had been so idiotic as to cloak the spell. He carried his book with him at all times. Muttering angrily, he continued to search his book for the cursed spell.

*****

It had taken the rest of the day to reach the structure, even at their brisk pace, but Daniella and the others arrived at the building unmolested. A small insignia on the front doors said, "Hall of Records."

"Something tells me we shouldn't go in there," Tasha said uneasily.

"I agree," Tier added. "Something is very wrong with this place."

"I feel two presences inside," Tasha said suddenly. She seemed to be in a sort of trance. Her eyes were glossy, as if she was looking far beyond the door.

"What do you see?" Ivy asked.

"One good presence, one very evil presence," Tasha continued. "The good is being held captive by the evil."

"Let's save them, then!" Daniella cried, reaching for one of the brass door handles.

"Wait!" Autumn interjected, slapping Daniella away. "How do you know this isn't a trick? How do you know this supposed good presence is really good?"

"If Tasha says it's good, then it is!" Daniella replied angrily, pushing at the doors, which did not budge at all. She cried out angrily, giving the doors a hard kick and sending them crashing open. She stormed inside, the others in close pursuit.

Daniella understood then why the building was called the Hall of Records. It was a gigantic library, as well as a museum. Its cathedral ceiling seemed to stretch upward for miles. Stairways and balconies led to shelves of thousands upon thousands of texts. Some shelves contained unknown items or cases, some even bound in chains.

And in the middle of the room was a man. A black cloak shrouded him. He stood next to a large table. Half the table was littered with books. The other half played host to a gagged and bound Michelle Harmonium.

"Michelle!" Daniella cried, rushing forward across the lush carpet that covered the floor. Instantly, she knew that she'd made a mistake. She had rushed in stupidly instead of thinking, alerting the cloaked figure in the process.

"Ah, so she is indeed a keeper," the cloaked figure rasped, stepping away from the table and toward the gathered group. His black robe flowed, and he appeared to float.

The raspy voice spoke again. "Helius will be very pleased that I, Morpheus Eternia, Keeper of Death, have captured the lot of you."

He reached out for Daniella, long, bony arms with skeletal fingers ready to grasp her. Unthinkingly, she placed a firm fist into the figure's abdomen, causing it to retract its frightful arms and gasp in pain and surprise.

"Free Michelle!" Daniella cried, looking at Ivy. Autumn ran for the table, alongside Ivy. They reached the table as the figure recovered. It turned, raising one hand and pointing it at them.

"Time to die," Morpheus snarled, producing a dark ball of purple lightning. He threw it at Ivy, who screamed. It bounced off her as the protection spell took the full force. Ivy stopped for a moment, then proceeded to free Michelle of her bonds.

"What?! That's impossible! I nullified the protection!" Morpheus shouted, conjuring another ball of lightning. Ivy knew then that if he threw that ball at her, she would be killed. The spell was not strong enough to block a second assault of equal magnitude.

"Nullify this," Autumn spat, conjuring a fireball and flinging it at the evil keeper. It hit him in the chest and engulfed him quickly, the flammable fabric of his cloak helping the flames to spread. He screamed, wildly trying to bat the fire away. Around and around he twisted, finally falling to the floor in a burning heap.

"That will teach you to mess with my friends," Autumn shouted angrily, shaking with fury and fear.

"Well done," Ivy said firmly, clutching Autumn by the shoulders. "It's…"

Whatever Ivy was going to say was suddenly cut off as the charred, smoking figure rose, shedding the burned and darkened cloak. Tasha screamed as the figure rose out of the ashes. Long, shining bones emerged from the remnants of the cloak. The true Morpheus Eternia was at last revealed.

"For that outburst, foolish girl," the skeleton hissed, "you will die."

Daniella pulled one of the larger books off the shelf and threw it at the skeleton. It turned just in time to dodge the projectile nimbly, counterattacking by sending a bolt of lightning at Daniella. The bolt knocked her to the ground, skidding her across the floor. Adam ran to her side to help her up.

"Weak fools!" Morpheus cried happily, turning to Tasha, who was frozen in terror. He picked her up by the throat. "Your turn!"

He threw Tasha, sending her spinning across the room and into one of the large bookshelves. She fell to the ground amid a pile of books, lying still. Tinuviel spoke a spell, causing the floor to shake and throw Morpheus off balance as he sent a bolt at Tier. Tier jumped out of the way as the bolt struck the floor, burning the carpet and charring the stone. Morpheus sent more lightning coiling out, striking Tinuviel and throwing her out the open doors of the Hall of Records.

"Do something!" Tier cried frantically, looking at Autumn.

"What?" Autumn cried as Morpheus advanced toward the frozen Tier.

"Anything!" Tier screamed as the skeleton reached out for her.

"Have you ever been near death, girl?" it asked, picking her up as she screamed continually. "Such a pretty voice," Morpheus commented, bringing her closer to give her a kiss.

Repulsed, Autumn was determined to stop that thing from touching Tier's face. She made the quickest move she thought possible. A few words conjured a bolt of white lightning, sending it screaming through the air at the white bones. The lightning found its mark, striking Morpheus before he could kiss Tier. He dropped her as the lightning hit him, blackening the bleach-white bones as it ravaged across them.

The figure did not flinch at the searing pain. It simply turned and looked at Autumn with empty, soulless black eye sockets. She flinched at its gaze, suddenly frightened out of her wits and unable to breathe. She fainted, collapsing from the dark power of the Keeper of Death.

"My power far outmatches your puny spells," Morpheus cackled hysterically, looking at Ivy and Michelle. "No one can match my power!"

Ivy readied her wand, but Michelle suddenly stepped forward. "The power of Heaven can!" she cried, advancing toward the skeleton. He clearly did not expect this outburst, as he took a few steps back to observe the suddenly powerful keeper.

"So you have power!" Michelle continued. "Big deal! The universal power is stronger than you are! As long as I know that, you can never defeat me! I am not afraid of you!"

She started to glow, a brilliant white that smashed out the tall windows of the Hall of Records. They exploded outward as the light expanded. The skeleton shrank back suddenly, knowing that he had made a grave mistake tampering with this girl and her companions.

"What is this magic?" Morpheus cried, trying to cover his face to block the light.

"The power of Faith," Michelle replied in a lofty voice Ivy had never heard before. It was not Michelle's voice at all, but a voice of great and ancient power, perhaps a deity long forgotten by the sands of time. Michelle continued in the strange voice. *"You must go on your way, Morpheus Eternia. I send you to true death. The power of Faith sends you."* She reached forward and touched the skeleton, making it howl with pain and terror.

Morpheus screamed in terror, feeling a jolt of white magic course through him. How could this be? How could he have lost? He was the Keeper of Death! Death could not die! *"It doesn't matter anymore,"* a voice said soothingly in his ear. His time had come. He was finished.

He stood silently, giving in to the warm energy that was ripping him apart. With a glow and a final cry—or a sigh of happiness, for no one ever knew—the skeleton that was Morpheus Eternia exploded, throwing shining particles of dust into the air. The good magic that had destroyed him returned itself to Michelle, who in turn returned to her normal, non-glowing self.

"Wow," Tier managed to choke out, still quite shaken. "How did you manage that?"

"The power of Faith is capable of many things," Michelle replied enigmatically. "But it can be found, even in the darkest of places."

"But who…who was that?" Tier asked in reference to the lofty voice that had come from Michelle.

Michelle said nothing. She simply smiled.

*****

CHAPTER XXVII: THE TEMPLE OF THE INFERNAL COUNCIL

HELIUS HAD BEEN RELATIVELY COMFORTABLE IN HIS throne, enjoying his victory over Gavin. He had decided to open one of his very best bottles of wine, for this was an auspicious occasion. He was still sitting and enjoying some of the berry wine when he felt a disturbance.

Morpheus had been destroyed. Though he tried to tell himself it was an impossibility, Helius knew deep down that it was the truth. Morpheus was gone, joining the other slain keepers in true death, where Helius dared never to enter. He was unwelcome and would be all too eagerly taken by true death, never to return to the outside world. He could only cheat death so much. So Morpheus was gone forever.

Helius tried to contain his fury at the keeper's demise, only worsening it when he crushed his glass and cut his hand. Dark blood trickled from his palm to his wrist, flowing smoothly and uninterrupted. It was then that Helius knew a solution to his problem. He would call upon the dark forces to aid him, preferably in the form of the Infernal Council.

There were four members who composed the Infernal Council. Though they were dark gods, they were not as powerful as he was. But they did have one thing he didn't have—the Sight. Gavin had been born with the gift—Helius had not. They could see into the future and enable Helius to divert any more disasters. Helius decided he would go to their temple and awaken them. Surely, they would be able to help him dispose of Moonstone's troublesome keepers.

Helius smiled as he thought of the awakening of the Infernal Council. The last time they had been called upon was when Helius had asked for guidance in creating Chaos. Now they would be awakened once more to aid him.

*****

The Chimera bucked and twisted as Regina and Burgundy rode on its back. The three heads focused on their destination—Fearsome Keep. "Yah, horsy, yah!" Regina whooped, grinning and enjoying the ride. Burgundy, however, looked extremely ill.

"Regina…" he started. "Slow this beast down…I think…I'm going to be…sick…"

"Oh, don't be such an infernal fool," Regina giggled, turning her attention back to her beloved pet. "Good horsy."

"I'm insane and love it, but this is just crazy," Burgundy hiccuped as the Chimera continued its relentless trek toward Fearsome Keep, stopping for nothing.

*****

Maximus was relieved. Jasmine was up and walking around, seemingly fine. It appeared almost as if her fainting spell had never occurred. She looked healthy, and she was definitely not dehydrated. Her face was flushed slightly, back to its normal color, and her lips were red and beautiful once again.

It still bothered Maximus, though. If Jasmine was pregnant, that would mean she would be exiled, stripped of her queenly rights; worst of all, she would become human. He knew how it worked, the rules the harpies had set in place. Both Helius and the harpies forbade taking a lover. It meant certain death.

Maximus worried over this until he got an awfully wonderful idea. Apparently, Gavin Moonstone's keepers were alive and well, wreaking havoc throughout Chaos. If he captured or killed some of them, Helius would know for certain that he was evil. After all, the keepers were most likely searching for the prisoners. Many of the prisoners were being held captive at Hell's Gate to await Helius's orders.

Maximus smiled, causing Jasmine to walk over to him. She sat on his lap, her eyes glittering. "Thinking, my darling?" she asked.

"Yes," Maximus replied, holding her and closing his eyes. He felt her delicate fingers combing through his hair. The sensation sent shivers down his spine.

"About what?" she asked softly, staring into his eyes.

"Our child," he replied shortly, his breath catching in his throat. It felt odd talking about the child they were to have.

"Why?" Jasmine asked sleepily, edging herself against Maximus's chest.

"I have an idea that will save both us and the child," Maximus replied, deciding to reveal his plan to Jasmine. "If I capture or kill some of the good keepers, Helius will see that I'm still evil. That way, we should be able to hide until after the child is born. No one else knows, save for Torizar and Penelope."

"Your thoughts are acceptable," Jasmine answered, snuggling close to him. "But let them come here. Don't rush off to find them."

"Of course," Maximus said, lightly kissing Jasmine.

*****

"There has to be something useful in one of these books!" Daniella cried, frantically leafing through the pages of a large manuscript. The other keepers and Ivy talked quietly.

"So you were teleported here?" Ivy asked anxiously, looking at Michelle.

"Yes, by a gorgon," Michelle replied.

"What about the others?" Tinuviel asked.

"They were fine before I was teleported," Michelle answered. "We rescued Asterel…"

"Asterel?" Ivy cut in. "She's safe?"

"Yes," Michelle said. "I am not sure where the others are now, though."

"What about Mae and Thistle?" Ivy asked.

"They were not with us," Michelle said, frowning. She had never met Mae Snowfall or Thistle Sunfire, but she knew she would recognize them in an instant. They certainly had not been with Ginger and the others.

Ivy was cut off from responding as Daniella let out a triumphant cry. "I found a map!"

"A map?" Tasha echoed. "Of what?"

"This world, silly!" Daniella said excitedly. She walked over to the others and unfolded a large map, throwing books aside to set it on the table. Indeed, it was a map of Chaos, charting out all the landscape.

"We're here," Daniella said, pointing to a small building marked, "Hall of Records."

"And?" Tinuviel asked impatiently, irritated that she was now bruising on her back from being thrown out onto the stone steps.

"There are many unmarked locations on this map," Daniella replied, pointing to a building northwest of their current location. "Whoever made this map never got to finish it. Maybe one of these places has the people who were taken prisoner! Now that we've found the Crystal Palace, we can send the prisoners somewhere safe once they've been rescued. Then we'll find a way to defeat Helius."

"So you're telling us we need to visit these unmarked sites?" Tier asked.

"Yes," Daniella answered, smiling. "Starting with the building northwest of here."

*****

Ginger's head throbbed from the hit she'd taken. The fall against the rock had hurt a great deal. She wondered if she'd suffered a concussion. But she dismissed the idea immediately as she wasn't groggy and her head wasn't bleeding. The bridge they were crossing, however, did make things worse.

"Ginger, are you all right?" MJ asked cautiously, looking at their leader.

"My head hurts a little from being thrown into a rock, but I'll live," Ginger replied, shrugging off MJ's concern.

"Ginger…" Aurora said slowly.

"I'm fine!" Ginger insisted angrily.

"It's not that," Aurora replied. "Look."

Ginger followed Aurora's direction to the other end of the bridge. She finally saw what Aurora had meant. An army of the dead stood waiting for them. Omicron was at the very front. Though it was dark outside, Ginger could see that he was grinning triumphantly.

"We have to fight," Ginger said. "If we go back, we'll be trapped."

"What about Omicron?" Serenity asked.

"The necromancer's mine," Ginger growled. "We defeated him once. We can do it again. If we destroy him, his control over the army'll be broken, and they'll scatter."

MJ gave Ginger the necessary element. She put a fire spell into the sword Ginger held, allowing it to kill the dead, not just wound them. If the sword struck against an undead creature, it would truly kill it.

"Brace yourselves," Asterel said as they neared the other side of the long bridge, approaching the waiting army and Omicron.

*****

Morpheus was dead. Hexus had felt it. *Pity*, he thought. Morpheus had been a powerful man. Though Hexus was much more powerful than the Keeper of Death was, he was still a bit worried. Morpheus had also failed, and Gavin's keepers were proving to be much more threatening than he ever imagined. They seemed to be getting stronger, not weaker. Plus, he had not found the spell he sought.

Annoyed, Hexus opened his book to search again. He was surprised this time, however, when he found that he had opened the book to the exact page he had been looking for. A smile crossed his face as he left the book open. He would wait for them, wait to see the fear in their eyes. Then he would use the spell and send them all where they belonged…the Nether Realm.

*****

Helius stood in the large, circular stone room, staring at the four stone statues on a raised dais, against one of the walls of the vast room. They were magnificent. Dark gods, powerful and exactly the way they had looked the last time he saw them. It sent chills of glee up his spine.

Helius looked to the first one. It was a man with a skeletal-like figure, dressed in a dark robe. Hades, the Great Lord. He was one of the four and the leader of the council. Helius remembered that Hades was a fierce leader with a fiery temper much like his own, easily angered and vengeful.

Shiva was next in line. Despite his odd, almost feminine name, he was quite handsome, as well as powerful. A nickname he had favored was "The Destroyer." He changed moods frequently, the color of his eyes indicating the particular mood. He carried two large broadswords, matching his red and gold uniform.

Shiva's wife Kali stood by his side, the third of the four council members. Kali, much like Shiva, enjoyed destruction. She enjoyed destruction so much, Helius had heard, that she had almost killed her own husband by dancing on him at a battle when they had emerged victorious. She wore a matching dress of red and gold, appearing weaponless. But weapons were not always swords and daggers.

The last of the four council members was Adonis, a god of supreme darkness and death. Adonis was the only one of the four who was most human in appearance. He wore a white robe embroidered with gold. Only his dark eyes gave away his true nature. He carried a golden scepter in one hand.

Helius, feeling absolutely humiliated at having to bow, knelt in front of the four statues and lowered his head. He spoke the ancient verse fluently, remembering well how it had called them forth the first time.

As Helius finished the old verse, the figures sprang to life, taking their places at the designated chairs that stood in front of them on the dais. After they were seated, the silent deities carefully observed the evil emperor. Hades finally spoke.

"Master Helius, why have you summoned us?" His words were like thunder and ice, booming but chilling the room and making Helius shiver, despite the fact that he was accustomed to the cold.

"I have come in hopes of receiving assistance from the higher powers," Helius said, his face reddening with humiliation.

"Once you have called upon us, and once we have assisted you," Adonis replied. "Forbidden, it is, to summon us a second time for your own selfish purposes."

"But I need assistance!" Helius cried in exasperation, standing.

"The laws of magic that we are bound by, both good and evil, forbid us from aiding in a war that is not our concern," Shiva said sternly, glaring at Helius, who seemed to shrink under the forbidding stare.

"It was forbidden the first time as well!" Helius suddenly screamed, his face purpling.

"We felt pity for you. That is why we assisted," Shiva said. Kali, who immediately spoke, cut him off.

"We were severely punished for aiding you in the construction of your dark world!" she roared, clenching her fists on the arms of the chair and causing pieces of stone to splinter and chip off.

"Calm yourselves," Hades replied darkly. He waved his hand, causing a large cauldron to appear in front of the group. "Though we cannot physically aid you, we can give you one piece of advice toward the betterment of yourself. We shall consult the future." He stood and walked to the cauldron. Another wave of his hand made the liquid in the large cauldron swirl violently and change colors.

The other council members stepped up to the cauldron, leaving Helius to wonder. After what seemed an eternity, they turned to Helius. Hades' soulless eyes gazed right at Helius.

"We have seen nothing," Hades said bluntly. "Your future is empty."

"That is not possible!" Helius cried, suddenly fearful at the words of the great god. "The prophecy of long ago said that I would conquer all!"

"The true prophecy you do not know," Adonis answered. "And the true prophecy you shall never know."

"What will I do?!" Helius shouted.

"Allow Fate to carry out its plan," Hades replied. "We have offered all the help you shall receive. Do not call us again. Goodbye, Master Helius."

The gods and the cauldron disappeared, leaving Helius alone. He screamed with uncontrollable rage, slamming his fists against the cold stone floor. A shuddering of the structure indicated that Helius had cracked the main supports. The temple was crumbling. He stood silently and walked out of the temple as it crashed to the ground behind him.

*****

"Well, that plan's shot," Tinuviel grunted as they watched the billowing plume of smoke in the far distance. They had been ready to leave the Hall of Records when they heard a loud crash or explosion. Looking out the window, they had seen the smoke in the distance.

It was quite hard to see because of the darkness, but the darkness was slowly giving way to the light of a new day. Time seemed to be moving so quickly. The structure on the map disappeared, showing only ruins.

"Oh well," Michelle said happily. "Let us find someplace else to travel to."

CHAPTER XXVIII: THE CHAPEL OF SHADOWS

"I WONDER WHAT THAT WAS ALL ABOUT?" TIER ASKED quietly.

"We have to go!" Daniella protested, starting for the door. "There might be people there!"

"There weren't," Tasha replied softly.

Daniella turned to Tasha, her eyes questioning. "What?"

"There weren't any people there," Tasha repeated. "I would have felt them die. Nothing there died. It must have been an abandoned building."

Daniella visibly calmed, her hand dropping from the door to rest at her side. She relaxed, walking over to one of the large, now broken windows and staring out at the diminishing trail of dust and smoke. "They weren't there," she said with relief.

"That means they are still out there somewhere," Adam said to Daniella, putting an arm around her.

"Which means that Mae and Thistle might be with them," Ivy said excitedly. "We must find them!"

"From the time I spent with them very briefly, I sensed that they were both self-sufficient and very powerful. They're probably looking for us right now," Tasha said reassuringly.

*****

The fairy princess had awoken, struggling once again. Victoria was getting exhausted. She couldn't take it anymore. The girl was becoming annoying with her silence.

"I'll ask you one last time to tell me what you know, and then I'll make you tell me," Victoria threatened, her face now permanently flushed a dark red color.

"I'll never tell you anything," Mae said stubbornly, a bruise forming on her cheek where Victoria had struck her earlier. One of her eyes was swollen, and a small trickle of blood leaked out of one of her nostrils.

"My friends will come for me, and you'll be sorry," Mae continued.

"Wash away your hope, for the Gates of Sorrow await!" Victoria spat disgustedly, throwing down the stick she had been intending to use. She had heard enough.

"I'll send you somewhere you'll never escape from!" she shrieked in Mae's face, her blue eyes changing to red. Mae squeaked with fear, realizing that Victoria was about to kill her. She could not escape, much less do anything. She was prepared to die, and that was that. There was nothing she could do, except let out a terrified shriek. It was the end of her, for sure.

Mae wished that her mother was there to comfort her. Ivy always seemed to be able to help, even in the stickiest of situations. And Mae also thought of Thistle, and what they could have had together. A solitary tear rolled down her cheek for him. He would die of a broken heart once he discovered that she was dead, or die trying to avenge her. She let out a shuddering sigh and prepared for the inevitable.

*****

Freedom was blocked, and they were trapped once again. Aster and Veronica could not penetrate the heavy oak door that led out of the dungeon. It was bolted from the other side and protected by a magical energy field.

"Blast!" Veronica cried in despair. They could not give up now. They had fought their way to the exit, and they were going to find a way through.

"Mages!" Aster bellowed, temporarily taking command. "Prepare a counter-spell for this energy field! I want this door open now!"

*****

They had managed to escape somehow. Ginger's enchanted sword had done the trick. It had seemed impossible at first, until Ginger had thrown her sword and decapitated Omicron. With the dead necromancer decapitated and forced out of life, his power was dispelled, scattering his army with it. They had fled in terror from the powerful keepers, slinking away into the darkness as light had begun to emerge for another day. Still, the group had rushed past, fearing that Omicron would rise to attack once again. But he did not.

It had taken an incredible amount of traveling time, from sunrise to sundown, for Ginger and the others to finally locate another structure. The light was disappearing over the horizon when they reached the small fortress.

"I wonder if it's…" Serenity's question was cut off abruptly as a shriek was heard from inside.

"Someone needs help!" Ginger cried. She tugged at the door madly, realizing that it was sealed tightly. Asterel suddenly joined her.

"Let's break it down," Asterel said quickly and calmly. "I'll help you." With the combined effort, the two smashed through the door, just in time to see a woman in a burgundy dress raise a dagger to stab another woman, who was chained to a wall. The chained woman was none other than Mae Snowfall.

"Get away from her!" Asterel screamed, grabbing Victoria by the hair and throwing her. The confused woman crashed into one of the stone walls and slumped to the ground in an unconscious pile.

"Mae!" Asterel cried, trying to pry the shackles off the weak girl. The shackles didn't budge. Ginger strode over to the unconscious Victoria and found the key, throwing it to Asterel. Within seconds, Mae had been freed.

"Asterel, you're here! You came for me!" Mae said weakly, tears falling from her eyes. "I knew you'd come!"

"It's all right. It will all be okay now," Asterel said soothingly, hugging the princess tightly. Mae was around the same age as Thistle, and she reminded Asterel so much of him.

"Is Thistle with you?" Mae asked hopefully, wiping away her tears painfully as she touched the bruise on her face.

"No, dear," Asterel replied, her heart aching. They had found Mae, but Thistle was still missing.

"I think we can find him," Ginger growled, picking up the now-conscious Victoria and throwing her into the strong shackles. Victoria's nose bled profusely, trickling down her lips and onto her chin.

"Time to get some information," Ginger said, grinning wickedly.

*****

The sun was setting as Daniella and the others reached a bridge spanning across the lake. They had been walking alongside the lake for a few hours, and they had finally found something that seemed almost relevant.

"I think it's safest if we cross the bridge," Daniella said aloud. "Seeing as the dead can't cross water…"

"But there's a bridge!" Autumn protested wearily. "We can't burn down every bridge we come across!"

"We can set up some strong wards," Daniella replied. "The dead usually don't like to cross any form of water. They'll be discouraged as it is, and we're safer across water than on the land here."

"Daniella's right," Ivy agreed. "With our combined powers, we should be able to cast a powerful enough ward to protect us until the morning. We should sleep and travel again at daybreak."

Without another argument, the keepers and the fairy queen crossed the bridge. It seemed to take them forever, and they realized how exhausted they really were. They had not had anything to eat for a few days, and they were starving.

"We'll see if we can find something to eat tomorrow," Ivy said wearily as they trudged along the long wooden bridge.

After what seemed like an eternity, they reached the other side of the bridge. Ivy, with great effort, produced her wand and waved it at the base of the bridge. A faded blue glow appeared, indicating that Ivy's Spell of Protection had taken hold.

"Touch the shield to empower it," Ivy said loudly to the others. They each touched it, changing it a different color with each power. Its final color was a cool blue-green, almost sparkling with the power it held. The shield spread to encase a small area around the keepers.

"We'll continue our journey in the morning," Ivy said, lying on the ground. The keepers mimicked her, Daniella and Adam snuggling close to each other. Tinuviel settled against a nearby tree, snoring almost immediately. Autumn, Tier, Tasha, and Michelle found selective spots and settled down for the night, heavy eyelids closing with relief, however temporary it may be.

*****

Helius had received no help from the Infernal Council, aside from the fact that he should alter his plans to avoid the certain doom and emptiness they had predicted. He snarled to himself as he arrived back at his castle in a blast of black fire.

"It doesn't make sense!" he shouted to the blackness of the night. Receiving no answer except silence, he grunted, throwing open the castle doors and storming inside. He waved his hand and lit the many candles lining his expansive great hall.

Things just kept adding to his fury. Five of his keepers now lay dead, none killed by Gavin Moonstone. Where had he gone wrong? Killing Gavin should have solved all of his problems, but it hadn't. The keepers were still functioning without the good emperor to aid them.

"How can this be?" Helius asked softly, entering his throne room and sitting upon his large onyx throne. He was tired. Perhaps he would consume a few souls to regain his strength.

Still, he felt continually empty, and dismissed the soul consumption idea for the moment. His first impulse was to hunt down Gavin's keepers and kill them. But the words of the Council rang through his head. If he continued with his current plan, he would be destroyed. The time would come for the keepers' punishment. It just wasn't yet. Helius would be patient.

Perhaps he would take a nap. Sleep would clear his head and allow for a change of plans. He would be victorious. He could not lose to some filthy keepers. He would ensure victory. Standing and stretching, Helius headed for his bedchamber.

*****

A dark figure glided toward Daniella, reaching out its hands for her. She tried to run, but her legs wouldn't move. As the figure closed in on her, she realized who it was. Helius, dark and menacing, was reaching for her, pulling her into his horrid grasp.

She tried to scream, but no sound came out of her mouth. She couldn't run, couldn't call for help. The hands reached out farther, clutching her throat to strangle her.

Daniella jolted awake with a gasp, having broken out in a cold sweat. Adam's arms were wrapped around her. He still slept. She had not caused him to stir.

She lay still for a few minutes, allowing her heart to slow and her breathing to become normal once more. Helius was not here, trying to strangle her. It had been just a bad dream.

Daniella snuggled closer to the sleeping Adam, taking comfort in his warmth. Slowly, her eyelids started to grow heavy. She was about to fully close her eyes when something moved, jolting her completely awake. There was something hiding in the bushes, just outside the protective shield. Something indistinguishable. Daniella shook Adam, causing him to snort and slowly open his eyes.

"What's wrong?" he asked sleepily.

"Something's watching us," Daniella whispered. She hadn't realized that her voice had come out as more of a squeak.

"What?" Adam asked, sitting upright, now fully awake.

"I don't know," Daniella said, crawling across the ground and shaking Tier.

"No, Ma, go away," Tier mumbled grumpily, turning over and starting to snore. Had it not been such a serious situation, Daniella would have laughed at her friend. Sadly, it was not. A slap from her woke Tier instantly.

"Tier, give us light," Daniella said quickly.

"What? Why?" Tier asked, yawning.

"Something's watching us," Daniella replied, cutting short Tier's yawn. Tier nodded immediately and clapped her hands, causing a bright glowing orb to appear.

"Come out, whoever or whatever you are," Daniella's voice boomed, causing the others to wake. From behind the shrub, a figure slowly appeared.

*****

Cinder hid behind a large shrub, watching the sleeping people. He dared not come any closer when he smelled the reek of protective white magic. Whoever the newcomers were, they stank of power. There had not been normal humans on Chaos for an eternity. And no human had been to Lost Isle for eons.

Cinder was a shadow, but not just an ordinary one. He had once been a great sorcerer, knowledgeable and powerful. A struggle for the position of Keeper of Shadows had broken out between Matthew Hexus, the true keeper, and himself. Cinder had felt Hexus was unsuitable, and decided to challenge him.

A bad mistake. Hexus had killed Cinder in the battle, enslaving him and banishing him to the inner reaches of the Shadow Realm. Cinder had clung to the outside, however, gathering power to one day come back and take revenge upon

Hexus. Now that he had clawed his way out, he was ready to fight again.

Perhaps these newcomers could help him. They felt extremely good. He had never actually encountered true pure magic, but he had studied it much. Perhaps he could help them, in return for their assistance.

He shifted in his dark, cloud-like form, realizing immediately that this had been a mistake. The bush rustled, alerting one of the humans who had been asleep minutes before. She aroused the man sleeping next to her, then stood and woke another woman.

A bright light appeared, followed by a voice that shouted, "Come out, whoever or whatever you are!"

Knowing he had been discovered, Cinder shuffled out of the shadows, his shadowy hands held up in a defensive, surrendering position. He stepped forward, remaining aware of the shield that now glowed not five feet in front of him.

"Who, or what, are you?" the woman called, coming closer to see Cinder better in the light of the shield. There was no question about what he was…a shadow being.

Fearing she might destroy him at any second, he spoke, his hollow voice sounding almost like an amplified whisper. "I am Cinder the shadow being, Mistress."

The woman seemed taken aback by his politeness. "A shadow being?"

"I was once a great sorcerer," Cinder explained, carefully observing the woman. She was quite beautiful, now that he was able to see her clearly. She also held a great deal of power.

"What is your purpose here?" the woman commanded, snapping Cinder out of his small daze.

"I have a score to settle with a man named Matthew Hexus," Cinder replied, studying the formidable woman once again. "He is the Keeper of Shadows under Helius Rue."

"Matthew Hexus…" the woman replied, thinking over the name. "Why are you looking for him?"

"I said, I have a score to settle," Cinder repeated. "He killed and bound me in a power struggle over that title and banished me to the Shadow Realm. He must pay."

"I see," the woman replied. "Why were you watching us?"

"I thought you might be able to help me," Cinder said weakly.

"Help you? But you're evil!" the woman cried.

"I can be trusted!" Cinder retorted angrily. "Upon my word, I will not harm you or your friends!"

"Why should we help you?" the man asked, walking over to the woman and standing next to her.

"Because I am sure I can help you in return," Cinder replied.

"How?" the woman asked.

"Let me in and I will show you," Cinder answered.

"Don't do it, Daniella," the man said to her.

"I am quite insulted," Cinder broke in irritably. "I offer my help and my word of honor, and I still cannot be trusted?"

"Come in, Cinder," Daniella muttered, stepping backward. Cinder cautiously stepped up to the shield and walked through with ease.

"Thank you," he said. "Now, why are you here?"

"We come from a planet called Terra-Quenlist," Daniella explained. "Our planet was destroyed by Helius Rue, and our people are being held here on Chaos."

"So you seek them?" Cinder asked, more to himself than to anyone else.

"Can you help?" Daniella asked.

"Why, of course!" Cinder replied. "Back when I was a sorcerer, there used to be humans on this world. Most were captured and held either at Hell's Gate or the Castle of Souls."

"They were?" Daniella asked. Cinder mentally smiled. She was already getting excited. "Do you know how to get there?"

"Absolutely," Cinder replied.

"We have a map that we found," Daniella said, unfolding the large sheet that she had tucked in her pocket. "If you could point them both out, we'd be grateful."

Cinder pointed out the two locations with ease. Daniella hastily marked them, scribbling down their names. "Now it is your turn to help me," Cinder said. "We must travel to Shadow Keep."

"What's that?" Daniella asked. Cinder sighed, pointing out a small building on the map.

"It is where Hexus lives. It is also a gateway to the Shadow Realm. A hydra guarded the door…"

"A hydra?" said another woman, walking over to Cinder. "I saw a hydra."

"Who are you?" Cinder asked questioningly.

"Michelle," the woman replied.

"And you say that you have seen a hydra?" Cinder asked.

"Yes," Michelle replied. "The hydra was near this odd door with chains. A dark hand came out of the door when it was opened and grabbed the hydra. We shut the door and ran."

"The gateway to the Shadow Realm," Cinder whispered. "Was Hexus there?"

"No one was there," Michelle replied, "save for my friends."

"Hexus must be at the Hall of Spirits, then," Cinder mumbled thoughtfully, pointing out the building so Daniella could mark it.

"Wait a minute," Daniella said, confused. "We crossed the bridge over the Helio River, and we never saw a building on the other side."

"Hexus must have cloaked it," Cinder said thoughtfully. "Which means that he is there right now. We must go!"

"Very well," Daniella said wearily. "But we must visit every dwelling we can along the way, just in case some people are being held captive."

*****

"Good horsy," Regina said happily, patting one of the Chimera's heads. It growled, sounding almost like a purr. The eyes of all the heads closed, enjoying the attention from the Keeper of Confusion.

They had reached Fearsome Keep. Though it was dark outside, Regina could tell. The keep seemed to absorb the darkness and hide from the light. Home sweet home.

"Ugh! You're actually PETTING that thing?" Burgundy said, completely repulsed.

"It's my pretty pet," Regina replied. "I think I'll call it Buttercup."

"And I thought I was nuts," Burgundy mumbled, scratching his head as he stepped away. "Maybe you should be the Keeper of Insanity."

"Make yourself useful and open the door, silly twit," Regina said between coos to the Chimera.

Burgundy, neither smiling nor giggling, grumbled and pulled open the doors. Regina grinned and led the Chimera through, disappearing into the darkness. Burgundy sighed and followed, closing the doors behind them.

*****

"Well, isn't this convenient?" Ginger said sourly, glaring at Victoria. The woman's nose had stopped bleeding, drying now on her fair face. Victoria blinked, feeling nauseous and completely confused.

"Who are you?" Asterel asked forcefully.

"I'll say nothing!" Victoria burbled, trying to speak despite the dried blood plastered to her face.

"Fine," Ginger replied. "MJ?"

"A spell of truth I cast on thee. Deceit and all confusion flee," MJ said quickly, making motions with her hands. Victoria went rigid for a moment, then stilled.

"Same question," Asterel said, staring at Victoria.

"My name is Victoria Bloodmoon, the Keeper of Despair," Victoria answered mechanically. Though she answered automatically, Asterel could see her internally fighting MJ's spell. She would have to be quick with her questioning.

"Where is Thistle?" Asterel commanded.

"If you refer to the boy who was with the princess, he is being held at Nightmare Keep," Victoria replied.

"What is Helius planning to do to the people he has captured?" Ginger asked forcefully.

"He is planning a massive soul extraction," Victoria responded. "He will take all the souls and use them as he needs them. He will keep them…Ah…"

The spell broke, and Victoria was free. She glared at Asterel. Ginger thought she saw Victoria's eyes flash. Instantly, Ginger realized Victoria had done something when Asterel turned and started choking her.

"For Helius, you will die!" Asterel's mouth moved, but the voice wasn't her own. It was Victoria's.

"Help…me…" Ginger rasped weakly as she tumbled to the floor with the possessed Asterel. MJ and Cody jumped forward, trying to pull Asterel off the suffocating Ginger. Aurora, however, jumped forward and slapped Victoria across the face, breaking the magical stare she was using to keep Asterel in her hold.

"MJ…" Ginger choked. "Bind Victoria's powers."

Quick as a flash, MJ's fingers flew and words flowed from her mouth, saturated with power. Victoria had not the reaction time to recover from the slap and mutter a counter-spell. The binding spell hit her with full force, breaking the chains and slamming her against a wall. She sobbed in pain, fury, and total humiliation, crawling on all fours out the door of the keep.

"Let her go," Ginger said as Cody started after her. "She can no longer use her powers. She won't be back."

"At least we know where Thistle is!" Mae replied cheerfully, trying to lighten the mood.

"But we don't know where exactly Nightmare Keep is," Asterel commented, biting her bottom lip nervously. "Worse yet, we now know what Helius is planning to do to the prisoners."

"We have to find them," Serenity whispered.

"It's time for a new plan," Ginger announced.

*****

Cinder had guided them safely to the other end of Lost Isle, fending off the few creatures that dared try to attack. Light had just started to appear as they crossed the bridge, leaving the island. It was a small comfort.

"Won't the light kill you?" Daniella asked.

"No," Cinder replied. "I have become powerful enough to stay safely in the light."

"Oh," Daniella mumbled, falling silent as she followed behind the shadow being. He did seem to be trustworthy, but she would still be on guard. He was helping them, so he was to be trusted…for the moment, at least.

After what seemed like hours of walking in the weak light, the group finally stopped for a rest. "How much farther until we reach any type of building?" Tier asked sullenly.

"If I remember correctly, we are very near to a keep," Cinder replied absentmindedly.

"Well, what do you know?" Tinuviel grunted, pointing. "He's right."

A few miles away stood a dark tower. It seemed the light did not touch there. No longer was the grass a pale shade of green, but a disturbing brown. Cracked and windblown, the weathered grass swayed gently in the soft, chilly wind.

"What is this place?" Daniella asked finally as they reached the grounds around the tower.

"Unless its name has changed, it is called Fearsome Keep," Cinder replied. "Terrible place. Home of Regina Zeal, Keeper of Confusion. Or, at least she was before I was banished."

"Should we go in?" Michelle asked quietly.

"We don't have a choice," Daniella replied grimly. "Even though the sunlight is weak, it still gives us some advantage."

"Very true," Cinder agreed. "That is, depending on what is inside. If there are shadow creatures, you will have an advantage. If not, I doubt the light will be of any aid."

"Do you know what's in there, Cinder?" Autumn asked.

"It is hard to tell," the shadow replied. "Normally, I would guess there were no shadow beings in there. But it has been a long time since my exile."

"We have to take a chance," Daniella said. "It's possible that there are prisoners being held here, right Cinder?"

"Perhaps," he replied thoughtfully. "There is only one definite way to find out."

"I'm ready to go in," Tinuviel growled, cracking her knuckles.

"I don't have a choice, do I?" Tier said glumly, nodding in approval.

"I'll help where I can," Ivy said quietly, readying her wand.

"I am probably not of much use in a fight, but I shall assist," Cinder said to Daniella, smiling slightly.

"Thank you," Daniella said to the shadow being. Turning to the others, she nodded and said, "Are we ready?"

Solemn nods confirmed her question. She took a deep gulp of air, her heart beginning to pound. Part of her mind continually asked why she was putting herself and her friends in danger. Another part replied by justifying that she had to know whether or not some prisoners were being held within the walls. Whoever or whatever resided behind the walls, she was certain she could face anything—especially with the help of her friends. After all, they had beaten death, or more accurately, the Keeper of Death.

Hands trembling slightly, partly from anxiety and partly from fear, Daniella pulled on the heavy doors, surprised at how easily they opened. A rush of cold air made her shiver but did not deter her from opening the doors widely. Cautiously, she stepped inside.

What an odd place Fearsome Keep was. It seemed a complete blur inside, as rooms continually shifted and changed.

Every time she tried to concentrate on one specific spot, it was impossible. The rooms were changing too quickly. The only room that did not change was the room she stood in.

A loud, blood-curdling noise made her look to the other side of the room. The rooms ceased their spinning as she looked hard. And now she realized why. A woman, undoubtedly Regina Zeal, stood next to a growling, three-headed beast. A strange, wild-looking man stood next to her smiling, though not out of happiness. More out of insane giddiness.

"My, what an unexpected surprise," Regina said sourly, her eyes narrowing.

"You forgot unpleasant," the man chimed in.

"Silence, Burgundy!" Regina spat sharply. She patted one of the beast's heads and grinned.

"I must admit, you have surprised me. You're more powerful than you look."

"Yeah? Well, I work out," Daniella replied, snorting.

"I see," Regina replied curtly, sniffing. "Nevertheless, I'm to dispose of all of you. Prepare to die."

The room became charged in the very essence of air particles. Regina's hair stood straight out, catching static out of the air. Her eyes were glowing with electricity, as were her hands. She pointed them at the good keepers.

"Counter-spell, now!" Cinder shouted at Daniella.

"But I don't..." Daniella started. Her words were cut off by the roar of electricity whizzing through the air...straight at them.

"Avans carnes!" Cinder shouted, but not quickly enough. His counter-spell only shielded Daniella, Adam, Ivy, and Tinuviel. Tasha, Autumn, Tier, and Michelle fell to the ground in a confused heap.

"Well, that was fun," Burgundy giggled, helping the confused Regina to her feet. A slap in the face knocked sense back into her.

"So it didn't affect all of you," she said blandly. "How inconvenient. But no matter. My Chimera shall dispose of the rest of you. And you, Cinder!" she cried.

"Traitor! Traitor to Helius!" Burgundy shouted, clasping his hands together. "You will pay! To the Chapel of Shadows, Regina! We'll contact Helius's astral form to give him the information he needs on the location of Moonstone's keepers!"

Burgundy reached into a small pouch attached to his side and pulled out a pinch of sparkling dust. He threw it to the floor in front of Regina and himself, and they disappeared in an explosion of black smoke.

"Kill them, my darling," said an incorporeal voice that was Regina.

The Chimera's heads growled with pleasure as the unreal creature advanced toward the terrified group. It would have a filling meal, indeed. So many people…who would it choose to devour first?

"Uh, Daniella?" Adam asked frantically.

"I know!" Daniella shouted fearfully.

"Hmm…a Chimera," Cinder said thoughtfully. "Tough creatures indeed. Well, you will just have to kill it."

"Oh, easy for you to say!" Daniella shrieked as the beast took another thundering step toward them.

"It is not that difficult if you know a little about them," Cinder chided. "Set it on fire and it will die."

"Autumn's a little preoccupied!" Daniella cried, pointing to the dazed woman who was busy chewing on her nails.

"Crack open a fissure in the earth and boil it in magma, then," Cinder snorted disapprovingly. "Really, I thought you were not that dull."

"Tinuviel, can you do it?" Daniella asked quickly. Without a word, Tinuviel raised her hands. The ground trembled and shook violently, unwilling to split. At last, it surrendered, shuddering and cracking around the beast.

The Chimera paused when it realized the ground it had been standing on was no longer there. With a roar of despair and anger, it plummeted down the crevice and into the waiting magma of the very deep underground.

"No time to wallow in triumph," Daniella said shortly, patting Tinuviel on the back. "We have to catch Regina and Burgundy before they contact Helius. If they do, it's all over."

"They will be at the Chapel of Shadows," Cinder cut in. "I shall take you there."

"Let's hurry," Daniella said. "And isn't there anything someone can do to snap the others out of their stupor?"

"I'll work on that," Ivy said shortly.

"I had forgotten about Burgundy Alabastor and his treasured Telepowder," Cinder grunted, floating over and picking up the bag that Burgundy had accidentally dropped. "We will use this."

*****

A flash of dark smoke, some coughing, and they had arrived. Regina and Burgundy were inside the Chapel of Shadows. Dark pews matched the black marble walls and death-oriented atmosphere perfectly.

"Curses!" Burgundy cried angrily. "I've dropped my Telepowder!"

"You idiot!" Regina hissed. "They'll use it and be here in a matter of seconds!"

"Mistress Regina and Master Burgundy," said a cold voice. "What brings you to the unholy Chapel of Shadows?"

"We need to use the power of the dark priests to talk to Helius, Lucas," Regina replied quickly, turning to face the dark priest.

Lucas lived up to his profile perfectly. The soulless black eyes, the pale face, the dark hair…they all suited him wonderfully, down to his black cloak and glossy black boots. Regina had always admired his authority, though his voice still gave her shivers.

"Of course, Mistress," he replied, motioning to the altar at the other end of the vast room. "The other priests will form a circle around the two of you and begin the summoning chant."

"There are good forces on their way here to thwart our plans," Regina added hastily. "See to it that they do not succeed."

"It shall be as you command," Lucas replied, bowing. Regina and Burgundy rushed to the altar, where a group of priests was starting to form a circle.

*****

Ivy had brought sense back to the others, doing exactly as Burgundy had done to Regina—giving each of them a slap across the face. With senses regained, Cinder used the Telepowder Burgundy had dropped. Whirling, spinning, the world around them had disappeared. They were everywhere and nowhere at the same time, hurtling through time and space. And in the same instant they had disappeared, they reappeared in completely different surroundings.

"Where…" Adam started to say. He was cut off as a staff flew through the air and hit him from behind. He collapsed in an unconscious stupor.

"Adam!" Daniella shrieked.

"Duck!" Tinuviel cried as the staff flew through the clearing smoke. Daniella ducked and rolled, covering her face. As the smoke cleared, the wielder became visible.

"A dark priest?" Ivy questioned.

"Lucas," Cinder rasped.

"Get out of the way!" Michelle cried as the staff was swung again. It was aimed at the defenseless Tasha.

"No!" Tasha cried, thrusting out her hands to protect herself. And Lucas froze in mid-motion.

"She froze him?" Cinder asked in disbelief.

"No time!" Tier cried, pointing. "Look!"

A circle of dark priests surrounded Burgundy and Regina. A field of dark magic created by the priests had encircled the two keepers. Within a few seconds, Regina and Burgundy would be in contact with Helius.

"Too late…" Cinder whispered.

"Cover yourselves!" Tier cried frantically as she began to glow. Then she shouted, "Give me light!"

Tinuviel and Tasha covered Cinder as Tier's pillar of light appeared once more. It shattered the barrier, throwing the dark priests in all directions and stopping Regina and Burgundy's summoning spell. "No!" Regina shrieked, jumping to her feet and grabbing a nearby sword. She ran at the keepers, swinging wildly in blinded fury and shrieking like a crazed animal.

"Tasha, freeze her!" Ivy cried. Tasha thrust out her hands as she had done before and Regina stopped, motionless.

"Quite clever," Cinder said with approval. "I never doubted you."

"Right," Tinuviel growled. "What do we do?"

"Bind them, of course," Cinder replied. "Without their powers, they cannot directly link themselves to Helius."

"None of us knows how to perform a binding spell!" Daniella protested from her spot next to Adam.

"But Lucas does," Cinder answered, motioning to the dark priest, who was still inanimate.

"We'll get it, then," Tinuviel said. She grabbed Lucas by the throat, causing Tasha's spell to break. He, however, could no longer attack, much less breathe.

"Bind the powers of those two, now!" Tinuviel commanded.

"Never…" Lucas choked out.

"Bind them, or I'll feed you to the shadow," Tinuviel said fiercely, motioning to Cinder.

"Yum," Cinder said, a malicious smile creeping across his face.

"No! Not him!" Lucas cried, recognizing the shadow now as Cinder. "I can't! Helius will kill me!"

"And we'll kill you if you don't," Tinuviel replied flatly. She dropped the now-sobbing priest, and he executed a series of symbols that encircled Regina and Burgundy. They unfroze, falling to the ground and crying out in pain.

"My powers…" Regina croaked.

"Are bound," Ivy said forcefully, causing the blonde-haired woman to shrink back in actual terror. "We're finished here." And with that final statement, Ivy turned back to the others. "Let's go."

*****

CHAPTER XXIX: THE HALL OF SPIRITS

HEXUS PACED BACK AND FORTH. THEY HAD TO BE arriving soon. He had felt a great disturbance. Regina and Burgundy, as well as Victoria, had been defeated. He could feel their restrained powers, as he was magically connected to them all. And he did not like it. The powers of the whole were ebbing rapidly, and this caused him great uneasiness.

There weren't many left who were powerful enough to stand up against Moonstone's keepers. Excluding him, only Torizar, Bracchus, and Maximus were standing against the forces of good that were growing impossibly strong. If his comrades were beaten…

Hexus chuckled nervously. Helius could surely defeat the keepers if his minions failed. If worse came to worst and all the evil keepers were beaten, Helius could defeat the good threat with ease. *Which he probably should have done from the start*, Hexus thought. *What an idiotic twit.*

As always, Fate had a plan. Hexus would just have to be patient. When the keepers eventually came to him, he would be ready. He would kill them and enslave them, making them shadow beings, mindless and waiting to be controlled. He laughed as the cloaking shield around the Hall of Spirits vanished. Soon…

*****

"Ha…can we not be here?" Autumn squeaked nervously. The stories Cinder had told before they had teleported to their current location made her shudder. Midnight Village, in Cinder's time, had been home to a colony of vampires led by Linus, oldest of them all.

She had studied vampires back home on Terra. The books about them used to terrify her. Their vivid depictions turned her stomach. Now, she was truly sick at the reality of the existence of vampires.

"Let's check quickly and leave," Autumn added nervously.

"I agree wholeheartedly," Michelle chimed in.

"Hush," Cinder said as he led the way to the large manor at the other end of the town. Not waiting for someone to allow them entry, Cinder muttered a spell, blowing the doors inward.

"Linus!" he bellowed, lunging inside with Daniella and the others in close pursuit.

"You need only to have knocked," said a lofty voice. Standing at the top of a staircase was a handsome man who was undoubtedly Linus. He had long, jet-black hair and dark eyes, matching his youthful face and red lips. He wore a red velvet shirt with a sort of black cloak over it.

"Are you harboring prisoners of Terra-Quenlist?" Cinder asked.

"Why is it of your concern?" Linus asked curiously, slowly descending.

"These good people behind me are looking for them," Cinder explained forcefully.

"Alas, I was not allowed," Linus said as he stepped off the staircase. "Helius has other plans for them." Ivy felt a pull as she suddenly glided toward the vampire elder. "You, however, I can have."

"Touch her and you die," Tinuviel growled, her fingers curling around a bottle of holy water in her pocket.

"Just a taste," Linus said softly, brushing his lips against Ivy's neck. Before anyone could make a move, Tinuviel threw the bottle of holy water. It hit Linus in the face and he yelled, pushing Ivy away and clutching his face.

"I warned you," Tinuviel growled, reaching for another bottle.

"Cursed woman!" Linus screamed, his face red and blistered. "Look what you've done to me!"

"I suggest we leave now," Cinder said calmly. "We know what we came to find out."

"Never!" Linus screamed, lunging at Tinuviel. She jumped out of the way as a war erupted. Bottles of holy water soared through the air at Linus, most finding their target. Linus cried out in pain and frustration, trying in vain to cover his face.

Vampires began to emerge from everywhere to help their defenseless leader. "Let's go, now!" Daniella shouted to Cinder. "Next closest place?"

"Nightmare Keep!" Cinder shouted.

"No choice. Hurry!" Daniella cried as the vampires swarmed upon them, Linus's bellowing voice drowning out all other noise.

*****

"Ginger," MJ said slowly. "Was that building there before?" She was pointing to the north at a large building that had, indeed, not been there earlier.

"No," Ginger replied shortly. "Which means it was cloaked. And whoever cloaked it's waitin' for us. Of that, I've no doubt."

"So, do we go?" Aurora asked.

"I don't believe that we have any other choice," Asterel said.

"Let's think about this," Serenity said quickly. "Is this really the best idea? If someone was powerful enough to hide an entire building from us, should we really go and face them?"

"We owe it to the prisoners," Ginger said. "They're dependin' on us."

*****

"Away, spawns of light!" Bracchus cried, throwing a chair at Daniella. She ducked as the chair soared over her head and crashed into the wall.

"Where's Mae?" Ivy shouted, ducking as another chair flew past. She swept her leg across the floor and knocked Bracchus off his feet. He crumpled to the floor, rolling away.

"Free Thistle!" Ivy shouted as she ran after Bracchus. The keeper, who had not expected such a sudden assault, yelped as Ivy tackled him, grabbed him, and slammed him against the floor.

"Where…is…my…daughter?" she cried, slamming him into the floor with each word.

"Really, this is getting us nowhere," Cinder snorted. "I helped you find a prisoner. Now you have to help me. Let us now go to the Hall of Spirits."

"I bind thee!" Ivy cried triumphantly, pointing her wand at the gasping Bracchus. The evil man wordlessly skidded across the floor and stayed where he stopped.

"Thistle, dear!" Ivy cried, hugging him tightly.

"I think Mae's in trouble," he said quickly. "We have to go."

"Right," Daniella said. "Cinder?"

"Here is the last of the Telepowder," he replied, throwing the mixture to the floor. "To the Hall of Spirits."

*****

Victoria ran for the safety of anything. Her nose was bleeding once again, and she couldn't seem to quell the flow. Her mind was spinning. She couldn't manage to focus on anything. She didn't even know where she was.

Those stupid keepers, she thought, sobbing in frustration. She had been so close to killing the princess, and they had saved the brat—and defeated Victoria in the process.

The realization came like a slap in the face. How could she begin to explain this to Helius? Her powers were bound, and the prisoner had escaped. Against her, at least, Moonstone's keepers had prevailed. She had failed, miserably and utterly failed.

Tears of frustration streamed down her face to join the blood as she ran. She had been disgraced. And it suddenly occurred to her that she could not return to Helius. She had failed, and now would be cast out forever. She could go nowhere. Stopping in mid-sprint, Victoria collapsed from total exhaustion. It was all over.

*****

"So, d'we go?" Cody asked impatiently. "I'm gettin' even more freaked out just standin' here while we talk."

"We're still undecided," Ginger said at last. "I say that we gotta go. Whoever's there undoubtedly knows where we are. They're probably expectin' us."

"Which is why we shouldn't go," Serenity insisted. "What if it's Helius, waiting for us so he can kill us?"

"We'll have to kill him first," Ginger replied.

"But without the others, we can't beat him!" Serenity practically screamed.

"We have to take a chance," Asterel said quietly. "We've already taken a few chances and managed. One more can't hurt."

"Besides," Aurora added, "we can't be sure that it's Helius. And if it is, we will fight to protect the people."

Aurora suddenly felt a strange twinge in her stomach, something she had never quite felt before. It felt as if someone had just forced her to swallow a small bolt of lightning, but she didn't have time to dwell on the feeling; it disappeared almost as immediately as it had begun.

"Is something the matter?" Asterel asked.

"I'm not sure," Aurora replied, shaking her head slowly and brushing her hair aside. "I don't think it's anything."

"Okay everyone, it's time for a vote," Ginger said loudly, forcing all eyes to look to her. "Are we goin', or're we stayin'?"

"Let's go," Mae said decidedly.

"For the people," Aurora added.

"It is what we do, after all," MJ said.

"Yee haw!" Cody whooped anxiously.

"I'm outvoted, aren't I?" Serenity asked miserably. "Fine, I'm game."

"When do we leave?" Asterel asked.

"Right now," Ginger declared.

*****

Torizar yawned with boredom. It was useless to sit here all by himself. After all, wouldn't it be better to gather the keepers to fight all of Moonstone's allies? He suddenly laughed to himself when he realizing how paranoid he was being.

Or was he correct? He just couldn't ignore that nagging little voice in his head. It kept telling him to run and hide, that Moonstone's keepers were more powerful than anyone could ever have imagined, and that his doom was practically knocking at his front door.

"Ridiculous," Torizar grunted as he sat down. "I have great power. They can't win." He frowned as the insistent and nagging little voice told him that the good keepers most likely would.

*****

"Cinder, we have to find Mae!" Ivy protested angrily as the group appeared in front of the Hall of Spirits.

"If she is indeed being held at the Keep of Liars, there is nothing to fear," Cinder replied coolly. "I am quite sure that she is safe for the moment. Besides, the keep is not very far from here. It is due south."

"But…" Ivy started.

"I will take you there after we destroy Hexus," Cinder said firmly. "We must attack now, while his guard is down!"

"How do you know his guard is down?" Daniella asked.

"Come on," Cinder growled, ignoring the question and turning to the doors. With a magic that had been previously hidden, he blew open the doors in a cloud of fire, jumping inside. The others followed.

"So you have finally come," boomed a voice throughout the large chamber. Tall, elegant windows lined two of the four expansive walls, letting in the weak light. A large table was centered at the heart of the room, large chairs seeming to hold it in place. At the farthest chair sat a man with silver hair and dark eyes—a man who was none other than Matthew Hexus.

"Hexus," Cinder hissed, slinking forward, his red eyes glowing fiercely.

"The worm," Hexus replied, standing and shifting the weight of a large book into the crook of his right arm. "I thought I banished you for all eternity to the far reaches of the Shadow Realm. Apparently, eternity was far too short."

"I came back," Cinder retorted. "You, however, will not."

"Are you threatening me?" Hexus asked, his voice icy.

"You beat me the last time, but not this time!" Cinder cried. "I have waited a long time for this moment! I shall not be denied my revenge!"

"Out of my way!" Hexus shouted. "I have some meddlesome keepers to deal with, and they are much more powerful than a grub like you!"

"No! This is my fight!" Cinder cried angrily. His eyes glowed, and a fireball erupted at Hexus. The keeper calmly waved his hand, dispelling the flame.

"A fireball?" he asked quizzically. "After all this time, that is the best you could come up with? You are an even weaker entity now than when you were alive."

Cinder screamed with fury, and a fiery sword appeared in one hand. He raised it to swing at Hexus, who didn't seem the least bit surprised. As Cinder brought the sword down, an icy sword appeared in the outstretched hand of Hexus, blocking the shadow's deadly attack.

"You almost caught me there," Hexus said, smiling wryly. "Almost."

A flick of the wrist, and Hexus's sword was thrust through the shadow. Cinder screamed in pain, unable to escape the power of Hexus's magical sword. He wriggled in vain, causing Hexus to laugh cruelly.

"Again, I win," Hexus laughed triumphantly. "And this time, I will not make the same mistake. I banish you into the sword."

Cinder burst into flames, shrieking and trying to escape the biting grip of the icy sword that began to draw him in. He turned to Daniella, shouting, "Hear me! The light dispels the shadow! Use it!"

In a wave of heat, Cinder the shadow being was no more, banished into the icy metal of the sword. He was destroyed, permanently this time. His words still hung in the air, absorbed all too well by Daniella and the others. Smiling, Hexus looked at the sword, which disappeared.

"Now that I have taken care of that little nuisance, it is time to deal with all of you," Hexus said, grinning.

"Where are the prisoners?" Daniella asked forcefully.

"Safe, for the moment," Hexus replied. "They are being held at Hell's Gate and the Castle of Souls. The gate is not very far from here, actually."

"What does Helius want with them?" Ivy questioned.

"Dear me, you don't know?" Hexus said with mock surprise. "Helius is planning a massive soul extraction. He is probably transporting all the prisoners to his castle as we speak. You see, Helius can only survive by consuming human souls. Such is the price for his awesome power."

"You're disgusting," Ivy spat.

"Do you think I care?" Hexus asked. "In a very short time, nothing will matter." He grinned. "And I am happy to say that I will be the last thing you see before you die."

"That's it!" Tinuviel shouted angrily. "Shut up, will you? Tasha, freeze this jabbering idiot!"

Tasha did so, and Hexus paused, but only for a moment. He quickly shook off the spell. "Foolish girl!" he spat, laughing hysterically as Tasha shrank back in utter terror. "I am Matthew

Hexus, Keeper of Shadows! My powers are beyond incredible! I am matter! I am space! I AM ALL!"

A loud boom resonated through the hall, and Tasha was sent flying across the room into one of the chairs. The chair exploded in a shower of splinters, scattering through the air and across the floor. Hexus sent another spell whizzing past. Adam held out his hand and deflected the magic, sending it spinning wildly away. He was more surprised by this reaction than Hexus, who growled angrily and continued throwing spells at the remaining conscious keepers.

A bolt of lightning leapt at Daniella, who screamed. Ivy jumped in front of her, receiving the blow instead. She was hurtled through the air, only to collide with the nearest window. It smashed as she continued through it, tumbling to the ground outside to lie motionless.

Daniella rushed at Hexus, jumping and kicking. She stopped in mid-air, held motionless by yet another spell. Try as she might, Daniella could not budge an inch.

"Impudent moron!" Hexus hissed through clenched teeth, flicking his wrist and spinning Daniella away. She fell beside Ivy outside the window, now unconscious as well.

"I have beaten you!" Hexus cried wildly, grabbing Adam and throwing him aside. He opened his large book to its desired page, licking his lips and feeling the power that not even Helius could tap into—the power of total and complete darkness. "I've done what not even Helius could do! And now, I will send you all to the Nether Realm!"

Shadows from apparently everywhere rushed at Tier and Tinuviel, holding them firmly in place. Laughing with glee, Hexus began chanting. Tinuviel clutched her throat, looking at Tier, who was doing the same. They were choking. Tinuviel couldn't breathe. Something was choking her, draining her life force. Though she had never before experienced it, Tinuviel knew she was dying.

She heard a familiar voice yell, but she couldn't turn her head. It was over. She was dead for sure. As her eyes started to blur, she saw something odd.

Hexus was lifted from the ground and thrown aside, dropping his book in the process and halting the spell. Tinuviel and Tier gasped as the spell ceased and the shadows retreated. The book slid across the floor into Tinuviel's grasp. Turning, she searched to see who her savior was.

*****

Ginger and the others had almost reached the strange fortress when they heard the shattering of glass. A woman, none other than Ivy Snowfall, smashed through one of the large windows and hit the ground, staying where she landed. "Mother!" Mae cried, running forward. A few seconds later, Daniella was thrown through the same window, landing next to Ivy.

"Mae, tend to them!" Asterel cried. "The rest of you, get inside!"

"Go!" Ginger shouted. The keepers charged inside, MJ leading the way. They saw all the other keepers unconscious, save for Tier and Tinuviel, who were being held captive by a group of what appeared to be shadows. A silver-haired man holding a large book was chanting. He was psychically strangling their two friends!

"Serenity!" MJ cried. "Hit him!"

Realizing all too well what MJ meant, Serenity waved her arm, sending Hexus flying. He dropped his book, halting the spell and causing the shadows to retreat. The book lay unattended where it had been dropped.

"Slide the book to Tinuviel, quickly!" MJ cried. Serenity did as she was told. The book slid into Tinuviel's outstretched hands, safely away from Hexus. Tinuviel turned around, smiling with relief when she recognized MJ and Serenity. Grabbing Tier and dragging her, Tinuviel crawled across the floor to them.

"Take the book," she wheezed, handing it to MJ.

"There's an inscription," MJ said aloud, looking at the book's inside cover. "It says, 'Nothing but might can quell the flow of darkness from mine pages own.'"

"Might? Oh, light!" Tier cried suddenly. "Light dispels darkness! That's it!"

"Oops," MJ said. "It is light, not might. My mistake."

"Give me that book!" Hexus screamed, jumping to his feet with fury and a rush of uncontrollable power.

"Blast him, Tier," MJ said. "And don't miss."

Tier stood and turned to the advancing Hexus, glowing. He froze in mid-walk, suddenly deciding that going the other way was a much more favorable option. But too late. The pillar of light hit him before he could duck, filtering right through his body. He screamed in horror as he suddenly started to shrink, to melt into a puddle of unrecognizable goo.

"How…could this be?" he gurgled, disappearing into a small pool on the floor. In a blast of black fire and smoke, Matthew Hexus was no more.

*****

CHAPTER XXX: HELL'S GATE

HELIUS JOLTED AWAKE WITH PAIN. HEXUS WAS DEAD; he had felt it. But all too late. There was nothing that could be done. Hexus, his trusted second-in-command, was no more.

Helius's eyes burned red with fury. He screamed, tossing a few fireballs out his window and igniting the tall dry grasslands below. The fire spread quickly, surrounding the Castle of Souls in a matter of minutes.

"Get through the fire, keepers," he hissed, "and I'll be waiting."

*****

As Hexus had said, the harpies had begun their mass transportation of the prisoners from Hell's Gate to the Castle of Souls. Only Jasmine, Maximus, and Penelope were to stay at Hell's Gate.

"Well, this is exciting!" Jasmine said with giddiness.

"I suppose," Maximus grunted.

"Think of it this way," Jasmine said. "It's one less thing for us to worry over."

"I love the way you talk," Maximus replied, grinning and kissing her briefly. "And," he added, "it makes it harder for Moonstone's keepers to rescue them."

"Once the souls are extracted, Helius will have enough life force to live forever," Jasmine said, an almost depressing tone in her voice. "But Moonstone's keepers will have no motivation, no cause, after the deaths of all the prisoners."

"Quite right," Maximus agreed. "And I'm sure that they'll see the harpies in the sky. And when they do…"

"They'll come to us," Jasmine finished. "And we'll rid ourselves of them for good."

*****

The keepers had now been restored and revitalized at their reunion, along with the help of Mae's powerful curative magic. Not only had Mae helped, but a large flask of pure magical water from the goddess Tara had aided in revitalizing them. Mae and Thistle were now huddled together in what looked like a constant embrace. Mae's eyes were closed with relief as Thistle held her and gently stroked her hair.

"I believe, Ivy dearest, that we have a lot to look forward to in the future," Asterel whispered, indicating the prince and princess.

"I do believe you are right," Ivy replied softly, smiling. An elf and a fairy together…a magical union indeed.

By this time, the groups had exchanged information from previous explorations and plights. From Cinder the shadow being to Omicron the necromancer, they explained everything to each other. And once again, they were all together and stronger than ever.

"I'm quite interested in those writings you mentioned," MJ said to Daniella. "Do you mind if I have a look?"

Confused at first, Daniella remained silent. But when she realized what MJ meant, she said, "Go ahead."

MJ touched Daniella's forehead and tapped into her mind, searching for the information she needed. Finding it at last and seeing the runes as if they were as clear as day, MJ began to translate.

"They read, 'In the beginning were light and dark. Light created the gifted Thirteen, as did dark. For in the future, the Thirteen of both sides were to battle. Each had a special power. On the side of good, these powers included: love, dreams, wisdom, peace, life, truth, hope, justice, the five basic elements, faith, light, and two for the…'"

"Why did you stop?" Daniella questioned.

"The prophecy stops where you stopped reading," MJ explained, opening her eyes and dropping her hand back into her lap. "Unless whoever wrote it never got the chance to finish. I wonder…"

"What does it all mean?" Tier, who had been quietly listening, asked.

"It means," MJ said, "that we were destined to be here to fight against the evil Thirteen. What I'm curious about is the fact that only eleven of the thirteen powers of good were mentioned. What are the other two?"

"And who are they associated with?" Daniella asked.

"One of the unknown powers must belong to Aurora," Ginger, who had also been listening, said. "The thirteenth was…"

"Gavin's power," Aurora finished, sitting down next to the others. "It must have been. My father used to have a book. It talked of a 'Universal Power,' an ability of great magnitude that tied all magic together. It was often referred to as 'The All.'"

"So, what is your power?" Ginger asked.

"I really don't know," Aurora replied. "The All had two parts, feminine and masculine, but they could only be used by a god and goddess. I suppose those two elements make up the missing two parts of the Thirteen."

"Well, Gavin was a god," Ginger said solemnly.

"And he would have represented the masculine part of The All," Aurora replied. "As for me, I couldn't represent the feminine entity. I'm no goddess. Gavin must have made a mistake. I have no power."

"You sound as if you're mad at him," Daniella commented.

"I am!" Aurora shouted suddenly, surprising the group as tears started to fall. "All my life, I dreamed of meeting him and marrying him. I had seen him when I was younger, and I was immediately in love with him. I hate him for dying! I hate him for going away before I could tell him how I really felt!"

By this time, everyone was silent, intent on Aurora's sudden outburst. "Aurora…" Ginger said.

"And I hate myself for not telling him before he died!" She was sobbing now, tears streaming down her face. "I…"

"Aurora," Ginger said, hugging her tightly. "It'll all be okay. I miss him too." Tears fell silently from Ginger's eyes as she hugged Aurora, surprising herself at the sudden burst of maternal instinct and hidden emotion.

She let the sniffling Aurora go and looked her straight in the eyes. "No one could've prevented what happened. It wasn't your fault. But it's all the more reason to make Helius pay for what he's done. And we can still prevent that from happenin' to others."

"You're right," Aurora said, wiping her eyes with her sleeve. "He is going to pay. If he comes near anyone or hurts any of you, I'll kill him myself."

She felt the twinge in her stomach once again, and the room suddenly disappeared. All she could see was darkness, but she could hear a voice speaking. It was Gavin, reciting a spell. And she remembered the spell. MJ had recited it for everyone much earlier, before they had split. Though she had been speaking it quickly to imprint it in everyone's minds, Aurora had remembered it quite well. It called upon something named Oblivion. Whatever it was, she had the strange feeling that it was somehow important, the key to freedom. And…

"Aurora!" She felt herself being shaken by someone, and she slowly opened her eyes.

"What happened?" Aurora asked.

"You tell us!" Ginger answered, releasing the girl's shoulders. "One minute you were fine, and the next minute, ya fainted!"

"I heard Gavin's voice, Ginger," Aurora said. "He was reciting the spell to summon Oblivion."

"Are you sure you're all right?" MJ asked with worry.

"I'm fine!" Aurora insisted, almost angrily. "I know what I heard!"

"Okay, we b'lieve you," Ginger said soothingly, smiling. They ended the conversation with that. But Aurora could tell that Ginger and the others were concerned about her; she could see the smallest hints of worry etched into their facial features.

"So now what d'we do?" Cody asked anxiously.

"Locate Hell's Gate," Ginger said decidedly. "If we're lucky, we'll be able t'catch the harpies 'fore they can take the prisoners to the Castle of Souls."

"Too late," Mae whispered, pointing out the window. Dark clouds carrying distinguishably human figures littered the sky, all headed to the north. They were too late; the harpies had begun their journey.

"We might still be able to stop some of them!" MJ cried. She picked up Hexus's book and shoved it into Gavin's black bag, then reached back inside and pulled out a wand.

"Gavin's wand?" Ginger asked with confusion.

"I think it might be able to enchant the carpets once again," MJ quickly explained. "They're our only hope of reaching Hell's Gate in time, if we're already not too late. Rodaine never had the chance to enchant them. Someone has to try. Everyone at the Crystal Palace seemed quite drained."

She waved the wand and shouted, "Carpets of Terra! To us!"

In a whirlwind came the carpets, restored and renewed. Though she never quite figured out how they had gotten into Gavin's bag, MJ was grateful. They hovered in a great line, waiting for their commands.

"Everyone on!" MJ shouted, thrusting the wand back in the bag and snapping it shut. She climbed onto a carpet, and the others followed.

"Take us to Hell's Gate!" she shouted, shrugging. She wasn't even sure if the carpets knew where Hell's Gate was.

Apparently, however, they did, for they shot out of the Hall of Spirits toward the south.

*****

Bracchus ran until he could run no more, both furious and terrified at the same time. How had things gone so wrong? Nothing mattered now, except finding someone he recognized. It seemed, however, that time was running out.

Bracchus fell to the ground, gasping for air. Powerless, he could do nothing but lie where he had fallen. Closing his eyes, he waited for the heavy veil of darkness to envelop him.

*****

Regina and Burgundy ran, hoping that they could somehow find Victoria. They had managed to travel all the way to Rueful Vista, but now they were breathless and exhausted.

"Don't you have any more Telepowder?" Regina asked at last.

"Oh, right!" Burgundy giggled, producing a small vial from one of his many pockets. "I forgot about my secret stash!"

"I hate you. I'd kill you right now if I could," Regina croaked wearily. "Use it to get us to Victoria."

"Yes, of course," Burgundy replied. Throwing the vial to the ground, they disappeared in a blast of thick smoke.

*****

Across the sky the carpets raced, staying lower to the ground in order to avoid the sharp talons of the harpies. Far in the distance, a small tower was visible. "That must be Hell's Gate!" Ginger cried over the rushing wind. "We'll land near the doors!"

Within several agonizing minutes, the keepers had touched down outside the large tower. Wasting no time, Serenity jumped off her carpet and blasted the doors open. She smiled inwardly at how impressively her powers had developed over the course of such a short amount of time.

*****

Torizar jumped to his feet as the front doors of the Keep of Eternal Darkness exploded inward. Without warning, the keepers of Gavin Moonstone rushed in. All of them.

"Where are the prisoners?" an Amazon-like woman shouted at him.

"Prisoners?" he asked, stepping backward. Clearly, he was greatly outnumbered. "Surely, I know not what you mean."

"He's one of Helius's keepers," the Amazon woman announced. "He should be bound as well before he can do any damage."

Torizar knew he had run out of options. He had been caught off guard and would pay for his arrogance and stupidity later. His fingers curled around the small vial Maximus had given to him as a war gift many years ago. It had the power to teleport him wherever he desired. For now, anywhere was better than here.

"Those who fight and run away live to fight another day," Torizar hissed, throwing the vial on the floor. It smashed, and he disappeared in a flash of yellow, the glow of his green eyes still reverberating through the room.

*****

"What the…" Serenity started.

"Forget it!" Ginger cried. "We went to the wrong place! We must not've gone far enough south!"

"If we'd been paying attention, we would have known to follow the trail of the harpies!" MJ said angrily.

"There's still time!" Ginger shouted. "C'mon!"

*****

"The last of the harpies have gone, Mistress," Penelope confirmed as she closed the front doors of the small palace.

"Excellent, Penelope," Jasmine cooed. "Bolt the doors to bar entry."

"Yes, Mistress," Penelope replied, sliding the heavy metal bars in place. She twisted them until they clicked, then she exited to leave Maximus and Jasmine to themselves.

"Well…" Maximus started, stopping immediately as the room flashed. As the flash subsided, Torizar stood in front of them.

"They're coming!" he cried in despair. "All of Moonstone's keepers are on their way here to rescue the prisoners!"

"What do we do?" Jasmine asked. "Surely, they can't be that powerful."

"The three of us stand more of a chance together than apart," Torizar said. "Maximus, I will be your loyal friend always. I hope you know that."

The keepers shook hands, and Maximus drew his sword. Torizar and Jasmine turned to face the bolted doors, readying themselves. "Cosmo," Maximus said to his trusty sword, "do me proud."

*****

A large palace loomed before the keepers as they touched down. It seemed to blot out the sky, darkening both the air and the sunlight that managed to filter through thick clouds surrounding the palace.

"Is this Hell's Gate?" Tasha asked.

"Dark, menacing, and evil…yep," MJ replied. "It looks like we're too late."

"Never!" Ginger argued. "We'll rip this place apart until we find the prisoners!" She ran to the enormous front doors and pounded on them, trying to smash them open.

"Help right now would be kinda nice!" she yelled. Serenity ran over and tried to help. She psychically pounded at the doors, wanting to help the desperate Ginger.

Daniella's mind began wandering. She suddenly turned around and was staring at three unfamiliar people, who in turn stared at her in surprise. Turning the other way, Daniella reached forward and pulled out the bolts that held the front doors in place, dropping them to the floor.

And she was back outside. Back out in the cool air, nowhere near the front doors of Hell's Gate, much less inside. She blinked with confusion until she heard the crash of the now-open doors. And it all became clear. She had astral projected to the other side of the locked doors, unbolting them. Then she had returned to her physical body.

"They're open! It's rescue time!" Ginger shrieked, whooping and rushing inside. MJ followed her quickly, as well as Serenity and Daniella. The others were not far behind.

"Release the prisoners or be destroyed!" MJ cried as they entered the great foyer of Hell's Gate.

"You're too late!" Jasmine cackled, standing between Maximus and Torizar on the other side of the room. "You fools are too late! My harpies have transported all the prisoners to the Castle of Souls! You have failed! How does it feel?"

"I've been better," Serenity replied sourly, waving her hand. Jasmine somersaulted backward, catching her balance and hovering in the air.

"That's an interesting power you have, witch!" Jasmine cried, pulling out the diamond dagger from one of the many folds in her gown. "But you won't get a second chance to use it!"

The war between good and evil had spilled into the desolate foyer of Hell's Gate. Jasmine sprinted through the air at Serenity, readying her dagger. Maximus charged, Torizar closely behind.

"Away!" Serenity shouted, waving her arm. Jasmine halted temporarily, but Maximus and Torizar continued their offensive.

"Stop!" Tasha cried, throwing out her hands. Torizar froze, struggling to move. After a couple seconds, he was free of the spell.

"Ginger, they're too strong!" Tasha cried.

"Nonsense! Try harder!" Ginger replied hastily. "The prisoners're countin' on ya!"

Daniella closed her eyes, concentrating. She projected herself behind Torizar and stuck out her foot, tripping him. She quickly returned to her physical self, watching as Torizar fell face-first onto the stone floor. "Yes," she whispered triumphantly.

Tinuviel held out her hand, feeling for cracks in the floor. She found one and pulled at it with her earth power, causing it to spread. The crack multiplied and scattered across the floor, becoming larger.

"We can't be doing that!" Jasmine cried. She flung the dagger at Tinuviel, finding her mark. The diamond blade sank itself into Tinuviel's stomach, knocking her over. She lay still, her breath becoming ragged. MJ dove toward the fallen Tinuviel, quickly forming a healing spell. She sent the gold energy through herself and into Tinuviel's wound as the dagger was removed.

By this time, Maximus had reached Daniella. "Die, witch!" he cried, swinging his sword. From behind Daniella, a different sword was swung. It blocked Maximus's fatal blow. Daniella ducked out of the way as Ginger stepped in.

"Mind if I play?" she asked with mock innocence, grinning devilishly at the Keeper of War.

"Not at all," Maximus growled. He and Ginger fought, sparks flying as they parried across the floor. Adam and Autumn were fighting Torizar in hand-to-hand combat.

Autumn was sent sprawling when Torizar gave her a well-placed kick in the chest. Adam leapt high into the air with inhuman force and kicked back, knocking Torizar all the way across the room.

Torizar jumped to his feet, his green eyes glowing. "Let injustice take you!" he hissed at Adam. A green aura surrounded the good keeper, and he turned from the helpless Autumn to Michelle, who was standing still in shock.

"H…Help!" she cried as he ran toward her, his hands outstretched. He fell just before he reached her; Aurora had stepped in and hit him from behind with Gavin's bag.

"Sorry, Adam!" she cried, grabbing Michelle and dragging her away.

"I'll fix you!" Autumn cried to Torizar as she sat up. He looked at her quizzically, laughing.

"You? What can you do?"

Autumn grinned at the mistake of the keeper. "Lots," she replied, throwing the fireball she had conjured. It struck Torizar and sent him crashing through the door on the other side of the room.

Meanwhile, Jasmine and Serenity were battling. Jasmine threw herself at Serenity, clawing at the girl. Her long fingernails left scratches across the keeper's neck, but Serenity continued to fight with her telekinesis. It seemed the two had reached a stalemate.

Ginger and Maximus swung their swords at each other, both relentless in their fight. The other keepers watched intensely, waiting to see where they could help. Cody saw an opportunity.

He created an illusion, making a duplicate of himself. Both the duplicate and the real Cody charged at Maximus, interrupting him. He swung his sword and hit the duplicate, causing it to disappear. The real Cody rushed past, snatching Maximus's sword away from him.

The evil keeper swept out his foot and caught Cody, tripping him. Cody bounced across the floor, still clutching the sword tightly. Maximus walked up to him.

"Give me the sword, and I might not kill you," he commanded.

"Tinuviel!" MJ cried. "Crack the foundation! Bring down Hell's Gate!"

"But…" Tinuviel started.

"It's the only way!" MJ shouted. The floor started to heave, splitting and exploding as Tinuviel's magic touched it. Some places sank in as the large pillars around the foyer began to crumble.

"What the…" Maximus said, turning around. He lost his balance and fell backward—right onto the sword Cody still held…his own sword.

"Ugh?" Maximus grunted, falling on his side and immediately ceasing his assault. He made no more noise.

"Maximus!" Jasmine yelled, ignoring Serenity now and rushing to her fallen lover. Cody crawled away as more cracks appeared in the floor.

"What have you done?" Jasmine shouted in fury, pulling the sword out of the keeper's stomach and holding him close to her.

"Time to go!" Tinuviel shouted hurriedly. "The place is coming down!"

"Autumn!" MJ cried. "Use the spell Rodaine gave to you!"

Autumn nodded, the words flowing out of her automatically. "Return us now from whence we came, for we all now have much to gain. Distort space and cause no pain, return us now across the plane!"

In a bright flash of light, the keepers disappeared, leaving Jasmine and her lover alone in the crumbling palace. Jasmine sobbed in pain and anger, clutching the limp form of Maximus tightly as the room around them began to crumble. The horrible fountain of dancing demons shattered and toppled over, joining the quickly-piling rubble as Hell's Gate groaned in agony. Only one thought remained in Jasmine's mind as the room grew dark around them…they had failed.

*****

Hell's Gate collapsed, sending smoke and rubble high into the sky. Penelope, who was quite a safe distance away, giggled with delight. The keepers had done it! They had killed Maximus and Jasmine!

The pleasure overtook her. She would be queen now for sure! How delightful! Her time to shine had come at last! Though Hell's Gate was gone, she could find another palace—or construct one. And wasn't that destruction, the sealing of Jasmine's fate, just absolutely splendid? Dancing down the dirt road, Penelope thought of what she would do first as the new queen of the harpies.

*****

CHAPTER XXXI: FINAL BASTION

REUNITED ONCE MORE, THE KEEPERS APPEARED AT the gates of the Crystal Palace. Standing quietly for a moment, they absorbed what had just happened. After a couple minutes, Asterel clapped Ginger on the shoulder.

"That was a wonderful display of leadership, my dear!" she said to Ginger. "All of you were excellent!"

"I don't understand how you got that sword!" MJ said.

"It came outta Gavin's bag," Ginger replied, pointing to the bag Aurora was holding. "It was the only thing I could think of—the sword, I mean—when I reached in the bag."

"I see," MJ said, raising her eyebrows in approval. "So it seems that we've fought our way to the top. That leaves only Helius and the prisoners to deal with, I think."

"We'll go into the castle and prepare," Ivy said. "Whether we like it or not, the final battle approaches."

"I know," Ginger said, sighing. "And I hope we'll be ready."

*****

Regina and Burgundy had found Victoria. She had collapsed in the middle of nowhere, falling in a bloody mess. Her nose had stopped bleeding, but the blood had dried in her hair, ruining her complexion. And she was unconscious.

"Wake up!" Burgundy cried, kneeling next to her and shaking her lightly. "Regina, what do we do?"

"We have to get her cleaned up and get back to the Castle of Souls," Regina decided. "It will probably be easier to clean her up once we get to the castle's protection. From the way things are progressing, Helius may need us anyway."

Picking up Victoria, Regina and Burgundy looked at each other. He pulled out the second and final vial he'd stored in his pocket and threw it. Regina was too tired to even comment on his utter stupidity. In one last and great explosion, the surviving evil keepers teleported to the safety of the Castle of Souls.

*****

"They have all been defeated, you say?" Rodaine asked.

"Yes, Rodaine," Ivy answered. "Helius seems to be the only remaining threat."

"What's more," Asterel added, "we've located the prisoners."

"Where are they?" Rodaine asked.

"That's the problem," Ivy replied. "They're being held at Helius's castle. We have to find a way to rescue them and defeat Helius."

"We'll see what we can do," Rodaine answered, turning to the throne and pulling out a large spell book from beneath the cushion.

"Which reminds me!" MJ said when she saw the book Rodaine had produced. She opened Gavin's bag and pulled out the large book Hexus had dropped.

"Don't open that!" Ginger cried.

"Why?" MJ inquired.

"Because that book almost killed Tier and Tinuviel!" Ginger responded. "Let's keep whatever's in there right where it is."

"I didn't think of that," MJ said sheepishly, putting the book back in the bag.

"I think I have some spells that might help you," Rodaine interrupted.

"And we still haven't used the power of Leviathan," Tasha added. "Torrent's gift can still come in handy."

"The council told us to use it well," Ginger replied in agreement. "I guess we just didn't need it yet."

"Besides, it might be useful against Helius," Tinuviel interjected.

"In any case, I have some useful things," Rodaine continued, slightly annoyed.

"What've you got for us?" Ginger asked.

"Protection spells, mostly," Rodaine answered, "to protect you from physical and magical harm. I also have a few to enhance the projection of your powers."

"Cast away," Ginger announced.

*****

Veronica and Aster had failed. Just as they were running toward the palace gates and their freedom, the dreaded harpies had appeared, prisoners clutched tightly in their talons. In a wisp of air, the escaping prisoners were carried back to the dungeon, along with the new prisoners.

"Let me go!" Veronica shrieked as she was thrown back into a cell. She turned around to shout at the harpy that had thrown her in—only to have her breath freeze in her throat. Staring back at her was the face of darkness, of evil…Helius Rue.

"Well, isn't this quaint?" he asked mockingly.

"Let me go or I'll…" Veronica started threateningly.

"Or you'll what? Kill me?" Helius roared with cruel laughter. "You're pitiful! I'd almost feel bad killing you if I didn't know your soul would be so essential. You waste my time."

Laughing again, Helius turned away from the captive commander and walked back up the stairs. His cruel laughter rang through Veronica's head. It was too much to bear. She broke down crying, unable to sustain her warrior-like composure for any longer as despair crushed down upon her like an icy fist.

*****

"We have been observing the landscape since your last visit," Rodaine explained to the party. "Our magic can't extend to the very center of the terrain. A large desert and some mountains seem to enclose something, but our magic is not able to ascertain what lies beyond."

"It has to be the Castle of Souls," Ginger said flatly. "It's the only thing I can think of that'd have enough power coursin' through it t'block other magic."

"Then that's where we have to go," MJ said, looking at Ginger. "There's no time to waste. If we're quick enough, we should be able to rescue the prisoners before Helius has a chance to do anything to them."

"Are we ready?" Ginger asked at last, breaking the small silence. "This's it, everyone. The final battle approaches."

*****

CHAPTER XXXII: THE CASTLE OF SOULS

REGINA AND BURGUNDY STUMBLED INTO THE THRONE room, still trying to support the unconscious Victoria. They had tied her matted hair back in order to clean her face. Now, they looked to Helius for guidance.

"What in the name of unholy thunder…" Helius bellowed as they approached.

"Moonstone's keepers," Regina said shortly. "We were all defeated. We tried to contact you, but those idiotic keepers stopped us!"

"Fools!" Helius spat. "You've probably led them right to me!"

"N…n…no, Helius," Regina replied, trembling. "We used some of Burgundy's Telepowder!"

"You have failed me for the final time, you insolent, pathetic, no good, useless MORONS!" Helius cried, overturning a chair as he advanced toward the frightened keepers. "Clean up Victoria and get back down to the throne room immediately!" With a slight whimper and a nod of affirmation, Regina turned to Burgundy. He nodded fiercely, and the three exited, leaving Helius alone.

"All my keepers, defeated," Helius whispered. "How can this be?" He told himself that perhaps some had escaped alive.

After all, Regina, Burgundy, and Victoria had escaped barely unscathed.

"We shall see," Helius said darkly, sitting back in his throne. "In a few hours, the prisoners will be ready for my grandest plan. With the mass extraction, I will live forever and have power enough to conquer the galaxy!"

*****

Bracchus awoke, blinking with confusion. He thought he was dead at first, but then he chuckled stupidly. How could he be dead if he was looking around?

He stood up slowly, wincing at the pains from his sore muscles and aching bones. Success had no longer become one of Bracchus's top priorities. Right now, he felt the need to sleep.

Finding a nice patch of particularly brown grass, Bracchus curled up contently. He had failed, plain and simple. He'd eventually be dealt with, and Helius's wrath seemed unfavorable to think of at the moment, so sleep seemed to be his most favorable option. He closed his eyes, his thoughts fading to black.

*****

Once more, the wind whipped past as the keepers and the royals flew through the air on the eager carpets. Ginger let her thoughts wander. It had seemed such a long time ago that she'd first flown on a carpet. But, of course, it had only been a matter of many days. She wasn't even sure how many days had passed. Her thoughts drifted to Gavin. She remembered his smile, his laugh. He had always been so happy, up until…

She shook her head, refusing to let the horrifying memory of the emperor's death interfere. This spurred her out of her daydreaming state and back to the task at hand. Helius would pay dearly for what he'd done. Terra, the people, Gavin…she would avenge them all.

"Look, Ginger!" MJ cried. "Look below!" The unchanged, desolate landscape had given way to a large desert, which seemed to stretch forever. A sudden cold wave passed over the party.

"We can't beat him," Serenity said with despair.

"What?" Michelle asked.

"We'll lose for sure," Cody commented.

"What are you talking about?" Michelle cried.

"He'll kill us," Daniella agreed. "Just like he killed Gavin."

"What is the matter with all of you?" Michelle gasped.

"We're crossing the Desert of Despair," Tinuviel answered, holding up the map she had taken from the babbling Daniella. "That must be what's affecting them."

"It must not affect me because of Faith," Michelle said. "But why doesn't it affect you?"

"Because despair can never beat hope," Tinuviel answered simply. "Haven't you ever heard the story of Pandora and her box? The dreaded box held all the troubles of the world. Pandora was told never to open it. Curiosity overcame her one day, and she opened the box, releasing the world's troubles. Knowing her fatal mistake and trying to undo it, she slammed the box, trying to stop the troubles from escaping. And her action was not in vain. One trouble at the back of the box still remained locked inside for all eternity."

"Despair," Michelle breathed.

"Yes," Tinuviel replied. "As long as despair still remains imprisoned, hope can prevail."

The speech of Tinuviel seeped with white magic. Her words drove the despair away and brought the others back to their senses. They looked around, breathing sighs of relief.

"Despair's an awful thing," MJ commented angrily.

"We're fine for the moment," Tinuviel replied. "But we have to be cautious. Who knows what else lies ahead?"

*****

"Find the Crone and bring her to me!" Helius bellowed to one of the little gremlins cowering in front of him. "I want her here now, or YOU will be the main dish for my supper!"

The small creature shrieked in terror, running away to do Helius's bidding. Helius grinned cruelly. Underlings were so easy to torture. It was almost as fun as torturing a human. Almost.

The Crone appeared a few minutes later, shuffling in with a sort of limp. She was an awful creature, only slightly resembling an old woman. Her face had been permanently contorted into a horrid grin, her beady eyes and stringy gray hair furthering her hideousness. A limp and a deformity on her twisted back made her walk slowly and with a cane. She smiled at Helius with rotting teeth, wrinkles etching her decrepit face.

"Master Rue," she rasped. "Strange of you to summon me. Why have you?"

"I've run out of options," Helius replied icily. "The Infernal Council has helped me naught. You see the present and the future. Show them to me."

The Crone cackled wildly. "You banished me to the depths of this castle for my unwillingness to see the future! Or have you forgotten? My Sight was clouded, as you told me before! Is it still, or has it suddenly cleared?"

"Shut up!" Helius shrieked angrily.

The Crone laughed triumphantly. "Then give me my freedom!"

"Very well! You are free!" Helius shouted impatiently. "Now tell me my future!"

The Crone's eyes clouded over with a fine film. She stood motionless, apparently looking at something much farther away than Helius. Her eyelids shut, and she stood completely lifeless.

"What do you see?" Helius asked quietly.

"I see the good keepers of Gavin Moonstone," the Crone answered mechanically. "Across the landscape they race, eager to battle you and avenge the fallen and their dead world. They are powerful, and they are protected by something incorporeal; something elusive and strong."

"Where are they now, Crone?" Helius demanded.

"They have crossed the Desert of Despair unscathed," she replied. "And I fear the Mountains of Illusion will not stop them for very long."

"Now tell me the future. Tell me what you see," Helius ordered.

The Crone's eyes opened. "I see nothing," she said blankly. "Either you have no future, or something is blocking my Sight."

"Yet another who has failed me," Helius spat, cursing. "If you cannot show me the future, why do I still keep you around?"

He answered his own question, waving his hand at the Crone. She screamed, bursting into flames and disappearing. Her cane clattered to the floor as she vanished.

"I forgot," Helius said. "I no longer need a useless old Crone."

"Helius!" Regina called, emerging from the entrance to the throne room with Burgundy and Victoria, who was now cleaned up and conscious.

"We're ready to help!" Burgundy chimed in, giggling nervously.

"I no longer require your help," Helius snarled. "You are all useless fools! Get out of my sight!"

"But…" Victoria mumbled.

"Leave, now!" Helius screamed, shaking the foundation of the castle. "Useless, worthless idiots!"

The three keepers bowed and slowly vanished, leaving Helius alone. He obviously had a plan to put to action. Why else would he dismiss them?

Helius turned away as they vanished, fuming. Why had he entrusted his awesome abilities to a batch of useless imbeciles in the first place? A critical flaw in his grand design, he reasoned. Nevertheless, there was a big problem still at hand…Gavin's keepers.

They were on their way to the castle, most likely to rescue the prisoners of Terra-Quenlist. Surely, they could not plan to fight him? He had killed Gavin, demonstrating that he had the more powerful abilities. They couldn't possibly be stupid enough to face him.

Very well. If their intention was to face him, all for the better. With them out of the way, his grand plan could be put to action immediately and without interruption. He couldn't risk the mass extraction until the keepers were dealt with accordingly.

They must not be allowed to free the prisoners, much less enter the castle. He would wait in the entrance hall for them to arrive. It would all end there.

*****

The path was completely blocked, from earth to the endless sky. Mountains that stretched to infinity wound themselves together to completely block the view of the other side. "Now what?" Tier asked with exasperation.

"I can try to move them," Tinuviel suggested.

"Why not? Give it a shot," Ginger said encouragingly.

Tinuviel closed her eyes, trying to move the mountains. Any part of them would do. She opened her eyes and shook her head after a few seconds.

"Nothing's happening," she said. "I can't explain it. Normally, I'm able to feel every little pebble. But I feel nothing. It's like the mountains don't exist. I just can't explain it."

"What do you mean, there are no mountains? They're in our way!" Tasha commented.

"Unless there really is nothing there," MJ said. Everyone looked at her in confusion until she continued. "What if the mountains are just a mirage, put there to discourage us?"

"We have a way of finding out," Cody said quietly. "I can create illusions, so I s'pose I'm able to make them also disappear."

Quick as a flash, Cody executed the spell to dissipate an illusion. The mountains melted away, revealing a sea of flames. Beyond the flames stood the most terrifying structure the group had ever seen. It seemed that the Dark Master himself had built it.

Black towers with sharp apexes pierced the sky, seeming to challenge the heavens themselves. Odd stones and statues could faintly be seen jutting out of various spots. A small courtyard of stone led to the castle doors.

"It's the Castle of Souls…" Tasha murmured.

Mae pulled herself farther into Thistle's embrace. "I'm afraid," she whispered.

"So am I," he whispered back, clutching her tightly.

"All right, everyone," Ginger said, her voice wavering slightly. "We need a strategy."

CHAPTER XXXIII: THE THRONE ROOM AWAITS

"ONCE WE'RE INSIDE THE CASTLE, WE'LL HAVE TO split up," Ginger said apologetically. "One group has to distract Helius. The other has to find the prisoners and get them out as quickly as possible."

"A small group will be less noticeable," Asterel commented. "I suggest that Ivy, Mae, Thistle, and I find the prisoners and rescue them."

"An excellent idea," Ginger replied. "I 'spect Helius'll be waiting for us. My group'll charge in attacking, while your group sneaks in behind us. If Helius's waiting, he'll be too busy fighting us to notice you."

"Sounds like a plan," MJ said.

"I hope it works," Ginger said, voicing her concern, "because we're here."

*****

Helius stood just outside the throne room. He would be ready for them when they came. He clutched his Belladonna wand tightly, finding comfort in the dark magic that coursed through it.

The creatures of Chaos had failed. His keepers had failed. The Desert of Despair, Mountains of Illusion, fiery grasslands…all had failed. But Helius Rue, Emperor of Chaos, would not.

This would be a spectacle to end all spectacles, a war to end all wars. He held the power. He had the authority. And he would use both to exterminate the keepers forever.

*****

They could feel the heat of the flames on their backs as they landed in the courtyard of the Castle of Souls. Ginger realized that they needed to do something about the blazing fire in order to safely evacuate the prisoners.

"Autumn, do somethin' about the fire please," Ginger commented.

"No problem," Autumn replied. She turned around and pointed to the dark clouds, closing her eyes and mumbling something to herself. The menacing clouds overhead erupted in a rain burst, quelling the flames and completely eliminating the fire in a matter of minutes.

Taking a deep breath, Ginger said, "Here we go, everyone. Good luck to all of you. May the light protect us."

"Taran!" Ivy cried suddenly, breaking the solemn moment. In a way, Ginger was glad.

Ivy rushed to the statue that sat next to the steps, touching it in disbelief. Asterel followed her, putting a hand on her shoulder. Ivy did not respond.

"Ivy, dear," Asterel said, "we'll come for him later. Time has run out for the moment. We must focus or risk losing more lives than that of Taran."

Ivy nodded slowly, turning to join Mae and Thistle. She hugged them both and stood silently. Asterel smiled and kept her composure as best as she could, joining them as well.

"Does everyone know what t'do?" Ginger asked.

"I'll astral project myself to fight Helius," Daniella said.

"I'll conjure a shield to protect everyone," MJ replied.

"I'll throw fireballs," Autumn confirmed.

"And I'll hide," Aurora cut in miserably. "Give that jerk a couple extra smacks from me."

"With pleasure," Ginger said, cracking her knuckles. She nodded to the royals, then turned and walked up the steps to the front doors. "Serenity, will you do the honors?" she asked, grinning nervously.

"Of course," Serenity replied. With an earsplitting crack, the doors exploded in a sort of splinter rain, leaving only fragments of rusty hinges.

"Let's go!" Ginger yelled, giving a war whoop as she charged inside.

*****

Helius fired a disarming spell as soon as the entrance doors exploded. The Amazon woman, who had charged in first, took the full force of the blow, spinning aside and collapsing. Another woman with glasses ran in quickly, holding out her hand and chanting. A silvery shield encased her and the Amazon woman.

"Clever move, witch," Helius snarled, advancing. He was thrown backward when Serenity hurried in and waved her hand.

The rest of the keepers rushed in, executing their spells and chants. Fireballs flew through the dank air, and an astral form of Daniella was fist fighting with Helius.

A wave of his wand and Daniella was jolted back to her physical self. She gasped, causing Helius to laugh harshly. He easily deflected the spells thrown at him, countering by pounding at the protective shield. And his attacks were working.

MJ's hold on the shield finally gave out. She was thrown backward by the force of Helius's magic, landing on top of Ginger. The protection spell vanished, leaving the keepers unprotected.

"MJ," Ginger whispered. "Use the stone. Summon Leviathan." MJ reached into her pocket and produced the small stone, throwing it at Helius. It landed a few feet away, glowing.

"A rock?" Helius snorted, bursting into furious laughter. "This is your defense?"

He was silenced when the rock changed into a large serpent, snake-like and menacing. It hissed at Helius, low and guttural. Helius shrank back a little, clearly intimidated.

"So, you're able to summon Leviathan," he said, backing up. "Impressive." Leviathan sprang at Helius, smashing the both of them through several of the castle's walls. Only the tip of the serpent god's tail was visible.

"Asterel, now's your chance!" Ginger cried. "Go!"

Asterel and the other royals sprinted inside, looking for doors. They found a large wooden one in an opposite corner of the room. Running for it and hoping it would be the correct choice, the royals smashed it open and charged inside.

"Phase two of the plan!" Ginger shouted to the other keepers. "Get out! Stay at the edge of the desert until the prisoners arrive! Then take them across to the Crystal Palace!"

"Ginger, what about you?" Aurora asked, already knowing the terrible answer.

Ginger opened Gavin's black bag and withdrew a silver spear, smiling sadly. "Someone's gotta distract Helius," she replied solemnly, handing the bag to MJ. "Go!"

Each of the keepers, to Ginger's astonishment, either bowed or saluted. Then, in a great rush, they exited the castle. MJ executed one last symbol, throwing it to Ginger. The mark glowed, spreading across Ginger's body to protect her.

And the keepers were gone. Just in time, as a matter of fact. Leviathan was suddenly thrown back through the walls as Helius started his offensive. Finally, in a frenzied rage, Leviathan collapsed, melting back into the little blue gemstone, which Ginger promptly grabbed and stuffed into her pocket.

"Don't you see?" Helius shouted, emerging through one of the walls. "I am immortal!"

"And I'm someone who's about to prove ya wrong 'n grind your ugly face into the dust," Ginger spat, readying her spear. And they suddenly charged at each other, locking in a tight battle.

*****

CHAPTER XXXIV: WAR OF THE EMPERORS

IT SEEMED THAT LUCK WAS FINALLY IN THEIR FAVOR. The door Asterel had picked had led to the dungeons. But the prisoners would not be rescued without a fight. Helius was ugly and evil, but he was far from stupid. He had left the harpies—among others—as guards to ensure the hold on the prisoners.

Creatures upon creatures blocked the way, denying access to everyone but the horrible emperor himself. The royals, luckily, had been prepared. Asterel drew Luna, Mae and Thistle drew the swords they had received from MJ, and Ivy readied her wand. With newfound strength, they began fighting their way through the impossibly large hoard of demons.

*****

Regina, Burgundy, and Victoria watched from the shadows as Helius and Ginger fought. She was an excellent fighter, and they were actually enjoying watching the battle. Regina turned to her companions.

"Should we help him?" she asked.

"He said he didn't need our help," Victoria retorted angrily. "So…no."

"I'm having fun just watching," Burgundy giggled. "We'll help if he's in real trouble, but he's fine now on his own."

"Fine," said Regina, shrugging. "We'll just keep watching."

*****

Ginger and Helius were still fighting strongly, and it appeared that Ginger was winning. She had successfully dodged or deflected all of Helius's magic. Plus, she had been able to hit him a few times with the blunt end of her spear. Aurora would be pleased.

He was backing toward the open doors of the throne room now, still flinging spells at her. She deflected them quite easily and prepared to take another jab with her spear. But Helius had anticipated this.

His wand shuddered and changed into a sword, giving him the chance to block Ginger's attack. They had now carried the fight into Helius's throne room. Tables and chairs were carelessly thrown aside as the fight continued. The large pillars that lined the throne room supported only that particular room. It seemed as if the heart of the castle was a separate entity from its body, the rest of the stone structure.

Sparks flew when Helius's sword collided with one of the stone pillars. Ginger ducked and rolled out of the way, panting. She was starting to tire. And that, she thought, could be a fatal problem.

*****

Eden Starglass sat among the prisoners, thinking to herself. She had known that she would be captured, just as she had known that she would also be freed. She had been sitting, patiently waiting for the rescue she knew was to come. Now, as her moment of freedom drew near, was the time for action. There were a few things that she needed, and she knew exactly where to get them. They were in the black bag carried by MJ.

Eden smiled. She had always loved her gift in the Sight, because it had made her so happy. Now it had come in handy yet again. Closing her eyes and ignoring the clash of swords that signified freedom, Eden called for the items.

*****

MJ dropped the bag when it began to shudder. She backed away as it burst open, a carpet and a wand exploding from it. They sped away together, leaving her in a state of complete shock and awe.

"What was that?" Cody asked in surprise.

"I'm not sure," MJ replied slowly. "But I think it might be a good thing."

"I do hope Ginger's all right," Tasha said, her voice filled with worry and concern.

"I'm sure she's fine," Daniella said reassuringly. "She's a strong woman. If anyone can beat Helius, it's her."

"I thought there were only twenty carpets," Cody said with confusion.

"There are only twenty," MJ replied. "We have them."

"Then where did that one come from?" Cody asked, indicating the carpet that had burst from the bag and rocketed away.

"Good question," MJ answered.

*****

Asterel laughed triumphantly as she began to break the locks on the cell doors. Prisoners began to pour out in crowds, including Aster and Veronica.

"My Queen!" Veronica said to Asterel. "You're unharmed!"

"Yes," Asterel replied shortly. "We haven't much time. You must escape with the prisoners. Get out of the castle with them and find the keepers. They're waiting just on the edge of the desert to escort everyone to safety."

"But…" Veronica started.

"That is an order, commander!" Asterel said sharply. Veronica snapped to attention and saluted, grabbing Aster and disappearing in the crowd. Slowly, the prisoners began filtering out of the dungeon and upward to their freedom, Aster and Veronica leading the way.

"Asterel, Mae, Thistle!" Ivy called, firing another jet of snow from her wand. "Go! I'll hold the creatures off!"

Without argument, the other royals escaped with the prisoners, helping to lead them. Ivy, with one final blast of snow, followed. She stopped in the doorway leading to the dungeon steps, fixated on the battle between Helius and Ginger. It appeared Ginger was tiring quickly; she had to help, or Helius would kill the keeper.

Ivy slammed the door to the dungeon behind her, enchanting it to hold the remaining evil creatures inside. Charging into the throne room, Ivy prepared to blast Helius with an ice spell. She was surprised, however, when a renegade spell bounced off one of the pillars and hit her in the stomach. All she now knew was that she felt cold…very cold. She froze in place, struck by the same spell that had turned Taran to stone. She, too, now suffered his fate.

*****

The wand was caught by a shadowy figure, just outside the entrance doors. With a solitary tear from one of the eyes of the figure, Taran changed from a cold statue to his regular, animated self. He stammered, looking for words. But he had been frozen so long that he couldn't form any. The figure gripped his shoulder in reassurance.

At that moment, Asterel, Mae, and Thistle emerged with the prisoners. Asterel gasped with awe when she saw the normal-looking Taran, then began to weep uncontrollably when she looked to the other figure. A hurried gesture sent the prisoners, the royals, and the commanders on their way, including Taran, who ran beside Asterel.

The figure turned away from the group and started up the steps, slowly but surely. The small wand glowed, and the hand that held it tightened further. The figure knew exactly what must be done.

The carpet that had come with the wand twisted around Eden, who emerged in the entryway. She jumped onto it, waving at the approaching figure. "I will be watching, as always," she cautioned, flying past the figure and away. The figure continued its silent route into the Castle of Souls.

*****

"Who is that?" Regina asked in awe, pointing at the shadowy, obscured figure that stepped into the entrance hall.

Victoria bit her upper lip. "I'm not sure. But I think we may find out soon."

"I'm ready!" Burgundy laughed, clapping his hands. "Bring it on!"

"No," Victoria said, holding up a hand as a silent warning went off in her mind. "This is none of our business. It concerns Helius, not us."

*****

"You foolish little wench!" Helius roared as his sword shimmered back into a wand. He unleashed a beam of darkness at Ginger and knocked her to the floor. She had dropped her spear a while ago and was now huddled in terror, one corner of her lip bleeding. One of her eyes was swollen, and one arm was badly bruised.

"Did you really think you could beat me?" Helius screamed in rage, spittle flying from his mouth. "Six of my most powerful keepers are vanquished, and Hades knows where the others are!"

"All're destroyed or bound," Ginger said smugly through bruised lips, coughing and getting back to her feet. "Including your precious Maximus. He fell on his own sword."

Helius's face purpled, his eyes bulging unnaturally out of his head. "I'll kill you!" he shrieked, unleashing a red beam of light. Ginger countered it with magic of her own, dispelling it.

This, of course, further enraged Helius. He screamed with fury, causing the foundation of his throne room to shake. Ginger fell over from the tremor. It seemed that the tremor had sapped the last of her strength.

She looked over at Ivy, who was frozen in stone. The queen's look of utter surprise angered Ginger. Despite her physical ailments, she refused to allow her soul to give up. Standing once more, she readied herself.

"I see you were observing my newest statue," Helius said with amusement, motioning to Ivy. "Now, she joins your beloved Moonstone in death!"

He cackled, and Ginger was suddenly blinded by an uncontrollable fury. Helius had killed the queen, her friend. He had killed Gavin. He had killed Taran. He had destroyed her world and everything she held dear. Now, he would pay.

With a scream of rage, Ginger charged at Helius. He had not expected such a sudden outburst and had not the time to dodge before Ginger tackled him, knocking him to the floor and slamming her forehead into his face. He lost the grip on his wand, and it skidded across the stone floor, impacting with a pillar and snapping in half.

"NO!!!" Helius screamed, stretching out his arm to try to absorb the power that escaped from the wand. Determined to stop Helius from absorbing any magic, Ginger did the one thing she had always been the best at—she sank her sharp teeth into his arm and bit down as hard as she could.

Helius yowled in pain and fury, slapping her until she released his arm. She toppled backward and he rushed to his wand, but too late. The power was gone.

Every bit of his awesome power was gone. All that he had worked for to preserve was now gone. And it was all because of that snotty little wench.

His lips curled into a sneer when he noticed the spear lying next to one of the pillars. He lunged for it, bony fingers curling around it tightly. Ginger stood up, a large gash on her right leg. She took one glance at Helius and realized it was the end.

Helius threw the spear and Ginger closed her eyes, waiting. She hoped it would be quick. She thought of all her friends, Storm, and Gavin. Eden flashed through her mind as well, her weathered and smiling face still quite lucid.

The spear bounced off Ginger as candy bounces off gelatin. Ginger opened her eyes, wondering why the spear had not killed her. Helius appeared astounded as well.

She turned around and smiled with comforting disbelief, her heart warming to the bursting point. Gavin, alive and well, stood in the doorway, a hand raised. His hair was tussled and he had cuts on his face, but he seemed strong…and extremely angry.

"HOW?!" shouted Helius, backing against a pillar. "I killed you! I threw an avalanche of rocks on top of you!"

"Things are not always as they seem," Gavin said sourly, limping into the throne room. He noticed the statue of Ivy and limped over, leaning against it.

A solitary tear ran down one of his cheeks. He brushed it off and rubbed it on the statue. And, as a flower blooms, the stone of the statue crumbled away, revealing a perfectly normal Ivy. She stumbled away and grabbed Ginger, whispering a prayer to Gavin as they headed for the exit.

"Ivy!" Ginger said. "We need t'help!"

"Run, child!" she said sharply. "You will not want to be here now!"

They exited the throne room, slamming the heavy doors behind them. Helius shrank away from the advancing form of Gavin Moonstone. He was flat against the pillar now.

"Without keepers, without magic, without power," Gavin snarled, all hint of happiness gone from his voice as he raised his wand. "You have lost, Helius Rue."

"Gavin," Helius said, laughing nervously. "Would you really kill your own brother?"

"You will never again be my family!" Gavin shouted, wand shaking furiously in his grip.

"Well, if there's no convincing you…" Helius said. With lightning reflexes, he swept Gavin's feet out from under him and grabbed the wand.

"Now who holds the power?" Helius cackled crazily, pointing Gavin's wand at its owner. He stood up, his eyes bulging dangerously out of his head.

"Go ahead," Gavin said coldly. "I have nothing left to live for! The life I had can never be replaced! But if I'm to die today, I'll make sure I take you with me!"

He yelled, lunging at Helius. The evil man, taken aback by this sudden change, tried to stammer a spell. However, he was cut short when Gavin's strong fingers wrapped around his throat and choked off his air supply.

They rolled across the floor and stopped, Gavin banging Helius's head continually against the floor. Helius gurgled and finally managed to throw the enraged ruler off.

"I never thought you had it in you!" Helius rasped, jumping backward and exploding off the ground.

"I will kill you before I allow myself to die!" Gavin yelled, exploding from the ground in a cloud of yellow fire. Higher and higher they climbed, crashing through the domed ceiling of the already damaged throne room and rocketing into the darkness of the hazy black sky.

*****

CHAPTER XXXV: OBLIVION

GINGER WATCHED IN HORROR AS THE RULERS exploded through the roof of the castle's throne room, locked in battle. She whistled for her carpet, but Ivy stopped her. She spun around angrily to glare at Ivy.

"No, don't!" Ivy said sharply. "It will only lower Gavin's guard! You must not distract him!" Lightning cracked across the lifeless sky, sparking out of the wand the emperors were fighting over.

"Ginger!" Serenity cried over the lightning, running up to her. "What's going on?"

"Gavin and Helius are fighting!" Ginger replied, her lip beginning to bleed once again.

"Gavin's alive?" Tinuviel cried in disbelief, looking to the sky. "But we saw him get crushed by a rockslide!"

"He's alive…" Aurora breathed softly, hope in her rising once more, along with a feeling she could neither express nor control. Perhaps it was relief. "I believe in him completely."

Helius rocketed into Gavin, and the two smashed back through the castle roof like comets. Rubble and dust were blown in all directions, and a shock wave caused the keepers to stumble. None, however, fell.

"Gavin!" Ginger yelled, rushing back toward the castle. She ran to the open doorway and jumped through, dodging the flying debris.

"Ginger, wait!" Aurora cried. "Don't go in! Don't try to help him!"

Ginger, immediately followed by Aurora, burst through the doors just in time to see Helius point the wand at Gavin and fire a beam. Gavin turned and looked at them as the beam hit him. He smiled slightly and fell to his knees, his arms stretched to the sky. His figure stiffened and turned gray and cold.

"No!" Ginger yelled, rushing at Helius.

"Not this time, you little wench!" he cried, pointing the wand at her and firing the same beam. Ginger froze in her tracks, uncontrollable fury etched into her features. She became stone as well.

Ivy rushed in with the other keepers when she heard Ginger's cry. Asterel, Thistle, Mae, and Taran were still evacuating the hostages. Horrified when she saw the stone figures, Ivy unthinkingly sent the rest of the keepers after Helius.

One by one, they fell. Helius delighted in knocking them over with such ease. Tinuviel was last to fall, her eyes ablaze with revenge. The castle shook as she used her remaining energy to bring down the rest of the destroyed ceiling. It bounced away from Helius as it crashed to the ground.

"Your attempt failed, you idiot!" Helius cackled, suddenly gasping when Ivy jumped on his back and started choking him. He swung at her, slapping her in the face and knocking her off. She crumpled to the ground, standing no longer. She had been knocked unconscious by the powerful slap. Aurora was left standing alone, the only remaining keeper, forced to observe her fallen comrades and the man she loved, all gone.

"Aurora!" cried a voice from above. Aurora and Helius looked up to see Eden Starglass perched on a carpet.

"YOU!" Helius cried.

"Use your strength and call him! Call Oblivion!" Eden shouted, floating up and avoiding the beams Helius shot at her.

Aurora knew what she had to do. MJ had told her the entire incantation, and she remembered it like the back of her hand. It was time. All the pieces had come together. The twinge in her stomach, the vision…they were all connected to this incantation—to this very moment. She could feel it in the fiber of her very being.

"When night is day and day is night," she started.

"A silly incantation?" Helius cackled.

"Our powers we combine to fight," Aurora continued.

"You think it's going to help you?" Helius roared with laughter.

"The evil that has brought us down," Aurora continued, feeling stronger.

"Go ahead, then. Finish it," Helius chuckled.

"We summon you, Oblivion!" she finished. But nothing happened.

"Fool!" Helius laughed cruelly. "Only an emperor imbibed with the powers of the Thirteen can conjure Oblivion. Ha!"

"I am Aurora Lightly, daughter of Garth Lightly and the emperor's counsel," Aurora replied. "And I declare myself, in the absence of the royal emperor Gavin Moonstone, Empress of Terra-Quenlist."

"Wow! That was scary!" Helius said as Aurora fell to the ground. "What was that supposed to do? Bore me to death?"

"Shut up," Aurora gasped.

"You are truly the most pathetic creature I have ever encountered," Helius mused as Victoria, Burgundy, and Regina appeared. "A keeper who doesn't even have any powers. Pathetic, indeed."

The spell took full effect and sprang to life in front of everyone. Helius's laugh was cut short when a blinding white light split the sky, shooting downward and illuminating the throne room. "It cannot be!" Helius shrieked, trying to remain formidable when, in truth, he was terrified.

Seven angels floated down, the most beautiful sight Aurora had ever witnessed. The central angel was the most beautiful of all, with a gold-etched white robe. "I am Oblivion," he spoke, turning to Aurora. "All will be forgiven."

"No!" Helius yelled, pointing the wand at the angels. Oblivion waved his hand, and the wand exploded, scorching Helius's hand and causing him to scream.

"Helius Rue," Oblivion said, "your reign of evil is over. I have been summoned to destroy you."

Helius shrank back, screaming as Oblivion reached for him. The angel grabbed him and lifted him off the ground. "Help me!" Helius screamed in terror.

"Sorry, Helius," Victoria said, slinking backward and shaking her head.

"Yeah," Burgundy giggled nervously, backing away.

"We dare not, Helius," Regina squeaked, also backing away. "It's over. We're through."

Helius screamed louder as his traitorous keepers disappeared from the room and ran away like the cowards they were. Oblivion turned to Aurora again and said, "Look not to the outside for the solution. It lies within."

Oblivion shuddered, turning into a black hole of antimatter. Helius screeched, pulled in headfirst. The other angels followed and the hole closed, leaving the throne room silent. Oblivion and the angels had disappeared…and Helius was gone. Gone forever. Aurora rushed to Ivy, who stirred and sat up slowly.

"What happened?" Ivy asked.

"Helius is gone forever," Aurora said. "I used the incantation and summoned Oblivion. He wasn't evil at all. He was an angel. He swallowed Helius and disappeared. It's over. We've won."

All at once, the realization hit Aurora. The other keepers were dead, killed by Helius. Their broken bodies were strewn across the throne room. And Gavin was dead as well.

"Once again, we've arrived too late," Taran said sorrowfully as he stepped into the throne room with Mae, Asterel, and Thistle.

Aurora's eyes filled with tears, and she walked slowly over to the statue of Gavin, her fallen angel. She touched his stone-cold face and leaned close to it. "I love you," she whispered, her cheek brushing against his. A solitary tear landed on Gavin's cheek and stayed there. Aurora crumpled to the floor, sobbing. "Please come back to me."

Gavin's warm embrace shattered her sadness, brightening the room. He sat there on the floor with her, holding her and gently stroking her hair. She stared at him in disbelief.

"The tears of an emperor are quite powerful," Gavin said knowingly. "Or in this case, empress. And if it's any consolation, I love you too."

He held Aurora's face in his hands, staring right into her eyes. "Of all the powers I have utilized, love was never among them. I now see what the Oracle meant when she said my power was in my happiness. With love now opened, my power is complete. And you have proven—beyond a shadow of a doubt—that you were always meant to rule."

"What do you mean?" Aurora asked.

"Will you marry me and become Empress of Terra-Quenlist?" Gavin asked.

"I would, but Terra no longer exists," Aurora replied.

Gavin stood and took her hand. "With the power of The All now reunited, masculine and feminine, all can be remade." He started to glow, causing the other royals to step backward.

Aurora began to glow as well, and a large golden beam emanated from them, coursing upward into the sky. It seemed to flow into everything, into everyone. Life flowed back into all of the keepers, bringing them back to the world of the living.

The glow did not stop, though. It coursed through the atmosphere and into the stars. The pieces of the destroyed planet came together, and the planet of Terra-Quenlist sprang back to life, more beautiful than ever before. The buildings were back, and the Crystal Palace and all people and creatures alike were returned from whence they came. The spirit of the planet, in its lonely bottle, disappeared, flowing back into the physical mass of earth and sighing contentedly.

"That…was past amazing," Ginger breathed as she stepped over broken stone shards that had encased her moments before.

"Come," Gavin said to everyone, smiling and nodding as all in attendance bowed with respect and happiness. "There is still much work to do."

EPILOGUE

When the Dark Castle doth appear,
All of Terra has much to fear.
The Great Evil shall then come seeking his token,
And at last in ruin shall Terra be broken.
A ray of hope shines soft and bright,
To wash away the darkest night.
Though good's chances of victory are rare,
Love can pierce the dark despair.
When The Savior's part is done,
The broken shall at last be one.

-Phoenix, Firebird, and Pegasus

AURORA AND GAVIN WERE MARRIED IMMEDIATELY AT the Crystal Palace. All were in attendance. Rodaine conducted the ceremony, smiling with pride. Flowers of all known species were strewn throughout the palace grounds.

The keepers and the royals, as well as the Royal Army and all citizens of Terra, bowed as the newly-weds walked through the courtyard, nodding and smiling. They stopped when they reached the keepers and the other royals.

Gavin smiled when he saw Adam and Daniella holding hands, then grinned widely when he looked upon Mae and Thistle. "My, my. It appears that we have much to look forward to in the future."

Ginger, unable to control herself, rushed forward and hugged Gavin. "I'm so happy," she cried. Turning to Aurora, she said, "You got a prize here, sister. It's a shame I didn't get to him first."

Gavin and Aurora both laughed, and Gavin patted Ginger on the back. "I think your duties are not yet over."

"What do you mean?" MJ asked.

"With Helius gone, Chaos has no ruler," Gavin replied. "We'll need someone to take control. Who better than the keepers?"

"Are you saying…" Ginger began.

"Go to Chaos and rebuild it the way you see fit," Gavin continued. "You fulfilled all of my expectations and beyond, and you are ready to be a queen."

"But…" Ginger started.

"Take whoever wishes to go with you," Gavin responded.

"I'll go," Cody stated. "After all, somebody's gotta keep Ginger sane."

"As will I," MJ added, beaming with pride.

"We'll all come with you," Serenity said happily.

"It's settled, then," Gavin said. "Use the Onyx Castle as your link between the worlds and reform Chaos." He stopped, then handed his black bag to MJ. "Take it. Consider it a gift from me to you." Then to all, he said, "You'll do wonderfully."

The keepers, including MJ, all smiled, bowing and walking away. Ivy, Mae, Thistle, Taran, and Asterel were left standing in front of the rulers. They smiled at Gavin and Aurora.

"All is back to normal," Asterel said.

"And Helius is gone," Ivy added.

"You all did so well," Gavin said, looking at Aurora, who continued.

"And the two of us would like to say thank you," Aurora added. "Without you, I could not be where I am now."

"Perhaps we'll have this much fun again sometime," Taran said gruffly, smiling wickedly. Then the royals walked away as well. A solitary person now remained.

"I am proud of the two of you," Eden said warmly, hugging Aurora and Gavin. "You have saved us all, and all is now as it should be."

"Thank you, Eden," Aurora replied.

"Oh no, my dear," Eden said mysteriously. "Thank you."

She disappeared, leaving Aurora to ponder. "Don't hurt yourself, dear," Gavin said, laughing. "No one's ever been able to figure her out."

*****

Back on Chaos, the destruction was still quite visible. Hell's Gate had been completely destroyed, imploding from the assault by the good keepers. And it would stay that way.

Torizar pushed himself out of the hole he had fallen into, brushing off and wincing at the pain in his arm, which was most likely broken. Helius was gone. His presence on Chaos was merely a trace, no more.

Digging madly through debris, Torizar had a new purpose, a new motive. He had a new job. He had to find his friend, his comrade. Somewhere, under all the rubble, Maximus and Jasmine were buried. He had to find his friend and the queen, even if they were…

The dread welled itself in his throat. Untiringly, he continued to search for them as a new dawn illuminated a clearer, brighter Chaos.

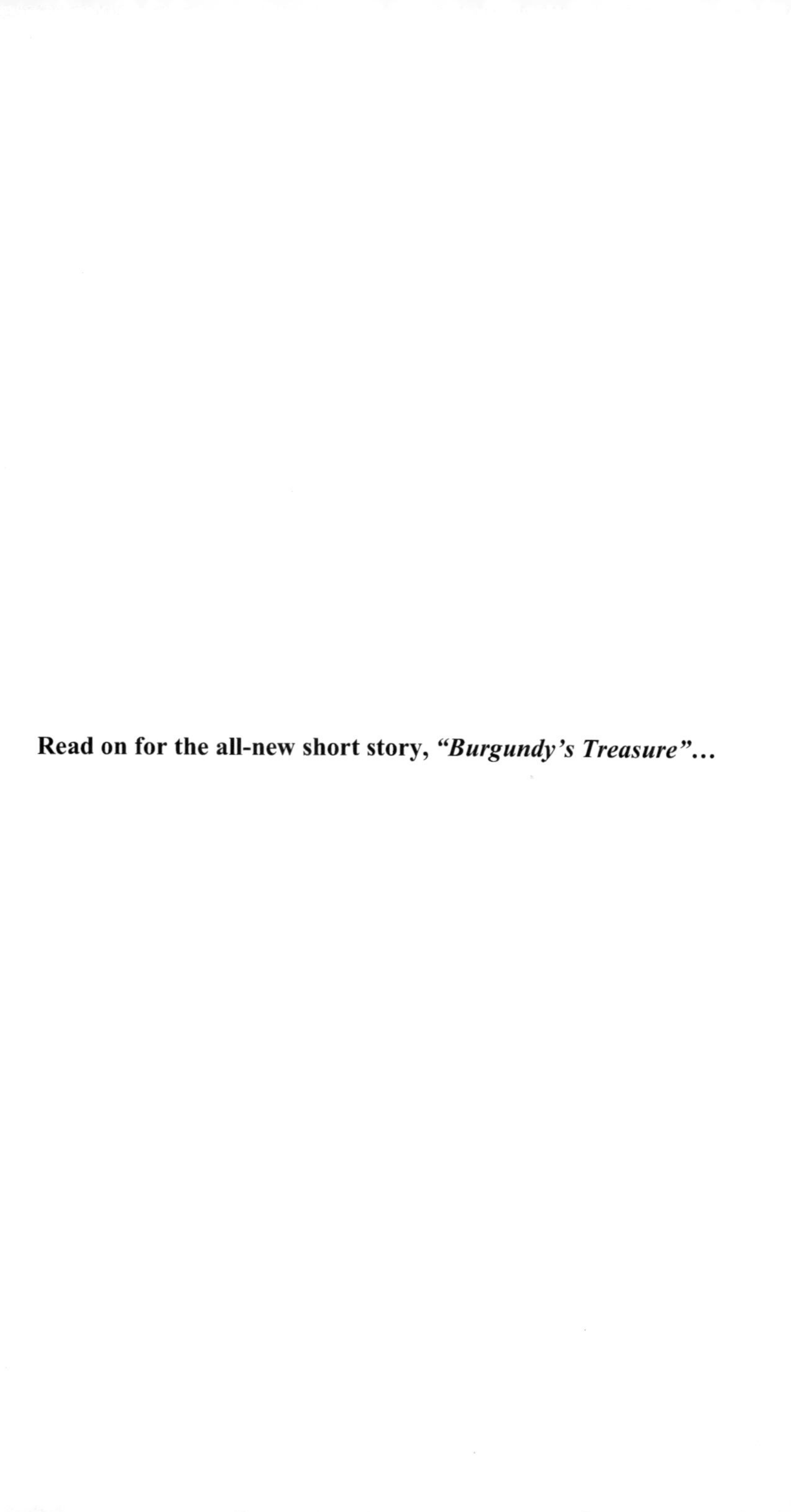

Read on for the all-new short story, *“Burgundy’s Treasure”…*

"Burgundy's Treasure"

A *Chronicles of Terra* Short Story

"Riddles here, riddles there,
Hidden treasure everywhere;
If look you, hard, and this treasure find,
It will surely help your pow'rs unbind."

-Gravnolde, Keeper of The Moga Box

It has been ten years since Helius Rue's demise at the hands of Oblivion. The Army of Chaos is fractured and in need of a leader to reunite its shattered ranks that continue to dwindle. Matthew Hexus, Morpheus Eternia, Maximus Altair, Torizar Fairplay – all the obvious leaders are dead or presumed dead. Helius's remaining keepers – Victoria Bloodmoon, Regina Zeal, Bracchus Moonshine, and Burgundy Alabastor – are the only ones capable of reuniting the Army to defend what's left of their dark world. But without their powers, they are not able to withstand the might of the encroaching goodness that threatens their evil world. But Burgundy, in spite of his insanity, may have found something that can solve all their problems and save them from the ever-growing forces of light that threaten to destroy their beloved world of Chaos....

*****

"Ow!"

"Hush!"

"But my finger...."

"QUIET, REGINA!" Victoria Bloodmoon, Keeper of Despair, clasped her hand over the mouth of the woman next to her as they huddled in the shadows behind some shrubbery, watching the Amazon-like woman as she spoke to her stoic-looking commander outside the gates of her semi-constructed new city and palace.

"But you stepped on my finger!" whined the Keeper of Confusion as she teared up and cradled her hand.

"I'll step on more than that if you don't SHUT UP!" Victoria hissed ferociously.

Regina whimpered but said no more. Since their miserable defeat by Gavin Moonstone's keepers only a mere handful of years ago, the remaining keepers of the now-vanquished Helius Rue had deferred leadership of their decimated ranks to the Keeper of Despair – partly because Victoria had a habit of naturally taking charge, and partly because the other three remaining keepers were just plain idiotic.

After Helius's demise at the hands of the angel named Oblivion, and the subsequent destruction and continual de-compartmentalization of the world of Chaos with his fall, the task of trying to hold back the forces of good had fallen to Helius's remaining keepers – none of whom was currently in any shape to be battling the forces of Gavin Moonstone. With their powers bound, the four remaining evil paragons were basically useless. They had been on the run for years now since the defeat of Helius, hiding and scrounging and finding any dark place that would still welcome them. There were many spots on Chaos still friendly to dark beings – but they were becoming fewer and fewer with each passing, agonizing year. Now, only a handful of dark bastions remained.

That was all to change soon, however. At least, that's what Victoria hoped.

Victoria's eyes narrowed and her lips curled into a sneer of hatred as she observed the Amazon-like woman – Ginger Molloy, that was her name – conferring with her new commander, a man named Bracken Pennyroyal. Ginger had recently been named Queen of Chaos by Emperor Gavin Moonstone, who had assumed, in his conceit and error, that he had the power to bestow such a title to so unfit a person, especially when it concerned a planet that was none of his business. A meddler, to be sure, and one who had ruined the lives of not only Helius's keepers but also the state of darkness and Chaos and, of course, Helius Rue himself. And unfortunately for the remaining forces of Chaos, Ginger was doing an excellent job of getting right to business and doing her part to purge the world of its dark forces.

Victoria felt her fists clench at her sides as she lurked in the shadows and watched the conference. The new queen had wasted no time in beginning construction of a new palace – right over the ashes of Hell's Gate, the nerve! – and had dubbed it the "New Kingdom." As if she could ever hope to accomplish spreading light to a world born of darkness.

"How's the army doin'?" Victoria heard Ginger ask. She cringed at the sound of Ginger's voice, her eye twitching in irritation. Imagine...a crude, horrible wild woman with fractured speech being the new Queen of Chaos? It made her woozy with disgust and repulsion.

"We are still meeting with heavy resistance, Queen Ginger," her commander replied, his unease clearly visible. "We have taken some heavy losses within the last couple days. It seems Helius's army will continue to fight, even without him to guide it. We are fortunate enough, though, to have the army scattered throughout Chaos."

"How's that fortunate?" Ginger asked as she frowned.

Stupid woman, Victoria thought, her lips once again curling into a sneer.

"It's fortunate," Bracken replied, "because the fractures of the army still have no leader to unite them again. With Helius's best keepers dead and Helius himself gone, the army has no guidance. It's amazing that it has kept cohesive for this long without leadership."

Victoria snorted in distaste. Helius's best keepers all dead, indeed. If they were as great as they'd claimed to be, they would have still been alive. And yet, here she sat – powers bound, true, but still alive…and ready for revenge.

"Once we get our powers back," Victoria whispered, "we can reunite the Army of Chaos and drive those two pathetic fools off our world forever."

"Oh goody!" Regina giggled. "That should be fun!"

Victoria rolled her eyes in annoyance as she observed the other woman's wild hair bouncing around crazily, the insane static which clung to it causing it to appear even more unkempt and homely than usual. Regina was a stupendous moron, no doubt…but at least she didn't have to deal with Burgundy at the same time. At least, not at the moment. She turned her attention back to the exchange between Ginger and Bracken.

"What about Helius's remainin' keepers?" Ginger asked.

"Their powers are bound. I don't see them as a particularly pressing threat," Bracken replied.

Victoria's teeth ground together in fury.

"The Castle of Souls?" Ginger questioned.

"Sealed with magic, as you commanded," came the reply.

"Good," Ginger responded. "Even if there's nothin' dangerous left in there, I don't wanna have t'deal with unnecessary attacks, like the one this mornin'."

Victoria cursed softly to herself. The morning's exploration to the Castle of Souls, after waiting in quiet seclusion in hiding for five years to return a second time to search it after Ginger's security detail had grown lax, had been a near disaster. She and the other three keepers had ventured back to the castle's welcoming darkness, having stayed away since their last attempt to search five years before that, looking for…something…anything, really, that might give them guidance and perhaps help to restore their bound magics. Unfortunately for the evil keepers, though security had loosened considerably since the immediate days after Helius's demise and since their last attempt to search the ruins, Ginger had still kept several royal guards there, anticipating the dark keepers' return at some point in time. A battle had ensued, and the four had barely escaped into the depths of the castle before Ginger's reinforcements had arrived. All because of Burgundy.

"Why are we still watching them?" Regina's nasally and incredibly irritating voice broke into Victoria's thoughts, causing the woman to let out a low growl.

"Because, you twit, we are making sure Ginger did not discover the hidden passage into and out of the castle." Victoria turned back. "Besides, I want more information as to what Ginger is up to. I also want to make sure that she is nowhere near the Castle of Souls when we go back."

"To find Burgundy's treasure! Yeah!" Regina crowed – a little too loudly.

Ginger and Bracken whipped around at the noise, scanning the surrounding area. "What was that?" Ginger asked. Victoria saw the Amazon woman's hand venture toward the spear she'd propped against a nearby tree.

"You IDIOT," Victoria snarled in a low tone as she grabbed Regina's arm and backed the two of them slowly away from their hiding place as Ginger and Bracken advanced cautiously toward it.

"You'll never take us alive!" Regina suddenly screamed, breaking out of Victoria's grip, bursting out of the shrubbery, and insanely rushing the shocked Ginger and Bracken. She let out a wild, monkey-like screech, took a flying leap, and tackled Ginger, clawing at her face and pulling her hair.

"Moron!" Victoria yelled at the crazed Regina as she charged in and jumped on Bracken's back, punching the commander in the back of the head and knocking him to the ground as she continued to pummel him. "Not a threat, am I? How does that feel?!"

Bracken flailed and tried to throw off Victoria, but she continued to slam his face into the ground while Regina yanked crazily at Ginger's hair, causing the faux queen to scream in pain. Regina giggled and screeched again in victory as she gave Ginger a well-placed kick and then sprinted away toward the safety of a path leading away from the New Kingdom.

"Regina!" Victoria cried, abandoning her attack on Bracken and racing after the fleeing Keeper of Confusion.

"Guards!" they heard Ginger bellow as they raced away. "GUARDS! Stop them! Seize them!!!"

"Run!" Victoria screeched. The two women charged ahead down the path, hearing Ginger's shouts slowly fading – and the tramp of soldiers' boots growing steadily louder as they were pursued.

"I can't…keep…running…" Regina panted as she stopped and abruptly fell over into a confused pile.

"Regina, get up!" Victoria hurriedly tried to pull the keeper to her feet, to no avail. Regina was staying put, which meant that Victoria could either abandon her…or she could stay and fight – without magic.

The Keeper of Despair whipped around to face the oncoming battalion of royal guards – only to be knocked off her feet by an enormous gust of wind that came from above. She looked up, as did the guards, to see a giant bird crash to the ground between her and the guards. It was Callus Nightshade's pet Roc, ridden by Bracchus and Burgundy.

"Need some help?" Bracchus drawled as he patted the creature's head. The Roc screeched at the battalion of guards who were still trying to advance, pecking at them and causing them to back up with uncertainty.

"It's about time! Where were you?" Victoria huffed as she threw Regina onto the Roc and climbed on herself. "And where did you find the Roc?"

"Which question would you like me to answer first?" Bracchus said lazily as he gave the Roc a kick with his heel. The bird screeched and lifted off, its wings knocking aside the battalion of royal guards like bowling pins as it lifted into the sky with the keepers.

"Never mind!" Victoria shouted over the rushing wind. "Did you find anything useful, aside from the Roc?"

Bracchus turned to grin at her, then looked over at Burgundy, who was nodding idiotically and giggling. "You won't believe what we found."

*****

Ginger sat outside the steps of the New Kingdom's palace, scowling as she rubbed her sore head. Despite being the first among Gavin's keepers, she still didn't have a full handle on her powers – such as being able to always detect a dark presence when it was nearby. If that had been the case....

The queen shook her head. No need to dwell on it. Victoria Bloodmoon and Regina Zeal were a nuisance, nothing more. They lacked the strength and unity that Helius's other defeated keepers had possessed. And without magic, they were harmless...mostly.

Ginger scowled again and winced at the throbbing toward the back of her skull. Powerless as they might be, they WERE still a problem that needed to be dealt with. It was possible – however, unlikely – that they could be capable of uniting the remaining the shards of the Army of Chaos. It would be a task of great magnitude, but still possible – even if they had been unsuccessful at it for the past ten years.

Bracken rushed up to her side with a small battalion of shaken-looking royal guards, interrupting her scowling. "Queen Ginger, this is the battalion that pursued Victoria Bloodmoon and Regina Zeal. They were unable to apprehend them, however. A giant bird made of stone descended with two more of Helius's keepers and swept them away."

Ginger felt her blood run cold. They had accounted for most of the missing dark keepers, so the two who rescued Victoria and Regina were undoubtedly Bracchus Moonshine and Burgundy Alabastor – both of whom had been driven away from the grounds of the ruined Castle of Souls only a short time earlier. By themselves, they posed very little threat. Now that there was evidence they were all united, however....

"Commander," Ginger found herself saying as she stood up, "I think it's time we strike harder. We need t'wipe 'em offa Chaos for good and stop whatever it is they're up to."

Bracken raised an eyebrow. "Do you really think they could organize the army against us, after all this time?"

Ginger paled. "I dunno – but I don't wanna wait any longer t'find out."

*****

The Roc landed at the edge of the Mountains of Illusion, the ruined Castle of Souls visible in the distance, its once grand and commanding sky-reaching towers crumbling and shattered. Victoria's heart still ached when she beheld its now-destroyed visage. Ten years ago, the War of the Emperors, as it was now being called, had most certainly caused its share of damage; Victoria was surprised that the castle hadn't completely collapsed by now with all of the structural damage it had sustained in the battle between Gavin and Helius.

Burgundy hopped off the Roc, patting its beak and giggling maniacally. He turned toward Victoria expectantly. She rolled her eyes and grabbed Regina's arm, pulling the whining keeper after her. Bracchus stretched out on the Roc's back, reclining lazily.

"Good idea, Bracchus," Victoria growled sarcastically. "If we need an escape, you will be able to secure that."

"I want to stay too," Regina whined. "I have a cramp from running."

"The only cramp you have, Regina Zeal," Victoria ground out as she grabbed the other woman and hauled her away, ignoring any reply that Bracchus might have managed to muster, "is in your brain." Victoria returned her attention to Burgundy. "Well?"

The idiotic keeper cleared his throat theatrically, then produced from the folds of his clothing a small piece of paper. "I present, to you, my find from this morning's search."

"A piece of paper?" Regina exclaimed. "THAT'S your find?!"

"My dear Regina." Burgundy affected an offended tone. "It isn't just a piece of paper. It's a treasure map."

"A treasure map?" Regina, even in her state of perpetual confusion, was incredulous. "You dragged us back to the Castle of Souls and are risking our lives for a TREASURE MAP?"

Burgundy's insane grin continued to widen. Instead of his customary response of continuing to provoke and engage Regina, he turned instead to Victoria and handed her the piece of paper. Growing impatient, the Keeper of Despair snatched the paper and opened it up, only to feel herself recoil in shock as if someone had slapped her. Burgundy giggled and clapped.

"This isn't just a map," Victoria said slowly and quietly. "It's a set of instructions as well."

"Yep!" Burgundy crowed.

"Where did you find this?" Victoria asked.

"It was stuffed under the cushion of Helius's throne when we searched the throne room!" Burgundy replied. "Happy birthday, Victoria!"

"Idiot," she replied automatically, turning away to study the paper. She had read tales of the fabled Moga Box, but up until now, she'd had no reason to believe it to be anything other than a myth. Now....

"Do you know what the Moga Box does?" Victoria asked quietly. Now, even the lazy Bracchus was paying attention, having sat up at hearing Victoria's words.

"No one does!" Burgundy crowed in a singsong voice. "That's why this is such a great treasure!"

"But if Helius knew about the Moga Box, why didn't he use it?" Victoria mused to herself. "Perhaps he thought himself greater than its power." She grunted and walked back toward the Roc, absentmindedly patting its beak as she studied the map scrawled on the paper. "Regina, Burgundy, Bracchus...I've begun to form a plan."

"What kind of plan?" Regina asked suspiciously as Burgundy jumped up and down, clapping.

"The four of us are going to take back Chaos," Victoria said as she clutched the map to herself. "We have hidden and sulked and brooded and wandered for too long without our powers, without a plan, and mostly without support. We have allowed the forces destroying this world to push us around and ruin our home for far too long. This plan will take time – years, most likely – but we can do it. It will require us to work together as never before." She turned toward Bracchus. "And it will be your powers that will make it all happen."

The Keeper of Deception toppled off the Roc in surprise, scrambling to his feet and sputtering. "But...but...but...Victoria – I don't have my powers, remember?"

The Keeper of Despair's lips curled into a malicious smile – or perhaps a sneer, for her face was not made for smiling. "Not yet. But you will. Soon, we all will. And then...they will all pay."

*****

"Ginger, I don't see how...possible...when...have... powers...begin with." The shimmering image of MJ Holmes flickered in and out, cutting off pieces of what she was saying – though Ginger understood most of it. The Keeper of Strength and Wisdom was currently studying inside the Cave of the Prophets, searching through the scrawlings on the walls to absorb more of Chaos's prophecies and ancient texts. The keeper's face appeared to still be studying the walls as she spoke to Ginger.

"That's a relief, then," Ginger answered, "but I still got a bad feelin' in my chest. Somethin's wrong."

"...Can continue...things out...but...is weak...."

Ginger understood. Either due to the drain of sustaining the spell to communicate or due to the magic contained within the cave, MJ couldn't hold the distance image steady for long. "No worries, MJ. If y'say there's nothin' t'worry about, then..."

"Hang on," MJ's image said abruptly. The feeling in Ginger's chest immediately dropped to a cold, icy dread that lodged in the pit of her stomach.

"...Found a text...details the...of a...the Moga Box." The image got fuzzier and dissolved into static for a moment before returning. "...Says...used as...sort of wishing box to...upon...guardian to...release...and...powers." MJ's face had gone slack, save for the tension in her eyes. Ginger understood all she needed to.

"Where?" she asked as MJ's image began to dissolve into static again.

"Not sure...near...of Darkness...an island...out in the middle...guarded..." The image completely dissolved, shattering into sparkling flecks of light within the surface of the mirror Ginger had been using to communicate with the keeper. The queen paced across the surface of the outer courtyard of the yet-unfinished New Kingdom's palace and grabbed her silver spear, whistling for her carpet as she did so. It zoomed underneath her, sweeping her up and carrying her into the air.

"T'the Ocean of Darkness," she commanded, the dread growing. "An' let's hope I'm not already too late."

*****

"Drat," MJ growled as the connection to Ginger broke. She didn't know if the queen had gotten all of her message or not, but it seemed as though the Amazon-like woman had understood the core of what she was trying to tell her.

She paced along the tunnel, the words on the walls glowing with a fiery light as she passed them. Even if Ginger managed to find the obscure island in the middle of the Ocean of Darkness, she had no idea what awaited her.

"And knowing Ginger, she's rushed off to combat whatever threat she can feel brewing," MJ mumbled. "She needs to know what awaits her."

Focusing her concentration, MJ projected herself to the New Kingdom's crystal mirror again in the hope of catching Ginger – only to have the call answered by Bracken Pennyroyal. "MJ?" he said in confusion.

"Bracken," she said quickly, "Ginger might be heading into trouble somewhere in the Ocean of Darkness. She may need your help if that's the case."

"...Didn't...that," Bracken said worriedly.

"Ocean. Of. Darkness," MJ enunciated slowly. Bracken understood. "Ginger. Trouble. Sending carpet. Go now."

Bracken nodded and MJ exhaled in relief. She summoned her carpet and sent it on its way to Bracken. He saluted, and his image disappeared.

The Keeper of Strength and Wisdom slumped to the floor in exhaustion. It took more magic than normal to project when inside the Cave of the Prophets. Perhaps her next project would be the development of a new communications system.

"Stay safe, Ginger," she said quietly. "May Bracken be there to protect you."

*****

The Roc crashed to the ground in a small, sandy clearing at the edge of the isolated island, hidden in the middle of the Ocean of Darkness. It had been hard to locate, due to its dull black sand camouflaging it against the murky black water, but Victoria and Bracchus had succeeded in the end. There were actually two small islands in the Ocean of Darkness, but the map had indicated the smooth gourd-shaped island rather than the jagged, mountainous one.

Victoria smirked as she hopped off the bird, pleased with herself for assuming command with a plan that actually worked. She had dispatched Burgundy and Regina to scour some of the still-dark parts of Chaos and rally the scattered troops of the Army of Chaos. It would be a difficult task without one of the stronger keepers to keep the army in line and convince them to accept command from the remaining keepers, but Victoria was confident that the Moga Box was the key to helping restore the glorious darkness of the true Chaos – and Helius Rue's legacy.

Her plan was quite simple, really. Once the shattered remains of the Army of Chaos were put back together into something coherent, she would take control as the interim ruler – the Regent of Chaos – and then allow Bracchus to instruct them in the ways of deception. The army would assume new tactics for combating Queen Ginger and her soldiers; they would spread out in a perimeter throughout all of Chaos and execute strategic hit-and-fade, aggressive battle tactics. Then, they would disappear and move to another location like shadows.

Time consuming, yes, but necessary. And right now, it was the best plan for them all to survive. Victoria was privy to that. Once their powers were unbound and restored, the Army would follow without question.

Bracchus's snort of distaste roused her out of her musings. "What a desolate place. It's no wonder we never knew it was here."

Indeed, Victoria thought to herself. But another thought disturbed her even more: if Helius had kept this place hidden from even his most-trusted advisors, what other secrets had he taken with him when he was swallowed by Oblivion?

She shuddered and turned toward a semi-overgrown path of broken stone that led away from the sandy black beach and toward a half-dead, brown and black forest. "Let's go, Bracchus," she sniffed. "The sand is getting in my shoes."

Consulting the map as they stumbled along the ruined path, Victoria felt her excitement growing. They were getting closer; she could feel it. And once she was in possession of the Moga Box, their plan could proceed exactly as she envisioned.

Victoria was not completely sure what sort of powers the Moga Box contained; she only knew that it contained great power, and that was enough for her. She could draw out the finer details once she was in possession of the box.

The shattered path led into a small, decimated courtyard – or at least, it seemed to have once been a courtyard. The broken pathstones were arranged in a sort of circle, and broken columns of stone ringed the damaged courtyard. The central stones of the courtyard's path were tinted a different color. But aside from that, there was nothing else there.

"Well," Bracchus drawled, "it looks like there isn't anything here."

Victoria studied her map again. No – the location was correct. So what, then?

She whirled around as something crashed to the ground behind her. A large boulder, apparently appearing out of nowhere, had landed near the path that led back to the black beach.

"What...?" Victoria's remaining words died in her throat as the monstrosity that had thrown the boulder stalked out of the dead trees along one edge of the courtyard. Horribly disfigured and composed solidly of grotesquely-scarred muscle, the near-ten-foot-tall creature began its lumbering strut toward Victoria.

"Cyclops!" Bracchus shrieked, tripping backward over his own feet and crawling away from the advancing nightmare.

Victoria, her momentary petrification now past, shook herself and stomped her feet on the discolored bricks of the central circle. "In the name of Helius Rue, Emperor of Chaos, I demand you cease and obey me! I am Victoria Bloodmoon, Keeper of Despair!"

The cyclops roared at her, brandishing a giant club from behind one of the broken columns and waving it threateningly at her as it continued to advance.

"No wonder Helius had the cyclops race wiped off of Chaos!" Victoria shrieked. "They are too stupid to obey even the simplest of orders!"

Instantly, the cyclops's deliberate tromp toward her changed to a sprint. Victoria screamed and fell over as the cyclops leaped and crashed down in front of her, windmilling its club and bringing it up to smash down on her. She rolled out of the way as the club thundered down, pulverizing the discolored stone circle upon which she had just been standing. In an explosion and a cloud of dust, the inner circle of the ruined courtyard blew up, rolling Victoria away and pitching the cyclops into the woods like a stone skipped over the water. The shattered circle emitted a deafening boom, then....

Silence.

Victoria coughed out rock dust and slowly crawled over to the smoking hole that had once been the courtyard's central circle. "Boomstone," she croaked. "I knew I recognized it." Boomstone, an incredibly rare stone harvested from the volcanic deposits deep inside the Hills of Fire, had long since been thought of as both precious and extremely lethal, due to the hazards of collecting and mining it, as well as shaping it and placing it. Direct, smashing impacts caused the sulfuric and charcoal-based components within the stone to ignite, the end result being an explosion.

Which meant that something had been hidden beneath the central circle of the courtyard.

Victoria peered over the edge of the smoking hole and into the crater, nearly tipping herself into the hole with glee. A small, intricately-carved wooden box sat at the bottom of the crater, perfectly unscathed.

"It's mine," she hissed, slithering carefully down the crater and crawling over to the box.

As she reached forward to grab the box, she suddenly found herself tumbling head-over-heels as a section of the rubble beneath her exploded. She sailed over the box and crashed into the rubble on its other side, rolling over sharp stones and debris as she was thrown like a rag doll over the chaff. She let out a cry as she rolled across an especially sharp stone and came to rest – next to the box once again.

"Curse...that...boomstone..." she ground out between pain-clenched teeth as she reached out and pulled the box toward her.

"Victoria!"

She looked up, clutching the box to her, to see a disheveled Bracchus peering over the lip of the crater at her. "Help me out of here," she managed. "I don't know if I can get up by myself."

Bracchus looked over his shoulder fearfully and slid down the side of the crater with unusually surprising speed for normally being so slothful. He hit the bottom of the crater and pulled Victoria to her feet none too gently.

"Watch it!" she snarled.

"Apologies," he said as he scrambled up the opposite side of the crater, dragging her along, "but the cyclops is back."

The gargantuan beast was suddenly in front of them, jumping from the opposite edge of the crater and pounding the debris at the bottom to powder when it landed at Victoria's feet. She lashed out at it with one of her struggling feet and kicked it squarely in its mammoth eye. It roared and toppled backward, allowing both her and Bracchus to scrabble up the crater and flee for their lives.

"Run for the shore and let's get out of here!" Victoria cried through her pain as they took off back down the path that led toward the beach. "We have what we need!"

The pain was bearable but still excruciating. Everything hurt. Victoria was fairly certain that the boomstone detonations had damaged her hearing, as well as caused some subsequent broken ribs when she was thrown into the side of the crater. If they could just get to the shore and back on the Roc....

Her lungs burned. They were almost there, though. She could see the path starting to change to the black sand of the beach and the waiting shore. Just a little further....

She screamed as she heard a bellow from behind her and knew the cyclops wasn't far behind. She pushed her body to move faster as she and Bracchus burst into the clearing of the shore – and bowled over an oncoming Ginger Molloy. The three of them rolled across the beach in a confused, screaming pile.

Victoria kicked and thrashed wildly, punching Bracchus in the process and kicking Ginger away from her as she disentangled herself and crawled toward the waiting Roc. She heard another roar and then a strange whizzing sound. Instinctively, she flattened herself to the ground – just as the cyclops's club flew past like a missile and smashed the Roc into a billion sparkling pieces of rubble.

"Noooooooo!" Victoria could hear herself screaming in despair, a long, wailing, blood-curdling shriek that could have frozen fire solid. She rolled herself out of the way and back into the brush of the forest, crawling through the foliage as she heard the cyclops's club smashing things apart behind her. She crawled frantically faster, away from the fading sounds and back into the depths of the island forest.

After minutes, or hours, or days – she couldn't really tell anymore – Victoria collapsed in a pain-wracked, gasping heap in a very small clearing of trees. She could no longer hear the crashing or bellowing of the cyclops. Perhaps it had decided to abandon its assault on her and direct its attention to eating Ginger instead.

"If only," Victoria growled as she propped her bruised form up against one of the trees of the circle. She carefully positioned the Moga Box – her prize for such trouble – on her lap. And then, she opened it.

Inside, there was nothing. The Moga Box was empty.

Victoria felt her heart sink. It seemed as if the universe had played its cruelest joke ever on her. She sat there, unable to move from the sudden physical and mental fatigue, staring at the empty box. And then she began to laugh. She laughed until her sides hurt even more than they already did. And after she was laughed out, the laughter turned to tears.

A noise interrupted her self-misery. Wiping her blurry eyes, Victoria looked around for the source of the noise. When she looked down, finally, she almost dropped the Moga Box in shock. Standing inside the open box was now a little creature, unlike anything she had seen before. It resembled a miniature gremlin, but it was a creature she had never before encountered. It cleared its throat again – that was the noise she had heard – and spoke.

"Mistress Victoria, why do you cry?
Whyfore are you sad? Did somebody die?"

The Keeper of Despair froze. This strange little creature knew her name. All was not as it appeared to be. "Who are you?" she asked.

The little gremlin-like creature grinned from ear to ear and clicked its heels.

"Be not afraid – I'll not give you a pox;
For I am Gravnolde, Keeper of the Moga Box."

Her heart leapt into her throat. The box had not been empty after all. This little creature – Gravnolde – was the keeper of the Moga Box. And that meant he – or she – was the keeper of a lot of power.

"Your name is Gravnolde?" she asked. The creature bowed in response. "What does the Moga Box do?" she asked.

"The better question yet is, what does it not?
Seeker of knowledge, ask and you've got."

"Can you get me and my fellow dark keeper out of here?" Victoria asked.

"Oh Keeper of Despair, you have been marked;
So long as your pow'rs are bound, you'll remain in the dark."

Victoria growled. "Yes, my powers were bound. But you possess great power. Can't you use that great power to unbind my powers and transport me off this island?"

The little creature shook its head.

"My dearest Victoria, misinformed have you been.
My powers are knowledge; my strength lies within."

"What?!" Victoria exploded. So, it seemed that the legends were not true after all. The Moga Box had no real power. Neither, apparently, did Gravnolde. "So you can't help me?"

"Keeper of Despair – said that, I did not.
With my knowledge and wisdom, you've just gained a lot.
In first part of question, to unbind powers bound,
Seek out High Priest Lucas; he'll bring them around.
In second part of question, look o'er to that tree.
For when you step through it, it shall set you free."

Victoria looked over, following where Gravnolde pointed its knobby little finger. At the other side of the little circle of trees stood a gnarled old ash tree, its bark as black as midnight, its branches coiled and dead. "It's an ugly old tree," Victoria said. "I don't see how walking through it is going to get me anywhere."

"The ash is a tree from which great magic springs;
use its potential, and see what it brings."

Gravnolde's matter-of-fact, singsong tone was becoming unnerving. "Very well. I'll have to just…."

"Victoria!" Bracchus thundered into her sanctuary like a dragon in a cave full of gold. "Ginger killed the cyclops and now she's after me! Run!"

"Idiot!" Victoria cried as she jumped to her feet, holding tight to the open Moga Box. Gravnolde seemed completely nonplussed. "With the Roc dead, we're trapped here!"

"Dearest Victoria, you know that's not true.
The tree's over there; just walk right on through."

"What is THAT?" Bracchus said in disgust.

"Shut up," Victoria replied, then looked at Gravnolde. "If you're wrong, I'll make sure to kill you myself before I die."

"Beautiful keeper, mistakes I don't make;
In a world full of sleepers, I'm solely awake."

"What did he mean?" Bracchus asked.

"Gravnolde told me that all we had to do to get off this island was walk through that ugly ash tree in front of us," Victoria replied.

"Gravnolde?"

"The keeper of the Moga Box. Keep up, rock brain," Victoria snarled. "It seems we don't have a choice. I can hear Ginger crashing toward us."

Bracchus looked behind them with worry. "She's crazy, Victoria. Even crazier than Burgundy. And that's saying something, since he's completely insane."

The Keeper of Despair grabbed his arm and pulled them over to the tree. "Then let's hope this is not all for nothing." She took a deep breath, one hand holding tightly to the box with Gravnolde and the other firmly clamped around Bracchus's wrist, and stepped through the tree.

*****

Ginger fumed as another gnarled branch slapped her in the face. Bracchus Moonshine was as slippery as a greased eel on a rainy day. He'd somehow maneuvered her into fighting – and killing – the cyclops that protected this island, and he had escaped in the process. Luckily, he was anything but stealthy, and she'd followed his rasping, exhausted panting through the forest, to where she could now hear him talking to someone. It was undoubtedly Victoria. Either that, or he was talking to himself.

She edged closer and just caught the tail end of a garbled, singsong voice saying something about "awake." So, there was someone else there, as well. She gripped her spear and took a breath. Then, she jumped into the clearing where she heard the voices.

The clearing was empty.

Bracchus and Victoria – and whoever else had been with them – were nowhere to be seen. They had simply vanished. Ginger roared in frustration and whistled for her carpet. If she was right, Victoria was now in possession of the Moga Box. And with that power, who knew what the evil keeper could accomplish?

"I needta get back t'the New Kingdom," Ginger said as her carpet scooped her up and whisked her away. "I needta tell Bracken t'prepare for war."

*****

They had stepped into darkness. Victoria felt blind. Wherever the tree had transported them to, it was dark. She grunted as she felt around in the darkness for something – anything, really – that would bring a little light.

"Lumen," she heard a singsong voice say. Her other outstretched hand, which still held the Moga Box, suddenly lit up with a soft glow. Gravnolde stood in the center of the box, holding a glowing orb.

"You DO have magic!" Victoria exclaimed. "I knew it!"

"Victoria, Keeper, have powers, I do.
But what you need is knowledge; it's of greater value to you."

She scowled and held out the box with the little keeper inside in front of her like a lamp, ignoring Gravnolde's commentary and looking around her in observation. It was a small, empty stone room. There was nothing in it; no windows or doors, no furniture, nothing save for the glimmering bit of light from the portal through which they had just arrived.

"This room has no exit," Bracchus said flatly. "We're trapped."

"Statements of the obvious," Victoria sneered. "There has to be a way out other than the portal we just came through." She ran her hand along one of the walls, searching for a false wall or perhaps a cloaked door. Her hand bumped over an irregular stone carved into the surface of the wall, not noticeable to the naked eye but noticeable when touched. Strange, since the wall was otherwise relatively smooth. She ran her hand back over the irregular stone, noticing it felt a bit loose. So she pushed on it.

A slab of stone above their heads slid aside, and grim light poured into their small room. Victoria looked up to see pale sky. Gravnolde's glowing orb vanished, and the Moga Box's keeper sat down, looking incredibly smug. Victoria hoisted the box up out of the room, then pulled herself up. Bracchus scrambled up behind her. Only when she stood up and looked around did she realize where they were.

It was the throne room of the Castle of Souls.

Helius's throne, on its dais slab of stone, had slid backward enough to open the hole in the floor that led to the portal room. Apparently, the Castle of Souls held secrets that no one but Helius himself knew.

"We're home," Bracchus breathed, "and you have the box. What do we do now?"

Victoria looked at Gravnolde, who blinked at her expectantly. "We get Regina and Burgundy and go to the Chapel of Shadows. High Priest Lucas has some work to do."

*****

"Ginger, I understand the sense of urgency. I felt something dark stirring again from all the way over here, as well," Gavin Moonstone's image said in the mirror at her palace's half-finished throne room. "Are you sure that it's Helius's remaining keepers, though? With their powers bound…."

"It may be them indirectly," MJ piped up, standing next to Ginger after recovering her strength and having traveled back to the New Kingdom to aid. "I was studying the writings at the Cave of the Prophets, and the entries on the Moga Box are few and obscure, but they are nonetheless very unsettling. If this box can do all the things the writings claim it can, and if Victoria does actually have it…."

"Then we're in a lotta trouble," Ginger finished. "With the box, it may not matter if their powers'r bound or not. They may be able t'use magic by usin' the box."

Gavin's image frowned, his purple eyes changing to blue. "It's odd that Helius would be in possession of such an item and not use it. I remember something, very faintly…an item from another world…." He trailed off, shook his head, and re-focused on Ginger and MJ. "Sorry, I lost myself for a moment. Perhaps the writings are just superstitions?"

It was MJ's turn to frown. "That is possible, I suppose. But the writings in the cave have so far been all too real. That leads me to believe the writings concerning the Moga Box are not just superstition or purely exaggerated. We may be dealing with a very serious uprising of darkness soon, perhaps one that hasn't existed on Chaos since before Helius's death."

Gavin's frown deepened. "This is very concerning, then. What do you need from me?"

Ginger looked at MJ, who shrugged. "You are the queen. I just study things."

"We'll need some extra protective magic," Ginger responded. "I have this feelin' that an army's comin' here. Our troops'll need extra help."

"Done," Gavin answered. "I will send some elemental mages your way to assist."

"I'll go ready the troops around the palace," Bracken said, turning and striding out quickly. Ginger, in her flight back to the New Kingdom, had been fortunate enough to intercept the commander as she'd raced back. She had filled him in on their return to the palace as best as she could.

"That's the best aid I can give you for now, Ginger," Gavin said, smiling slightly. "But I'm confident you have everything you need already."

"Thanks, Gavin," she replied. "Sorry t'bother ya. I know you've got your hands full."

"Not to worry," Gavin responded with a smile. "Aurora and I can multitask with the children and still come to your aid when you need us. All you have to do is call and we'll be there."

"Thank you for your help, Gavin," Ginger said. "We couldn'ta done it without ya."

The Emperor of Terra-Quenlist smiled again. "You know I'm always here to help." He reached into a pocket in his cloak and withdrew a small chain, to which was attached a ring. Standing, he reached through the mirror and handed the object to Ginger. "It's a talisman. To protect you," he added, "from any darkness."

"But I've already got my amethyst from you," Ginger responded, clutching the pendant around her neck.

"Well, I'm sure you'll find a use for it." Gavin's eyes twinkled. "I will send along those mages to aid you. Call if there is anything else Aurora and I can do."

"I will," Ginger answered solemnly. "Thank you."

The emperor nodded. "Be safe." His image vanished, leaving Ginger and MJ alone in the New Kingdom's throne room.

Ginger turned to MJ. "Did Cody answer when y'called him?"

The Keeper of Strength and Wisdom snorted. "No. He's probably taking a nap or listening to music that is too loud to hear anything else, such as someone speaking. I will try again momentarily."

Ginger nodded. "While y'do that, I'll start rallyin' troops with Bracken. We need to…."

The ground shook violently, cutting Ginger off and throwing both her and MJ to the floor. The windows of the throne room that were finished exploded in showers of glass and twisting stone and metal. Ginger crawled toward the doors to the throne room's balcony, wrenching them open and looking out. Her stomach turned to lead.

Approaching from all four directions were pieces of an army.

"MJ..." Ginger started.

"I see it," MJ yelled over the suddenly screaming wind. "The Army of Chaos seems to have re-formed. We don't have time to mount a proper defense! Gavin's mages won't get here in time!"

"We gotta try!" Ginger yelled back. "We NEED t'get to Bracken. If we can't repel 'em, we're doomed."

*****

Victoria stood triumphantly atop a small, floating platform, along with Regina, Burgundy, Bracchus, and High Priest Lucas. Lucas and his dark priests had responded to her requests with lightning speed. With Gravnolde's instructions, all of the keepers were now unbound, their magics returning almost instantly. The spells that had bound Burgundy, Regina, and Bracchus's powers had been relatively easy to break. The binding spell that had entrapped Victoria, however, had taken far longer than she had cared to wait. After much impatient waiting, and with the help of Lucas and his dark priests, the binding spell that had kept her cut off had at last been shattered.

No sooner did she have her powers restored than Victoria took command and set her plan to immediate action. With Burgundy's powers freed, he could once again make Telepowder. Using the Telepowder, the other three keepers set to massing the Army of Chaos quickly and efficiently. In no time, the call for an all-out attack on the New Kingdom and the false Queen of Chaos was under way.

The little Keeper of the Moga Box had, indeed, proven his worth. Gravnolde had armed her with some elementary spells for both attack and defense. His wisdom was invaluable and essential. The Moga Box was, indeed, powerful.

She held the box in front of her now. It was only when she realized about the powers locked within the box and how to access them that she had understood both its and Gravnolde's true power. The true power of the Moga Box itself, its ultimate secret, was to amplify one's power. When she held it and focused her powers, they amplified a thousand-fold. Her abilities of Despair had physically manifested in the weather now, as they marched on the New Kingdom. Ripping winds and shaking earth slashed away at the pitiful echelon of light amidst the once-more growing darkness of Chaos. She would use her army to squeeze them in a pincher grip until they were crushed into a fine powder.

Victoria turned to Bracchus and handed him the box. Gravnolde looked up at the Keeper of Deception and gave him a toothy smile. "Use your powers, Bracchus," Victoria instructed. "Show the Army of Chaos how to hit and fade."

She then turned to Regina and Burgundy. "Then, you two will project your powers against the New Kingdom and its forces to crush their minds beneath the weight of confusion and madness." Burgundy clapped and cheered idiotically, babbling something about a really fun tea party, while Regina stared at her blankly in vacancy.

Victoria turned to Lucas, who simply bowed and said, "Mistress." Yes, her plan was working perfectly. They would go in, cause as much chaos and destruction as possible, and then vanish, only to strike again like a poisonous serpent. Her fingers curled and uncurled in anticipation. Oh, yes. It was indeed gratifying to feel and use her powers again. To do so as commander of the Army of Chaos....

Her lips curled into a sneer of delight as Burgundy and Regina's powers, transformed from passive to active with the amplification lent by the Moga Box, twirled together and crashed like a tidal wave toward the New Kingdom. It was delightful to see the normally passive dark magics amplified so intensely that they BECAME active and tangibly visible. The Moga Box was, indeed, unbelievably powerful. It would all come to pass. Her plan would be fulfilled. Soon, all would be hers.

*****

Ginger and MJ had managed to make it out of the half-finished palace before it began shaking apart. As soon as they exited into the courtyard, chaos once more ruled. Tidal waves of multiple energies slammed into them, bowling them over and knocking them both out of breath.

All around, people were screaming. Guards ran past, caught up in insane delusions of non-existent specters. Others were sitting down, rocking and crying. The blasts of dark energy had reduced Ginger's haphazardly-gathered army to chaos and rubble in the blink of an eye. They were nearly defenseless and completely open to the full-scale army that was hemming them in from all directions.

"MJ!" Ginger cried over the catastrophic winds. The Keeper of Strength and Wisdom crawled to her feet and began firing off spells: protection, warding, defense, repulsion, strengthening...she was blasting them in all directions in an attempt to help anyone nearby.

Ginger used her powers, too – something she rarely actively did. Her powers of love radiated away from her in gentle rings, their soothing energy restoring anyone close by. Ginger projected the waves of healing love as far outward as she could push them, visualizing the expanding rings of energy just as Gavin had taught her so long ago.

Fortunately for Ginger, most of her gathered army was still near the courtyard, so her projection was able to free them from their personal torments...at least momentarily. "Fight it!" Ginger roared over the wind as she continued to push. "Don't let the darkness win!"

"Well, isn't that sweet," a curt voice echoed through the wind behind her. "The power of looooove will conquer all. Ha!"

Ginger turned around to see a floating dais crash down at the courtyard's entrance. Victoria Bloodmoon, Keeper of Despair, sneered and hopped off of it, followed closely by Burgundy Alabastor, Regina Zeal, Bracchus Moonshine, and a dark-cloaked man she didn't recognize – until he pulled back his hood and she realized it was High Priest Lucas. MJ turned toward Victoria and began to weave a spell. Victoria smiled, held up a hand, and telekinetically slammed MJ to the ground.

"I suggest you stay down. Don't interfere," Victoria snarled as she approached Ginger.

The queen took a step back out of both reflex and shock. How could Victoria be that powerful? She had never had that kind of power. With a single flip of her hand, she had knocked MJ senseless. How was that possible? Unless....

Then Ginger noticed why Victoria was only using one hand. Clutched in her other hand was a box that could be none other than the fabled Moga Box. Its stories had just proven all too true, as MJ had predicted. With Victoria using its energies, she had gone from a minor nuisance to an incredibly dangerous foe.

"I see you are admiring my new toy," Victoria said. "It has proven to be quite useful to me." She looked down at the box and said, "Gravnolde, why don't you say hello to our beloved queen?"

A little creature jumped out of the box, standing atop its open lid and doing a small jig in Ginger's direction. In a singsong voice, it said:

"Greetings, Ginger, queen untrue; Why so sad? Why so blue?

You see the power wielded strong; a queen no more – you don't belong."

Burgundy cackled from behind Victoria, clapping and yelling, "More! I like the little imp-elf!"

Victoria's smile was cold and predatory, devoid of any emotion other than a mad, cruel glee as her lips curled into her usual disgusted sneer. "I'm going to enjoy this immensely."

Ginger reacted instantly and dove out of the way as a discharge of electricity blew a hole in the stones where she had just been standing. She rolled and jumped to her feet, twirling her spear and hitting the next electrical orb like a baseball, rebounding it back at Victoria. As Victoria dodged, it whizzed past her and slammed into Burgundy, sending him shooting like a rocket backward and down the main street. Regina shrieked and went running after him as hoards of the Army of Chaos began streaming in and advancing.

"Leave the queen!" Victoria shouted. "Destroy everything you want – but Ginger Molloy is mine!"

"Ginger!" MJ, who had roused herself, cried, "You need to separate her from the Moga Box! It must be destroyed or we are all going to die!"

"Oh, I'll separate 'er all right," Ginger growled as she held out a hand and sent a wave of pink energy outward. Lucas dove for cover, Bracchus was sent sprawling, and Victoria just stood smirking as the energy dissipated around her to no apparent effect.

Ginger ducked another lightning discharge and rolled, jarring herself and dropping the chain and ring from Gavin out of her pocket on the way. She jumped to her feet and threw her spear at Victoria.

Gravnolde spoke, Victoria held out her hand, and Ginger's spear reversed direction. "Time to die!" Victoria snarled.

"Look out!" cried Lucas to Victoria and MJ to Ginger simultaneously.

Victoria flailed and threw the Moga Box as she was hit from behind, crashing to the ground in a confused pile as the box and its keeper bounced across the ground and into Ginger's hands.

The spear dropped in mid-flight like a stone as Ginger gripped the box and Gravnolde screamed.

Bracken Pennyroyal stood over Victoria, the hilt of his sword ready to strike her a second time. Victoria rolled away and scrabbled across the ground toward Ginger. "Give me that box!"

"Smash it with your magic, Ginger!" MJ screamed.

The little Gravnolde kept shrieking as Ginger slammed the lid on the box, closing him inside, and, using her magic to amplify the throw, hurled the box against one of the courtyard's stone pillars. Victoria found herself shrieking incoherently as the box struck the pillar with a tremendous crash and exploded, shattering into a hundred pieces.

"Kill her!" Victoria screamed as she crawled toward the destroyed box. Bracken stepped in front of Ginger to guard her as the two of them were swallowed by a torrent of the Army of Chaos. Victoria crawled up to the broken box and picked up one of its larger pieces, feeling already that all of its power was gone. She stood slowly, looking down in anguish at the remains of the box she held, feeling the weight of despair falling upon her instead of allowing her to use its might against others as she so often did.

Then, she felt a pressure on her leg, little crawly fingers scrabbling and wiggling along the bottom of her shin. Repulsed, Victoria looked down to see the dying Keeper of the Moga Box clutching at her leg and rasping in what attempted to be speech. She bent down in an effort to hear him. His breathing was ragged and he was clearly near death, but he managed to gasp out one last rhyme:

"Hear me, Victoria, Keeper of Despair, for what you seek is neither here nor there.
In gilded moonlit pages, find the might, and return the darkness to our sight.
Pages enchanted, do hold the key; when spoken aloud, will return them to thee."

The little creature's grip slackened, and with one final rasping, rattling breath, Gravnolde died. Victoria stared in dismay at the little creature as it vanished before her eyes, her heart sinking. The Moga Box was destroyed, its limitless supply of magic and knowledge vanished. Its keeper, holder of all its secrets, was now gone as well – and, just like Helius, he had taken the answers she so desperately sought to his grave.

Gravnolde had, however, just given her an immensely useful piece of information in his final moments. In his last rhyme, he had told her that she could resurrect her fallen comrades – a piece of her grand plan that she had been mulling over, due to the immensity of power involved and the means by which to bring them back. With the remaining keepers' powers now restored, however, that part of her plan could once more be pursued. He had given her renewed hope that Chaos would once again be the glorious dark world upon which she had so loved to exist. His rhyme had told her that she needed a book to resurrect her comrades. But there were literally hundreds of thousands of books locked away on Chaos, mostly inside the Hall of Records. It could have referred to ANY book.

A thought suddenly occurred to her, as she stood there shivering. No, it wasn't just any book. It was a special one. His riddle held another clue – the book's pages were "gilded moonlit," and they were also enchanted. And there was only one book that, to her knowledge, held that specific description, particularly when it came to revivification – and that book was the Book of Resurrection, a text so powerful and so advanced that few, if any, had been able to properly wield its power; it was a text so dark that it had been locked away. To her knowledge, the last person to successfully access its power and understand its mysteries had been none other than Matthew Hexus, who had transferred many of its spells and secrets to his own personal spellbook before once more locking it up.

Gravnolde's rhyme had rung true – it gave her the knowledge to do what was intended. Though he had given her what she sought – the knowledge needed to resurrect their comrades – it would still require a lot of supplies, beings willing to wield dark magic, and a lot of time and very careful planning. And, unfortunately, patience and secrecy. The book they needed, if she was correct and if the Book of Resurrection was still where it was supposed to be, was sealed behind several very complicated magical barriers, not to mention most likely guarded both by Ginger's guards and by the ever-irritating, book-absorbing MJ Holmes.

"Victoria!" Bracchus came running up to her, snapping her out of the mental trance she had been in. She looked down and realized she still held the shattered fragment of the Moga Box.

"I'm fine, Bracchus," she responded automatically.

"Good, but that's not why I ran over here," he said. "The Army is being attacked by elemental mages sent by Gavin Moonstone and…." He stopped, seeing for the first time the remains of the Moga Box. "The box?"

"Destroyed," Victoria answered.

"Gravnolde?"

"Dead." Victoria turned to look at him. "The box's destruction changes nothing. We will remain with our plan of strike and vanish."

"But the box…."

"We have our powers back," Victoria replied. "We have re-unified several fragments of the Army of Chaos. With our powers restored, we will continue to do so. If it takes years, I intend to be the poisonous thorn in the side of Queen Ginger and those do-gooders. And," she replied as she dropped the fragment of the Moga Box and began to calmly and unaffectedly walk away from the battle raging around them, "I have all the information we need to proceed to the next phases of our plan."

"What about the Army?" Bracchus called.

"Tell them to vanish and re-group at the Chapel of Shadows," Victoria answered. "Their task here is done for now. We have proven our strength and humiliated Ginger and her allies today. For now, that is sufficient. I intend to drag out her misery and humiliation and make her suffer with twice the amount of pain she has inflicted upon us."

Bracchus ran away to do her bidding, no longer bothering to question her natural leadership. She strolled nonchalantly away from the still-raging courtyard, collecting a babbling Regina and a stunned and semi-electrocuted Burgundy as she strutted proudly away from the chaos at the New Kingdom – the chaos she had instigated. Lucas joined her silently.

"Is Ginger dead?" Regina snarled.

"I doubt it," Victoria replied, "but no matter. The longer she lives, the more grief we can cause her." She turned to Burgundy. "Thanks to your treasure map and your treasure of the Moga Box, we have all the information we need."

"We do?" Burgundy asked, giggling as his hair stood out as wildly as Regina's. "Yay, Victoria! Yay!"

"Indeed," Victoria answered, permitting herself a rare yet small genuine smile. "Use your Telepowder. Bring us to the Chapel of Shadows. There, we will continue our process of reuniting the remnants of the Army of Chaos." Her voice continued to rise with the passion of her conviction. "We will bring Linus and his vampires into the fold to cause even more uproar and destruction. We will travel to the Hall of Records and steal the Book of Resurrection. We will unlock its secrets together and use its dark power to resurrect our fallen comrades." She turned to face her allies fully, her eyes flashing and her voice nearly insane with power. "It will take years to do this. It will take years to unlock the secrets of resurrection. We must do this with the utmost care and the utmost secrecy, so that we shall succeed without interruption. And all the while, we shall once more have the glory of Chaos!"

Burgundy and Regina cheered, jumping idiotically up and down and clapping. Lucas asked, "But my lady, once all of this is accomplished, what then?"

Victoria smiled at him with a set of predator's teeth. "We will have laid the foundation for our greatest task of all. Once all of that is completed...we will use our combined powers to resurrect Helius Rue." In a cloud of Telepowder, the group exploded through time and space, back to the darkness of the Chapel of Shadows to begin the next stage of their sinister plan.

*****

In a flash, the suddenly unified Army of Chaos had vanished as quickly as it had appeared. Ginger was still reeling from the swiftness of the attack and the damage it had caused. The unfinished New Kingdom was now set back several years in construction, many of its established structures and architecture now damaged beyond repair and in need of a total rebuild. Fires were still burning throughout the city and the central courtyard. The palace was a wreck, basically reduced to ruins by the Army of Chaos – as great as the ruins of Hell's Gate upon which it had been built.

Ginger realized after the army vanished that Victoria's plan had never really been to kill everyone, but to shame and embarrass Ginger. And in that, she had succeeded all too well. Because of her underestimation of Helius's remaining keepers, her work and her progress with transforming Chaos had been set back terribly. She had grown lax and had forgotten the most important lesson of all...though Helius's remaining keepers were bumbling idiots, they were still evil, and they were still more than capable of destruction and devastation. It was a mistake and an underestimation that she would never make again.

Bracken came walking over to her, proudly wearing the talisman she had given him in recognition for saving her life – the talisman that she had only a short while ago herself received from Gavin. She smiled weakly at him as he approached.

"How are you feeling, my queen?"

"Tired and hungry, but I'll live. How's everyone else doin'?" She looked around her.

"The casualties are slim to none, actually," Bracken said with a smile. "And, if I may say so, things can always be rebuilt." He gave her a little bit of a playful nudge, then seemed to remember who she was and stiffened back to his military posture.

Ginger smiled, in spite of herself. "Excellent work. And thanks, Bracken. You saved my life."

"My queen." He bowed and stepped back as MJ and a bleary-eyed Cody took his place.

"What'd I miss?" Cody asked sleepily.

MJ slapped him and turned back to Ginger. "We're glad you are all right, Ginger. Victoria did a number on the New Kingdom, but we can rebuild it. It will just take some time." She turned around, pushed her glasses back up the bridge of her nose, and glanced back over her shoulder at the group of mages sent by Gavin. "And with the elemental mages here to train and support the troops, we have an additional advantage. All is well."

Ginger grunted and got to her feet, turning fully to face her friends. "I dunno, MJ. I think this's the start of bigger things t'come. There's no tellin' what Victoria and the others'll do now that they have their powers back. They've gone back into hiding, and even our forces couldn't take 'em on if they decided to stand against us in full force at the Chapel of Shadows. It's one of the places left on Chaos we just can't seem to conquer."

"Hmm. Perhaps," MJ replied thoughtfully. "I have some ideas that may help protect the New Kingdom. I will get to work on them immediately." She turned to leave, then turned back around. "Oh, by the way. I will be constructing a spell to transport the entire Cave of the Prophets nearer to the New Kingdom, and I will most likely need help with casting it, as it is going to require more magic than I can use on my own. Since I have been spending most of my time there anyway, I figured it might be a good idea to be closer, should anything like this happen again. Once I have gotten what I need from the Cave of the Prophets, I plan to start scouring the Hall of Records more in depth to uncover its knowledge more thoroughly, as well."

She turned back around, dragging a half-asleep Cody along with her. Bracken slipped back beside Ginger and stood, looking out into the distance as the sun began to set. "Are you sure that you are all right?"

Ginger looked outward toward the sunset as well. "I am. But it's time for me t'start really bein' a queen. We must be prepared if this ever happens again. I've no idea what's to come…."

She turned to Bracken, who looked at her expectantly, and continued in much more formal speech. "I have no idea what's to come, but when it does, we'll be ready for it. We'll rebuild and make this world a better place, and we'll meet any opposition that comes against us. Together."

To be continued...

About the Author

Phillip J. Adamczyk graduated from the University of Wisconsin-La Crosse with a bachelor's degree in secondary English and history education in 2011, before beginning his additional career as a business owner. He owns and operates a wellness center in Townsend, Wisconsin and is also in process of historic restoration and preservation projects, as well as the eventual opening of a university in Laona, Wisconsin. Phil is also a state licensed and board certified massage therapist. When not teaching, running his businesses, or seeing clients, Phil continues to further his work in writing, hoping to emerge with even more new and exciting ideas as his work progresses, develops, and expands.

About the Illustrator

JoMarie Bentzler has drawn and painted her whole life in Wisconsin and has completed a multitude of projects since 2007 as a freelance/commission artist and illustrator, finely tuning her talents by attending courses in Wisconsin and earlier in Iowa. She has since completed numerous commissions, has been featured in the Timber News for her achievements three times, and her work has been featured in a few select shops in Colorado. She specializes in both traditional and digital mediums: watercolor, ink, and digital artistry. JoMarie currently works part time as a freelance artist and works full time by caring for the elderly. She has resided in Colorado Springs since 2013 and currently lives there happily with her daughters, Alaina and Alexis, and Kevin, her loving partner.

Made in the USA
Monee, IL
26 February 2023